KILLING IN

PETE HAYNES

KILLING INNOCENTS

In memory of mum and dad.

1

Stephen leaned towards the table in front of him and studied the letter he was holding. It was from the oncology department with news he and his wife, Jessica, had been waiting for with great apprehension. Stephen read the words in the letter two more times, looking closer at it each time before finally leaning back in his chair. He exhaled heavily as his eyes searched frantically around points in the room for something to focus on and make sense of what was happening in his life. Finding it difficult to swallow, he began to breathe slowly, concentrating on counting the seconds of each deep breath, but he knew, ultimately, it was useless. His worse fears had now been confirmed in a formal letter from the hospital. It was written in a clinical manner, stating a medical fact, and it was cold. A thick cloud of heavy emotion moved from his chest into his throat and mouth, making breathing difficult and his dry mouth could not produce saliva. His hands began to shake as fear travelled up his legs, through his body and heated his face, and his heart beat faster. As he became conscious of a painful band constricting around his head, Stephen thought of Jessica, his wife and his love. A feeling of weakness broke inside him and he cried out, rocking forward, tears breaking uncontrollably as he sobbed his wife's name.

Five weeks earlier Jessica and Stephen were sitting opposite a female doctor who looked sadly from Jessica to a computer screen on her desk, and then to a letter she was holding. She began to speak, but it was as if both Stephen and Jessica had become deaf to everything she said after hearing her words, 'The risk of having ovarian cancer increases with the more years a woman ovulates, whether she has given birth or not.'

'What is this?' Jessica said, her words sounding absent as they fell involuntarily from her mouth. Stephen's breathing became constricted and he heard a rushing noise in his ears that deadened all other sounds around him. He looked into the side of Jessica's face and gave her hand a reassuring squeeze, but she continued to look at the doctor, shock and fear was quickly embedding itself and had seemed to age her ten years.

Jessica and Stephen had become experts on the facts and figures about infertility during the previous couple of years as Jessica tried to conceive, but without success. Stephen held Jessica's hand as he thought back over the trials and tribulations that he and Jessica had experienced in the pursuit of having a baby. They learned about the different factors involved in the trouble couples have conceiving, and how, in a fair number of cases, there just is not an identified cause. Jessica had tests for different conditions and had been given explanations for lack of regular ovulation. They were told about factors relating to infertility from weight, alcohol, smoking, sexually transmitted diseases and environmental factors, which at one time made them consider moving to an area with less pollution. The journey started at their family doctor, who referred them to their local clinical commissioning group, where they learned that funding for IVF treatment was not available for Jessica as it has additional criteria ruling that women over thirty-five years of age are not eligible.

As Stephen thought of the things that had happened and what they had been told over the past couple of years, he remembered Jessica saying, 'I feel excluded from a club that everyone else is in.' He thought of the blame she once directed at him for not being able to conceive, because it might have been his fault for not having good quality semen; although she later apologised and felt upset for what she had said. Stephen had to remind himself not to blab out that someone they knew was pregnant, or of how so and so's child was getting on at school, and there were times Jessica felt she couldn't go to christenings when having been invited. There are forums on the internet for women who have recently had babies, but then there are sites offering support for women having trouble to conceive where they share their experiences. These sites use acronyms, which was something Stephen became familiar with, but was confused when first hearing Jessica using terms like, HPT, which is home pregnancy test, or BFP, meaning big fat positive, but for Jessica it was always a BFN, a big fat negative when getting the result of a pregnancy test. Stephen would try to lighten her mood by making up jokey acronyms, but it was a struggle and something Stephen treated in a very sensitive manner.

Jessica noticed the looks from some of the women she knew or came into contact with who had a child. She became upset as she felt left out and different, and to make matters worse some women gloated at what they had achieved in contrast to her situation. Although the fertility sites are intended to give support, Jessica felt the language and terminology made it a separate world, a world where there is tension at being a failure and feeling different from all other woman that

5

seemingly conceive at will, as she once said, 'Often unknowingly and after a bawdy night of lust and alcohol.'

It upset Jessica, she had encountered spite and resentment, a condition that has been called, 'primary fertility envy' and she was also upset at joining a world that she saw had become an area of debate and research with psychologists making a living out of the subject. After all, it was her life, her 'experience of failure,' as she called it, that these people were profiting from.

After about seven months they decided to pay for private treatment in an effort to conceive because the NHS had 'cut back' on some treatments. They were told the treatment they wanted was available, but it would be expensive and there wasn't a guarantee of success. Their family doctor advised them on choosing a clinic licenced with the HFEA, the Human Fertilisation and Embryology Authority. They never envisaged wanting a child would lead them into an experience of coming into contact with so many organisations, specialists and different theories. There were glossy brochures with tariffs giving the costs of treatments, the medical terminology and warnings about having to be mindful not to be deceived by people wanting to financially profit from their situation, because they are only interested in exploiting their desperation to have a baby. Their doctor recommended a list of doctors who work in the private sector and told Jessica and Stephen to look at their 'profiles' carefully before deciding which one they felt would suit them. They spent hours looking at the private healthcare site and reading the profiles, backgrounds and experience of the doctors. Jessica chose a woman she thought sounded open minded, interesting and someone she could get on with. She was a consultant obstetrician and gynaecologist who spoke of her interest in complimentary medicines, such as acupuncture and meditation to calm the mind and body.

It was in this doctor's office where Jessica and Stephen were sitting. When first meeting her she told them how the cost of IVF can be over five thousand pounds for just one cycle of treatment, with extra costs for consultations, tests and medicines. It was a lot of money, and they had considered going abroad, but rejected the idea when looking at the risks. The benefits are lower prices, especially if one travels further afield, but there are legal issues to consider as laws at home are more stringent, which safeguards against receiving inferior treatment in substandard fertility clinics. Another concern of having treatment in a foreign country, is the impracticability of follow up appointments, which would entail an awful lot of travelling.

6

It went on for three years, the consultations and meetings, and all the while Jessica's emotions became increasingly strained by the torment of having treatment without success, and struggling to pay for it. As Stephen sat in the chair his mind went over the experiences Jessica and he had been through in regards to Jessica inability to conceive; it had been four years since they wanted a baby. After trying for over a year, they decided to go to their doctor to see if there was any problem underpinning the reason why Jessica couldn't get pregnant. At first there were ideas about artificial insemination, and Stephen remembered the tone of the doctor's voice, dry detached and without emotion as he said, 'Artificial insemination involves the deliberate introduction of sperm into the woman's uterus or cervix for the purpose of achieving pregnancy – the artificial insemination techniques available are intracervical insemination and intrauterine insemination,' and he carried on explaining the process.

The artificial insemination route was blocked after fertility tests showed Stephen's sperm as normal. They were eventually advised to go with IVF; but at a financial cost. At the time NICE, National Institute for Health and Care Excellence, recommended that IVF treatment should be available for women on the NHS if the woman is aged between twenty-three and thirty-nine years of age, but they learned that local NHS resources were not available for funding IVF treatment because Jessica was over thirty-five years of age.

Stephen thought back to the times he had waited in different rooms, reading leaflets giving information, with, what he sometimes thought to be, childishly drawn pictures explaining ovulation and the process of pregnancy. He read how the ovaries release an egg about fourteen days before a woman's period, and the egg then travels down one of the fallopian tubes and when sperm penetrates the egg it's called fertilisation or conception. The fertilised egg, or embryo, then travels to the woman's uterus, or womb, and attaches itself to the lining in the uterus and begins to grow. It felt to Stephen that he read about it a hundred times, and had been doing so for a hundred years, but then his attention was drawn back to his present situation in the office. Back to *reality*, his life, his wife, Jessica, having cancer. It was *his*, *their*, reality.

In the previous few months Jessica had tests to find out if she had IBS, irritable bowel syndrome, and then to see if she had PMT, pre-menstrual tension, but it had turned out to be ovarian cancer. She was feeling very tired all the time, thinking it was down to the stress of infertility, but now they had found out why Jessica was feeling the way she was.

7

'I came with hopes of finding a way to have a baby, and am now told I have cancer – that's my baby – cancer,' Jessica blurted the words out, and then began to cry. Stephen looked at her, he felt completely helpless and broken inside, not having the strength to say anything meaningful he just caressed her hand and said nothing.

2

Later that day, when back in their home, Jessica and Stephen sat in separate chairs, looking from one another to objects around the living room, a room that the pair of them had put much love and consideration into, but now had an empty and cold feel. The silence was broken only by the sounds of sighs and of them shifting position in their chairs. The doctor at the fertility clinic had said she would write to their GP and for them to book an appointment with him as soon as possible. Jessica rang the surgery as soon as they got home and an appointment was made, although not with their regular doctor because of a waiting list, so they were to see a locum doctor the next day. They continued to sit quietly, it was only when Stephen asked Jessica if she would like a cup of tea or coffee that something was said, but she just shook her head and every so often held her head in her hands and sobbed. Stephen watched Jessica, the woman he loved, his heart breaking as he held back tears; tears of anger.

Stephen Charles Dale and Jessica, nee Jessica Andrea Bowland, had been married ten years. They met when Stephen went into a building society where Jessica worked to open a new account. He told Jessica that he had not long left the army, which he had been in for six years, having joined up at eighteen years of age after working a year in a warehouse. That was four years before they married. The first thing he noticed about Jessica was her lovely smile, it was natural, not a corporate duty, but pure and friendly. Her eyes showed kindness that reflected a soul, which Stephen thought, had understanding and compassion. He told Jessica he had to leave the army because he suffered an injury to his back while in action, which flared up when engaging in physical activity, and for this reason he was going for an interview in the tax office for a sedentary job.

Jessica wished him the best of luck and listened intently as he told her about his injury. She noticed how he held back from fully explaining the situation he was in, noting how he refrained from talking about details of violence and boasts of courage displayed in that situation. She saw him as chivalrous, a decent person of substance, modesty and depth, attributes she felt was lacking in a lot of people she came into contact with, and she hid a smile as she saw him as old fashioned; and she liked that quality.

As Stephen sat in the chair in their living room watching Jessica, he thought back to their first date, and the day he went back to the building society hoping to see her. He remembered how he felt a pang in his stomach when seeing Jessica behind a desk, and of the way he hung around, walking in a circle until she noticed him. Later on, they spoke about that moment, laughing at his shyness and how awkward he was. Jessica told Stephen it made her love him all the more when thinking of that time.

Stephen went into the building society two more times after that with made up reasons to ask questions about his account, just so he could speak to Jessica. He then went in and told her he was successful in getting the job at the tax office, and stood looking at Jessica without saying anything. She congratulated him, and seeing how shy he was, took the initiative by saying he should celebrate the occasion. Jessica asked him if there was someone 'special' he was going to celebrate with, and when he looked down with a smile breaking on his flushed face, Jessica just knew he wanted to ask her. She helped him, saying she was single and that she liked going out for a nice meal. Stephen looked up at her, relief showing clearly on his smiling face, and then he tentatively asked her if she would like to go out with him. The look in her eyes was something he had never forgotten. It always warmed him when thinking of it, and the fun they had when having the meal as Stephen made a fool of himself by ordering the wrong food, not knowing he had ordered a desert for the main course. She laughed, her eyes showing love and kindness for the well-meaning man who had entered her life and given it greater meaning.

Stephen watched Jessica as she stood up and left the room without saying anything, only to return a few seconds later carrying her laptop. She sat back down, still not saying anything she tapped on the keyboard, and all the while Stephen watched her carefully, noting every movement and facial expression she made.

Jessica sighed as she typed and said the words, 'ovarian cancer' in a resigned way, as if it had been part of their lives for years. She moved from one site to another, 'Being diagnosed with ovarian cancer,' she said in a flat tone and continued to read aloud with no change of expression, 'Mainly affects women who've been through the menopause.' Stephen hoped she would stop looking it up, he could see the cracks forming beneath the façade she was presenting.

'Ovarian cancer, or cancer of the ovaries, is one of the most common types of cancer in woman,' Jessica looked at Stephen, to see if he was listening before returning to the screen. 'Causes of ovarian cancer – exact cause is unknown, although risks of getting it are increased with things like, being over fifty years of age, a history of ovarian or breast cancer in one's family – risks increased by inherited genes.'

Jessica became silent, swallowing hard she blinked as she looked at the screen, her act was fracturing and she was getting close to breaking. Stephen continued to watch her, his heart quickening in pace.

Jessica's breathing was becoming laboured as she licked her lips and began to read aloud. 'Ovarian cancer occurs – when cells in the ovaries multiply uncontrollably, which produces a lump of tissue called a tumour.'

Jessica broke from reading to take a deep breath, and bracing herself she continued, 'There are older studies that linked infertility treatment to ovarian cancer, although these studies have been replaced with new research, where the thinking is that it is more probable that being infertile increases one's risk of getting ovarian cancer rather than the treatment for infertility…'

She broke, finally, her head dropping to her chest she let out what sounded like a mixture of a cry and a heart rendering howl of total despair. Stephen stood up, too quickly and at an awkward angle, which triggered a searing pain to burn through his lower back, and for just that second, he wasn't in their living room. A voice barked an order inside his head, 'Shoot him.' Stephen stopped on hearing the voice. Taking a deep breath, he steadied himself and slowly approached Jessica. He looked at her in way he had never done so before, but would be doing so many more times in the months to come.

3

Jessica and Stephen saw the locum doctor the following morning, who spoke very little as he looked at the computer screen on his desk and made arrangements for Jessica to see a specialist at the hospital. He said the referral should take no longer than two weeks, and he was right, ten days later Jessica and Stephen sat in an office looking across a desk at the specialist they had been sent to see. While waiting during those ten days, Jessica had been scanning the internet, picking up leaflets giving information on who there is to talk to, and of course, talking to her mother; her father had died of cancer when she was twenty-six, leaving Jessica with her mother and younger brother Chris.

The specialist talked to Jessica about the symptoms that are common with ovarian cancer. Speaking in a calm voice she said, 'Unfortunately, symptoms of ovarian cancer are vague and difficult to pick up until the latter stages when it is often too late to treat the cancer successfully – four to five thousand women die every year in this country because of ovarian cancer.'

Jessica and Stephen stared at her.

Jessica did have the classic symptoms, and this was discussed and investigated while having the infertility treatment, treatment that was private and cost a lot of money. She had pain in the lower part of her stomach for a long while and felt bloated, she was also tired out all the time and was treated for irritable bowel syndrome. The feeling of fatigue was so great it stopped Jessica wanting to engage in activities, and although they didn't do any really active pastimes, because of Stephen's back injury, they did enjoy walking and taking holidays to visit places of historical interest, among other countries they had been to were Peru, Israel and China.

The consultant told them how it seems women who have children are less likely to get ovarian cancer, and indeed, the more children the less the risk. She said that infertility itself can be a cause and that it was once thought the treatment of infertility by the use of drugs caused it, although research has now changed the medical profession's understanding of its causes. She said, 'Women who haven't had children are at a greater risk as their ovaries don't get a rest during the nine months of pregnancy, and therefore continue to produce eggs each month.'

The appointment ended with Jessica being sent for blood tests and an ultrasound scan. It was then decided to send her for a CT scan because it shows the ovaries more clearly. As Stephen waited for Jessica while she was having the CT scan, he thought about a television programme he had seen the previous evening. It was a documentary about homeless ex-servicemen, although it's not only men, but it is predominately men not women. There were statistics giving the amount of ex-service personnel who were, as they put it, living on the streets. The number was in the thousands, with some reports saying one in ten homeless people in London had served their country in the armed services. The numbers shocked Stephen, and his emotions stirred at the thought of their plight and how lucky he was, but then that thought was immediately blighted as it crashed into his mind that Jessica had cancer.

The documentary ended with giving information for getting help if viewers were 'affected' by what they had been watching. There was a list of charities that help the homeless, and some specifically for people who had been in the armed services. A separate number was given for ex-service people suffering mental health problems, physical disabilities or drink and drug problems. Stephen couldn't get the documentary out of his mind. He knew his emotions were disturbed because of what was happening with Jessica, but he felt upset and angry when thinking about his comrades in the army, men who he could trust his life with in situations that most people in the society he was part of knew nothing about. Some of the men had served in the same places he had been, but now they were sleeping behind churches in a carboard box and telling stories of being physically attacked by drunk louts at night. One man had been set on fire as a gang of young men and woman laughed and 'high fived each other.' Another man told of how he was turned away from a local authority housing office, and another spoke of his drink and drug addictions. The scars on his head and face showing his decline into a world devoid of comfort, now existing in a subterranean world of fear and violence, with a constant reminder of his alienation from the society he had put his life on the line for in the cause of maintaining it.

Rejection. The word formed in Stephen's mind, but rejected from exactly what? That was the question he pondered, turning it over in his mind, really thinking about what *society* actually was and what it is meant to be. He had heard the name many times, of course he had, and he had used

13

the word, of course, but had he really thought what it meant? Realising he was holding his breath, he breathed out and in doing so felt tension release that had built up in his chest. He took his phone from his pocket and pressed buttons to bring up Google, but then stopped as his eye caught a small notice on the wall asking people to turn off their phones. His immediate response was to turn it off, but what stopped him from doing so was seeing other people in the waiting room using their phones. A brief wrestle with his conscience took place, which resulted in him continuing to pursue his research on Google. He didn't think about it at the time, about not following the request, or order, to turn off his phone, but he would do at a later date.

He searched through definitions of the word *society*, reading how it is commonly understood as meaning an established group of people sharing the same values and culture. Stephen followed the links, reading the different definitions of *country*, meaning as an area of land with borders defining it as a country. He went on following the links and read about the crown, the monarchy, the royal family, with the queen being head of state, although not having the power to make and pass legislation, the laws, they are made by an elected people in parliament, the politicians, although she has, as the royal family have, an important role in representing the nation. *Patriotism*, he read, is a love and support for one's country and the head of state, while *loyalism* is an allegiance to a political ideology and rule.

Stephen thought about his sense of *duty* towards his country and the *respect* he had for the *leaders* of the country. He just saw it as the right thing to do; he had *faith* in authority. Stephen wanted to serve his country and the established rule, and wanting to do so without a second thought, without awareness of how it is actually made up with the different people and the influences they have in shaping the *system* we all live under. A thought came to Stephen that *we* don't *all* live under it at all, because our experiences aren't shared, and an elite group of people live completely different lives to others because of their privileged positions. Stephen tapped in the words *armed services*. Nothing was really on his mind, he just did it, and sat back as he read, following a link to the word, *military*. He read how the military is an organised body armed with weapons that has been given the authority to use lethal or deadly force to support the interests of the state, while defending the state and its citizens. Made up primarily of the army, navy and air force, the military is also used in other situations. It gave examples, such as being used in times

14

of natural disasters to construct bridges, support other public services in guarding duties and internal population control in times of civil unrest.

Stephen thought back to various situations he was involved in, remembering what he was doing at the time, of how he felt and the people who were there, his fellow army pals and the locals. It struck him that he hadn't kept in touch with his army comrades, but then, when thinking about it, there was only a couple of them he felt that close to. He smiled as he remembered how much they all depended on one another in life-threatening situations. Their training drummed it into them that they work together, for each other, for the regiment and with pride. Not everyone shares the same feelings about the different things in life, but in a situation when one's life is under threat it became a family, a close family of camaraderie and above all, a trust in one another. To *trust*. Stephen thought about the word and its meaning, of how it felt and where he had seen and experienced examples of it. A strange feeling came over him as he thought what *trust* really meant to him. It was a sensation he had never before experienced that kept running through his body and wouldn't go away. He realised how the feeling came when examining his understanding of the word *trust*. This was the first time in his life he had really thought about what it meant and what it means to others. His mood darkened when thinking of his past, of his actions and *beliefs*. The beliefs he had about what he had done, what he thought at the time when he was a boy scout, and then when in the army. His attitude and thoughts when in contact with those representing authority, those in charge, in command, those in *control*.

4

The results of the scan were not good; they were what Jessica and Stephen had been dreading. It showed conclusively she had cancer, so further investigation by having exploratory surgery wasn't necessary. The letter from the oncology department had arrived earlier in the morning. Jessica and Stephen had read it together in the kitchen, and then sat there for over an hour after Jessica had broken down. Jessica went to their bedroom to be alone, leaving Stephen sitting at the table studying the letter. He thought of how it had been just five weeks since the private consultant at the fertility clinic had said Jessica needed to see her doctor. Five weeks had slipped by, yet it felt like that day was years ago. Stephen placed the letter on the table and sobbed, all the while repeating Jessica's name.

Five days later Jessica and Stephen sat in the doctor's office, both slumped in their chairs, exhausted their strained stares glazed at the doctor as he explained how it has been thought that there is a link between infertility and ovarian cancer. The doctor went on, explaining how during IVF treatment an egg is removed from a woman's ovaries and fertilised with sperm in a laboratory. The fertilised egg is then returned to the woman's womb to grow and develop. But to harvest the eggs medication is used to encourage the body to produce more eggs than normal, and those eggs are collected by inserting a needle in the ovaries, which some have said causes increased cell division and damage to the cells. Also, the drugs used during IVF treatment stimulate the ovaries to produce multiple eggs rather than just one, which stresses them, and stress on cells can lead to cancer.

The doctor told them how there is research showing results of the possible risk of developing ovarian cancer in the three years after having IVF treatment, which has led to some researchers saying there is a link between IVF treatment and ovarian cancer. Jessica and Stephen sat listening, not asking questions they felt totally helpless as the doctor told them the cold facts about an illness that had intruded upon and ruined their lives.

That evening passed slowly with large periods of silence as Stephen and Jessica sat in the living room hardly speaking to one another. Jessica sat curled up in a chair, reading on the internet about the link between IVF and cancer. She started to speak without looking away from the screen. 'There could already be the propensity for getting cancer, and the IVF treatment triggers it.' She continued to look at the screen and began to read, 'An explanation might be that the underlying problems making a woman infertile also put her at risk of developing cancer – so, IVF treatment might increase the risk in women that are susceptible to ovarian cancer in the first place.'

She stopped reading and bit her lower lip for a while before continuing to read. "Some studies suggest that women are at greatest risk of getting cancer about three years after starting IVF treatment – there are doctors that have been calling for routine screening for women undergoing IVF treatment, and to even make it a policy for it can be seen, or has been said, that any phenomenon that decreases ovarian activity may reduce the risk of developing ovarian cancer, so any intervention to stimulate the growth of eggs may increase the risk of developing cancer."'

Jessica looked at Stephen, as if waiting for him to respond, but he didn't, he just shook his head very slowly and gave a slight shrug at the hopelessness of it all. Jessica looked down at the screen as she began to speak. 'I can't help thinking how much the whole industry around this knows things they don't make the public aware of.'

Stephen looked at Jessica, his expression gravely serious, and what she had said triggered in him a feeling that caused him to say, 'In what way, Jess?'

'Well,' she said, while looking at the screen, 'Even though women are told about the risks involved with the treatment, it makes you wonder if the medical profession, or industry, play down that risk as it's worth the gamble because the chance of developing cancer and of there being a direct conclusive link is so low – or that's what they say.'

Stephen looked confused. 'Why?' He asked, staring at Jessica with his full attention.

Jessica spoke in a way that was distant, although in a voice that was becoming convinced of what she had been thinking was correct. 'Well, maybe it isn't just all about the woman's health and chances of having a baby. Maybe money has something to do with it – like large companies and

17

individuals losing out on the opportunity to profit from an area where there are so many desperate people.'

Stephen continued to look at Jessica, feelings deep inside him were causing him to feel uncomfortable, and it showed in his eyes. The unsettled feeling didn't leave Stephen during the rest of the evening as he watched Jessica read from the computer screen. His heart was breaking as he watched Jessica trying to make sense of what had happened to her, but there was something else forcing itself into his mind. He wasn't sure what it was, but he could feel it as something physical, pushing and entering into his very core.

Jessica went on forums, reading out what people were saying about IVF treatment and links to financial profit. There was a lot of criticism out there where people spoke of how doctors have to serve the interests of shareholders above everything else. This prompted discussions around ethical practice and conflicts of interest, as assisted reproduction technology often takes place in IVF clinics that have been established to make financial profits and are being floated on the stock exchange.

The evening was long and hard going. Jessica was a fighter, as was Stephen, and they knew they had a fight on their hands, but they were facing it together. Stephen stayed in the living room for a short while after Jessica went to bed, he just wanted some time to himself, time to go over thoughts that hadn't yet formed in his mind. He stared into space for long periods as he tried to pin down what was flitting around his mind. It wasn't that the thoughts were elusive, but he knew they were going to be troublesome, so he was reticent in addressing them full on.

Stephen had a dream that night, it was a flashback to what happened to him in Iraq when driving down a dusty dirt road. A sudden explosion spun the world upside down, and when it settled a broken vehicle was lying on its side, it was the vehicle he had been in. Stephen's Sergeant shouted an order, 'Shoot him.' Stephen shot at a young man standing nearby, and he fell to the ground. Stephen went over and looked at him, noticing how young he was, but now he was dead, bullets have torn off half his face and head.

The dream was very real in every detail, the smells, colours and sounds Stephen had not though about, or consciously remembered. They were vividly clear, and the dream stayed with him al the next day. It left a strong perception of how he felt at the time when the incident happened and gave him a far clearer insight into the feelings and thoughts he had at that time than when it actually happened. He felt upset and loss, but there was also a melancholic feeling Stephen found difficult to fully interpret. It was a feeling that something was wrong, that it was sick, and that it was unfair.

5

The following evening, after Jessica had gone to bed, Stephen stayed in the living room watching a twenty-four-hour news channel on television. It seemed to Stephen that the programme told the same four stories over and over until the next day, and then another four stories are repeated and discussed by *professionals*, some in detail and to an extent that one *expert* repeated what the other one said. Stephen thought it was meaningless and nothing more than a superficial display, when what really matters is never brought in for discussion. Turning down the sound he picked up his laptop and began to search through links related to Iraq and the time he served out there; this was the first time he had done this, and he was conscious of it being so as he did it.

He read men's accounts, in their own words, of their thoughts when they were in Iraq. The ex-solders told of how they felt when they killed someone, many said how there isn't time to stop and think, chaos breaks out and one's training kicks in automatically. It was common for them to say how thinking of what happened comes later, because there isn't the time and it's not the situation for reflection. Ultimately, it's all about survival and the whole time a person is away he or she is still in the battle environment and responding to army discipline. It is when one comes home to a completely different setting, one that might be familiar, but one all the same that isn't within army culture, that a person begins to reflect over what has happened. They spoke about how at the time it was like being in a trance-like state, something similar to hypnosis where they were transfixed on what they were doing and there was nothing else in their minds. Some said how they were not aware that they had been in a way programmed, like a machine, and an order from authority would, without thinking, trigger the correct reaction because instinctive mechanisms were put in place through constantly repeating an action. One man said that it's 'muscle memory,' and another said that the people one is shooting at and engaged in battle with aren't people, but the 'enemy,' and that they are to be 'neutralised.' Others told of how people that are the 'enemy' were seen as nothing more than objects, and to kill is a reflexive action without introspective deliberation.

Ex-soldiers spoke of gathering their thoughts when in a situation away from the army and battle situations. Some were upset and some had guilt, but most agreed it is wrong to kill and the act of

0

killing someone has to be taken seriously, yet they were following orders. Stephen read how there is a big discussion on the percentage of soldiers in war who don't fire at the enemy, but shoot over the heads or away from the people they are meant to be shooting at; although it was conscripts in the First and second World War they were primarily talking about. Links took Stephen to sites discussing war-related psychological injuries and the debate around post-traumatic stress disorder, PTSD. On one site he read how over the course of one year in the US military more people died from committing suicide while on active duty than were killed in combat-related deaths. There were articles investigating the effect it has on a person when he or she kills someone and concluded that soldiers themselves are casualties. It looked at mass killing from a distance with bombing to close contact killing, where it is far more personal, and because of that it seems far more damaging for the soldier who has killed someone. The closer the contact, the worse it is because one cannot turn a blind eye to what he or she has done. A soldier cannot easily disassociate from his or her actions in that situation, however much one is programmed and trained to do so, whether on grounds of race, religion, ethical standards or even dehumanising the *enemy* as a disease ridden rodent or insect.

Stephen read how research has shown that those who actually killed another person were at a greater risk of suffering psychiatric problems than those that did not. So many stories were the same, of troops returning home devastated at what they had seen, done or failed to do. The secrets they promised themselves to stay just with them are too strong, and so the guilt and haunting fear grows until it spills out into a society unprepared to address it, and often not caring to bother. One man spoke of feeling a sense of betrayal in that those who are our 'leaders' gave orders, which were carried out by the men as they were trained to do, even if the men might have personally thought what they were doing was wrong, but the moral consequences of those actions were not thought through by those giving the orders, or they didn't care what the men have to live with. The debate haunts and disturbs those that were involved in battle and is significant in leading to many of them developing mental health problems. The writer of the piece believed it is a matter of questioning the responsibility and culpability of those given the authority to direct actions that kill, maim and destroy peoples' lives, whether that be the enemy or innocent civilians.

One man told of his experience when told to open fire on a van, and when opening the back of it they discovered six children ripped to pieces by bullets designed to pierce heavy armour. The feelings of betrayal felt by this ex-combatant are shared with others. One man spoke of society not caring, and even worse, lots of people criticise people like him personally, calling him, cannon fodder, a puppet, mentally thick and a psychopath. The man spoke of the criticism there was towards him and also how he was upset with the government. He went on, saying how politicians and the authorities gave reasons to put troops into a country and of why it was so important, only to pull out without anything having been resolved, and in some cases the situation was made worse. The man continued, saying the rhetoric changes when there is a change of mind and that's that, it's just ticked off as a matter dealt with only to send troops in somewhere else, with again all the reasons of why it's so important. Another man said how the biggest injury he suffered was to discover the moral depravity shown by some of 'our leaders.' He spoke of how they preside over situations where men are sent to give their lives for a cause, only to get there ill-equipped and poorly supported, and then to find out some of *our leaders* not only have financial interests in companies supplying arms and equipment for that battle, but also have business interests in that country they were sent to fight in.

Stephen read a post which told of a man who had become addicted to the painkillers he uses as a result of an injury sustained from a roadside bomb in Iraq. Stephen thought about his own injury, just like the man, a roadside bomb in Iraq and he considered himself lucky as he rarely took medication, although the injury was always there, and at times immobilised him. A link took Stephen to a thread discussing the effect close combat has on a person's personality. He read about a condition called Confusion States, which encompasses a variety of nervous conditions from basic anxiety to becoming psychotic. As Stephen read, he remembered, only too clearly, the mood swings men suffered from, of wanting to hide away, some curling up in the foetal position wanting to escape their situation, the poor food, lack of sleep, the constant discomfort and fear, never relaxing, yet having to put a brave face on it all when one's insides are screaming for release. He saw men who became negligent, beyond caring they walked aimlessly disregarding the possibility of stepping on a mine or being caught in the sights of an enemy sniper. Stephen remembered the men he saw erupt into flash rages and drop to the ground shaking. Some became paralysed with panic, and he particularly remembered one man of about twenty years of age becoming hysterical after receiving a wound and thinking he had finished with the battle, only to be patched up and told he had to return and fight. Stephen remembered his eyes.

He closed the site down and took a deep breath. What he was doing was something he told himself he would never do, to rake over the past and examine things he can't do anything about. He had to get on with things, he had been told, 'get on with your life,' and 'move on.' Also, it wasn't all about him. There was Jessica, that was his main priority, and so it should be, he loved her and felt about her like he had never felt about anyone before. And now she had cancer. Again, he took a deep breath at the thought of it, but his stomach tightened so much it restricted his breathing. To distract his thinking about Jessica he clicked on a story that was in the news. It was about something the present Chancellor of the Exchequer's younger brother told a reporter, which was controversial, and so he back peddled in an effort to make amends for what he had said.

Stephen read how the chancellor, Graham Mears, had defended his younger brother, Luke, over what he said concerning soldiers returning from war. A reporter approached Luke Mears as he was leaving a business convention and asked him about the morality of investing in businesses in a country where this country has troops fighting a war. The reporter asked him if it could it be seen as insensitive in regard to the number of soldiers returning from that country with physical and mental difficulties. Luke Mears was dismissive, saying he wasn't a spokesman for all business investment in that country. The reporter persisted by asking if he thought his brothers' cabinet members have considered how difficult it can be for a soldier trying to participate in normal society, especially when struggling with different issues, including PTSD. He told Luke Mears that there are a high number of ex-service men who are now homeless with many getting into trouble with the law and ending up in prison, and when the reporter asked him if he thought the government should provide more adequate provision for the troops returning home, as it is surely the country's responsibility, Luke Mears responded with flippant disrespect. He told the reporter that this is nothing new for the 'nambies' to 'get upset about,' and he quoted a reporter for the New York Times who commented after the American Civil War on the massive increase in crime and violence, 'That's what can happen if you turn Rough Material upon society.'

Luke Mears later apologised for what he said, defending himself by saying it was insensitive, but he more than most supports our troops and the evidence is in the charity work he is involved with that works on behalf of the military. It was pointed out in the article of how the charity Luke Mears is involved with has recently come in for examination for their tax and administrative practices, the name of the charity is, Support and Development – For Those That Served. The article concluded by saying how 'sad and disgraceful' it is to think there are those prospering from the loyalty and bravery shown by our service people.

Stephen looked away from the computer screen and thought about his experience in Iraq, conjuring up the face of the young man standing near his vehicle when it was blown up. He had thought in the past that the young man wasn't actually involved with the incident. It would be highly unlikely if he detonated the bomb because he wouldn't be that close, but of course, in the heat of the moment there wasn't time to think about it. His sergeant shouted an order, 'Shoot him,' and he did. Stephen thought of the young man's face, or what was left of it. He was the last person Stephen shot at. A short while after, when the adrenaline wound down, Stephen realised he was injured. A piece of shrapnel in his lower back was pressing on nerves in his spine, an injury that finished his time in the army and had plagued him ever since. He thought back to his time in the hospital, the two operations to remove the shrapnel and then the waiting to be sent home.

His army career was over, and Stephen felt a mixture of embarrassment and of being a failure. It was a strange feeling, one he had never experienced, because it felt like guilt at having done something wrong. Stephen remembered how he felt at the time, getting ready to fly back home, filled with apprehension instead of excitement and relief, which is the normal way to feel when returning home, but the roadside bomb changed it all. He took in a deep breath, and while exhaling put the thought from his mind and began to reflect over what he had been reading, about what people had written, of when in battle, the army culture, of how one does not *think* so much as *respond*, because to do so could make one *dysfunctional* and a soldier needs to be *functional*. When out of the army and away from that situation, *thinking* evokes feelings that aren't encouraged in one's training. So, it's a matter of don't think, just act, but when one *really* thinks, *blind faith* comes in for examination.

Stephen looked up definitions of the term, 'blind faith.' He thought about the notion of putting one's faith into someone or something without having evidence to the claims that person or whatever is making. It is common to believe and support a doctrine or system based on convictions coming from socialisation rather than one having proof that the doctrine or system is what it presents itself to be. Stephen thought how he had heard on many occasions people say things like, 'Oh, they don't really think, they just follow with blind faith,' and he thought how it is stupid to follow, support and even offer one's life for something that rests on blind faith. He had been told this very thing about the 'enemy' in Iraq, of how they shared this ignorance, of how they are people who blindly follow a belief and are willing to lay down their lives for that belief, or for a person whom they believe embodies the power he or she professes to have. When, in actual fact they have no proof of this being so. They are just blindly following that person, religion or regime. Stephen thought about how it might be acceptable to follow a football team without question because one's father did and it's a family tradition to do so, but, in matters as important as laying down one's life and being prepared to take the life of a person one hasn't met, well, that's a different thing all together.

Tension had built up in Stephen's chest and shoulders, an unpleasant feeling had settled itself inside him and he became aware that he was holding his breath. Taking deep breaths to relax himself Stephen continued with his research. He was persistent, his eyes fixed on the screen, Stephen wanted to learn more and find something that satisfied his curiosity that had begun to burn inside him. Stephen asked himself why was it that important at this time of all times? He had opportunities in the past to contemplate such thoughts, but now with Jessica and the cancer, and everything they were facing, why was it so important? What had triggered it? Putting that question out of his mind, he looked up information on the area of blind faith, what *faith* actually is and how it is relevant in getting people to follow unquestioningly an army, a political leader, a religion and religious leaders.

His research led him to read about cults and how they can provide emotional comfort. For many, there is a need to give one's self over, or ally oneself, to a political party or group and share the values of that group or party one aspires to be part of. It is required for one to think and act in a way associated with those particular beliefs and values that the person, group, religion or whatever embodies. The benefit can be to alleviate feelings of insecurity, fear of standing alone and making choices in a confusing and threatening world. It is felt to satisfy a common human need to feel safe and have a sense of belonging.

Stephen read an article about political leaders who make bogus claims and employ strategies that are intended to exploit the fears people have, although not as extreme or as personally intrusive as a cult in telling people to disown family members and sever ties with friends. Ploys that have been used throughout the years by rulers, and people that want to rule, is to give warnings of imminent financial disasters and impending threats to one's country's security and culture, even when the opposite of what they are saying is evident. Yet, for many people, the fear of looming doom maintains allegiance and faith in that party or person they have aligned themselves with. Stephen thought how it isn't real, meaning some of the things people believe in, and yet they are even willing to give their lives for. He thought about how deluded people are, and that their feelings of security, brought about by believing in something as having depth and substance, can often be nothing more than an illusion. He saw them as having been deceived by false promises and tricked into having a sense of well-being by doing the right thing for the right cause.

Stephen followed links taking him from 'cults' to 'mind control,' reading accounts of how people have been 'brain washed' and of how they very quickly lost the ability to think critically or independently, but adhered fully to the values and beliefs of a cult, religion or political ideology. They often follow a leader who controls through a charismatic personality, whether the figure has powers bestowed upon him or her from divine sources, or that their personality is so appealing, it inspires devotion from others. He read examples of where young men and women from stable middle class families joined cults, all believing what they were doing was for the best, not only for themselves, but for other people and the future of the planet. They were duped into doing unpleasant things, actions they certainly didn't have in mind when they joined the cult, but console themselves in thinking it is ultimately for the good of the world. Not thinking for themselves they robotically follow orders, rationalising they are doing it in the name of a greater power than themselves. There were examples given of how they go through a series of rituals and events that *reshape* the person into a compliant individual, just like a soldier, like Nazis throwing children in gas ovens and justifying it by saying, 'I'm just doing my job.' 'Just following orders.' He read articles about the need for *faith* and *trust* in the process of developing a strong belief in someone or something. This caused Stephen to think about himself, of his relationship and feelings towards the scouts and the army. He thought of how he felt about security, of a need in himself to feel part of something bigger than himself and that the scouts and army gave a feeling of safety. Questions filled his mind and he became confused. A foreboding sense of doubt wouldn't leave him. The feeling grew and it nagged at him, and then Stephen panicked as he felt he was losing confidence in himself and control over what he thought he was.

The word *thinking* came clearly into Stephen's mind and he typed it into the search engine. He then typed in the words, 'to think for one's self,' and followed links taking him to the words, *rationalise*, *logic* and *justification*, which led him to read about *reason*. He looked up the word, *consciousness* and thought about himself, of being aware and perceptive, and the notion of independent thought and conscience. He thought about acting conscientiously in making one's own choice over whether something is morally right or wrong, and to be faithful with one's conscience in knowing what the truth is and what isn't. He asked himself questions around the subject of supporting or going along with something when knowing it is false, such as following the principles of a person in an esteemed position having influence over others, even when knowing that person is a hypocrite.

Stephen looked at the television screen and seeing the face of Graham Mears on it, the Chancellor of the Exchequer, he pressed the button on the remote to increase the volume. As he looked at him, without really listening to what he was saying, Stephen thought about what Mears's brother had said concerning troops coming home, calling them 'Rough material.' Stephen reflected over what he had been reading about, of analysing consciousness, to really think, and he became aware of the way he was thinking at that very moment. He thought of how he was questioning things and people like Graham Mears and his brother and who they actually were. Stephen asked himself if they were actually anything like what they present themselves to be, and what were the real intentions of these people, and others like them. He went over memories of when at school and of the things in history he was taught, of how the political leaders of the country were portrayed, and of how people in authority are supposed to be *pillars* of society. Stephen thought of how he had heard people say of these leading figures, 'What they say and what they actually do is completely another matter.' He wondered how corrupt some of these people are, of how they serve their own interests while projecting an image of caring for one's country and the people in it. Stephen thought about the morality of it all, and of how much these *leaders* really share common aims and feelings with the people they profess to be responsible for?

A jabbing pain bit into Stephen's stomach. It was dull and deep, and anger filled him as he watched Graham Mears talking. He stared at the television, his expression grim and not changing as he turned it off and slapped the remote down on the sofa; it was an aggressive action that was uncharacteristic for Stephen.

Stephen lay in bed unable to sleep. His mind racing, it wouldn't settle as he thought about what he had been reading on the internet about cults and individuals with charismatic personalities who attract devotion from people. He thought about mainstream politics, the political leaders, the very establishment itself and of how many people find it all acceptable and *normal*, giving little thought to the 'way of things,' as people say. He thought how they support individuals, political parties and their policies while having no or little knowledge about them, often only that from a bias media with interests in persuading people to support a political party, or from when they were at school when one is given, mostly, a view that isn't critical of the country and its past. Stephen thought how most people wouldn't see themselves as *devoted* to the political party they traditionally vote for, or, devoted to the leading figures making up the establishment. He thought about a type of personality that is *dependent* on an authority for one's own personal sense of security.

Stephen considered *why* he was thinking the way he was, what had brought it on and what had possessed him to pursue this line of thought so fervently. The word *dependent* kept popping into his mind. It led to him thinking of a *need*, a reliance he has had on authority and the establishment of the country he grew up in. It was the place where he was born, he felt part of its history and had thought the rulers of the land did all they could, their *duty*, to bring about the best for the country and the people they are ruling over. He had thought that, although he might have disagreed with particular decisions, but in the main, he had given unquestionable support and compliance in following and respecting the country's laws and the intentions of its leaders.

A chill prickled Stephen's skin as he thought that maybe he had a personality that was dependent, like the people he had read about who followed cults and had the need to be led. Afterall, he had followed a system and its leaders, a power greater than himself, because he thought that ultimately it was for the best. Then maybe he didn't think, but merely supposed it was for the best. After all, thinking is not encouraged when one is a soldier; it is to respond. He thought about the accounts he had read earlier of the soldiers' experience when in battle and taking the life of another person, just as he had done. He gave a sudden violent twitch. 'Yes,' he said to himself, and he thought that was him, programmed not to think, but to respond, because to think is a negative response, and one that could cost the lives of one's comrades. It is also the action that challenges order, and in civilian life, maybe that order needs to be challenged from a moral point of view. There isn't that luxury in a battle situation to debate and consider theories and thoughts concerning working towards the betterment of all people and to raise the quality of life for those not yet born, whether that be human, animal, or the natural environment that we need for life to continue.

He went over the word *dependency* and its meaning opposed to independent thinking. It made him feel weak, he hadn't followed a cult and he wouldn't blindly align himself with ideologies like the Nazis. He had been faithful and did his duty for a normal and respectful cause, his country's interests, which surely is in the interests of the people that live in it. Stephen thought how it's called, *discipline*, but ultimately for whose interest? He thought of the current political figures that were in the news, and his mind settled on Graham Mears. Stephen knew things were changing for him, not only his life with Jessica, but there was a change developing inside him.

He lay in bed, motionless, his eyes wide open staring up at the ceiling, Jessica lying by his side, asleep, 'but for how long,' were the words that skimmed across his mind. The thought evoked a feeling of disgust in thinking such a thing.

Stephen noticed how the shock of being told she had cancer had affected Jessica. The myriad of information online is tremendous, much of it shouldn't be looked at as Jessica was told to focus only on reputable sites. She was encouraged to learn more about her illness, the disease itself, so that she could 'actively participate' in the decisions made in addressing her treatment. Her sleeping was disrupted and she exhibited the usual signs a person would do when suffering from such a shock and worried out of her mind. Walking on eggshells would be an exaggeration, but Stephen was careful in what he said to Jessica, and found himself frequently holding his breath as he anticipated an outburst, such was the stress Jessica was feeling. Some of the language surrounding the whole area infuriated Jessica to a point that she shouted out, 'Oh, for Christs sake – bloody hell – my "negative feelings" might be stopping me from, "moving forward" – God!' Stephen didn't know whether to smile or how to react; he just wanted to hold her.

He listened to Jessica as she told him of her fears and of no longer wanting to go out because her life was shattered. She talked to Stephen of feeling isolated, not only from him and her family, but from everything. Jessica spoke of being terrified, the immensity of it all was crushing her, and she resented the reality that a new language, with all the medical terminology, was now part of her life. After the initial disbelief when told of the cancer there was anger, the moods and outbursts, sometimes at Stephen, but he knew it was Jessica crying out for help. Jessica became irritated when told to learn about her cancer so that she could be involved in the 'decision-making process,' because it's 'important' and 'empowering' when taking control of one's treatment and able to 'make an 'informed decision.' Jessica screamed out, 'Oh shut up – just shut up,' when reading about being 'informed' and the detailed reports written from research undertaken on different treatments and patient's responses. She said, 'What difference does it make?' Jessica was referring to a recent visit to the hospital when she asked concerning a type of treatment she had read about and if they had information regarding some research that was happening in America. The response to the first part of her question was that the particular treatment she had mentioned wasn't practiced in this country, and the information about the research was met with ambivalence.

Jessica's treatment was based on the stage and grade of her cancer. Tests showed the size of the tumour and the grading examined the cancer cells, which, showed how fast the cancer is growing. Jessica's cancer was classed as stage two, two B, which they were told is advanced and that it had spread to other tissues in her pelvis. An appointment was made for her to meet a specialist gynaecological team called the Multidisciplinary Team, MDT, which would guide Jessica through the 'appropriate treatment.' On the evening before Jessica's appointment, when she was to meet the Multidisciplinary Team at the hospital, Jessica and Stephen were in the living room, Jessica looking at her computer and Stephen looking at the blank wall in front of him. He was thinking about what he had read concerning the theories around dependent personalities, the symptoms involved and even a thing called Dependent Personality Disorder. Stephen thought again of how the theory of the dependent personality can be linked to himself, and most others in society for that matter. After all, it seemed to him that most people don't really give these things a second thought, because they don't really think about conditions outside of their control that impact on their thinking.

He went over what he had read about Dependent Personality Disorder, and of how a particular personality is satisfied when reassured that things are taken care of if one is behaving and responding in a manner that is approved by that person, group or authority that one seeks reassurance from. Stephen thought about how many people go along with things they think might be personally wrong, but they consent all the same. He thought about how many people are scared to have a strong opinion that they will defend, as if they don't think they have the right to think for themselves. Stephen wondered if the reason for this was fear, of not wanting to be an outcast and different from the norm, and that it is easier to assent with authority, to be with others and not stand alone. He thought that people are afraid when realising they lack any real control over matters affecting one's life, so it's a relief to feel connected with a power that takes care of that fear. Stephen thought about these things and of how it is fear that controls people, and that we are socialised by the education system and media to be fearful, but not to worry because the great, all-powerful *state* will take care of it all so it's best to believe in it. It struck him how many people are weak and barely functional if not given support, direction and reassurance, because for many people living one's life without assistance is just too hard to cope with. It could mean nearly everyone in society is mentally ill, and that to be deluded is the normal condition. He questioned that maybe this state of thinking has been constructed by those with the power to do so because it's in their interest for it to be so.

Jessica asked Stephen what he was thinking about, and so he told her about what he had been reading, which had led him to think whether he had a dependent personality, and that maybe the powers that be want people to fit into the *system* and not question things, which makes people deluded, yet maybe they prefer to be, because it gives them a sense of security. She listened carefully as he spoke about his time in the scouts, then the army and how he had never really questioned authority. Concern creased her forehead as she spoke, telling Stephen that it was 'odd' for him to be giving thought to such things considering what they were facing. She was upset, although not showing it she stood up and told Stephen she was going for a walk and wanted to be alone. He asked Jessica to let him go with her, but she was adamant, and gave him a look he didn't like; it was a look of doubt. He watched Jessica through the window as she walked away, his heart aching, and he questioned his own strength of mind, and of how autonomous, if at all, his thinking had been throughout his life. It bothered him why he kept thinking about this subject, but he persisted, recounting the discipline he had experienced, and mostly enjoyed receiving when in the scouts and the army, seeing it as furnishing him with the skills, attitude and fortitude to help him through his life in all situations. He had learned to respect one's superiors, a sense of duty to others, to work as part of a team, yet capable and willing to work alone and make decisions to work things out to help oneself and others. Stephen thought back to the scouts, and he smiled as he remembered reciting the pledges he made, such as the scouts' *oath,* or *promise.* Stephen got up and walked into the smaller bedroom they didn't use. He pulled a suitcase down from the top of the wardrobe, and as he dropped it onto the bed a feeling excitement came over him.

The case contained memorabilia going back to Stephen's early childhood, most of it to do with the scouts and army. He carefully selected items, which were all in order with different things relating to each other. On the left side of the case were bits to do with the scouts and cubs, such as the woggle, scarf and jumper. He thought of the scout's oath as he looked through his treasured artefacts, and he said aloud the scout motto, 'Be Prepared.' Stephen took a book from the case, and holding it carefully as if it was very precious, he read aloud the title. 'Always A Scout.' The book was written by F. Hayden Dimmock. Stephen looked at the cover, back and front, and then opened it, flicking though pages his eyes feasted on what he was looking at. Placing the book on the bed, he returned to the case, taking out different badges for achievements and awards. A thoughtful expression shaded his face as he looked at the Activity Badges and Challenge Award badges. There were many of them, and the ultimate, the Chief Scout's Gold Award. As he looked at it, Stephen remembered how one of the leaders would encourage him and always say, 'resilience, commitment and determination.'

Stephen remembered how proud he felt as he showed his mother and father the scout's three fingered salute, explaining to them the significance and origins of the salute and why three fingers are used. Remembering by heart the three aspects of the Scout's Promise, he told his parents the meaning of the salute was to, honour God and country, to help others and to obey the 'scout law.' Stephen looked up from the suitcase, staring vaguely at the wall he thought about his mother, and of how worried she was about Jessica and him, and he thought about Jessica's mother, of when they met and of how they get on well. Jessica's father also liked Stephen, and Stephen liked him, but then he died. It was a terrible time for Jessica, although it brought her and Stephen closer together as Stephen's kindness and support helped her immensely. Jessica's brother, Chris, hadn't bonded with Stephen, it's not that they didn't get on, it's just that they were different types. He thinks Stephen is a bit of a bore and told Jessica that being in the scouts and army suited him because activities were organised and structured. Chris did the university thing of travel, liked extreme sports and wanted to live in a developing country with ideas of working in education. He saw Stephen, as he once said to his mother and sister, as 'straight' and unquestioning of the 'way of things.' On one occasion he told Jessica that Stephen was nice enough, but, 'limited in his conceptual perception,' which was a reason why, 'he accepted without doubting dictates from the government.' Jessica told Stephen what her brother had said, but he just shrugged it off saying, 'Everyone's entitled to their opinion, that's why I fought for the country.' Jessica's mother liked Stephen, although at times she found him closed as a person, but always pleasant and good to, and for, her daughter.

Stephen thought about his father, who he had never really had any conversations with about emotions or feelings, and he supposed how it was probably the same for many people. Stephen had one sibling, an older sister, Val, he really only saw her when she visited their parents with her two children, but they were now older. Stephen had never shared a great deal with her, although they were on friendly terms. Val, as others, saw Stephen as a bit of a bit of a loner, a quiet person doing things alone, and, although not having the desire to be accepted by the in-crowd, he liked to work and act within the rules of an organisation.

Although Stephen enjoyed the scouts and army, he had always preferred to solve his own dilemmas without wanting to ask for help. He worked for the best interests of a group he was part of, which he thought had been demonstrated by his commitment to his country in putting his life on the line for others he worked alongside and people he had never met. Stephen had never wanted or felt the need to pose in *team* photographs. He saw it, at times, as insincere when people use the *team*, or *group*, as a means to propel themselves forward when they wouldn't have the guts to do so by themselves.

Stephen had no contact with his sister's husband, a company man his life is defined by the company image and his work in computers, but he's good to his sister and that's all Stephen is concerned about. Stephen's parents like to go on holidays, his father has just retired with a small pension, his mother has a tiny pension, but they are careful with their limited finance; drinking and smoking hasn't taken their money. Stephen's father wasn't involved with the scout movement as some other families were, with fathers, brothers and other family members joining and becoming fully engaged in scouts' culture. Besides the scouts there were one or two boys Stephen would hang around with, but he didn't develop long-lasting relationships with them, and his relationship with his parents wasn't as close as the one his sister had with them. She had children and they liked being grandparents, but all the same, they all got on well together and they were proud of him.

Stephen looked down at the suitcase, his mood becoming sad as he thought of his family, of his life, and a weak feeling came over him as he saw it all as very small. He saw them all as not having any power to challenge the authorities that control and influence the factors determining the course and quality of their lives. As Stephen was thinking this, he picked up a plastic wallet and read aloud the words on a card inside it, 'Be Prepared.' A trace of a smile opened the lines in his face, and in doing so took away the signs of stress that had eaten into from the recent anguish. Although, it was only a momentary release as his eyes focused in concentration while reading, The Scout's Promise.

35

He then picked up Baden Powell's book, Scouting for Boys, it was an old edition that had been bought for him as a Christmas present. Stephen's interest was fully taken as he looked through the book, his mind going back to how he remembered the nine essential points laid down in 1908 by getting his mum to test him. He read the nine points making up the *scout law*, starting at number one and working through them. He remembered the commitment he felt to the values laid down in the *law* and of what a privilege it was to be part of such a great organisation. Stephen thought about the word *honour* and of how he and his fellow scouts discussed its meaning. It was important to be truthful and carry out one's duty, to be trusted and have trust in other scouts to do the same, and if not, they had to hand in their badge and would never be able to wear it again. The principle of *loyalty* is paramount in the *law* to one's King or Queen, country and superiors, for it is a *duty,* and a scout is responsible to help and do what is *best* for others. Memories flooded back as he read the *law*, remembering when he and other scouts discussed how everyone should be respected and when meeting someone, he or she should be accepted for who they are and to never look down on a person. The young Stephen was enthused to talk and think with other scouts as the adults led debates on how bullies are cowards, not to be cruel to animals and to help those that are vulnerable. They spoke of how being prudent is a virtue, money is not to be wasted, but given to those in need if one has it, to always help rather than do harm, to present a smile even when suffering and that a scout follows an order and fulfils his or her duty.

The words Stephen was reading appeared to him to be static and frozen in time, but they served as a reminder that things do not change, and they are as important, and true, now as when he first read them. Stephen felt that he had returned home, it was a cosy feeling of being close to something special and personal. He read through what he had written at the time, which was about the origin of the scouts shaking hands with the left hand, a practice filled with symbolism, honour and respect. The left arm is closer to the heart, and it is said when Baden Powell went to shake hands with African warriors from the Ashanti tribe, the African man offered his left hand, a sign showing trust to a brave person. Baden Powell had fought with, and against, the Ashanti in Africa. The left hand held the shield, so to lower it and use it to shake demonstrates the trust and respect they had for him.

Stephen read what Baden Powell had written about the Ashanti being brave fighters who defeated the British. They would run towards their enemy who had weapons of far greater power because of their technological advantage, but pride and bravery spurred them on to be feared and respected. Baden Powell learned advanced scouting skills of surviving in the jungle from Africans during his time fighting in the Boar War. He acknowledged his debt to the African warriors in his writings, and stated that without their aid his army could not have survived in the conditions they encountered in Africa. It wasn't only shaking hands with the left hand that impressed Baden Powell, the African warriors had a significant influence on the boy scout movement. The respect he had for the warriors is shown in the shape of the scouts' badge, which is based on the design of the Zulu warrior's shield.

Stephen flipped through pages of an exercise book, in which he had written down points to remember. As he read, Stephen remembered the stories that were told, some of real people who demonstrated the values a scout should adhere to and respect. The stories were about people who did their duty and served their nation, people from all walks of life, role models who demonstrate loyalty, honour and bravery while seeking to help others and do the right thing. There were fictional stories that exemplified how using the skills and knowledge one is shown and given can be put into practice and possibly save a life, even one's own. Reiterated throughout is the message to obey the law and rules, as the great effective leaders obeyed before leading others. Stephen's mood become sombre as he continued to read. He read aloud, the *promise*, 'To do my duty to God and to the Queen.'

He looked at the words, thinking about their meaning and he remembered how he felt when he was a child, his pride and commitment to his country, his loyalty to the leaders of the country and of how he felt part of a people fortunate enough to be sharing this *great* nation. He was told how the royal family, the prime minister and the government worked selflessly for the good of the people in the land. *Authority*, Stephen wrote the word on a blank wall in his mind. He looked at the word, and thought of how he has felt about its meaning and of how it made him feel. Stephen asked himself a question, what did he *really think* about *authority*, and what does it really mean?

8

There was a strange quietness in the waiting room that was different from a waiting room in the orthopaedic part of the hospital. It was an air of stillness and solemnity, the people in there were cancer patients, or friends or relatives with those having cancer, and it showed in their faces. Jessica and Stephen sat mainly in silence, every now and then holding hands, but their eyes constantly alert as they waited for a nurse to enter the area and call Jessica's name. They were being introduced to the cancer specialist team, which included a surgeon that specialises in gynaecological cancers, a clinical and medical oncologist, a clinical nurse specialist, dieticians, physiotherapists, psychologists, a radiologist, a pathologist, an occupational therapist and a counsellor. Jessica's 'treatment options' were to be discussed with her, and she was asked to think of any questions she wanted to ask the 'team' as it might help in demystifying parts of the process she was going through.

When meeting the specialist team Jessica found them to be friendly, informal and helpful. There were five people in the room with Jessica and Stephen, although the surgeon wasn't present for the meeting. Jessica was told she had epithelial ovarian cancer of a type that was serious, and it was explained to her how the cancer evolved and spread. As Jessica and Stephen were taking in the information about the cancer, one of the team, the specialist nurse, talked of possible treatment. It included surgery to remove as much of the cancer as possible, a procedure she called 'de-bulking,' and then for that to be followed up with chemotherapy to treat cancer cells unable to be seen with the naked eye and shrink the remaining cancer that couldn't be taken out during surgery.

The amount and substance of the information was immense, and the pace at which things were moving stunned Jessica and Stephen. Jessica was told she has a say in the decision of the treatment she is to have, but it seemed to her there wasn't really any choice if medical experts specialising in cancer thought she should have a particular treatment. Before leaving the meeting, Jessica was told she would be contacted in regard to a date for her next appointment, and was given the number of the specialist nurse to phone whenever she needed help. She was told the nurse is there, 'to hold her hand along the way, so never think twice before contacting her.'

The journey home was quiet, very quiet, Jessica did her best to stifle tears, but eventually gave in, and Stephen was glad that she did. It was a familiar routine when getting home, the laptop was scanned and doubled checked with other information on her phone. During those couple of weeks Jessica must have researched every site related to ovarian cancer that was written in English. The atmosphere in the living room was fraught and Stephen couldn't think of anything to say or do to break the mood. He nearly asked Jessica if she would like him to phone up for a takeaway meal, going out for a Chinese or Indian meal was something they used to like doing until recently, but her appetite and interest in things like that had completely gone. They spoke about the treatment she was going to have and how surgery and chemotherapy effects one's body. Stephen found it difficult to find the right thing to say when Jessica looked down and said dolefully how she would probably lose her hair. He knew it wasn't suitable to make lighthearted quips, he wanted to say something to brighten her spirit, but couldn't think of anything, and then Jessica snapped at him, 'Well, say something – just sitting there nodding at me.'

She stared at him for a few moments before her gaze became soft. Stephen could see she was sorry, and just as he started to speak, Jessica stood up and said she didn't mean to be nasty and that she was going into the bedroom. 'See you, love,' Stephen said quietly as he watched her leave, and she flapped her hand at him in an apologetic gesture while forcing a smile, which twisted a pain in his stomach.

Stephen turned the television on, keeping the volume low as he looked through things on his phone, and without thinking he realised he had typed in the words, 'chemotherapy and its effects.' He sat for a long time, the evening turning into night, but, for Stephen, time had lost meaning. His attention was diverted to the television, a man was speaking about the government, politics and business. The man said, 'Tax avoidance is endemic in high finance.' Stephen turned up the volume and concentrated on what he was saying. 'It's not illegal because the laws are made to benefit those avoiding tax, and if an occasion does arise where things have transgressed the law, well, then the law is changed to accommodate the avoidance, for that is the objective.' The man went on to say how money isn't made available to important services because of lost revenue to the government, but the news then changed to something to do with a forthcoming boat race. Stephen turned off the television and stared at the blank screen, his mind unable to focus on a specific point. He continued to sit, becoming increasingly conscious of his presence in the room. It felt uncomfortable and strange. He got up quickly, so quickly a spasm shot across his lower back. Stephen decided to go for a walk, he felt annoyed at not being able to concentrate on one particular thing, and it was because of feeling angry that things in life aren't fair.

As soon as Stephen stepped outside, he was reminded that the winter months had already started, but not wanting to go back indoors and get his heavier coat he zipped up his jacket and continued on his way. After walking for about twenty minutes he jumped on a bus that drew up at a stop he was walking by, he didn't look to see where it was going, and he didn't care. The driver barely acknowledged Stephen when he had nodded and wished him a good evening, although he stared at him with eyes that looked like they had seen a great deal of suffering and injustice. The man's eyes showed he was suspicious of people's motives, however well-intentioned they might be. Stephen took a seat near the driver and watched him, and the driver knew he was being watched, his cold eyes pierced through Stephen when their gazes met in the rear-view mirror. The driver reminded Stephen of men he had seen in Iraq, and the way he was looking at him took Stephen back to when he was in battledress checking people's ID's and patrolling neighbourhoods that had all remnants of progressive civilisation beaten and blown out of them. Maybe the man came from Iraq, Stephen guessed he was from that part of the world, and for a crazy second he wondered if they had met before and the man recognised him, and should he ask him where he came from.

Stephen took a deep breath and looked out of the window. He looked at the passing shops, all closed with neon lighting splashing across the pavements and reflecting on the windows of the bus. And there they were, those cold, dark eyes, framed in the mirror, watching Stephen, diverting direction when Stephen looked up, but only to return again. Stephen leaned forward in his seat, blowing hard onto his clenched fists, his mind flitting from his time in Iraq to the hospital that afternoon, the way Jessica snapped at him, of how powerless he felt in helping Jessica, back to Iraq, Jessica crying, his impotence in his inability to change the situation, the specialist cancer team, the specialist nurse, her nodding and smiling, Iraq, and there he was, looking at him in the mirror, the driver, his eyes showing a persistence that can't be broken, not even with torture by men with guns, dogs and implements and methods that are designed to instil pain and terror.

9

Stephen felt the driver's eyes fixed on the back of his head when getting off the bus, he lifted the short collar on his jacket in an effort to stave off a cold wind, but also to act as a shield from the bus driver's glare, and he began to walk in no specific direction He was now in a busy part of town and before long the faces of people that passed him lost all character and features. Stephen was tired and thought about going into a cafe for a hot drink, but decided against it after looking through the windows of a few of them. It wasn't so much the people in the cafés that put him off, it was that they seemed together, and the ones sitting alone seemed very alone. Stephen wanted to talk to someone, but he felt estranged from the people he had seen through the windows. A mood of solitary sadness was replaced by a feeling of being deserted, it was strange feeling and one he hadn't felt before. Stephen snapped out of it, guilty for feeling that way, Jessica was suffering and he had to be there for her. He *wanted* to be there for her.

Stephen came to a busy junction connecting three popular streets; the area throbbed with activity. He stood there quite a while, not thinking about anything, but just looking at the coming and going. The odd blast of a car horn taking his attention momentarily before he settled back to watching nothing in particular. Voices grew in volume and then trailed off. Laughter sounded sharp and hard, and then vanished into a backdrop of fragmented noises making up the whole sound, which is that of a bustling city. It struck Stephen how standing in the eye of hurricane is sometimes the best place for meditative thoughts, if one feels apart from the rush, that is. He continued to think of how a designated place for relaxation can somehow be seen as false, in that it is constructed for a specific purpose and demands certain protocol, and he thought how everything starts and ends within a person. His musings lingered and strayed until the cold began to chill him, taking his attention away from his thoughts. He looked around, thinking which street to walk down, and on seeing a sign for a train station he decided to go there and make his way back home.

The station was set back from the road, and running along the front and one side of it was a concrete wall. Within the enclosed space between the wall and the station were bits and pieces making up makeshift beds for people who were homeless and living on the streets. On seeing the bags and blankets, Stephen imagined how it must be terrible to sleep out in the cold weather, winter hadn't really started and the thought of it caused him to shudder. Just before turning into the station he stopped and took a closer look at some bedding next to the wall that was heavily marked with graffiti, and then became aware of a person standing in the shadows against the wall. It was a man, and he was watching Stephen. He saw the man's face more clearly as he took one step away from the wall towards Stephen. It was dirty and unshaven, dark rings around his eyes accentuated his grey pallor. The man was tall, having broad shoulders and although gaunt, his presence still retained some power as there were indications that he had once been physically fit.

'What you looking for?' He snapped, his eyes changing shape as he weighed Stephen up, who shrugged and answered in an innocuous manner, 'Nothing.'

'Thought you might be a cop,' the man said, and he took another couple of steps towards Stephen, 'Maybe looking for someone – on the prowl.' He stood in front of Stephen, 'But there's nobody here, pal, so there's no need to hang round, eh?'

Stephen nodded, the man didn't intimidate him, he had too much on his mind to really take that much notice. The man studied Stephen, wondering why he wasn't moving, but then he detected something in him. It was an essence he had seen and felt before in and about people who were beyond caring, maybe out of weariness, but also because they knew the hoping for what they wanted was hopeless, and no scruffy person emerging from a murky corner is going to make a dent in the way he felt.

'You all right Pal? Standing there like a dog who's lost his ball.' Stephen noticed how the man's voice was less abrasive and threatening, and there was also a way about him he recognised which was familiar and drew him towards the man. Stephen nodded, his manner congenial as he spoke, 'Suppose I have.'

'You don't look too bad, mate,' the man said, 'you could be in my position.'

Stephen looked at the man, remaining silent he surveyed the area where they were standing.

'Spent years in the army, giving it all for the country,' the man said, and he gestured with a tired wave at the rags and bags on the ground, 'What the Taliban couldn't do to me, this country and the people in it, did – bring me down.'

Stephen looked from the man to what he assumed were his meagre belongings on the ground. He thought about what the man had said, and he began to speak. 'I was in the army, for about six years.'

The man looked closely at Stephen before saying, 'I was in Afghanistan,' and he nodded at Stephen to evoke a response, 'You?'

'Iraq, got injured in 2003 – IED.'

The man's eyes surveyed Stephen, contemplating what Stephen had said he looked him up and down, evaluating who and what he was, and then he slowly nodded his head in confirmation that the man standing in front of him was bona fide. He put out his hand to shake, his eyes not leaving Stephen's as he did so. 'Ray, my name's Ray.' His handshake was strong, the grip nearly painful, and all the while he looked at Stephen, his eyes sallow, although telling a story of a man who was tough and never backed down if provoked.

Stephen gave a wry smile, 'We had the same assault rifle to keep us alive – standard issue.'

'The SA80 gear,' Ray said, and he nodded with irony, 'You know as well as me the things jammed up, they tested them in places that didn't come up to battle conditions, y'know, extreme like in Afghanistan and Iraq – we all know that.' He pulled a face and said sarcastically, 'Oh, British made and designed, so it's got to be the best – only the best for our boys.' He dropped the sarcastic voice, 'Yeah, that general, what's his face, he campaigned to keep the thing, saying it was up to the job – because of money, he was most probably an investor in it – cost hundreds of millions so they didn't want to research all over again and develop or buy a new one off the shelf.' He stopped talking and looked at Stephen, 'But you know this stuff, don't you?'

Stephen nodded, but only slightly, because he was embarrassed that he didn't know all the details, and also his mind was elsewhere, it was back in Iraq. He was walking behind a soldier, and another soldier was behind him, there was a line of them walking on the outskirts of village, knowing the enemy were hiding, waiting for the correct time to open fire, his stomach feeling upset and his mouth dry with nerves. He looked at the faces of the locals, they knew something was about to happen, they were also nervous, some not wanting to catch the eye of a soldier. Were they part of the ambush? Ready to give the signal? Or were they just fearing both sides? They were merely used as shields by the *enemy*, knowing their gruesome fate if they didn't comply with them, and Stephen gripped his rifle, tightly. Stephen's attention zoomed in on the faces of the locals, this is something he had often done in the past, remembering the looks on their faces, some innocent, just looking, although scared and bewildered by what their lives had become. There were those who were working as informers, and then Stephen saw the bus driver's eyes in the mirror. The eyes were watching him, just as Stephen had watched people in the land where the bus driver probably came from. The eyes narrowing as the man assessed who and what Stephen actually was, and Stephen looked away, just as the locals in the bus driver's land looked away when he had stared judgementally at them. Stephen became aware of Ray speaking to him, although not having heard what he had said because he was too deeply preoccupied with his thoughts. The bus driver had really unsettled him.

'Jesus, we envied the fuckers with their fifth hand AK's,' Ray said, 'You can bury them in the sand for months, dig them up and they still work.' He looked at Stephen, 'But you know that.'

Stephen nodded and as he mumbled a reply, Ray leaned in close to him, looking with concern into Stephen's face. 'What's up mate? You drifted off then – miles away.'

Stephen shrugged, and when Ray realised that was going to be his answer he continued talking. 'Went in there to stop international terrorism, and also to improve human rights in the country – construct a strong and stable state, and develop the economy, and all that goes with it. Yeah, when we went there in 2001 it was to take out the Taliban and wipe out Al-Qaeda – an American led invasion to counter terrorism.' He turned the words over in his mouth, as if they had an unpleasant taste before continuing. 'Then people laughed at us, calling us social workers, going out there only so girls can go to school – that's what they said, and it made people angry – it had parents asking if that was the reason their son died in the shit end of the world, so girls could go to school? Was that the reason?'

Ray stared at Stephen, 'Of course it wasn't.'

Stephen didn't say anything, and Ray carried on. 'That's the thanks we get – but then again, we're only servants – look at the Elizabethan wars with the Spanish, Queen Elizabeth the First's speech to the army at Tilbury, 1588 – look it up, another family argument, she gave him, the Spanish king, the cold shoulder, anyway, "and we do assure you, on a word of a prince" – that's what she said when promising to pay the men who fought for her and the country – "faithful and loving people" – that's what she called *her* people – yeah, giving it a lot of bollocks of how we're all in it together.'

Disgust showed on his face as he spat, 'But that didn't happen – typhus killed off most of the sailors, and she didn't pay them anyway, and the ones that survived, the few, are said to have died penniless, homeless and sick in the gutters of Margate.'

Ray looked about him, at the cardboard mattresses, at the dregs of the society, a place that he now existed and survived in, and he turned to Stephen, his words measured, 'So, not a lot has changed, my friend.'

Stephen also looked around at the filth and debris, existing only feet away from the enticing neon lustre and people competing to participate in something that has become no more than a memory to many of those inhabiting a world where Stephen was now standing.

'It's all been downgraded, and it's planned that way,' Ray went on, 'Use warriors to do the dirty work and then dishonour them, cos the government can't be seen as mean and nasty.' He looked at Stephen, maybe waiting for a response to what he had just said, but there wasn't one, so he continued. 'You know what I mean – get the booty, but that needs some rough hands, and the strategy is to cover themselves, send out confusing and conflicting messages, so the average Joe doesn't really know what's going on, and to a lot of people we're little more than a joke.'

Ray spoke how a lot of what they did for the country isn't taken seriously and it shows itself in different ways, 'Some of it is just pathetic. Take this fella I saw going to meet his kid from school dressed in a desert camouflage uniform, but I clocked it was American. It wasn't British, he'd unstitched all the yank stuff from the collars and sleeves, and the name from the left breast – the idiot had bought it in a shop, or online – I looked at him, he was holding the hand of a little girl. I wanted to say to him, 'Where did you serve mate? Fucking McDonald's? You fucking waste bag – and then maybe smack the cunt – but the little girl put me off doing anything. Yeah, then I started noticing other ones, probably desk job warriors, only thing they held was a pen – yeah, being met at the school gate by their *hero* – the kids had most likely done a project in school, about soldiers in Afghanistan, or Iraq, or wherever, and some of the kids had lied, saying their dads were out there, giving them some kudos so the other kids would like them – you can imagine it, can't you?'

Stephen thought about it, not knowing whether to smile he just slowly shook his head. Ray looked at him, maybe guessing what Stephen was thinking, and then he continued, 'I bet there are some kids who kick up a right fuss at home and force their old man to get dressed up like a *hero* – fuck me, any soppy cunt can buy the uniforms – they have shops full of them, look at these wankers who think they're hip or some shit, all camouflage trousers and boots, making out they're a rebel – maaan – or those dicks that go hunting – for squirrels – got all the gear on in case they come under enemy fire, when they're hunting squirrels – gives them a stiffy, when they'd really like to be killing people, but they're cowards as well as sicko cunts – could never face a real enemy, an army, men with guns, who want to kill them, sleeping rough, a couple of hours a night, and never really relaxed, sitting in a vehicle always wondering if that's going to be it – bang! A roadside bomb, an IED.'

Ray's eyes narrowed as he looked back through the years reflecting over a particular memory. 'I was involved in one – one second we were bumping along, being jolted around as we drove on a rough track road, and then it happened – suddenly the whole world is fucked in the air, screaming and shouting, I'm on the ground not knowing how the fuck I got there, and then realising what it must have been, and there was one of my mates, screaming, his leg completely gone, what's left of it, like strands of cheesy pizza pulling away from his hip – heavy on the tomatoes.'

An image flashed in front of Stephen's eyes of the young man he shot in Iraq, lying on the ground, his face and head broken and split apart, and Stephen tried to remember if he saw what he looked like before he killed him. He concentrated, trying to think what the young man would have looked like before his features were smashed and splintered, all life gone, the only thing left was a shattered and bloodied shell. A woman's son, a man's son, a brother. He was a person, maybe just innocently standing there, trying to get on with his life, just like anyone else; just like Jessica. Stephen thought about why he was thinking what he was. He was thinking about it in a way that he had never done before. Stephen couldn't stop thinking about it, of how the young man might have been running an errand for his mother, who was ill, or on his way to visit someone, like an elderly relative who was relying on him turning up, but he never came, because he was killed. He was shot by a man with a gun who was part of a foreign army, who didn't really know where he was or what he was really doing there. He shot him, because he was told to; so, he did.

Ray's voice pulled Stephen from his thoughts. 'Yeah, these wanna be soldier boys, lying in their beds, wanking themselves to sleep thinking up fantasies of shooting people – but having to do with shooting squirrels – because they haven't got any enemy in their lives, not a real enemy, someone who wants to kill them – who wants to shoot their fucking brains out, blow them to fucking bits – oh no, they don't know the fear of being captured and tortured – have your nails pulled out, and your eyes gouged out – cut your fucking cock off and wave it in front of your face – smash every bone in your hands, just for fun, and then tie you to the back of a truck and drive around their shit hole town – the skin ripped from your face and head, shredded to the bone, and the locals will come out and laugh, hit you with what they can get their hands on, the women and the kids, kicking you when you're dead and setting the body on fire – fucking great – it's a fuck lot safer shooting squirrels – get a night's sleep in your luxury bed, stuff your face with a full breakfast, take a shit in a clean, warm bathroom. Hey, and take a shower – then go out, dressed as a mercenary guerrilla soldier, packing your gun – you know what they're going to do, don't you?'

'Shoot squirrels,' Stephen said, his expression deadpan.

Ray nodded, disgust showing as a smile he gave a short nod in acknowledging that Stephen knew and that they understood one another. He then twisted his mouth and spat out words, unable to abide their foul taste, 'Heroes – what a fucking joke, it's all bollocks, just another thing some fucker came up with to make some money or a name for himself.

'Yeah, let's forget Helmand, it never happened – but it did – lack of support, equipment and intelligence – they don't want to talk about that, and the public don't know or don't care about it. I saw too many of our boys, good men, morphined to fuck and staring into a trance, not knowing what's happened and scared fuckless – bits of their bodies blown off. It shouldn't have been that

47

way.' Ray stopped and looked down at the ground, as if noticing for the first time how dirty it was. He looked up, his tone bitter, 'We were let down – we were combat soldiers, Jesus, take the way we were looking for IED'S, there must be better ways for metal detection – use dogs, more sophisticated kit, fuck me, a bunch of kids, give them a bit of training and send them out crawling about on their hands and knees searching with their fingers – it's worse than taking the piss.'

Ray's voice disappeared as Stephen had a flashback, to his time in Iraq. A young British soldier is lying on a hospital bed, his face looked like that of a young boy and his expression was childish, as if trying not to cry in front of his friends. His legs have gone and half an arm missing. He is trying to make the best of it by putting on a brave face, but Stephen caught him off guard. His face showed despair and the misery he knows will now be his life, forever, and Stephen thought about how he knew the boy will crumble when he is away from the army environment. And then what? To take his own life, as many do in that situation? Stephen thought how the *hero* thing rings very brittle after the handshakes and questions from people in one's neighbourhood, and then what? There is the alienation, isolated in a flat and bypassed in the street by those who shook his hand when he came back. Now a failure, and the state benefits aren't as supportive as one imagines they might be, and the bitterness at seeing others getting more sympathy and understanding from social workers...'

Ray was still talking; he talked continually. Stephen thought that maybe Ray hadn't been able to release his feelings onto someone he felt would understand him, but he had experience of what Ray had seen and was talking about. Ray spoke about ex-servicemen and the difference between 'front line' troops who saw action and 'pen pushers' who get the same wages and pension and aren't, percentagewise, going to suffer homelessness, trauma, drink and drug problems, family break ups, ending up in prison, violence or committing suicide. He spoke about the ones who had seen action and involved in combat, and when home wait ages for support, and because of that are more probable to be homeless and commit suicide.

'Sometimes they wait a couple of years for help, therapy, whatever – it's usually too little too late – people often just give up – they commit suicide.'

Ray stopped speaking and looked at Stephen, who didn't say anything, but just looked at him and listened carefully. Ray went on. 'I've met ex-vets who say their best friend is their dog – great, isn't it? Fight for your country and you end up on the streets, scared to sleep and the threat of getting beaten up by drunk idiots, and at the end having a dog for your closest companion.'

Stephen asked Ray how many ex-soldiers killed themselves. Ray shook his head and told him that he didn't know. 'Hundreds, I suppose – they don't wanna know. We're swept aside – the liberal elite call us cowards and murderers for invading other people's countries, and that we're unthinking pawns for the rich to prosper from – poor people killing poor people – that's what they say. The fact that we fought so they have the freedom to demonstrate and criticise is ignored and sneered at. They say we, the soldiers, are told that stuff about fighting for other people's liberty to keep us believing we're doing something worthwhile, when it isn't true, our actions in fact have made everywhere less safe for the ordinary person wherever they live – "don't believe you went there to help the people, do you?" That's what they say – and I had one spit in my face and call me a racist and a fascist when I had a go at her – yeah, we're burned up and fucked off out of the picture my friend – unwanted dogs, our function served.'

Nothing was said between Ray and Stephen, they stood in silence, each one going over thoughts and experiences related to their time in the army, and the silence continued until Ray broke it by sneering, 'Yeah, anyway, it's the domino effect, once things start falling down, it all drops to the ground – my wife left me.' He nodded bitterly, 'Of course she did, and being as polite as she could, said it was because of my,' and he pulled a face as he added with sarcasm, 'post war trauma.' He told Stephen how his daughter thinks he is 'weird' and doesn't speak to him, and that she once said to him, 'You're not a hero, just a saddo.'

Ray shrugged at the thought of it, embittered resignation to how hard life can be stained his face, and he spat, although nothing came from his mouth. 'When leaving the army, I found myself getting easily wound up by the no nothing's in pubs and bars – well, everywhere really. Yeah, wound up *too* easily. Work was crap and paid rubbish so I got into security work. I thought I might as well get paid for dishing out violence as I'm doing it for nothing to idiots – some of them with their twelve grand watches, paying hundreds of pounds for a shirt – all that crap, thinking they're someone, when they're nothing, and they mean nothing to anyone who's got any power – they'd be wiped away like dog shit from the bottom of a boot.'

49

He spoke of how he swapped from doing work in personal security, such as bodyguarding, to working as a mercenary soldier in different countries. He looked squarely at Stephen and said, 'Afghanistan wasn't the only place I despatched people with a bullet in their heads – no, my friend, I got the killing bug – not saying I'm proud of it, but it was like a lust, like having a hunger for war – a *need* for war.'

Ray looked around, his eyes discarding anything they seized upon, and then he looked at Stephen. 'Listen my friend, don't think PTSD only affects the good guys,' and he told Stephen about a time when he shared a prison cell with an ex IRA man who had, 'gone off his head' and got involved in dealing drugs when his life had hit rock bottom. Ray gave a shrug of incredulity, 'What numbskull would put ex IRA and British army in the same cell?' He shook his head, 'I served out there, in Ireland for fuck's sake.' Ray spoke of how the two of them became, 'buddies,' and swapped stories of what they had done.

Ray stopped talking and looked across the street for a few seconds before turning to Stephen. 'He topped himself – too much pressure on the outside. He feared a bullet when he got out – nowhere to go...' But Stephen wasn't listening to Ray, his attention was on a passing bus, and his heart stopped when he looked at the driver, he thought it was the same man who was driving the bus earlier on. The bus driver turned and looked at him, and Stephen was sure the driver turned in his seat and looked because he recognised him. His heart was racing and his mouth dried as he continued to look in the direction that the bus had gone. Ray tapped Stephen's shoulder and said, 'You okay mate? What's wrong – seen a ghost, or something?'

It took Stephen a few seconds to settle himself, but the sight of the passing bus had disturbed him, and he found it hard to concentrate for the rest of the conversation he had with Ray. He felt it was time to stop talking and told Ray he had to go, and then without intending to, he told Ray about Jessica having cancer. The words gushed out as he spoke of how the system was unfair, and that his wife's chances of keeping her life has been determined by people in power who most definitely have privileges in having healthcare ordinary people don't have. He told Ray everything, about the IVF, the private treatment, the diagnosis of Cancer, the treatment that's planned, how Jessica has read there is treatment that is unavailable in this country, or to people who cannot afford it, but hopefully they won't be in that situation. Tears filled Stephen's eyes as looked up to what were once called the heavens and he gritted his teeth in frustration. Ray stepped in close to Stephen and gripped his arm, 'Be strong – be strong – remember, swift and bold – swift and bold – you're not a quitter, we're not made that way, always at the front in a battle – and this is another one, doesn't matter whether they're sand kickers or pen pushers in government jobs lining their pockets – they're the enemy.' Ray looked deep into Stephen's eyes, and then gripping his shoulders he said, 'Action, we have experienced action – they haven't – we need to bring it home to them,' and he continued to grip Stephen's shoulders as he stared into his eyes.

Ray put his arm around Stephen and hugged him tightly. Stephen managed a weak smile as he acknowledged what Ray had said, 'Swift and Bold,' their old regiment motto, and he thanked Ray in words no louder than a quiet whisper. Stephen took a step backwards, and shaking his head to clear his mind, he told Ray that he had to go as Jessica was at home and he had work in the morning. Ray looked at him and said, 'Thanks for reminding me of what I've lost.' Stephen dropped his head and said, 'You know what I mean.' Ray gave a smile and said calmly, 'Yeah, I know what you mean, and I know you mean well, my friend.'

Stephen thrust out his hand and looked Ray squarely in his eyes. Ray gripped his hand tightly, and placing his other hand on Stephen's upper arm he squeezed it as he said, 'We don't fall – only when if we get shot.' Stephen smiled and turned, looking at what seemed to him at that moment as an assemblage of wasted luxury, with the garish lights that seduce to sell either trash, excitement or opulence, the passing cars intended to project status and the rushing people, each one playing their part in keeping the scene lit and vibrant. Stephen felt that beneath it all there was a fragility that is always constant, and is always felt by the people in the scene, but rarely questioned.

10

The only thought in Stephen's mind, as he sat behind his desk at work the next morning, was of Jessica. She had been told to be 'positive,' but as much as he told himself things will work out, he couldn't convince himself that there would be a happy ending. He looked up at a woman who had spoken to him, but he hadn't heard what she said as his mind was elsewhere. Stephen apologised, but it was met sarcasm as she asked him if being at work was keeping him from having a sleep. She told him a man was coming in for an interview and he was to take him to a room and then let her know, as she will be conducting the interview. He watched the woman walk back to her desk and sit down, her face taut with serious concern, she was diligent in her approach to work and tenacious in bringing those to *justice* who have defrauded the *system*. Stephen had noticed how she was servile to those authority, but treated colleagues she was superior to without much respect. He thought about the system where he worked, and where others work, a system that creates divisions, a fragmented workforce, each one working for themselves, even though a lot is made of working as part of a *team*. Stephen's position is called a Revenue Officer, which is a second layer job, the first being a Revenue Assistant, which is what he started as, a role seen as *menial* in that it consists of filing, basic data analysis, collecting information on a person under investigation and passing it to a Revenue Officer. The Revenue Officer collates the pertinent information and passes it to a Revenue Executive, a computerised letter is sent to the person under investigation to come to the office to be interviewed by the Revenue Executive; the woman who spoke to Stephen was a Revenue Executive.

Thoughts about Graham Mears entered Stephen's mind as his attention drifted from his work to an article he had read about Mears online, although it wasn't only about him, but other wealthy people in high positions of influence. It was a scathing criticism of how Mears, and many like him, do not have the personal morals or intellectual abilities they claim to possess. The myth is a successful tactic in the maintenance of a system that's set up to be primarily in the interests of themselves and to the detriment of the people who vote for them and pay their taxes. The writer of the article went on, pointing out that Mears failed in everything he tried when leaving university, even an exam to become a journalist, but not to worry as a family friend got him intern work and a job as an aid in Westminster. He was set up to follow that well-trodden route of the privileged. The writer of the article concluded with how the word 'virtue' isn't in their dictionary, while propounding the word *talent* as a reason they and their friends occupy positions of power in society. When in reality, people with a high intellect who are honest, hardworking and have studied for qualifications to do a job they can bring understanding and experience to, are not given the chance to do so, because things are run by an affluent elite making up an inner circle that exists in a parallel society to our own, which they exploit for their own interests.

What Stephen read in the article filled his mind and he couldn't stop thinking how futile his work was in making any meaningful contribution to bettering the society we live in. He was beginning to think more and more of how *ordinary* people do not want to redress the unfairness that exists. They are not only resigned to compete with each other in trying to make a life for themselves, but will turn against and lambaste people that are in a similar situation to themselves, rather than criticise a corrupt system with those people in positions of power that directly affect their own lives in negative ways. Stephen knew he was changing, he hadn't in the past thought about this subject as he was now with such interest. He didn't talk about how he felt at work, he wouldn't, but from what he had been learning, about the powerful with their corruption and hypocrisy, irritated him, especially when a tax officer gloated about nailing someone for tax fraud, when it was obvious the person wasn't getting away with hardly anything and their situation was dire with bad luck playing its part. Stephen knew it was because the tax officers couldn't change the system so they were striking out at who they could, but he felt, even if that might be so, it didn't mean he had to agree with them. He thought about Jessica and of how treatment for cancer was available, but not for everyone. He felt a growing sense of anger with hopeless despair, and then his thoughts were brought to an abrupt end when a young man, who worked at the 'desk,' came up to Stephen and told him the man had come in for his interview.

Stephen went out to the waiting room and introduced himself to the man before taking him to an interview room and asking him to sit down, but as Stephen turned to leave, the man started talking to him, telling Stephen he was a self-employed builder. He told Stephen that his wife had died eight years before from cancer. He spoke of how there were problems keeping up payments on a mortgage he wanted to see through, as he and his wife had planned to leave their house to their two children, who were both now married, or in relationships with children of their own, and, 'finding it tough going.'

The man went on, telling Stephen about how he wanted to help his children in the only way he could, but he also wanted to do it for his wife. Stephen didn't like this aspect of the job. His colleagues didn't have, or didn't show, sympathy, only saying it was their fault and they were knowingly defrauding the government and making other *honest* taxpayers pay for them. Stephen felt they didn't see, or didn't want to understand, that not everyone who they came across had set out to commit fraud. He believed that situations change people, causing them to act in ways they would never have thought of when their personal circumstances were different. Stephen thought about Ray, the man he had met the previous night, and of how he was a person changed by his circumstances and what he had experienced, and although one should to take responsibility for one's choices and actions, it wasn't too much to ask the country to help a person who was willing to give up his life for it. He continued to think about Ray, and many others like him that are experiencing hard times, and that there should be recognition of what these people have done, but it seemed many people in society were ignorant of their plight or didn't even care about it. Stephen started to speak, trying to be friendly he smiled as he told the man that he understood how things can go wrong and not as we planned, but the man rejected Stephen's amiable approach and said, 'That's what they tell you to say, to get me talking, that's your ploy, then stick the knife in my back – no mate, just get the other fella out here, or whoever it is, let's get on with it, I don't want to speak to the oily rag.'

What the man said startled Stephen. He had been sworn at many times during the course of his work, people get angry in these situations, but it was the way he said, 'the oily rag.' It made him feel uncomfortable and incompetent, like a man who is not of any real worth at all. He was nothing more than a person with a small and easily replaceable function in a system that has been designed to project an image of upholding the law, but is merely a façade.

The man looked at Stephen, pausing to giver greater effect to what he was going to say. 'I'll tell you a story, as it reminds me of people like you – it was when I was young, about thirteen years of age and I used to go to the cinema by myself on Sunday afternoons, if my friends weren' around. Anyway, I went to the cinema, and was disappointed to find out the only film to see wa True Grit, with John Wayne – who I couldn't bear – but I went in and sat halfway down on a

54

aisle seat. I sat there rolling myself a cigarette, because I began to smoke at an early age, and I thought it was all very grown up. The yobbos in those days would sit down at the front, in the front row, making a noise, being abusive, shouting things out and whistling, you know, that really loud whistle people do by placing their fingers in their mouth? They used to flick their lighted cigarette ends up at the screen and make remarks to girls going into the toilet – the carpet in front of the screen was dotted with cigarette burns – it was a constant problem in those days.

'So, I'm sitting there, very cheesed off because I've spent my money on seeing a film I didn't want to see, and then my arm is being tugged by a young fella who worked at the cinema. I would say he was about sixteen years of age, all thin and weak looking. He pulled at my arm and said, "Out you go, you've got to leave, no whistling – it's not allowed."

'I told him it wasn't me, but the lot at the front, it was them, they were the ones making a noise, flicking their fags in the air and whistling – and then I told him, and this is true, that I can't whistle anyway, and I demonstrated by putting my fingers in my mouth and blowing, but there was no whistling sound.

'Anyway, he wasn't having any of it – he tugged at my arm and told me I had to go, and I said that I had paid my money and I hadn't whistled – he told me I would be refunded my money, which instantly pleased me, as I didn't want to see the film and I'd be getting my money back. So, I willingly stood up and went with him – but, as we turned, I noticed him look down at the yobs at the front, and a nervous tic showed itself on the side of his mouth, and there was resentment in his eyes.

'He knew it wasn't me doing the whistling, but he was too scared to confront the mob at the front – worried what they'd say, or do – maybe he'd tried in the past and had been embarrassed at being called names, or threatened, and he was probably scared they'd wait for him outside and beat him up, or that he would see some of them around town another day. Anyway, I could sense his relief as we walked up the steps and out into the foyer, where a bored girl in the cashier booth gave me my money back. Three and six, it being old money then, but standing there was the manager, a man in a black suit, staring at the young man, and he didn't look very happy. The light in the foyer showed the acne spots and pimples on the young man's face, and his skinny body looked even more feeble than it did in the dark. He tried to avoid looking at the manager,

55

who I guessed had asked him to throw out one of the trouble makers at the front – and he had come back with me. The manager knew it wasn't me doing the whistling, and that the young man had picked on an easy target – because he was afraid. It wasn't so much disappointment showing in the manager's face, but disgust at the young man's cowardice, and knowingly throwing out an innocent person.'

The man leaned back, breathing in deeply he regarded Stephen with contempt and his expression intensified as he went on, 'And you know what?' But Stephen wasn't going to answer, because his mind had left the interview room and was back in Iraq. 'Shoot him,' the voice of Stephen's Sergeant sounded in his ears, and so he did. The young man was lying on the ground, stock-still, no breathing or no movement at all. Stephen thought of how the young man's body had stopped, and it would never move again. The face was broken and shattered. *He* had done that, Stephen Dale, he had done this thing. A fly landing on what was left of the young man's cheek, it was just like a doll with the stuffing spread out of the back of its head. Blood, veins, bone, tissue and gunge, and Stephen's mind returned to the room. He was finding it difficult to breathe and hadn't heard what the man had been saying, but nodded all the same and saw how he had become angry. 'Going after the easy targets, when knowing the real criminals are allowed to continue doing as they wish.' The man went on, 'Let off scot-free, because people are scared of them – and in the case of people like you, you must know this, in your heart, but of course, there's nothing you can do about it because of your position in the system.

'You see mate, you're just a maggot, like the rest of us – all slaves picking on each other because we can't have a go at the slave masters – isn't it? Eh? That's the way it is – that young man in the cinema, like the police nicking petty criminals, when the real criminals get away with what they're doing, because they run the show – just like you, chasing the likes of me, when you know the real tax avoiders are living it up at our expense – laughing at us, because they run the show with their mates in parliament – the politicians, pulling the same strokes as their crooked business friends – and we pay for it – they make the rules, and there's nothing a minnow like you can do about it, so you knowingly chase the little man, making out it's so important.'

The man stopped and looked at Stephen for few seconds before continuing. 'It must enter your mind at night when you're in bed, thinking about your mortgage payments, the car, a new kitchen, the kids, their future, what you can provide – and the rich, basking in the luxury we've supplied for them – and you work for a system riddled with hypocrisy, because it's run by the rich to give themselves favours – while sucking the shit out of the country.'

Stephen had to leave. The woman, the Revenue Executive, would be asking him why he had taken so long just to take someone to a room. He didn't say anything to the man, he just left, absently closing the door, his mind was elsewhere, again, drifting to places and people, to ideas and things he had read and heard others say; and then it locked. It was as if everything in his head seized up and solidified so that he couldn't think at all.

The thought of staying at work filled Stephen with dread and he just didn't feel he could see out the rest of the day. He was trembling with anxiety, his mouth was dry and his hands were shaking as he stood outside his office, trying to mop sweat from his face he prayed no one would come through the door. When back at his desk, he found it nearly impossible to concentrate, and there was a nasty taste in his mouth, of what it was he couldn't put his finger on. The Revenue Executive returned from having interviewed the man Stephen had spoken to, shooting him a contemptuous glance as she sat down. Stephen saw the look on her face, as if dismissing him as a person because he couldn't handle any real responsibility. He felt a burn cut into his stomach and his breathing shortened even more than it had been. Stephen wanted to say something to her, something like how he had coped with responsibility before and seen difficult situations though to their conclusion, so shuffling paperwork around and berating a person who has been doing a bit of work on the side without declaring the earnings to the tax office, pales by comparison to the life and death situations he had been in.

He felt awkward, more than awkward he felt incredibly self-conscious and thought people were watching every minute movement and activity he did. It made him clumsy, he fumbled with a file, which then dropped onto the floor, and when a colleague spoke to him, asking if he was okay, he couldn't answer because his mouth was so dry. The Revenue Executive looked at him, her contempt for Stephen showing clearly because of his incompetence. Stephen asked himself why he was so anxious, and then from nowhere he had to stop tears from forming and running down his face. He nearly cried out, the thought of Jessica and her suffering was so strong it physically shook his body. He looked over at the Revenue Executive, and a crazy idea came into his mind of going over to her and ask if they could go to a quiet corner so he could explain what was happening in his personal life, so he could tell her about Jessica, the IVF treatment and now

57

the cancer. He rebuked himself for thinking of such a thing, and then completely unintentionally he said out loud, 'What the hell is happening to me?'

Stephen looked around the office, a few people had turned and looked at him, one of them was the Revenue Executive.

11

The building felt strange, it was like a sports clubhouse, which was in a field away from other buildings, contained with its own rules that are observed by those who are *members*, or *guests*. It was because of the building being set apart from its surroundings that there was a feeling of disconnect, and that gave a potentially sinister feel. All activity was indistinct and without sound. The people serving behind a bar and the patrons did so silently, some animated in their actions, patting each other's backs and laughing, but without any sound. There were a few young children, their interests different from the adults as they ran around, one boy sliding across the floor on his knees, they were screaming and laughing, but there wasn't any noise. It was silent. It was as though it was all happening behind a screen, and the observer of this action wasn't part of it. He, she, they, were cut off and separate from the happenings, and it was also as if the observer wasn't invited. The observer turned away. The observer was Stephen, and on turning away he found himself in a large room. It was like an old-fashioned hospital ward, or a large mortuary with bodies laid out on slabs. Stephen felt scared, the place was horrible, he didn't know where he was or how he got there. He wanted to leave, and began searching for an exit from the disturbing place he had found himself in, walking around the side of the room, hoping to find a door, while trying not to look at the bodies. Nobody seemed to work there. Stephen came to what looked like a small room, he thought it might be an office, but it wasn't, it was a filthy washroom. The toilet was broken and excrement spilled across the floor. The wash basins were also broken and everything was dirty and squalid. Stephen looked up at the wall and saw a mirror, it was grimy and cracked. He took a closer look at it, and then closer, but then jumped back because the bus driver's eyes were looking back at him. Stephen woke in a state of shock, his breathing laboured and his chest was tight.

Jessica sat up, and asking what was wrong she turned the bedside light on. She looked at Stephen, who was sitting upright, staring at the opposite wall he was trying to control his breathing. He was thankful that the fear had subsided. Jessica waited for him to answer, but he didn't say anything, only taking deep breaths he continued to look at the wall, his eyes staring as if just having seen a horrific demon. Jessica asked him again, and Stephen turned and looked at her, licking his dry lips his breathing was still uneven, but still he didn't answer. Jessica was

59

scared by the way Stephen was looking at her. She reached out and smoothed his hair, feeling how his face and hair were wet with sweat she spoke in a calm voice, telling him to relax. Jessica had noticed a change in Stephen, but put that down to what they were going through, although this was something different; there was look in his eyes of tortured terror.

12

It was Jessica's second appointment with the Multidisciplinary Team, and while she had tests Stephen waited for her, finding a quiet space outside the chapel where a few chairs were lined against the wall. He thought of the dream he had a couple of nights earlier, that horrible washroom, the excrement on the floor, and the bus driver's eyes in the mirror, haunted, but steely in wanting revenge. Stephen forced the images out of his mind and looked around the corridor. A strange feeling came over him, it felt as if the area of the hospital he was now in had been abandoned, the only sounds being an occasional distant echo of some activity and on the rare occasion when someone walked by at the end of the corridor. It had a deserted feel, like a place that had been designated as out of bounds. Stephen thought it could have been the chapel that gave it that feel, maybe because it was place where one comes when everything has failed, the last resort. Fear caused Stephen to take a deep breath, he thought that maybe he would be going there sometime in the future. Stephen didn't go to church, but then he thought there must be people that go to the chapel and ask for the impossible who don't usually go to church. Prayer, the last hope for desperate people.

He thought about it and went through many situations where a person might come to a point where he or she felt there was nothing else to do, other than pray. He had been with young men in the army, usually gung-ho in spirit who, when finding themselves in a possible life-ending situation either shut their eyes tightly or stared into nothing and prayed. Stephen pondered how fear and hopelessness finds itself in many situations, and it seemed to be a great leveller. The rich, the powerful and the arrogant, prostrated and begging for help in a way they would never have felt possible for them to do so.

The time was going slowly, deciding to enter the chapel, Stephen stood just inside the doorway and looked around a room he thought to be surprisingly small. It wasn't really a church, although services were periodically held there, the place felt what it was, a small corner to get away from things, to pray, reflect, and ultimately, wait. It reminded Stephen of some of the makeshift places of worship set up in areas of battle, with the army chaplain reading an extract from the Bible or giving a memorial service for a soldier that had been killed. The towns and places the chaplain mentioned felt very different, not just belonging in the Bible they were now places that were familiar and real, now that he was in that part of the world.

When looking back, Stephen felt that his time in Iraq didn't seem real. He had to shake his head and tell himself that of course it was real. It happened, yet, there was something that didn't feel right about the whole experience. The word *surreal* came to his mind, and he thought of the word's meaning. He wasn't really sure what it did mean, but the experience he had been thinking about while in the army felt dreamlike, being real and then not actually real because in a way it felt fabricated. And a feeling ran through him as a thought popped into his mind that it was all designed to be that way. The place where it happened, in that Biblical land, a place that young children learned about as being special, and there he was, carrying a gun. Stephen asked himself if he was actually in the Bible? He then breathed out sharply, breaking away from the delirious thought he was having. Although a feeling stayed with him, dark and heavy it filled his chest and stomach, and it wouldn't go away. It gave Stephen a strange feeling and he thought that maybe the whole thing in Iraq had been contrived. Made up, just like a story in a disturbing film. A setting where people are sent to kill other people, the reasons for being there are invented to suit the objectives of those having the power to start wars and profit from them. Enemies are concocted as alien, threatening our existence and as different from us as invading *Martians* in cheaply made 1950's sci-fi films. 'Nothing is real.' Not fact but fiction, and it's sick, it's twisted fiction.

'Nothing is real.' The words meant something and Stephen wondered where he had heard them before, they were familiar and now they took on a significant meaning. An image of fields of flowers like poppies came to his mind. After a few seconds he realised it was Iraq, a time when he was standing next to poppy fields speaking to a young soldier. He said to Stephen, 'I said to my mate, these fields, they're going to be like strawberry fields, all red – red with blood when we're finished with them.'

Stephen thought back to an occasion when they had engaged the enemy in an area where there were poppy fields. 'Yeah, killing fields, poppy fields, it's all the same.' As the young soldier said this, Stephen conjured up an image in his mind of a field, completely red with blood dripping down every green plant, but then the young soldier brought him back from his imaginary fields as he said, 'Yeah, like strawberry jam, but you wouldn't want this jam on your toast,' and he laughed. It was a nervous laugh. Stephen watched the bones in the side of the young man's face as he forced an expression of great joy and nearly barked out laughter, but he couldn't hide the fear and anxiety he felt inside. Stephen thought about this as he looked at the young man. The bravado, the *army humour*, dark, employed to protect one's real feelings, although also used to negate and belittle an individual's emotions and thoughts, because it is only the army that matters.

'Nothing is real.' The words came to Stephen as he sat in the chapel, only this time there was music. They were words in a song, but he struggled to remember what song it was. He couldn't remember, and after a short while his attention was drawn to a figure of Christ. He hadn't noticed it before even though it was a prominent feature in the chapel. It wasn't a crucifix, but a sculpture of Jesus with his arms reaching forward, as if pleading. Stephen wondered what he was pleading for, it wasn't so much in prayer, but as if begging for something. There was writing on a brass plate fixed onto a wooden plinth at the base of the sculpture. Stephen stood up and walked over to it. YOUR FAITH HAS MADE YOU WELL. Stephen read the large writing and bent forward to read what else was written beneath them. *Luke 17:19 And he said to him*, "Rise and go your way; your faith has made you well."

There was a short explanation given of Jesus healing the ten lepers, and all that was needed was to have faith and one will be healed and feel no more fear. Stephen thought about the lepers, having a vague memory of the story from when he was a young boy at school. He thought about looking it up later, not that he considered himself to be a Christian, but it was probably the situation he and Jessica were in that had prompted his interest in Biblical reading. Taking a deep breath Stephen stepped back and looked at the ceiling. The word *faith* came to his mind, he thought about its meaning, what he had thought it to mean and felt sure he didn't feel the same about the word and its meaning as he once had. He remembered the evening when he was researching the word and its meaning on his computer, Jessica had gone to bed and he was restless. He was beginning to think that *faith* has been, and is, used as a strategy for getting people to *believe* in a cause. There was his example, the scouts, authority, the army, and as with others it was a *belief* that hadn't been questioned. Stephen thought about the concept of *faith* as a construction, something that didn't really exist, but an idea that is made use of by those with power and having influence over others.

Stephen sat down and taking his phone from his pocket he looked up Christian beliefs, what was said about living a *good* life and how greed is the root of evil. The pursuit of money, the love of money, to possess and dispossess others, to stop others having what they 'need,' which isn't the same as what they *want*. He thought about what he was reading, his mind immediately going to Mears, big business and corruption. It led him to different sites, some were about churches with religious leaders proclaiming the work of God. It interested Stephen, or amused him, as almost immediately there were cases of fraud and church leaders that had been arrested. He thought of Jesus and the irony of it all while reading how the charity commission is investigating a church, it was something to do with their accounts, and another church had a pastor sent to jail for fraud. There were other cases where there had been embezzlement of funds raised from parishioners. One church leader had an estate with a mansion and owned properties in several countries, and there was a photograph of him standing with his wife next to an expensive car.

Stephen tired with reading about the different cases telling of hypocrisy and fraud being committed by people using religion as a means to get money. He switched to looking up Mears's brother, Luke. Stephen thought how Luke was a Biblical name and he said the name aloud, 'Luke Mears' while thinking about how the Chancellor of the Exchequer's younger brother has business interests in countries where people like Stephen are sent to give their lives for their country. The reason given for sending them is to support the interests of the state and to defend the country and its citizens, and there was Luke Mears, the same as supposed religious people using *faith* to get what they want. Stephen thought about Luke Mears saying how he didn't care less about the morals involved or about soldiers returning home with mental health difficulties. Luke Mears didn't care about all the social problems that happen when a person has been away from their families and homes, fighting in an army that is actively involved in battle. He wasn't concerned of how it is common for a soldier returning home to encounter changes when having been away for a long time with their loved ones, friends and the areas they once knew and grew up in. It is also common for soldiers who have been engaged in battle situations to find that they themselves have changed, and that people see how they have changed. Stephen looked around the chapel as he tried to remember the name of the charity Luke Mears is involved with. He knew it was something like, 'those that served,' but he couldn't remember the whole name of it. He started to think about Ray, the homeless ex-soldier he had met outside the station, and he remembered what Ray had said about the queen at Tilbury, addressing *her* public, telling them how they were, 'faithful and loving people.'

And then from, seemingly, nowhere he remembered the song, where the words came from. It was Strawberry Fields Forever, The Beatles song. 'Nothing is real.' A sense of relief unfolded inside him, but he couldn't remember the other words. He didn't know the song well at all, it was a classic nearly everyone had heard of, but he didn't know what it was actually about and even many of the words. The words 'nothing is real' continued to play in his mind, the tune drifting with its swaying rhythm in a surreal feel. He looked the song up, put in earphones and played it. All other thoughts left Stephen's mind as he sat totally engrossed listening to the song, noting and enjoying the effects used on the instruments, giving a hallucinatory feel that was popular in 1960's drug-induced music with hidden meanings.

Stephen concentrated on the words in the song, taking in every nuance, the inflection in the singer's voice, maybe conveying a hidden meaning, an encrypted, message, like a code. A sensation of goose bumps ran down Stephen's body. He felt the song had a *message* that was not only significant, but important for him to understand. He played the song again, and then again, listening intently, enjoying the feeling that the song gave him, his senses fragmented and all he wanted to do was lose himself in the kaleidoscope of sounds and images that were in his mind. Stephen felt the song had given him means to unlock a door to a room that he hadn't explored before in his life. The sway and movement of the music fitting with his feelings and emotions, images of fields, red with blood came in his mind, just as the young soldier had told him, 'strawberry jam.' The words 'nothing is real' becoming an incantation in his mind, Stephen asked himself out loud, 'What am I? Who am I? What is my real self? My Psyche? My soul? My spirit?' The words formed from somewhere deep inside himself in a place he had never before been and he said, again, out loud, 'Where have you been?'

He listened to the words in the verse, 'living is easy with eyes closed, misunderstanding all you see.' They triggered a reaction in Stephen and his breathing became deep as he nodded in agreement to what he was hearing. Stephen didn't notice the time as it slipped by, his eyes remained closed as all other thoughts and concerns felt distant and below him, as if he was floating high above everything, transcending all matter, emotions and experiences he had ever encountered. He became engulfed in what appeared to be red clouds, they grew dark and were

65

crashing into one another. On looking more closely he saw the clouds were burning, as if in a furnace or rising from a vent of a volcano. He travelled into the clouds, the words, 'nothing is real' now appearing in the form of shapes within the clouds, floating and then whirling in circles until they disappeared. They were shapes Stephen couldn't describe because they were of a formation he had never seen before. Travelling deeper into the clouds he was surprised he could breath, although no longer able to see, but he couldn't feel any heat. The music had vanished as Stephen drifted slowly through the clouds in a soundless vacuum; and then he woke up.

13

Stephen left the chapel, his mood deep and introspective he had to wake himself to the present with Jessica, she would have had her tests and sitting in the waiting room. They were told to stay in the hospital as they would be called shortly for a more detailed discussion regarding the treatment for stage two cancer. It is advised to have someone else with a person who is going to hear important information, such as the case with Jessica, and not just for support, but to listen to what's being said as the person having the treatment is usually in shock and it is common afterwards not to remember what had been said to her or him.

Jessica and Stephen entered the room where members of the Multidisciplinary Team were sitting. It was reiterated that the cancer had spread outside the ovary within the abdomen and they were going to investigate to see if it had spread further in the body to other parts such as her lungs. Jessica was told she would have another appointment when the results of the tests she had just had were available. It was established that surgery was needed and chemotherapy will be used to shrink the cancer before the surgery. Other factors had to be investigated, such as the speed at which the cancer was growing and exactly where it had spread to. There was an uneasy silence after a warning was given that if the cancer cannot be cured there will be treatment to control the cancer for as long as possible.

Neither Jessica or Stephen spoke. They couldn't, but Stephen was aware of the looks on the faces of the people in the room, each one having a specific role in the treatment of a person unlucky enough to find themselves in the chair Jessica was sitting in. His gut felt that it was going split open, struggling to catch his breath he placed his hand on Jessica's knee, and although she looked as if she didn't notice, she softly lay her hand upon his, but all the while her gaze was looking at a place far away from where they were at that moment.

The journey home was becoming a familiar pattern, Jessica mainly silent, her contemplation painful to witness as Stephen struggled to find words that didn't unsettle her. This was the last time Jessica drove, they had been using her car to go to the hospital, and it was one more slip down a rung of the ladder they were descending when Jessica admitted she couldn't drive any more. The car was to remain parked in a space reserved for residents of the block of flats they lived in, and on seeing it standing unused was another dispiriting blow.

Jessica's friend, Sharron, had arranged to see her early that evening. She was an old friend of Jessica's from early schooldays and they had always been close, but during the time Jessica was trying to conceive Stephen had noticed there were signs of tension in their relationship. Sharron had two children, and although she didn't flaunt that fact, or was boastful in any manner, Jessica's failure to have a child did cause an unease between them. All that though had now vanished, Sharron was very supportive to Jessica and accepted her occasional outbursts of frustration and anger. She was a real friend, which was something that had caused Stephen to think about how he didn't have a close lifetime friend as Jessica did.

Sharron came to their flat just before seven, and after staying a short while she and Jessica went out for a drive in Sharron's car with intentions of having coffee somewhere. Stephen listened to the front door as it closed, and as it did so a feeling of silence filled the flat, just as he wanted it. He sat in the living room looking at the wall opposite to where he was sitting. Stephen became aware of the room as an entity, yet also of its inanimateness, just existing, impervious to the feelings of the people living within its confines. How could it not be? It was bricks and mortar and didn't have feelings. It didn't have a soul, but then a thought flashed across his mind that it was a *thing*, just as humans can be perceived as nothing more than *things*. Devoid of a soul without feelings, emotions or spiritual importance and something that is expendable

'Nothing is real,' the words and tune of the song drifted into Stephen's mind.

'It's not like shooting normal people, they're just idiots, stupid, I mean, let's get it right, fuck them...' These were the words said to Stephen by a soldier in Iraq. Stephen thought at the time that the young man who said them was scared. It was nothing more than bravado, which he needed in a dangerous situation taking place somewhere as foreign and hostile as where they were. Stephen thought about the young man, the way he looked, his facial expression, his accent, where he probably came from, where he was now and what he was up to, if he was around that was.

'And nothing to get hung about...' The words of the song came into his mind, drawing him away from himself with the tune and its drifting feel. Thoughts became muddled, fusing and melting

68

into an incoherent mass of indistinguishable images, words and sounds. He entered into a tunnel of shifting fragmented impressions concocted by a fraying imagination. And time became stilled.

Stephen turned the television on, but then almost immediately turned it off again. He went into the bedroom, switched on the radio, lay down on the bed and settled himself. This was something he had always liked to do, listening to the radio, not music, but programmes where people were discussing matters. Jessica found it an 'old-fashioned' thing to do, but since he was a young boy Stephen liked to listen to the radio when alone.

A programme was on about medieval musical instruments, Stephen found it mildly interesting, although it wasn't long before he started drifting to sleep. On waking he checked the time, seeing he had been asleep about half an hour he settled back and listened to what was being said on the radio. From what he could make out it was an interview with someone who was a stand-up comedian, and politics played a big part in what he was about. What he was saying interested Stephen, it was to do with matters that were current in his thinking. Stephen concentrated so that he could catch everything the man was saying, which he found difficult because he spoke at a fast pace, with irony present in nearly everything he talked about.

'Politics has become debased – the public's already foggy minds are confused even more by politicians and celebrities competing with one another to pitch their wares in the market place of popular culture, where there are financial rewards and status, and in doing so they falsely present themselves as modest, humble, in touch with the ordinary person and sharing common values of wanting to do good for others. Getting involved with a charity has proved itself to be a successful method to keep in the public eye, it can boost flagging careers while maybe gaining a new audience – oh yes, reinventing one's publicly presented personality, with the politicians doing their bit for equality by lobbying for policies to implement tax relief and exemptions associated with charities to encourage and attract interest for business investment.'

The man gave a list of names, among them were politicians and celebrities, and he went on to explain how some of them are involved in the same charities.

'There is no need for those who really run the show to use the services of politicians to serve their interests, they're just a sham anyway, not now they have celebrities to pass judgement on and sanctify our behaviour and values. The court jesters are, and have always been, good at fawning for a status and trinkets from the establishment, but things are different now when the most important person at a so-called big politics summit is a celebrity chef who was brought along to flip the burgers.

'Although, it isn't only chefs that have been canonised in our society, there are other self-engrossed, frenzied egotists offering their facile ramblings that are hitting a big audience. Do they really relate more with that person in the street? I doubt it, it's probably more to do with that poor sod in the street being punch drunk as a result of having been bombarded by all the conflicting fickle blather that comes from every direction, not just from our *leaders*, but also by celebrities who have been given a platform to preach on matters far beyond their original remit when setting out on their careers.'

Stephen listened carefully, what the man was saying struck a very large chord and he concentrated, thinking of Mears, the things he had read and was becoming aware of.

'Dee jays and radio presenters have often been reactionary airhead types, sounding their views and scoffing at the mentally ill and drunk on those awful late-night radio phone-in shows. It is an inexcusable act of bullying, but then we are learning all the time how bullying and self-interest is something that their *business* is all about as they shout down and ridicule people, while promoting personal friends and business associates on their shows to plug restaurants and books, as well as giving their view of societal matters.'

The man went on, saying how, 'The new lackeys for the establishment engage in a feeding frenzy for publicity to sell their profiles, whether they're an actor or politician there is little difference to many in the general populace, because it's just another media figure condemning or consecrating war, famine, civil unrest and our ethical standards.'

The man was interrupted by the presenter who told him that time was up and thanked him for coming onto her programme.

Stephen lay on his bed thinking about what he had just heard, feeling that some of it was a bit above his head. The guy most probably had the benefit of higher education, having been to university and coming from a family where occupying professional positions at work was not uncommon. He had mixed with others from his background, peers that openly voiced critical observations on matters in society, as authority was not a thing to blindly accept. Stephen thought about the way he spoke, having confidence in sneering at known politicians and prominent figures in the media. He ridiculed and questioned what the establishment had laid down as rules that were expected to be adhered to and accepted. The ideas and views of celebrities who cynically target an audience to consume in a mindless dream came in for scorn. The comic had reduced everything to sellers and buyers, traders and consumers. He used the word, 'pitch' when talking about politicians, businesspeople and celebrities. 'To pitch their wares,' that's what he said.

Stephen turned on his computer and researched the comic's name; it was Joe Tara. He thought it an odd name that was probably made up, and although Stephen spelt it incorrectly, he was famous enough for it to come up with the first search. Stephen looked at one of Joe Tara's shows, in which he covered some ground he had been talking about in the interview. After watching the show, Stephen typed in the words, 'charity, entertainment industry, politicians.'

He quickly found an article exploring the use of good causes in order to promote one's career and how it is a well-established practice in the entertainment industry, in fact it is an industry in itself that is fiercely protected. Anyone wishing to get involved and contribute towards the good work a particular charity is doing will find it very difficult to do so if known celebrities have their name associated with it. It is a guarded area of activity providing a valuable marketing medium for a celebrity, so managers and agents will go to great lengths preventing others from trespassing upon the holy grail.

Stephen read how celebrities are often identified with the charity work they do. Their character is even defined by it, thus making it part of that person, and because of that it comes to be seen as his or her property. So, having ideas to intrude upon such a valuable possession as charity work that has been designated only for certain people can have very nasty consequences, such as threats to ruin a person's career. Fabricating a past to further one's career is nothing new in the entertainment industry, although there are more than just mild cases of fraud where people just fib about their age or name. There is the serious deceit where mendacious celebrities lie about their past, who they are, what they do with a charity they are associated with and where the money goes. Involvement with charities has lucrative spin-offs, such as using the charity status to evade taxing profits on other businesses as well as avoiding income tax in this country, consequently denying money for essential services, like children's cancer units, which many celebrities brag about helping and criticise the government for not doing enough. A case was cited of a well-known female celebrity, known only for being famous rather than her acting or singing skills, who was the face and supposed spokeswoman for a charity providing guidance

71

and support for orphaned children in poverty-stricken areas, but it turned out she was being paid a huge wage for doing just about nothing with the charity itself receiving a paltry amount of money. There are cases of charities closing down and leaving a big dept as money raised was used to fund business enterprises rather than financing the supposed cause of the charity, and in one case donations to the actual charity were as small as one per cent of the proceeds.

Stephen nearly smiled in disbelief at the audacity of some of the things he was reading, which were criminal and some thoroughly nasty. One charity said they would provide a school and hospital in an area of the world beset with poverty, but nothing happened after some of the poorest people on the planet were forced from where they lived to make way for the new buildings. The money had run out before any building work started. Auditors showed how money was spent on individuals who had no connection to the charity with things like buying expensive cars, offices and even homes. A lot of money went on re-drafting architect plans and a massive lump just went missing. The list went on, giving examples of actors and singers who are involved with charities where money raised went on a range of costs from administration to buying costly personal possessions.

The article had a subtitle, 'From Saint to Sinner,' the style of it sarcastic, but ultimately condemning their behaviour as flagrant hypocrisy. It said how lying about one's age or height is forgivable and easy to understand, after all, the entertainment industry is a fantasy world the public plug into for reasons of wanting to escape from their daily worries and toil. Although it's another matter entirely to fool people into believing you are a person with deeply held moral beliefs who talks about the lack of integrity shown by business people and politicians, and that you are motivated to do your charity work because of these politicians and business people with their uncaring and unscrupulous ways. It can, and does enrage people. They feel conned. In a world where fact and fantasy has become blurred and people with a high profile, whether in the entertainment industry or politics, proclaim to have a pure heart with certain intentions, but are then found to be lying, can lead people to think that nothing is to be believed, whether the claims come from the news or showbiz world. It can all be seen to be the same, something that is not real.

Stephen looked at the floor, the words, 'not real' resonated within him as he thought of the lines in the song, 'nothing is real.' He continued to stare at the carpet, his mind flicking through thoughts and images, but too many feelings crowded in upon him to be understood. His capacity for thought overloaded, causing him to catch his breath and jump back as if in shock. Composing himself he looked at the computer and searched through different sites and blogs dealing with celebrities. He found an article about celebrities that have made false claims to further their careers. A list of well-known people was discussed and severely criticised. There was the case of an actor who pretended to have Native American ancestry, purely to boost the sales of a film he was in, as the part he played was of a Native American standing up against those stealing his land, and although they had greater technological knowledge, they had little in the way of morals. He later went on to exploit this fabrication and gain a high profile in human rights concerns, specifically for Native Americans, and also took advantage of other lucrative opportunities. Examples were given of American politicians and a television news presenter who made up stories about being in Vietnam and Iraq. To boost their careers, they told of how they fought for their country, the near misses they had and the dangerous situations they encountered while showing acts of selfless courage.

There were examples of female actors doing soft core sex films before finding fame, and of one whom later, because of now being famous, is in a position that allows her to proclaim her ethics and heartfelt principles in matters involving the treatment of women in the film industry. Before finding fame the woman worked in the seedier end of modelling, and men worked as escorts to sell their body to make a living. The writer of the piece spoke of how for the celebrities it was all the same, from stripping, exotic dancing, rubbing shoulders with drug dealers and mixing with criminals. The bottom line is that these types of people come across as desperate in their pursuit to attain fame. Stephen thought how terribly insincere it all was, and the people involved in that industry lacked integrity, but admiring celebrities and the famous is a massive thing in our society, and apparently, from what Stephen was reading, it was growing.

Stephen looked at articles about celebrities, their lifestyles, how people almost worship them and the cases when a fan goes too far and wants to be in the life of a celebrity. He read an article that said how celebrities have empires and a lifestyle out of the reach of ordinary people. They are called *stars*, and even *superstars*, they live in palaces and have relationships in a social scene made up of other media *Gods*. Their lives are scrutinised and monitored by their *public*, you can see them following updates of their idol on their phones, heads cast downwards towards a screen

73

as they concentrate on reading celebrity gossip. But it is in the *looking* and not the *thinking* that attachments are made, information zooms in and out at too great a speed for serious rumination. The writer of the piece asked why is it this way? Is it because so many people feel their lives are worthless or just lacking in a society driven by materialism with the pressure to have expectations for things beyond their reach? Is it because they feel compelled by the influence of the media to follow those having more interesting lives than their own? The writer went on to discuss how the supposed backstories of celebrities are constructed to connect with the public. They are often tales of rags to riches, one day doing a humdrum job just like the *fan,* the next day *living the dream,* chauffeured around in a stretched limousine from party to party and mixing in a world exclusive only to a VIP. The fans get a chance to peek into that hallowed land made up of excitement and opulence, and falsely believe they are part of a world made up of *winners*, which offers an escape from moping in the drudgery that exists in a world made up of *losers.*

Another person discussed how God has become meaningless to so many people, but not to worry because a replacement, or many replacements, have been created to fill that sacred void. Technology has driven into town with a menu of ever-changing deities. The new Gods are celebrities. They have become meaningful figures to many people, and some might argue that the claims certain celebrities make are as vaguely bizarre in their authenticity as those made in religions. The journalist wrote, 'After all, who needs truth when they have something to believe in?'

The article explored how the *fans* of pop singers and actors were once visible, a type that is a target audience for a particular singer or actor's PR and advertising department to aim at, but *idol* worshipping has now become a condition that is a significant part of our culture. Huge parts of the populace identify with their particular *deity,* and that condition is constructed, shaped and developed through the all controlling mediums utilised by the media. Celebrities market themselves through social media and any other means they can use to exploit a situation that has been created for them to do so. The media has an enormous influence on the thinking, interests, desires and aspirations of the majority of people in society, and the process is maintained through the use of emerging technology. The writer of the article asks, 'And for what real benefit? To worship the worthless?' She wrote about how the new Gods and Goddesses are media created and, seemingly, ubiquitously marketed. The essence of great power and influence is embodied

74

within a living human being, usually with bleached teeth presenting a false façade for admirers to identify with. The devotee believes he or she can interact with this higher being and pathetically feels his or her own potential can be compared to his or her idol. Uncles, Aunties, cousins, school teachers or a person that has shown integrity by working to better the lives of others, are now secondary to a figure people have never met and know nothing about, only what the marketing team spill out to update news feed so that their client remains in the public eye, and in the minds and hearts of fans. What is presented as *natural* has been edited, scripted and agonisingly perfected until the marketing team are satisfied with an image of the celebrity that they feel will benefit the *brand*. The writer ended by saying how there are factors that have proved important for lasting fame, with one's family background being an important one.

Stephen read another article where the writer spoke about the selling of glamour and sex and how it places physical demands on the celebrity who has to fit the image being sold, so staying young and attractive, or whatever the principal image might be, has to be maintained. Therefore, constant attention is taken in how the celebrity looks, as does the constant adjustments in the marketing so that the consumer remains interested. Publicists manipulate the media to sell their client as a manufactured object in a business that it is all about marketing. It is an operation with strategies and contingency plans, and along the way the brutal business involves hiring and firing people in order to get the product picked up by the consumer. For the celebrity, it's all about the self and being selfish is nothing to feel bad about, in fact it's a prerequisite and their disciples follow suit in their fascination with wanting to be associated with glamour. It's that simple and it's that basic. People seeing themselves as belonging with highbrow culture often need justifications, such as ethical or intellectual reasons, to like or associate with a public figure. For those people grouped in the lowbrow culture there can be sentimental reasons, although it's essentially a look-and-like rational. Either highbrow or lowbrow they are all the same in needing or wanting to look up and refer to someone else, whether it be for reassurance or whatever reason. The writer of the article said that it seems to be a human quality, and he concluded, quite gloomily, it is maybe this propensity for having this kind of dependence that accounts for our failure to have self-belief, which can lead to the popular support given to the most horrendous leaders that have existed throughout history.

It dawned on Stephen what he was doing, his wife was going through absolute hell and there he was researching stuff on charities, unscrupulous politicians and celebrities. He thought that if he was researching anything it should be about information on cancer treatment. Stephen tapped in words to trigger a search on cancer treatment and survival rates, but within seconds of sites and links appearing on the screen, his mind wandered to what he was thinking about before. He thought about Mears's brother and the charity he is associated with, but Stephen decided to shut down the computer and look him and his charity up some other time.

14

A date had been set for Jessica to go into hospital and have surgery. The medication had weakened her, and although her spirits remained high, it was a losing battle against the terrible tiredness she felt. She had been having chemotherapy to make it less difficult for the surgeon to remove the cancer, and although the side-effects were explained to her, the way she felt was beyond anything she had imagined. She was told about the tiredness, hair loss, feeling sick, vomiting, sores in the mouth, sores on the skin and diarrhoea or constipation, but nothing she was told could have prepared her for how she felt. They were told it is different for different people, some sail through while others suffer greatly. The physical and emotional suffering had bitten into Jessica and was quickly leaving its mark, which was something that caused Stephen to twist inside when looking at her.

Jessica had been told how some people ask for a second opinion and she could do so if she wanted, but she didn't as it seemed a simple matter of her having the cancer, and she had put her trust in the health professionals that were treating her. Both Jessica and Stephen had read an enormous amount of literature on the cancer she had, the stage it was and chances of survival. The prognosis was not good and the usual feelings one has when waiting to have an operation was not there, because Jessica knew it wasn't going to be straightforward. The coming date of the operation left them feeling flat as it was another stage of Jessica's decline and inevitable journey towards death.

They looked at wigs before starting the chemotherapy treatment to be prepared if she lost her hair. There was also an item of clothing called a chemo scarf, which is a head scarf for someone has lost her hair while having chemotherapy treatment. When Jessica asked if she should cut her hair before the treatment, she was told it wasn't necessary, although it can be recommended as it makes the transition to baldness less startling if one does lose one's hair. The emotional suffering with losing one's hair is traumatic and brings greater stress. Confidence and self-esteem are affected as one's image and sense of identity changes. Keeping it short can give a woman some feeling of control over something that is important to her when the going is very tough. Jessica didn't buy a wig, but bought a couple of scarves as the good wigs cost a lot of money, and they weren't certain she was going to lose her hair so it could well be a waste of money. Chemotherapy drugs do not differentiate between different cells, only targeting the cancer and leaving healthy cells alone. The drugs attack all cells that grow quickly, cancer cells are fast growing, but there are also others, therefore the hair is affected, although, as yet, Jessica hadn't lost her hair, but it was thin, dry and lifeless, as was her complexion.

Doctors were willing to adjust the medication as she went along to help lessen unpleasant side effects, but they were walking a tightrope, because the objective was to attack the cancer with as much power as possible. The chemotherapy can cause anaemia and leaves the patient vulnerable to infections as the drugs attack red and white blood cells, although there are things one can do to alleviate the side-effects. Jessica was asked to take it easy and persevere in trying to relax. She was told how stress can have a negative impact on her general wellbeing while she was having the treatment, and that research has shown how stress has a harmful effect on the cancer itself. Jessica had been advised to look into stress-relieving techniques such as yoga, meditation, massage, acupuncture, taking certain herbs and other methods she might find useful. A counsellor could be used if depression sets in to guide and support Jessica, but at that time she was very much in the frame of mind of wanting to *fight* what she was facing and was determined to use or try any options that might help. That was something Stephen found pitiful, Jessica's bravery, but also the desperation.

Among the many concerns was gaining weight. It wasn't the drugs, but a response to them in that it triggered cravings for certain foods, which went some way to lessen feelings of nausea and tiredness. Jessica's taste had changed, she now had cravings for things she never used to have, and disliked foods she had always liked, and were also healthy. She said they tasted metallic, and because of this she stopped eating nutritious foods, preferring ginger sweets coated with sugar and eating custard, as she said it soothed her mouth.

They had read how there is research that claims how it is bad, and especially so if having cancer, to eat not only fried, but grilled, barbequed and baked red meat, the extreme heat, apparently, creates carcinogenic by-products. As well as processed meats, excessive amounts of salt, sugar and oil should not be consumed, especially during the time if one has cancer. Jessica was given a list of foods that should make up her diet, or the majority of it. The list contained fresh fruit and vegetables, wholegrains, food rich in vitamin B, less processed foods and to eat small meals.

throughout the day rather than one large one, and to also drink plenty of water. A counsellor, who was part of the care team looking after Jessica, spoke about how she shouldn't make cancer the 'central focus' in her life, but to look at activities she enjoyed, such as travel, which would have to be arranged to fit in with her treatment. Stephen thought it was a sick joke, he recognised that not all people have the same experience, but in Jessica's case, considering the state of her health, it was obvious she wasn't healthy or fit enough for travelling, and having a life sentence thrown at her when trying for a baby had understandably shut down thoughts of booking a holiday.

The subject of sex and chemotherapy was raised by the counsellor. She wanted to know if Stephen and Jessica would like to talk to her about the subject and any concerns they may have. Jessica was told not to feel uncomfortable talking about sex with her doctor and that chemotherapy can affect one's sex life. Stephen understood when Jessica told him how she hadn't changed her feelings towards him in any way, it was just that she was so tired, and stress had caused her to lose interest in having sex. Jessica told Stephen how she was scared about her body being mutilated, and worried about how he will respond when seeing her scarred after surgery. The image she had of herself had changed, she felt ugly, different from how she did before, new feelings had come upon her and it was like she was losing sight of her old self. She was having hot flushes and had discomfort around her vagina. Jessica was embarrassed and guilty for bringing this to Stephen. She continued to blame herself, however much Stephen told Jessica that he loved her and it was only her he was concerned with.

Stephen entered the living room one early evening and sat in an armchair. He looked at Jessica who was sitting on the sofa and he smiled at her, but she didn't smile back. 'You don't want to sit next to me, then?' Jessica said, she was morose and looked straight at him in a way that said there was something wrong. This was another change, her sharp manner, the suspicion she was now showing, it just wasn't Jessica and he knew it was the illness that had brought this upon her.

'Well, say something then,' Jessica said, her voice louder with anger, but before Stephen could answer she started to speak. 'I've been reading about how romance and relationships finish when a cancer diagnosis is made.' Jessica continued to look at Stephen in order to let what she had said sink in. Stephen didn't respond, he looked at her, calmly, watching the way that she felt, and then Jessica shouted at him. 'Go on then, say something for God's sake, is this part of what I have to go through, to be alone, with you not saying anything, just looking at me as if I've suddenly emerged from the sea?'

Stephen was shocked, Jessica had never spoken to him like this before. The tone of her voice and the way she was looking at him upset Stephen. She went on, 'Am I that ugly as a person? Do I disgust you? Well, I'm sorry I was so selfish and got cancer – silly me, how stupid I am.'

Jessica continued to look at Stephen, and again he didn't say anything. He couldn't, words wouldn't come, his mind was swimming and he felt nervous. Jessica began to speak, her eyes hard, staring at him as she spoke. 'Statistics show that far more men leave a woman if she has been diagnosed with cancer than the other way around. A lot of men start off saying they'll stay and how they're with the woman one thousand per cent, but loads pull out because it gets too much for them. It's the reality, you see? It's too much.' She went on, saying the reasons for leaving vary from not recognising the woman they married because her looks change so much, and then there is the daily stress of treatment. To be a provider is one thing for a man, but to be carer is another, and there's the demands of work, of not being able to cope with their job and having to look after a woman they wouldn't be with if they knew what was going to happen.

Stephen found it hard to listen. He didn't say anything and the room fell silent, but only for a short while. 'I mean, Look!' Jessica said, referring to a young woman on the television, 'You can't stop looking at her – do you like her?'

Stephen didn't reply, he was surprised by what she had said, and the way she said it. He was shocked and he stumbled as he began to answer, but Jessica continued, staring at Stephen with intensity. 'I've seen you looking at women when we're out – in a way you didn't do before, and more and more as time's gone by.'

Jessica continued, and all the while Stephen was thinking of the right thing to say. 'Someone told me cancer can pull people apart, Jessica said, 'And the sex thing makes it worse…' Stephen interjected, asking her who had said that, but Jessica just shook her head. He told Jessica that he had read accounts of people getting through it all and staying together, but Jessica didn't answer, and fear began to show on her face. Stephen looked at her, and then speaking in a calm, but strong voice he said, 'But, forget what I've been reading, and what you've heard people say –

love you.' Jessica continued to look at Stephen, and then gently biting her bottom lip her chin dropped slowly onto her chest.

'Come on Jess,' Stephen said, 'We're together whatever happens – and we can beat this, together.'

'My body just feels dead,' Jessica said, her face had softened and her voice having lost its anger, 'That's how I feel – it just feels, like nothing, there's no feelings – nothing.' She looked at Stephen for a few seconds before continuing, 'Welcome to the new me, your new life with a woman you didn't fall in love with and marry – yet more good news – how lucky for you to share your life with…' She battled to get the words out, 'One of life's losers.'

As her head dropped, Stephen was beside her, taking Jessica in his arms he cradled her, soothing her gently as he rocked her. Jessica began to cry. 'Hold me,' Stephen said, 'Hold me love, hold me, come on,' his voice soft as he lovingly wiped tears that slid down her cheek. Jessica put her arms around him and spoke through her sobbing. 'I talked with the doctor about the way I feel, she said there is therapy available that might help.' She paused for a couple of seconds before crying out, 'I'm fed up with bloody therapy, every time something doesn't work they talk about therapy – therapy for this, therapy for that, it's the same old thing they all do, put on kind face and put on that soothing voice, all *really* nice smiles, all soft and caring – when it's all shit – I just wanted to have a ba…' She wept heavily, nearly howling, and the sound of her despair was too much for Stephen to take. He closed his eyes to stop tears spilling down his face, and swallowing hard his voice quaked as he told Jessica that he loved her and there was no need for therapy as they had each other, and that is all that matters in the world.

15

Stephen was always trying to keep the mood upbeat during the period of chemotherapy before the surgery. When possible planning a structure to their days and enjoying each other's company, especially spending time in nature. Activities were limited, but it was to be aware of the specialness of simple things and seeing them as important. Things like taking a cup of coffee to the park or woods and sitting on a bench were turned into occasions to be enjoyed. Although it was difficult, a feeling of impending doom was always present, stress and anxiety would overshadow most moments of pleasure when they were trying to put worries to one side, even for a short while. Stages had passed and Stephen knew there would be others to follow. At first the shock, then anger and then feelings of denial in believing what had happened and accepting it, and there was always the fear. Fear permeated their lives. There were feelings of dread when thinking of dying, Stephen woke one night in bed and found Jessica crying. She spoke of her fear and pain at leaving this life and not knowing what will happen to Stephen and her family. The feelings of fear, frustration and helplessness were worse during the night, and to such a degree there were times when Stephen didn't want to go to bed. Glimmers of hope were dashed before they took hold in any meaningful way. Jessica knew, Stephen knew, the cancer was advanced, they had read about the subject and it was obvious by the way health professionals spoke to them. Feelings of just being struck dumb occurred, finding it difficult to concentrate, the constant fatigue, being short tempered and having abrupt mood swings had now become part of their everyday life making up their new world. It was discussed with Jessica that she could well be suffering from depression, but she didn't want to look into it, telling Stephen that of course she was depressed, what do they expect, she had cancer and it had ruined her life.

Jessica was frustrated and scared, and there were feelings of guilt and blame. Stephen researched different ideas and practices that might help Jessica cope with her emotions. He researched support groups and counsellors, and read how people had different ways with coping. Some wanted to talk and express how they felt or what they were afraid of, while others needed to be alone or speak to their partners or close members of their families. There was not a blueprint that accommodated all situations, and at the end of the day it was the person's cancer and it was her or his life. The crashing shock of finding out Jessica had cancer was followed by a realisation that she had lost control in her life. It was a loss of control over the most fundamentally important thing a person could face; it was her very existence. All lessons and rules one had learned and adopted to cope with life before cancer go out the window. This brought further feelings of inadequacy and vulnerability. It seemed important to learn ways to relieve stress other than taking medication. This was something Jessica had been told and she was given information on complimentary methods such as meditation and yoga, as well as other techniques that are used to relieve stress and anxiety.

There was a huge amount of different therapies and theories, some making what should be considered unlawful claims about holistic and alternative treatments being able to cure cancer, prevent getting cancer and coping with it if you already have it. One woman told Jessica, when she phoned to enquire about her therapy, 'I aim to build the patient rather than the cancer.' The number of things out there was completely overwhelming, which not only caused confusion, but also anger at the contradictory so called 'evidence' and claims different people were making. Jessica went with her friend Sharron to see a woman who had set herself up as a holistic therapist. She was qualified, accredited by various bodies and associations and had her own website. The woman told Jessica that she needed to work on her spiritual connection with the universe, but to start with being conscious of fresh air, good water, pure foods, taking exercise, stress management and creating a simple and pure relationship with nature. Jessica returned home in a state, telling Stephen how the woman was talking 'at' her, rather than, 'to' her. 'It was like a script, me, my illness, my life is just a product that she's built her script on and makes her living from it.' Jessica cried as she explained how she felt like a bystander, a helpless observer watching someone who had 'hijacked' her life, her experience and suffering and had chosen to personally benefit from it.

The pain and helplessness Stephen felt was destroying him, but he had to present a constructive face as Jessica continued to look at the area of complementary and alternative therapy. She was told by the nurse in the team looking after her that some people are confused about the difference between complementary and alternative therapies, and often believe them to be the same. Every avenue Jessica and Stephen went down involved starting at the beginning and having to learn what it was they were embarking on. Jessica was told to consider carefully the claims that are sometimes made by those offering methods that had not been researched and tested by an

83

officially recognised body. Conventional cancer treatments undergo organised clinical trials to test their safety and benefits, while the companies and therapists using and promoting alternative and complementary therapies do so without any scientific testing, measurement or evidence, but often depend only on reports from people that have had the therapy. It was explained to Jessica how her doctor should be informed if she wants to take or use complementary medicines or therapies, as some of these treatments might interact and stop the conventional treatment she is receiving. Although, patients are encouraged to try certain complementary approaches as they have been proved to help with the unpleasant side effects that come with conventional treatment. Some complimentary methods have shown to ease stress and anxiety, which is believed to play an important part in the recovery of patients.

The importance of being aware of the, often miraculous, cures claimed by some people selling alternative therapies can be difficult at a time of great fear and vulnerability. Some of the alternative treatments can be unsafe and cause harmful side effects. Giving up one's conventional treatment can reduce one's chances of curing or controlling the cancer, and can maybe leave it too late, if returning to conventional treatment when having stopped it to practice an alternative treatment that proved itself not to work. Jessica was given a booklet explaining what the different complementary and alternative therapies actually were, many involved following strict diets, one recommended the taking of shark cartilage.

Some complementary therapies were free, although in some cases further treatments have to be paid for. There are cancer support centres, cancer support groups and charities providing complementary therapies, which can be a good way to pay less for treatment or get the treatment for free. Jessica was told there are many organisations and groups, and looking on the internet is a way of finding out who they are and contacting them. She was to inform her doctor if she decided on something, but reminded to take care and check for hidden costs.

Jessica wanted to find out more about meditation after reading how it can relieve tiredness, help with sleep problems, nausea and generally improve a sense of wellbeing. She spoke to a member of the team that was looking after her, who was very enthusiastic about the helpfulness of meditation and told her about the different types that were available. She explained to Jessica how it takes time and not to expect any quick fixes, but after a period of practicing everyday many people report how they feel calmer and less anxious. The claims made for doing meditation seemed to Jessica to be more modest than many other treatments that make assertions of reversing cancer. Jessica was told how meditation has been widely accepted as a method to reduce stress, which apparently boosts the immune system, yet doctors do not state that this can help the body to control cancer.

The psychologist assigned to the team looking after Jessica explained to her the different types of meditation. She told Jessica how important it was to have a professionally recognised teacher guiding her through the practice, and if looking privately Jessica should ask the therapist or teacher whether they are affiliated to a recognised body. Jessica was warned that in some cases meditation can cause anxiety if bringing awareness to fears that might worsen the symptoms. She should ask if the therapist has worked with people that have cancer, how long she or he has been practicing, what training have they had and do they have indemnity insurance in case of negligence. Jessica was told about different types of meditation, such as prayerful meditation, which is spiritual, visualisation, transcendental meditation and meditation movement, which are practices like tai chi and yoga, and there is mindfulness, a practice that has become popular.

After talking about meditation, and reading different sources of information, Jessica decided to try mindfulness and booked a session run by the NHS. The practice, very basically, draws one's attention to the present moment, concentrating one's awareness on feelings, sights and sounds at that instant in a relaxed observing manner. Stephen went with Jessica to give her support, and he could tell she was pleased that he did. The young woman's name facilitating the session was Kayleigh, after introducing herself, she took them to a room that had a bed in it, armchairs and large beanbags on the floor. She spoke for a while about meditation and mindfulness, telling them it can be practiced alone and anywhere one feels comfortable, preferably a place where one won't be disturbed so one can feel secure in being away from the everyday rush of preoccupations. The practice can be done sitting in a chair, lying on the floor, on one's bed or sitting on cushions, it doesn't matter as long as one is relaxed and feels at peace. She told Jessica that it was important to have a few sessions with a professional therapist, but after that it is perfectly 'safe and okay' to do it by oneself.

The session got underway with soothing music playing in the background as Kayleigh spoke in in a soft, calming voice. She told them to allow thoughts, sounds, feelings, worries, concerns or whatever to come fleeting into one's mind, and simply step back, observe them in a relaxed

85

manner and not to force them from one's mind, as the practice is to be done in a relaxed and peaceful way. Kayleigh spoke slowly, telling them to carefully bring attention to their breathing and to notice a 'gap of stillness' that exists between the breaths. While remaining conscious of their breathing they were told to count as they breathed in and to also count on the 'out breath.' She said that intruding thoughts are not to be seen as intrusive, but as friendly, soft, colourful shapes. 'They are spongy to the touch, let go of them and watch them come back to shape, slowly and softly, always, and now see them float away, slowly, over a great beautiful valley – you are now in the present moment, you are separate from your thoughts, they do not control you, you control them, be aware of your posture, your body's contact with what you are sitting on, of the blood inside you, of your breathing, the feel of the clothes against your skin, be aware of tastes, feelings and the sounds you are hearing, focus on them, on the place where you are at this moment, feel its atmosphere, and just relax thinking of the now.'

Kayleigh stopped talking, and the slow, drifting music continued to play in the background. A screen appeared in Stephen's mind with the words written on it like the title of a film, 'Nothing is real.' His stomach instantly tightened. He was frightened, he felt fear of the present, fear of existence itself and all that it means. The meditation was over and Kayleigh said, 'Take these feelings of mindfulness into your everyday activities,' but Stephen wasn't listening to her, his hearing had gone and he saw what he thought was his mind that had withdrawn into a small space and was hidden away from everything. He could see the space his mind had travelled into, but wouldn't be able to explain what it actually looked like or was if someone asked him to describe what he meant. But, then again, Stephen thought, who the hell would be asking him anyway? What was he thinking? He saw his mind slipping into a slim little drawer in a place that didn't look like a room. It just looked like, somewhere. It was white, without walls or features, and there could have been soft white clouds moving slowly around, but Stephen was confused about the drawer, asking himself what it was.

Kayleigh's voice was talking to him. She was smiling, opening her eyes wide, accentuating the action of opening her eyes, but Stephen couldn't decipher what the meaning of her doing that was, and he nearly said, 'Sorry, I can't read what you're saying.' Stephen noticed how Jessica was looking at him, embarrassment showing on her face. Kayleigh had finished the session, it was time for her to do something else, Stephen thought that maybe she had to do another meditation session with other people, he didn't know, and he continued to think about it.

'You okay?' Jessica asked Stephen, the look on her face more concerned than impatient. She was confused as to why Stephen wasn't responding. It was as if he had lost contact with his surroundings and bewildered by where he was and what he was doing there. Stephen stood up, feeling his inner self had retreated to a place to seek sanctuary and to hide away from everything that is disturbing. He told himself that from now on that is where he wanted to be, to feel separate from all and everything. He was conscious of shaking the young woman's hand, of performing the reciprocal procedure of smiling and nodding and bidding farewell, but it was as if he was an observer to the situation he was in, and he asked himself, 'Is it real?'

16

Jessica wanted to try another mindfulness meditation and had bought a DVD. She said it relaxed her, and anything that helps must be good, but Stephen didn't want to go to another mindfulness session. The last one had distressed him, and although not telling Jessica why, he told her that he didn't feel like going to another session. Stephen didn't want to tell Jessica how he really felt, of feeling nervous, the trembling inside, and having an uncontrollable sense of something nasty that was about to happen, and as strange it might sound, he felt that he could actually taste it. It was bitter and moved from his chest to his head and then to his stomach, like an impending doom it was dark and building in intensity.

The mindfulness session Jessica did was similar to the one in the hospital, but longer and it cost money. She told Stephen how she felt it relaxed her, and also the therapist gave her information about what she described as 'retreats' where a person can go for a couple of days or longer. Stephen and Jessica looked at the websites of the retreats that were recommended by the meditation therapist. Stephen thought it odd, or even insensitive considering Jessica wasn't healthy enough to travel abroad, as many of them were in Europe and other places like Sri Lanka and India.

'My God, look at the prices,' Jessica gasped, and Stephen joked, saying, 'Maybe they are retreats for the mindless, rather than doing mindfulness.' It was thousands of pounds for a week to share a room with a stranger in a supposed atmosphere that is intended to get away from life's concerns. Recurring words marbled the language used to describe the retreats and what went on in them, such as 'revitalising,' 'stimulating,' re-balancing' and 'transformation.' They littered sentences that were accompanied by seductive photographs of peaceful scenes and beautiful landscapes. The retreats in this country were so surprisingly expensive Stephen had to read how much the costs were a couple of times to make sure he had read correctly the first time. Just a few days was hundreds of pounds for shared accommodation and a meal. The retreats and the locations they were in were described in a way to evoke images and feelings of relaxation, but also basic simplicity, which Stephen couldn't link with the price it costs. The natural environment of where the retreats were located was emphasised, with descriptions of, 'enjoying long carefree walks in beautiful countryside.' Stephen couldn't help feeling that it was a lot of money just to go for a walk in the country, and he didn't feel it necessary to be told that such an activity was exclusively for people going on a retreat. After all, anyone can go for a walk. He wasn't impressed and was pleased when Jessica said she didn't want to go on a retreat, and added, 'God, these people all look well and healthy – it all looks a bit of a pose to me.' She shook her head, and Stephen could see beneath what she was showing Jessica felt let down. It hurt Stephen, but he didn't say anything, he thought it best to just let it go, and by the look on her face it was best not to say anything more about it.

Jessica went into the kitchen to make a drink for both of them and Stephen had a last look at the sites with the retreats. He noted the language used, supposedly, by people that had gone on a retreat. 'Really powerful experience.' 'I now have tools to deal with issues.' 'I'm learning to put myself first instead of feeling I have to please others.' 'I came here cos I used to be mental, but now I thank all the rubbish I've been through.' 'I no longer refer to myself in a negative way, I now feel good about myself.' 'Goodbye stress.' 'It's all about the *here* and *now*,' 'Yeah, mindfulness can do anything, also healing on a profound level.'

People gave accounts of how their lives had changed since practicing mindfulness. He read how mindfulness is a 'revolution' and not to miss out on this phenomenon. There was an article about a radio programme entirely devoted to mindfulness with endless talk of anecdotes about how beneficial the practice of mindfulness is. While reading, a feeling came over Stephen that was triggered by something, but he couldn't put his finger on what it was. Every time it nearly came to him, it dissolved and slipped away. He asked himself over and over what it was about this mindfulness *thing* that made him feel uncomfortable. There was something about the people involved in the business side of the mindfulness industry that reminded him of hippies. Stephen was too young to remember the hippy movement when it happened, but from things he had seen and heard in regards to the stereotypical lifestyle and attitudes of escaping mainstream culture, made him think what he was reading about was a modern version of all of that, except the principal priority now was of making money from those ideals. Money was a notable factor throughout the whole affair. Stephen couldn't help feeling critical about mindfulness, and not only mindfulness, but all the other stuff as well in the way it had become a big industry. The way they dress, talk, the exotic and peaceful places the retreats take place in, he didn't want to generalise, but he couldn't help feeling the way he did.

While reading around the subject of healing and therapy, Stephen followed links to research and articles written on the subject of PTSD. He thought about his experience of being injured in Iraq as he read about the effect terrible experiences have on soldiers coming back from battle. Someone had written an article criticising the mindfulness boom, seeing it as little more than a fashion, but that wasn't the main concern of the person that wrote the article, it was the potential danger involved when someone practices mindfulness without having advanced knowledge of nervous illness and the effects of past trauma. Stephen read what a Buddhist monk had to say about mindfulness meditation, which was basically that it can be helpful for a person who hasn't suffered a past trauma, but can be harmful to a person with trauma whose nervous system has been deeply affected. The monk spoke about the purpose of meditation and of how it isn't to 'de-stress,' but to develop and gain insights and awaken one's spirituality. It is a practice requiring discipline and adherence to training that is part of a greater knowledge, which should be directed by those having many years of experience, and who themselves are supervised by others with higher knowledge, so that they can guide a person safely and skilfully. The monk concluded by saying that it is worrying to think how diplomas are handed out accrediting people to hold mindfulness classes when considering the harm they can do.

Stephen read how mindfulness is the new fashion competing with dance classes and other fad activities that come and go. He read how mindfulness meditation is also used in the corporate world where it is sold as a product to give people an advantage over their business rivals. The idea is that the clarity of thought, supposedly achieved through mindfulness meditation, is conducive to greater awareness and will give a person the edge over business rivals. Other benefits are said to be the employee's personal satisfaction, which increases company profits by having a content and productive employee. One article cynically observed that in the corporate world mindfulness has replaced positive thinking to 'win the deal.'

An article looked at the claims of employees on mindfulness courses being more productive, but also the pressure put on companies by agencies providing training and courses who push the promise that mindfulness is an exploitable tool for achieving success in the business world These agencies push a concept called 'emotional intelligence' and claim that mindfulness car change an employee that is tired, unorganised and unhappy into a content person with ambitious enthusiasm. The idea of an employee being more productive and personally content is based on the popular belief of a happy workforce is a productive workforce. Companies are warned if they don't want to lag behind competitors, they have to make their own workers more dynamic, and the silver bullet that delivers this outcome is mindfulness. It is sold as a kind of meditation on-the-go with an image of a happy competitive careerist living a confident and functional life, healthily balanced with work and leisure, having an interest in their company's concerns and providing their family's needs. This ideal employee performs his or her role comfortably with a smile, showing gratitude to the company for financing their family, which they are also grateful for having. One meditates in the morning to train one's mind to focus on the present moment, and then carry that state of mind through the day while constantly reminding oneself that one lives in the here and now. By doing this one will pay greater attention to detail and not only see things more clearly, but will be looking at fresh, new ways of doing things one has done a thousand times before. The employee will be happy and enthusiastic about challenging and addressing issues to see if they can be done in a better way. The employee will have an open mind, looking at things in a different way he or she will be aware and conscious of thoughts and action while calmly leaving behind a mode of thinking that has limited one's perception.

Stephen stopped reading, realising he was holding his breath. He was irritated by what he was reading, but his main task was to make things as easy as he could for Jessica, and try not to think about the people involved in schemes to financially prosper from vulnerable people, especially those suffering with such a cruel disease as cancer. It felt to him as if these people were involved in the cruelty in that they were a part of the disease having to be suffered by those unfortunate to have the cancer. Stephen continued his search on the internet, looking at articles, sites and blogs, amazed at what he had encountered he felt strongly about the deception and how desperately ill people are targeted for financial gain. The word, *evil* came into Stephen's mind. He thought about the different gurus, leaders, teachers, therapists, mentors, or whatever they are called in the *healing* world and the tone of voice they use, intended to convey tranquillity and peace. Stephen thought of those in the *business* world selling the benefits of a calm and relaxed mind, which brings great rewards with one's mind tuned to a pitch that connects spiritually and intellectually at a level neither higher or lower, just at a different level, the level that gives the *enlightened* person an advantage, and don't forget the money.

His search took him to read debates about how the yogic and meditation traditions are at odds with the Christian belief. Finding it interesting he read further, following one link onto another. One hour passed into the next and still he read, focused and wanting to learn more. Stephen was totally engrossed with what he was reading about how some Christians view yogic, and other views and beliefs as being wrong and having a motive, which is to lead a person away from following the teaching of Christ and being close to the Lord, because it is the work of the devil. Teachings other than Abrahamic faith are seen as demonic and have objectives to mislead people by giving the answers they want to hear. They are seen to be appealing in an age where following God has become unfashionable, a situation brought about by the evil intent of demonic power. There was so much written on the dangers of yogic philosophy, and other methods of healing and therapy from the weird to the prosaic. Stephen read how some types of meditation demand a certain word to be repeated or even chanted to bring about a 'grounded' self, and in doing so the practitioner will become balanced, aware, strong, calm and safe. The reason behind the repetitive chanting is to invoke 'energy' to enter the person doing the practice, and aid that person in reaching a new depth in feeling of 'self.' It is like inviting a means within one's self to awaken a power that gives a great sense of well-being, and with it a greater knowledge, insights into self and things around us. With this sensation comes a sense of inner peace and of feeling love for all living beings. According to a Christian perspective, this euphoric feeling is all very good, but the chanting is an age-old method to summons evil spirits, which often creates a trance-like hysteria from which the practitioner emerges different and better in mind and body. Although, it is seen as little more than deception, a ruse the devil uses as the practitioner has been fooled by demonic manipulation.

The Christian belief does not see mindfulness, or similar methods used by Buddhists and other meditative practices, as something that is spiritually neutral. They believe that rather than a harmless activity to relax the mind, methods such as mindfulness unknowingly embrace religious or spiritual ideas that entrap the unsuspecting practitioner to engage in something that is very dangerous. The practice of mindfulness, from a Christian critique, is connected to other practices such as taking mind altering drugs, chanting mantras and putting one's faith in a shaman and other pagan medical people, which is no different from voodoo and witchdoctors. Stephen read how mind-altering drugs can cause an awareness to particular things in a person's life, and maybe to such an extent it is seen as an enlightening moment. The practice of meditation can also do this as the mind is stilled to observe it, but a flashing insight, a sudden realisation to an understanding, can seem like a revelation that may be felt of as a life changing moment. In the pursuit of attaining wisdom, consciousness and a relaxed fulfilled state, practitioners are being led down the dark path to sorcery. Stephen read how the Christian argument sees other beliefs and practices, whether New Age or old religions that are well established such as Hinduism and Buddhism, as ensnaring people and leading them away from following Christ. By practicing these other methods a person isn't getting to know or trust the true God, and is therefore inadvertently opening up one's self to demons. The practitioner is satisfied with one's own feelings and supposed greater insights into one's self, but when dying it is followed by eternal death as the evil power has won, unlike the experience of those believing in the true God, who will, supposedly, not perish but will have eternal life.

Stephen sat back, thinking about all the theories and ideas that people are wanting to propagate and sell. He thought of how some people could say Christians are protecting their *product* and not wanting any competition, but he didn't think about it for long as Jessica came to his mind, and he thought of how her suffering had led them to become acquainted with all these conflicting beliefs. He started to look at the different treatments for PTSD and read how a method in behavioural therapy, called Exposure Therapy, has been used with positive results. It basically involves exposing the patient to the source of the anxiety, or its context, by using immersive computer simulation. This therapy uses computer virtual reality programmes to create the situation the patient was involved in, and for the patient to be an active participant in the virtual reality exercise. The patient, hopefully, becomes desensitised to the fears and feelings associated with that event. Relaxation techniques are often learned by the patients before taking part in such therapy so that they can engage a relaxed state when confronting something they fear and have avoided because of it being so upsetting, which has resulted in repressing fear and increasing anxieties. By using this technique, the moment of what started the trauma is addressed and re-visited with coping strategies being gradually implemented in order not to shock the patients and re-traumatise them. Exposure therapy has been used with success with ex-combats returning from battle and suffering the effects of PTSD, although there is evidence that the therapy can have adverse effects on patients because it can increase their anxiety. For this reason, there is a call for only licenced professional therapists from the area of behavioural science to be used when conducting this therapy. It is seen as dangerous for someone who has only completed a short course, got a 'diploma' and guides vulnerable people suffering complex emotional problems.

Stephen read how mindfulness resembles exposure therapy in that the practitioner addresses his or her emotional experiences and aims to accept all feelings attached to a nasty experience, or the feeling that arises when thinking about it, and stop oneself from focusing on responsive feelings towards those negative sensations. Stephen went over how he felt when having the mindfulness session with Jessica in the hospital. He thought about the young woman, Kayleigh, who led the meditation, although she was a qualified person, just how qualified was she to be overseeing such a complicated procedure? And also, because of the popularity of it people can buy mindfulness DVDs from a newsagent, which is hardly a controlled therapy directed by a health professional.

17

Jessica went to another mindfulness session that was with others in a group, which she enjoyed and the teacher gave her the name of a woman who taught yoga. She told Jessica that the yoga teacher had a lot of experience of teaching people that have serious illnesses like cancer and that some people find yoga, like mindfulness, very beneficial. Jessica rang the woman, who seemed friendly and she told Jessica to come along with Stephen to a class for a chat. A few days later they went along to the class, which took place in a church hall that was used for different activities. As Stephen looked around at the people, he had to stop himself from pointing out to Jessica the colourful, childish drawings on the wall, she would have seen them anyway, and he knew it would sadden her. The women taking the class led Stephen and Jessica to the corner of the hall and told Jessica to do just one or two of the poses and that she would guide her through them. She told Jessica to stretch to only what is comfortable and let the movement follow the breath. She smiled at Stephen, prompting him to participate and told Jessica to focus her mind on one single thing, like the pose she was doing and not to stay in a position if it was uncomfortable. Stephen thought the woman spoke in a rehearsed manner as she rattled off very quickly to Jessica how yoga detoxifies the body and stimulates the immune system through movement, breathing and resistance. She said, 'You know, there is a lot in the power of the mind to heal cancer. Yeah? Using your mind to fight cancer, you know? Emotional and mental states play a significant role in helping a patient recover from cancer – and let me tell you, the stomach is our other brain, it's where we feel, where instinct and intuition are felt, the emotions are felt there in our stomach.'

She continued, saying how yoga helps to manage anxiety and stress when being diagnosed with cancer, and for Jessica to tell herself to, 'Go with the treatment,' however unpleasant it might be. She went on, telling Jessica to see herself as not separate from what she is going through, but as part of the process and it is positive to be part of a team with doctors and nurses and treatment that makes up a unity helping and working as one to cure her. 'Yoga helps to connect the mind to the body – that mind body dualism?' And she smiled rather smugly as she added, 'It improves flexibility, strength, endurance and the lymphatic flow in one's body.'

Stephen and Jessica did the class and at the end the teacher asked Jessica to hang back as she wanted to talk to her. She spoke to Jessica, every now and then nodding at Stephen to confirm what she was saying was true. She talked about studies that have shown how yoga can help cancer patients by lowering levels of stress, which is very important and maybe a factor in getting cancer in the first place. She went on, talking about lower cortisol, building energy levels, becoming less tired and calming the mind, which also helps one to cope and sleep better. She spoke of how performing the positions when practicing Yoga detoxifies the body and stimulates the immune system, one's body becomes more flexible, bone strength is weakened by cancer treatment, but that can be rectified by doing yoga, and as relaxation becomes easier one's sleeping gets better, which is good for health and recovery, and even post-surgery scar tissue and weight gain is helped by yoga. The woman made shapes with her eyes, which was something Stephen had noticed other people do from the healing world, as she spoke about how the yogic approach to cancer is holistic with a purpose to harmonise all facets of one's being, and that stress with continual anxiety can cause a person's thoughts and emotions to be negative and never bright and positive. She told Jessica that saying a mantra to oneself throughout the day helps to keep a positive state of mind, and to say something like, 'I am at ease with my experience, I feel the love and support of others.'

They didn't go again. Jessica didn't want to and Stephen didn't ask her why. The yoga teacher told Jessica about retreats and gave her a woman's card who did colour therapy, saying how 'wonderful' she was. When Jessica and Stephen got home from the yoga session Stephen went online to look up the yoga retreats, and Jessica looked up the therapist who uses colour.

18

The yoga retreats were basically the same as the mindfulness ones, mostly situated in beautiful environments in countries like Costa Rica, India and Thailand. Stephen looked at the cost of the retreats, whether in this country or abroad and thought them very expensive, some costing twice what an average person earns in a week for just a few days. He felt there was a designer asceticism aspect to it all, as if the people he was looking at in sun-drenched locations were playing the part, affecting a presentation of wanting to escape from the clawing demands of consumerism, but are spending more money than it costs to go on a conventional holiday, because they prefer to be with likeminded people having aspirations to be part of something that is a fashion. There was language used of 'rejuvenating yin and yang,' of 're-connecting' with oneself and of 'expanding one's mindfulness.' People stay in, 'eco-friendly beach bungalows' set in 'secluded beautiful locations,' and the 'vibe' is good and positive.

Newspapers seen as being at the top end of the market ran advertisements for retreats, with one company that had retreats with visiting teachers in several countries. It had a definite brand with an image of health, wealth and an emphasis on luxury and the *self.* Food is provided and described as 'inspiring' and wholesomely healthy with photographs of fruits and vegetables and smiling faces with everyone tanned and healthy. Stephen looked at an internet site advertising a retreat run by a man and woman. The man looked into the camera, his face was worn and wise, a man that was caring with an intelligence transcending concerns for material objects, but Stephen thought him to be a competitive man presenting a staged appearance of someone who is composed and compassionate, but his sharp eyes could not conceal a determined purpose that lay beneath. There was his biography, telling of the man's life and how he came to bring 'wisdom' and 'healing' and all his experience of different disciplines and practices together to help others, but before all this happened, he was in the music business. He started off playing guitar and singing in a band, but after not gaining the success he must have wanted, he then worked as an executive in public relations for a large record company. The blurb for his company told of how he brings 'fun' to his teaching, which is diverse in focusing on the mental, physical and spiritual. Whatever technique he uses it all works together in 'nurturing one's true self,' and in the future he plans to make a DVD made of his musical compositions, combined with his teaching of yoga and 'wellness.' Stephen looked at another website belonging to a man saying similar things, but he made the point of specialising in cancer patients, and it is all performed with 'love' … at $200 a session.

It felt to Stephen that there was something very wrong about some of the people he was reading about. He knew it was about money and it was just people advertising their wares, but it was wrong to target those who are ill, having cancer and other such illnesses makes a person very vulnerable. He thought of how there are those in the healing industry that peddle hope to people who are desperate, and of course they are going to bite, because they want to live. The retreats, yoga and meditation are all very well as an activity for relaxation and as a fashion one wants to be involved with, but it is wrong to make claims of healing the very ill. Stephen thought of how these people will try anything, it's about survival and it was beginning to upset him when hearing the hackneyed phrases people say, such as being 'brave,' 'open' or 'enlightened,' when it has nothing to do with any of that; Jessica, and anyone that has cancer, just wants to be alive.

Stephen found some articles that were critical of the complimentary healing industry. The word 'hedonist' came up, and he researched its meaning, not completely sure of what it was. A journalist was giving examples of certain retreats by showing photographs and films about them, saying how it seemed to be more about self-indulgence and seeking pleasure. Stephen agreed, everyone looked so healthy, and not at all like people with serious health problems and were seeking something that might help them hold onto their very existence. Stephen looked at the people in the films, they were nearly always young and attractive females, smiling, relaxing, doing a little yoga or meditation with others and then shots of them walking along a beach in trendy clothing, fashion to fit the environment. The locals were shown as humble people, smiling, going about the simple routines of work that make up their simple lives, and the people doing the yoga and meditation gracefully glide alongside this seemingly coexisting world. A world of no conflict, no resentment, a world where there is total acceptance and everyone is happy. It just wasn't real. The words came into Stephen's mind, 'Nothing is real.' The music followed, shifting and drifting, making shapes in his mind. A bitter taste came into his mouth, a band tightened around his head and his breathing was reduced to short breaths as his chest and throat constricted. While Stephen looked at the film of the so-called retreats, a sneer formed on his lips as the words unconsciously fell from his mouth, 'fuck you liars.'

19

Jessica had read about a man who made claims about curing and preventing cancer by choosing to eat certain foods. She wanted to find out more, it was terrible, living in hope of maybe finding just something that might help. Stephen went with Jessica for an introductory consultation with the man, the cost of the meeting was half the price of a single session and there were six sessions making up a course, which they were told to complete in order to get optimum results. It hurt Stephen, because he knew Jessica wouldn't be going to see this man if she wasn't so distracted with worry. He had made his mind up about a lot of the theories, from what he had read and the people they had met, but it wasn't about him, it was about Jessica and he would be by her side whatever she encountered along the way. The man talked about the fundamentals of the theory and practice, telling them it was essentially based on alkaline in the body. The plan is to eliminate acidic producing foods from one's diet with food that is categorised into three groups; alkaline, acidic and neutral. According to the man's theory, cancer can grow in an acidic environment, but cannot in an alkaline environment. Therefore, one should reduce acidic foods and eat a diet of alkaline producing foods, which can cure and even prevent cancer. He gave a list of foods that are apparently alkaline producing and spoke about the importance of minerals in one's diet. He talked about treating one's blood, Ionised Oxygen Therapy, of taking large doses of vitamin C and the benefits of a vegan and raw food diet. The man concluded with saying if these therapies and approaches prove to be unsuccessful it will not render the body vulnerable to an extent it cannot defend itself against even a common cold, and that can be fatal, which can be the case with chemotherapy and the other orthodox treatments where 'poisons' are put into the body.

The man's claims are part of a wider belief that the government are in cahoots with big business and have held back vital information on cures for cancer and cancer prevention because of money. They are in control of a very lucrative industry and have no desire to let it go, and to such a degree laws are established forbidding contrary cures to chemotherapy and available medication. In fact, chemotherapy is seen by those with these alternative views to cause greater harm in killing off more good cells than ones with cancer. Prominent in the debate among those advocating counter theories to the established treatment of cancer, is one's diet that should be made up of fresh organic vegetables, fruit and pulses, and there is always heavy criticism of orthodox medical treatment.

Jessica didn't want to see the man again, although she wasn't finished with searching for something. A couple of days later Stephen watched her as she spoke into her phone, making an appointment to see the colour therapist that the yoga teacher told her about, and the following day Jessica and Stephen were sitting in the woman's living room. Stephen felt it had become a process of attrition as the various therapies, practices and people they met were wearing him down. He felt the woman spent an unnecessary amount of time telling them about the history of colour therapy, how colour is such an important part of our lives and that we don't just see colours, but we feel them. She looked at Jessica and told her how colour has been used therapeutically for thousands of years, with evidence of its use in India, China and Egypt when ancient civilisations utilised wisdom now discarded. Colours, she claimed, is light of different wave lengths, so each colour has its own 'wavelength and energy.' She spoke of chakras, which are 'energy centres' situated in different parts of the human body, and how the energy of the seven spectrum colours, which are red, yellow, orange, green, blue, indigo and violet, resonate with the chakras, therefore, apparently, connecting vibrational energy sources that can be beneficial in healing the body and mind. The aim is to balance the chakras and create a state of harmonious energy fluidity between the energy centres of one's body, which is essential for overall health and wellbeing. That's how Stephen understood what she was saying, and he watched her as she told Jessica how one's chakras can be 're-balanced' with the use of colour, and that each colour relates to a different chakra which affects our spiritual, emotional and physical lives. 'Healing is possible through balance – there are important secrets out there,' she said, and made an expression that Stephen understood as meaning to convey that she has access to them. She said that everything in nature is here for a reason, and as a professional therapist she will guide Jessica in helping her to use her own capacity to heal herself. The woman told Jessica that every colour has its own significance and effect, but red is very powerful with the longest wavelength. She spoke of how light or colour therapy has various applications and one can use different coloured scarves or meditate on a specific colour, but the women felt using coloured lights is best, saying it is, 'A really good way to receive positive vibrational energy to re-balance the body and mind.'

She went on to say how visible light is broken down into different electromagnetic frequencies and each colour is determined by a particular frequency. Red light, she said, has been used successfully in the treatment of cancer, with blue bringing relief to people suffering depression. The woman said she had decided, in Jessica's case, to use red light and for it to be applied in two ways. One way is to look at the colour red, which can be done by looking at a painting that has a lot of red in it, and the colour reflects not only into one's eyes, but also onto one's skin. The other way is to take red light itself and shine it onto one's skin and into one's eyes to absorb the healing energy. Either way, one is receiving the healing energy of red light. She said how research has shown that red light has an effect of regenerating cells in one's body, and she gave a list of the positive effects that come from using red light's healing properties, such as stem cell growth, nerve regeneration and curing mouth ulcers. 'Certain cancers respond well to the effects of balancing and regenerating energy in cells,' she said, and that research shows how the colour red stimulated the sympathetic nervous system, which speeds up blood circulation.

The woman went on at length talking about claims and research showing the positive power of red, and gave an example that Stephen thought to be idiotic of men being attracted to a woman wearing a red dress. Fundamentally, according to this belief, red is the colour of survival and procreation, it energises and stimulates. She said that red light treatment is now commonly used to treat symptoms of cancer, and even the cancer itself through cell regeneration. The device she wanted Jessica to use would give her the healing power of infrared light, which is the invisible part of the red spectrum that is used in remote controls to communicate with the television, and she gave a warning saying that goggles have to be worn to protect the eyes. The woman spoke about different methods, but she felt Jessica should buy a device that had a deep tissue massage as well as infrared therapy. It was a hand-held device that came at a few prices, the highest, Stephen thought, was an extortionate amount of money.

Jessica appeared undecided, but Stephen was definite as he told the woman they would take some time to consider what they would do, but she was not going to be put off that easily. She spoke about how the different therapies correspond and work together, each one heightening the positive effects of the other with meditation and yoga have their place, but light therapy would

101

undoubtedly maximise holistic benefits. She went on with her sales pitch, the woman was slipping into salesperson mode, wanting to seal the deal and make a sale. Stephen felt that the doe-eyed sympathetic woman had taken a back seat, because now it was time for business.

Stephen told her again how they would like time to consider, and added that it can't be that easy or so successfully proven to work, or they would use it in hospitals and in the general treatment of cancer. The woman regarded Stephen for a few seconds before answering, and he felt she was giving herself time to come up with the correct answer, but also didn't like the thought of losing a sale. She spoke matter-of-factly, acknowledging what Stephen had said, but sticking to defending the claims she had been making. She told him that red light doesn't penetrate deep into the body so it has to be shone directly on the tumour, although not only having cell regenerative effects it is also good for other reactions associated with cancer treatment, such as poor skin, hair loss and aches and pains.

Stephen found it difficult to maintain a *positive* approach as they ventured down yet another avenue and met someone selling complementary and alternative treatments and cures. All this talk of the power of the mind to cure cancer, of visualisation techniques and the brain communicating with the body on a cellular level was baffling Stephen. He couldn't help thinking that if it has been that easy for all these years to cure cancer, why hasn't it become common practice? And also, people that have trained for years in the area of oncology can't be so stupid that they haven't even considered other theories to crack this terrible disease. He believed there might well be those with good intentions wanting to help people like Jessica, but there was also a horrible feeling of being exploited by ruthless charlatans that prey on people that are unfortunate to find themselves in desperate situations.

Stephen felt it cruel and nasty the way some of these people make such outlandish claims, and on the one hand state an alleged dislike and disbelief of the knowledge and methods practiced in orthodox medical science, yet were very conventional in the practice of charging money and protecting the interests of their business. He thought of the comedian he had listened to on the radio, Joe Tara, and what he said. 'To pitch their wares.' Stephen thought of how this was a good way to describe the people like the colour therapist and all the others with their fake compassionate voices, whether it's massage, sound vibrational therapy, reflexology, relaxation visualisation, art therapy, and the list goes on. He thought about it, seeing them to be like
102

vultures descending on those that are weak and vulnerable. He saw them waiting in a line, holding brochures, pillows, pads, fabrics, oils, bundled down with their props, each one dressed differently, wearing the costume fitting the role they are performing, their faces set in calm repose, gentle smiles, soft voices and looks of great concern as they tell you how much their therapy will cost. It always costs money, a lot of money for a person who is not wealthy. Stephen reflected how it was an industry, operating in a marketplace that specialises in desperate people, and there they were, the different traders. He thought about the different therapists he had seen and met personally, and he thought how he would like to ask them if they had ever done a favour for another person in their lives without wanting something for it, especially money.

A feeling was building inside Stephen, it was frustration when thinking of people gaining personally from Jessica and others like her. It was affecting him badly and he felt that he could actually hear himself breaking apart inside.

20

Jessica was referred by her team at the hospital to a woman who was a nurse that specialised in stress management. It was a week before the surgery and because stress levels increase at this time patients are often told about techniques to help them relax, such as breathing exercises and paying attention to maintaining a healthy diet. Jessica agreed to do this, but was tired with the *healing world* and had shut the door on anyone else pushing theories, courses, practices and potions. She was exhausted, and she looked it. And so was Stephen, he saw a lot of what they had heard and seen as shabby. He had decided that a lot of it was a sham, enticing those that are cunning to deceive people that were extremely ill, very scared and upset. He knew it wasn't all of them, but there was an unhealthy number in an industry where every person he met told him the financial costs of receiving their treatment. Some of the language made him cringe and the final straw was when a woman talking to him about Jessica's illness said, 'Has she considered transpersonal therapy.'

A pre-assessment appointment had been made where Jessica was to be checked to see if she was fit enough for general anaesthetic and to make a good recovery from surgery. She had various tests, among others a chest x-ray and blood tests, they also asked her to sign a consent form agreeing to the operation. Jessica was shown how to do leg exercises that help to stop clots forming and they decided she should come into hospital the night before surgery. Although Stephen was there with Jessica on her journey every inch of the way, a terrible feeling of separation was beginning to come over him. It was as if he was watching Jessica, feeling detached from her and moving further away, and he hated himself for feeling the way he did. He felt as if he was watching what Jessica was going through in a dream.

Stephen left Jessica in the hospital the night before the operation, she insisted that he went, stoically saying she wanted him to go home and rest, but he didn't go home. Stephen got on the first bus that stopped outside the hospital, not having anywhere in mind to where he was going. He thought about the bus driver he had seen before, thinking about his eyes and how they followed his movements and seemed to know who he was and what he had done. Stephen went from one bus to another, letting some go after seeing the driver wasn't who he wanted it to be, although, he didn't know what he would have done if it was him. Would he say something to him, such as, 'Did you have a son in Iraq who was killed? Well, I'm the bastard that did it – because I wasn't thinking, because that's the kind of useless person I am – I just do what I'm told.'

Stephen told himself to stop thinking about it, but he couldn't go home, not yet, he had to check a few more buses, just in case; just in case it was the driver. He then did something he was going to greatly regret the following day, he rang his mother and asked her to ring Jessica's mother and tell her from him that he loved her daughter so much. His mother asked him where he was and if he was okay. She knew something was up and had noticed how Stephen had been saying some strange things the last couple of months. She was worried and told him to go home, or if he wanted to go to her house, but Stephen declined the offer. He told her he would go home and that he was tired, and didn't mean to bother her, but he didn't go home. Stephen carried on travelling around aimlessly, and on one bus when a young couple, a young man and woman, sat near him, he leaned towards them and said, 'Nothing is real.'

21

Stephen was at Jessica's bedside the next morning, the first thing that struck him was how her face was completely drained of colour, and her wedding ring was the only piece of jewellery she was wearing. She had been given an injection thirty minutes earlier to relax her, which showed in her heavy eyes. Stephen looked into them, they were soft and caring, she quietly watched him as he held her hand, their communication conveyed extensive feelings and thoughts, even though nothing was said. Get well cards were on the cabinet next to Jessica's bed, Stephen had brought them in, most were from her colleagues at work. Stephen thought about his job as he looked at the cards. He kept his personal life, and feelings, to himself when at work, only mentioning what was happening with Jessica to one woman, a quiet and pleasant person who never involved herself in office politics and petty chit-chat.

Jessica didn't want her mother to be there before the surgery, she was distraught but supportive, and her friend Sharron was always there if Jessica asked her to be so. Stephen rang Jessica's mother before leaving that morning, the conversation was hard going, but he just wanted to share the feelings he had with her. She put on a brave face, but it was terrible, her husband had died of cancer and now it was her daughter. Jessica and her mother had a very close relationship, they told each other everything, and it was because they were so close Stephen felt he was intruding upon their lives. He was sure they didn't mean for it to be like that, but all the same, he did feel like an outsider. Stephen's parents told him he was doing all he could for Jessica and that her family knew he was loyal and loving. A nurse approached Jessica's bed; it was time to go. Stephen walked by Jessica's side as she was pushed down a corridor to the lifts, holding her hand he told her one more time that he loved her; and she was gone.

Stephen walked to the hospital cafeteria and phoned his mother before phoning Jessica's. He was told the surgery would take up to two hours, but then might be longer if the surgeon wanted to explore further. It did take longer, just over another hour and then Jessica was taken into the Intensive Care Unit where she would stay for at least two days. Her mother came to the hospital and joined Stephen as they waited to see Jessica. There were drips, tubes and drains on the wound and a nurse was fitting another tube that would constantly pump a painkiller into her body. Jessica's mother couldn't hold in her upset at seeing her daughter in the state she was in, and as soon as they left the room her head dropped as she began to sob. It was terrible. Stephen put his arm around her, thinking how she didn't have her husband to share this burden with, and she held on to him, gripping him tightly as wordless sounds came from her mouth. Stephen looked around the area they were standing in, the sounds and activity around them were loud and rushed, perversely bringing home to Stephen their insignificance in the grand scheme of things.

Later that day the surgeon spoke to Stephen and Jessica's mother about how the operation went. He said there would be a course of chemotherapy to shrink or eradicate the remaining cancer. Although not being told outright, they knew the prognosis was not good. Both ovaries, the fallopian tubes, her womb and also a layer of fatty tissue in her tummy were removed during the operation. The surgeon also told them that Jessica would be staying in hospital longer than what they might have been told or expected, as they wanted to keep an eye on her just in case there were any complications.

The next day a member of Jessica's *team* spoke to her about the menopause and because of having a hysterectomy she wouldn't be able to get pregnant. Jessica thought what the nurse was saying to be unnecessary as she knew these things, which were matters she didn't want to hear as a reminder of the miserable time she has been through. She didn't have the strength to say anything as the nurse went on, explaining how in some cases there is the availability of hormone replacement drugs if it is decided there is a conflict of opinion around the 'issue.' Jessica wasn't really listening to what was being said to her, which sounded like a recited piece of information. She was thinking about how she was thirty-eight years old, a year younger than Stephen, and she wanted children and strived to become pregnant, which led to treatments that led to the discovery that she had cancer, and now to this. Jessica looked around herself, at the tubes, bottles and machines, and then she couldn't think anymore as she closed her eyes and felt a tear slowly roll down her cheek.

22

Stephen got away from work early to see Jessica, he had taken a lot of time off and was aware of there being a lack of real empathy from his manager, even though the appropriate lip service was made. He didn't trust her and was beginning to think of her as the enemy. Worrying thoughts were crowding his mind, he had read how relationships change when in the situation Jessica and he was in, cancer destroys relationships no matter how one tries because the pressure is so immense. Jessica spoke to Stephen about their relationship a few weeks before going into hospital, she said that their relationship isn't an equal partnership anymore, but more of a patient carer affair as their conversations were always about the illness. Jessica mentioned how some people go to a councillor for support to help handle the situation, so they read about it and became familiar with terms like 'coping mechanisms.' Stephen told Jessica that he didn't want to speak to a stranger about him and the woman he loved. 'I don't need rubbish like "coping mechanisms" to be part of my life,' he told her.

They researched around the area of cancer and its effects, reading about statistics, theories, of other people's experiences, foundations, support groups and government policies that affect people with cancer. Jessica told Stephen of how it is far more likely for a woman than a man to be left by her partner when having been diagnosed with a serious illness, and even if the woman survives the illness, the stressful effects of the diagnosis and the changes that occurred in the relationship do not go away. The relationship fails as the man wants a divorce or separates from the woman. She said the findings indicate the reason why it is more common for men to leave the woman is because of a lack of control. Hopes, aspirations and things once discussed and desired come to an end as it is difficult to be positive about a future together. Stephen told Jessica that wasn't going to happen and for her to put that thought out of her mind. But Jessica had become to see herself as different, not as a strong woman who contributed fully to a relationship. She saw herself as someone who is weak, even inadequate and is cared for. Her relationship with Stephen had changed, they were no longer equals and that Stephen's role was now of a husband who was a carer and to be relied upon, which made his position in their relationship different. It concerned her, making her feel insecure and questioning whether he will stay with her.

After Stephen left the hospital, which was about eight o' clock in the evening, he went home and sat quietly. Jessica had been in hospital three days and it wasn't likely she would be home in the next couple of days. Stephen broke from his thoughts, there was nothing he wanted to watch on the television so he picked up his computer and began to randomly look things up, starting with the comedian Joe Tara, which he had done a few of times of late. It opened up a world Stephen had not been previously aware of, a world where there were comedians poking fun at the establishment, but it was more than that, he felt it was educating him. He felt more aware of the hypocrisy that existed in society, which led to him researching establishment figures like Graham Mears. It was a way of thinking he wasn't used to and hadn't had before. It was new to him, he hadn't known or mixed with people having these views and had never been conscious of this kind of critical thinking. Stephen was feeling how stupidly naïve he had been in his life.

He thought about the conversation he had with Ray the homeless ex-soldier, and how when listening to some of the things Ray was saying he thought of how his knowledge and insights were far beyond his own. He and Jessica never had any conversations about these matters, she was like him in just accepting the way of things and getting on with her life. Looking back, Stephen pondered over the state of being where there isn't any thinking and to blindly accept without question. He felt different now, that old way of thinking had gone, or *not thinking* as he saw it. The truth was important to him, and he was longer going to settle for being fobbed off with news and accounts of things that served the interest of a minority of people with power and influence. Now that he had become aware of these things, he saw it everywhere, the untruths and myths that pass as credible historical facts. A thought flashed in his mind, which was instantly followed by a feeling like a burning lance having passed through his stomach. The thought was of how powerless he was in helping Jessica. It left him feeling helplessness and weak. Stephen asked himself if he was fixating on matters like politics because he couldn't do anything to help Jessica? But then he thought, he also couldn't do anything about the political situation, and this caused a pain to constrict around his head.

He tried to put that thought out of his mind and continued searching things related to Joe Tara. Stephen watched one of his shows from a few years back, he had seen many of them, sometimes there was the full show rather than just a clip. He listened attentively, as a student might when taking note of what a lecturer might be saying, the subject intrigued him, and although Joe Tara

109

was a comedian, Stephen never laughed. He found what he was saying too serious a matter to laugh at and treat in a light-hearted manner. Joe Tara had recently written an article in a newspaper known for its political viewpoint that can be critical of the government. It was about the Royal family, their vast wealth and their associations with leaders of horrendous regimes in other parts of the world. He wrote about oil, arms and historical land acquisitions that had happened against the will of the people that lived in those lands, and how they were subdued in the most aggressively brutal ways. He made a jibe against the British army that carried out what he called, 'atrocities to serve the interests of the atrocious.'

Stephen came across a female comic called Jay Turn, while he was looking up things associated with Joe Tara. He read how Joe Tara and Jay Turn were friends and that she has often been dubbed a female equivalent of Joe Tara, and he was a male version of her. Stephen watched one of her shows from quite a few years back, and she was similar to Joe Tara in how she ridiculed and questioned authority. She also lampooned celebrityism as stupid and mind numbing, saying that it works in favour of the establishment to have a dumb populace. Stephen looked up other stuff about her, noting how she was always dressed in black and wore tee shirts with anarchist-like slogans on them. One was to do with the Spanish civil war having a woman shooting a rifle on the front. Another tee shirt had something about God and women on the front, and another about 'class war.' Her trousers were shapeless and ending above her black boots that she always wore.

It was completely different from what he understood comedy to be, but then he had never been that interested in comedians. He just accepted what was on the television and gave little more thought to it, but the use of comedy to challenge and make fun of those in authority was something else. Stephen liked it, he felt as though he had discovered something valuable. He sat on the sofa watching Jay Turn and Joe Tara for a while longer before going to bed, although it didn't cheer him up or lighten his mood. It did the opposite. It stirred frustration deep inside him as he thought of the hypocrisy, the inequality that exists and the unfairness of it all. Stephen got into bed thinking of Jessica, but also of how he had grown to hate people like Graham Mears, the Chancellor of Exchequer.

23

Jessica finally came home from hospital. They had kept her in nearly two weeks for tests and further observation. She was very weak and found it difficult to handle quite basic demands, such as Sharron coming to visit her. Stephen took time off from work to be with Jessica, and her mother also stayed for long periods during the day. Stephen was finding it hard going with Jessica's mother, and it made him feel guilty. He felt she would override certain things he said or wanted to do, and he couldn't help feeling, that in some way, she blamed him for what had happened to her daughter.

The challenges Stephen and Jessica faced weren't anything they would have dreamed of encountering, and to hear stories of other people in the same situation didn't lighten what they were dealing with. It was three weeks after the surgery that Jessica felt well and comfortable enough to move around the flat, being on the first floor made things more difficult because of having to manage the stairs, but she was beginning to feel a little stronger and more able. Jessica had to go to the hospital for courses of chemotherapy to sweep up any cancer cells that are not visible to the naked eye. The treatment was to be carried out in three-week cycles, with up to six cycles and a period of rest between each cycle to allow the body to recover. On the first appointment Jessica had a blood test, an x-ray and met her surgeon who asked her questions about how she felt. He discussed the subject of post-surgery depression and anxiety, and how the impact of stress can cause psychological trauma. The surgeon suggested that Jessica might benefit from counselling to put strategies in place to cope with upsetting emotions, and he gave her the name of a counsellor that specialises in this kind of work.

Later that evening Stephen was alone in the living room looking at his computer. He was thinking of going to see Joe Tara live, and as he looked for information on where he was performing, he felt it crazy to be thinking of doing this with Jessica being so ill. Even so, he did find comfort in what Joe Tara said, and maybe it was a distraction from the terrible time he and Jessica were going through. There were shows coming up in London and Stephen imagined walking into the theatre, alone, taking his seat among people that would probably be of a type he hadn't had any dealings with before in his life, in terms of socialising and informal conversation.

He made this assumption based on what he had seen on the internet, the audiences at his shows looked very middle class, and would most likely had been students who went into qualified jobs and shared an interest in a particular brand of politics. He would be uncomfortable with some aspects of sitting in a theatre with all those people, or intimidated was probably the correct word.

Stephen told himself it would never happen anyway. How could he go to the theatre and see a comedian while Jessica was at home suffering with such an awful illness? All the same, he continued to look at the places Joe Tara was performing, and then he looked at the price of the tickets. They were incredibly expensive. It astounded Stephen because they were so ridiculously expensive. He thought how it must be a joke, and that the price for a ticket was more than a lot of people get paid for a full day's work. Stephen found it shocking, and it confused him to a point he checked and re-checked the price to see if he had read it correctly. Stephen sat back looking at the details of buying tickets for Joe Tara's shows with mixed thoughts coursing through his mind and emotions troubling the way he felt. It puzzled him why the tickets were so expensive to see Joe Tara, a person that criticises materialism and its effects in causing inequality. The effect it had on Stephen was very powerful, and finding it difficult to accept he turned off his computer and looked at the blank television, taking in its stillness, which he thought was very much like himself in being silent and dumb.

24

Stephen went with Jessica to see the counsellor that the surgeon had spoken about. It was at the same hospital and in the same room where they had the mindfulness session. The counsellor was a pleasant young woman, her appearance and manner being so much like the others they had seen it caused Stephen to think that maybe they were cloned. She started off by saying how cancer not only affects the person with it, but also those close to her or him. She spoke of how a person with cancer faces not only physical pain and mental stress, but also feelings he or she had never before encountered. 'Shock and fear contrasted with denial has a heavy and destructive impact on the body,' she said, 'So one has to learn coping strategies to help manage this stressful time.'

On hearing the term 'coping strategies,' Stephen's mind went back to what he had read about PSTD and soldiers returning from battle, and he looked at Jessica, thinking how she had not returned home from her *battle*, but is still *fighting* it. As the counsellor spoke to Jessica, Stephen thought of when he was in *battle* and what he read about PTSD shock. He couldn't remember in much detail what PTSD really was, only that it was shattering for a person to experience unfamiliar feelings and confusing emotions that tear one's mind in all directions with anger, upset and fear. Stephen stopped thinking about the effects of shock and damaged emotions, it had set off a series of physical feelings, such as pins and needles running up his legs and back, and he wanted to open his mouth with the mad idea that it would expel a poison that was rotting his insides.

The counsellor was talking about 'disassociation' and how it can be seen as an unconscious use of a coping strategy. She went on to explain how there are different levels of disassociation, from mild daydreaming to avoiding one's unpleasant, stressful reality, and in more extreme cases of seeing the world as not real, and again Stephen shut off from what he was listening to and thought about the Beatles song Strawberry Fields Forever. The line 'nothing is real' played clearly in his mind, as clear as if he was listening to it coming from a speaker in the room. He was thinking of what is actually real and what people imagine to be real from *knowledge* that those in influential positions have told them to be true, from people like school teachers, priests, politicians and the media. Stephen continued to think about this, of what is really true, and then his thoughts disappeared as he became conscious of Jessica squeezing his hand. She was giving him a reprimanding look, and it wasn't the first time of late Jessica had looked at Stephen in this way. She had become impatient when seeing him slip into, what looked to her, to be something like a trance, staring blankly at seemingly nothing while she or someone else was talking about something serious.

The counsellor was talking about how the psychological distress suffered by a person with a life-threatening illness such as cancer is often unacknowledged by health professionals, although there is education in developing skills to gain more understanding in this area. She spoke of how it has been commented upon how the traumatising aspects suffered by a person with cancer are similar to what people experience when suffering mental illness. She went on, and on, talking about the effects of stress, and then talked them through subjects such as disconnection, aggression, poor sleeping, anxiety, disassociation and physical concerns like heart beat irregularities. Towards the end of the appointment the counsellor spoke about methods that are used to treat anxiety. She talked about the different types of counselling and what some people feel comfortable with, such as in a group or on a one to one basis.

Stephen thought of the different types of therapies Jessica and he had learned about, and here they were again. It was the same with the counselling, the cycle was continuing, although now everything felt doomed. The counsellor spoke about Cognitive Behavioural Therapy, which is what she mainly practiced, and how the therapy aims to change the way a person views and responds to emotions that are upsetting and destructive. She went on to explain more about Cognitive Behavioural Therapy, and Stephen saw how tired and upset Jessica had become. He asked her if she was okay, and the counsellor pushed a box of tissues along the table towards Jessica, and as she did so, Stephen noticed the way she placed her fingers on the box and slowly pushed it along the table towards Jessica. Stephen looked at the expression on the counsellor's face, and it caused him to think how the whole process, the therapy and counselling procedure is a business that is run like a production line and Jessica was just another unit in that process.

25

Stephen returned home from the chemist, having been to pick up prescriptions for Jessica. There was some confusion over paying for them as free prescriptions for cancer patients were abolished quite a few years back, although exemption can be issued by one's GP at their discretion, and in Jessica's case the doctor didn't hesitate in issuing the exemption. When entering the living room, Stephen looked at Jessica sitting on the sofa looking at her computer, and he noticed how tense she looked, and, he thought sadly, years older.

'I'm not going to beat this,' Jessica said as she looked from Stephen back to the screen, 'It's going to come back.' She was scared, and Stephen felt his stomach tensed as he saw how frightened she was. Jessica was looking at an online support group for people with cancer. 'God, I'm now part of an "on-line community" – reading about other people's experiences and comparing them to my "cancer journey."' She looked angry as she said, 'I'm now in a community I never wanted to be part of – it's all about how long one has to wait for scan results, or remission, aggressive cancer and people telling people to be "positive."'

Stephen watched her for a few seconds before speaking, his voice quiet and calm, 'Nor do any of the other people who join it love.' He was sorry for saying what he did as soon as the words left his mouth, but it was so hard to mind everything he said for fear of upsetting Jessica, or that's how it felt to him. Stephen was naturally sensitive, so he didn't need to consciously construct what he said, but all the same, he was finding it difficult, and draining, although he quickly reminded himself that it was far harder for poor Jessica.

Jessica's eyes became very still as she looked at Stephen, and speaking in a low, even voice she spoke without expression. 'I know that – of course I do, what do you think I am?' Her tone intensified as she screwed up her mouth in a way Stephen had never seen before, and she shouted at him, 'Of course I know that – do you think I'm stupid, as well as…,' and she stopped as she slammed further force into what she was going to say, 'As well as dying of an incurable bloody disease?'

She collapsed immediately after finishing her last word. Tears sprang from eyes that were constantly ready to cry, and knotting her hands into fists she began to beat at her legs as she shouted out, 'Oh God.'

Stephen held her, whispering close to the side of Jessica's face he told her how he loved her and that they would always be together, the two of them, whatever might happen, and he looked away to a place that does not exist, but it is a place people look at and into when feeling the way he did. Jessica sobbed out words hopelessly, 'First I went on the sites for infertility, where everything is about the world of not having something, and now I'm looking at people's lives, people like me, who do have something and don't want it,' and she broke again, falling against Stephen. The utter hopelessness of it all left her completely drained, desperate and scared. As Stephen held Jessica his attention diverted to thoughts of how things aren't real, and the line in the song, 'nothing is real,' but he told himself that this was real, what was happening to Jessica was very real, and it confused him why he should be thinking such a thing. He doubted if he was able to cope with what was happening, with something so massive he had no control over, and fear froze right into his core as he tried not to let tears form in his eyes and run down his cheeks.

26

The next appointment with the surgeon went pretty much as before. Jessica told him that she would think about seeing the counsellor again, but didn't tell him how she wasn't keen on the idea because she was tired of it all. The surgeon asked Jessica to speak to her oncologist and make an appointment before the one that had been planned. She asked him if anything was wrong, but all he said was they were taking precautions and it was best to keep a close eye on her progress. It darkened the mood on the way home. Jessica didn't speak, Stephen thought that she couldn't because she looked so defeated.

The following day was Jessica's birthday and Sharron had been in touch, wanting to visit her, but Jessica didn't want to see her and she didn't want to write to Sharron on social media. She asked Stephen to call Sharron and tell her she isn't up to seeing anyone at the moment. Stephen phoned Sharron early that evening, it had been a while since she had seen Jessica and he knew she would be shocked when she did because Jessica had deteriorated so much. Sharron wanted to give Jessica a present and asked if she could just drop round with it, but Stephen knew Jessica wouldn't want that, so he said he would come to her place and pick it up. Sharron was a good friend of Jessica's and was understanding.

It was eight that evening when Stephen knocked on Sharron's door, and while waiting he looked at the front of their house and a basketball hoop that had been fitted above the garage door. He thought how it seemed a settled house, a family home, perfect, the home Jessica and he would never have, but then the door opened and those thoughts dropped from his mind. Sharron was standing in the doorway asking him to come inside. She gave Stephen a warm hug, kissed his cheek and gave him a final squeeze before turning and leading Stephen to the living room. Stephen was uncomfortable, he had never been close to Sharron, although always finding her to be very nice, but the way she greeted him made him feel things had changed, as if something had passed and things will never be the same. He felt awkward as he walked into the living room, her youngest child, a small boy, was sitting in his pyjamas sliding on and off the seat until Sharron told him to stop it and, 'sit properly.' She told Stephen the older boy was upstairs in his room, 'playing a game as usual,' and that Phil, her husband, was out the back of the house and would be coming in as she had told him he was there. This made Stephen feel even more tense. The four of them didn't go out together, Stephen had only said hello to Phil a few times and had never spoken to him at any length or depth. Stephen was reminded of how shy he was, and he thought how he had always been, but now he felt so drained he just wanted to get out of their house. He couldn't stand the thought of having to answer questions about Jessica. Sharron told Stephen that she had been telling Harry, her youngest son, about him and that he was in the army and how he was a 'hero.' Stephen's insides froze on hearing the word, and a twitch began to shoot across his face a number of times as he tried his hardest to smile.

'Here he is,' Phil said as he entered the room drying his hands. 'How are you mate?' Phil extended his hand to shake, but Stephen didn't speak. He just couldn't say anything. It was impossible, it was all he could do to nod and shake Phil's hand. 'Yeah, we were talking about you earlier to Harry boy here, about you being in the army, and all that, being a hero.'

Stephen swallowed hard, trying to calm his breathing and asked himself what was wrong and why was he responding like this. Phil continued, he spoke a lot, Stephen remembered this from before and had found him to be a bit overbearing, and then Phil did something Stephen thought to be odd. He lifted up his shirt and slapped his stomach, 'Getting toned mate, go to the gym four times a week, 'aint a six pack yet, but it's on its way.'

Stephen nodded, not attempting to say anything, he just wanted to leave the house, but Harry took his attention, pointing his finger at him in the shape of a make-believe gun he made a noise of firing it at Stephen.

'Oi,' Phil said, 'don't shoot him, he's on our side – he's a hero.' Stephen tried to smile, but found it difficult, and felt increasingly self-conscious when he saw the expression on Sharron's face as she looked at him. It was thoughtful, and Stephen felt she had noticed how he was uneasy and that she was thinking of his situation, with Jessica being ill at home and what future were he and Jessica looking at. The little boy fired his imaginary gun again, pointing it at Stephen, but all Stephen could do was look down at him and nod, and then Stephen saw a Sharron and Phil exchange looks. It was about him, his behaviour, the way he was acting, his strangeness. Stephen froze, his mouth dried and a high-pitched tone filled his head. It felt to him that his hands were enormous as he fiddled with his door key, they had grown so large and there wasn't any feeling in them. Stephen panicked, he couldn't feel the key, it felt so small, and he wanted to scratch the side of his face, but couldn't because his hand felt too large and awkward to perform that action. Stephen could hear Phil's voice, but it took a couple of seconds for him to adjust his hearing in order to understand what he was saying.

'Yeah, I was telling Harry here about you in Iraq, not that it means much to him, he doesn't know where it is, but he was well excited when we told him you were coming 'round – a real life hero.'

Stephen didn't answer, he didn't look at Phil, but at Harry, and as he looked at the little boy he thought of how Jessica and he would never have this experience, of a child in the living room dressed in his pyjamas while another child was in his or her room playing on the computer. It was something they would never know. It was something they wanted so very much, but it was not to be. Stephen thought how Jessica and he would have shared the journey with their children, the early years, school, maybe university, a career, finding a life partner, setting up a home of their own, and then maybe having children, making Jessica and him grandparents. A high-pitched tone filled his head, his jaw tensed and he had difficulty breathing. He tried to take a deep breath, but lost his balance and stepped forward as if being tripped, and as he did so he took a deep breath, which brought him back to his senses. Continuing take deep breaths he apologised to Sharron and Phil, who watched him carefully. Sharron looked at Stephen with concern showing on her face, while Phil regarded him with suspicion.

'Sorry about that,' Stephen said, trying to breathe normally, 'I've been really tired today.'

Sharron looked closely at Stephen and said that Phil could drive him home, but he declined the offer, and having to quite firmly as Sharron insisted. Stephen was embarrassed by his behaviour, he just wanted to get out of their house, wanting to run out of the house, and keep running to try and escape from a voice inside telling him that his life has been destroyed. Phil started to speak, but Stephen felt he was putting on an act, finding Stephen odd yet having to be pleasant and jovial. Stephen felt trapped, and without thinking he bent down towards the little boy and extended his hand to shake his, but the little boy just looked at him with curiosity and confusion.

'Go on,' Phil said, 'shake his hand, you can shake the hand of a hero,' and he prompted the little boy to shake, guiding his hand with his own. The boy shook hands, but just going through the motions while continuing to look up at Stephen. The atmosphere was tense. Stephen knew it was, it wasn't just his imagination. He knew everyone felt uneasy and it was because of him. He had entered their family home and disturbed the peaceful setting. He had intruded and destroyed, just like he had when in the army, bringing death and chaos into the lives of people that hadn't done anything wrong.

The little boy was unsure as he looked from his mum to his dad, not knowing what to do he shouted out something Stephen couldn't understand, he then jumped down from the chair and firing his imaginary gun, he continued to shout as he ran towards the door. Sharron and Phil called after him, telling him to come back. Phil turned to Sharron and said, 'What's got into him?' But she didn't answer, she was embarrassed and looked at Stephen with deep sympathy, and he thought for a moment she was going to cry as she said, 'One final time, do want a lift? I'll drive and Phil can stay here with the kids. I won't come in, but it'll help love, you don't want to mess about on busses and trains.'

Stephen looked at her, he couldn't speak, and then couldn't breathe, his mouth dried, a buzzing sound in his head grew louder and his head, face, neck and body felt totally numb.

'Are you okay Stephen?' Sharron had said those words, but they didn't make sense to Stephen. He watched her as she continued to talk to him, but it was as if she standing the other side of a thick pane of glass, he couldn't hear what she was saying and so he leaned towards her in an effort to hear. And then the light in the room grew in intensity. Its brightness became painful, to such an extent Stephen had to shield his eyes. He realised he was shaking his head, but Sharron and Phil were just standing still, as if nothing had happened, looking at him like he was a curious animal in a zoo. He was an exhibit, that's how Stephen felt, an exhibit, nothing more than an object from war that is put on display for people to look at. Stephen intended to say, 'I think I better be going,' but he wasn't sure if he actually said those words, as he watched Phil leave the room with Sharron following him, but she turned before leaving and looked at Stephen. 'Yes, bring them in here,' she called out to Phil.

Stephen tried to move, but found it so difficult to do so, even changing his facial expression was difficult. Phil entered the room carrying a gift bag, his face now having serious concern, gone was his flippant banter. Sharron walked towards Stephen holding the bag out towards him, the smile on her face not convincing enough to hide the pinched look of worry that had been there seconds earlier. 'There you are love,' she said, 'that's for Jess, your beautiful wife.'

As Sharron said, 'your beautiful wife,' Stephen thought of Jessica lying in bed, looking nothing like his 'beautiful wife,' and his knees buckled beneath him, causing him to tumble onto the floor. He had no control whatsoever as he let out painful wailing and began to cry. Stephen was aware of Sharron standing in front of him, and forcing himself to look up he saw her looking at him with pity and fear showing in her face. Stephen couldn't stop crying, Sharron became a garbled mass as tears blurred his vision, although he saw her shape coming towards him as she knelt down and wrapped her arms around Stephen. She rocked him, patting his hair and gently saying words of comfort. Phil watched on, looking awkward and not knowing what to do. Sharron asked Phil to help her get Stephen up and sit him down on the sofa. He walked over, quickly, taking Stephen under his arms he lifted him from his kneeling position, but stopped immediately as Stephen let out a loud cry of pain. It was his back, his injury. Phil had pulled on his spine which caused an immensely sharp pain to sear though Stephen's back and hips. Sharron and Phil watched Stephen as he rested on all fours, his face creased in agony. 'What is it?' Sharron asked him, but Stephen couldn't speak, he just shook his head and making a huge effort he pointed to his lower back and said, 'Iraq.'

Sharron and Phil continued to watch Stephen, not knowing whether to try and help him to his feet or just stand there looking at him helplessly and saying the odd word of comfort. They really didn't know what to do and the looks they gave one another became increasingly worried. Stephen began to take deep breaths and braced himself to get off the floor, his head had cleared and the pain had subsided, but his embarrassment grew. What had happened to him? He asked himself this question over and over. It was no good, he had to face Sharron and Phil, he would have loved to just disappear, but that wasn't going to happen. Stephen slowly got to his feet, helped by Sharron and Phil.

'What is it mum?' A boy's voice called from the doorway. It was the older boy, probably having heard Stephen shout out he had come downstairs to see what was happening. Stephen looked at him and attempted to smile, but the boy looked scared. Sharron told him to go upstairs and that nothing was wrong, only that their friend had hurt himself. She had to tell him a few times, and he finally left after Phil barked an order for him to do so.

Stephen started to apologise, a flurry of words and reasons, which were mainly incoherent, gushed from his mouth. Sharron and Phil tried to placate him, saying how he was going through a terrible time, and they were there to help him and Jessica. He had calmed and felt more in control, but the embarrassment he felt was something he couldn't do anything about. Stephen continued to apologise as he walked towards the door with Phil and Sharron continuing to offer him a lift home, but he was firm in his decision to decline their offer. When outside Stephen felt better now that he was out of their house. He walked down the path, his head dipped low with his chin nearly touching his chest, and as he reached the pavement he turned and said, 'Please, don't tell Jessica about this.' They told him they wouldn't and that they were concerned for his welfare travelling home on public transport, but their words were waved away with his hand and an appreciative nod as he started to make his way up the road.

The huge relief Stephen felt when walking away from Sharron's house was so intense it warmed his body, he felt stronger and his mind was clearing. It was a great feeling, but it was marred at the thought of his behaviour. He saw himself kneeling on the floor, crying his eyes out, with Sharron and Phil standing over him, and then Phil trying to help him up, only for him to scream out, causing their child to come downstairs and see what was going on. The strange man who couldn't speak and made the boy's mum and dad nervous in their own home, which was probably something he hadn't experienced before. That is what he had done, ruined a child's feeling of security, of his home being impenetrable to the frightening things that happen outside, but not now, because the strange man had intruded and frightened his dad, for the first time he had seen his dad not knowing what to do, showing his vulnerability now that the bad that exists in the outside world had entered his home. And so close to Christmas too. Stephen thought about that, and hoped he hadn't spoiled their Christmas with the way he carried on, rather than laughter and light he brought darkness and fear. Stephen caught a bus, although he didn't see where it was going.

27

The doors of the bus closed with a wheezing sound of relief, now that the cold wind was shut out. Stephen looked around his fellow passengers, there wasn't that many and most of them looked shell-shocked from working long hours in boring jobs of work. Nobody was speaking and the lighting showed the tiredness in faces with eyes fixed on nothing as they thought about matters outside of the bus. They were in transit and this part of the journey was a necessary grind that wore at one's will. Stephen looked up at the mirror drivers use to check the inside of the bus. Nothing. There were no eyes looking at him. He was relieved, but then he realised the bus wasn't going in the direction he needed to go. Stephen pressed the bell and stood up, his mind spinning he caught his breath and tried to relax. The few people around Stephen didn't look up at him, but he knew they were watching him. It was as if everyone was cautious of others, everyone was a stranger and a possible threat. Their apathy bordered on hostility, reminding Stephen of patrols he had done in Iraq when looking at the locals, their faces, distrustful and showing disdain as they as they gave furtive glances at the foreign men in combat clothing.

Rain was beginning to fall from a black sky that held no thoughts of pity, fun or indifference. It just was. No stars were visible, urban lighting and pollutants congested the atmosphere, and the rain became heavy. Stephen held the bag, that Sharron had given him, inside his coat as he hurried along pavements where people walked in all directions. The way they moved made Stephen think of one of his favourite birds, the pied wagtails. He thought about the little birds as he tried to find out where he needed to go in order to get home, reading the destinations through droplets of rain on the glass-framed timetables was a difficult task. Stephen caught a bus that would take him to an area where he knew how to get back home. When getting on the bus, Stephen looked around at the people and immediately felt a sense of alienation. The guardedness of the people was getting to Stephen and he didn't like it. It made him disconcerted, his mouth dried as he took a firm grip on Jessica's birthday present. It felt to Stephen as though the people around him were a threat to Jessica, her vulnerability would easily be savaged by these people who had no sensitivity for what she was going through. Stephen wanted to shout out, 'My wife is suffering, and she's a lovely person, and I know I'm going to miss her because she is going to die – do you care? Do you understand?'

The bus stopped at a criss-crossing of busy streets that had entrances to an underground station on two corners of the intersection. Stephen got off and pulled up his collar in an effort to shield himself from the blustery weather. There was less circumspection and more anonymity in this area. A thought nearly formed in Stephen's mind of how in this part of town there were big names on big boards lit with big lights, yet the people bustling around the streets were small and unknown. The warm rush of air when entering the rail station and descending the escalator was welcome. Stephen thought there were a surprising amount of people about for the middle of the week, but then he considered how very few times he and Jessica went up town. A group of young men were loud, out for a drink by the look of them, having been to one or two places and now en route to another. Serious faced young women with shoulder bags carrying their work home passed him on the escalator, fast and sure footed as they sped neatly down the steps, alighting at the bottom and speeding off across the concourse in a zigzagging walk in order to avoid colliding with other rushing people. They also reminded Stephen of pied wagtails, their darting walk changing direction and then quickly changing again as they maintained their hurried pace.

An overwhelming sense of separateness from all around him came over Stephen. Not only did he see himself as isolated and different from everyone, but there was also a sinister aspect. He felt the people around him were in communication with each other and were monitoring him. They were watching him, taking a detailed account of his movements and behaviour, and Stephen wondered how they were doing it. They all looked to be in their own little worlds, going about their private little lives, but, Stephen thought, that was part of their training to appear like that. And who were they reporting back to? Stephen asked himself this question. Was it the army? The police? The Government? What on earth would the government be watching him for? It didn't make sense. But then, why would the army or the police be interested in his activities? Stephen changed the direction from where he was going, if they were watching and following him, he didn't want to lead them to his home. Not with Jessica being so ill. He had to protect her. He couldn't let anyone harm her.

28

It was Christmas eve, and time for another check-up at the hospital. Sharron had dropped off some presents the day before, and picked up the ones Stephen had hastily bought. She spoke to Jessica for about a minute, it was embarrassing for both of them. Christmas, for Jessica and Stephen was very much a low-key affair.

The night when Stephen went to Sharron's to get Jessica's birthday present was distant in his mind. The feelings he had on the underground hadn't passed, but had confirmed what he already thought. Stephen had got on and off trains, some going in the direction of where he lived, others in the opposite direction, but done so to confuse the people that he thought were following him. He checked faces to see if he had seen them before on another train or platform. Stephen nearly fainted as worry turned to panic, and again he controlled his breathing to relax himself. He got home very late, not wanting to worry Jessica he made up a story to explain why he was so late. Stephen couldn't tell Jessica about being watched and having to cover his trail, he had to protect her from harmful forces that existed out there.

Stephen sat with Jessica in the waiting room at the hospital.

They barely spoke to one another, their mood low as they both knew hope was running out and Jessica was like a condemned prisoner waiting to face the inevitable doom. Stephen began to think about the research he had been doing online regarding the Chancellor of the Exchequer, Graham Mears. He had researched Mears's family, looking at photographs of the different family members, at times spending a long time just staring at the face of one of them, taking in details and imagining how they spoke and what they were like. Graham Mears was married, his wife was brought up in a mansion in Belgravia, London, one of the wealthiest districts in the world. Her father is a property tycoon and her mother was born into a family whose company are well established publishers. He has two children, a daughter, Sophie and a son called Sam. Mears has two siblings, his brother, Luke and a sister, Amber. His mother has died, his father, Nigel, was chairman of the most exclusive gentleman's club in London. He is a retired stockbroker having made millions in the city where he was a senior partner in the firm he worked for, as was his father, and Mears's son, Sam also works for the company.

Stephen had read that Mears owns a luxury yacht, which he bought from his cousin who owns a luxury yacht company. He looked up the company, and out of curiosity looked at the yachts for sale. Stephen was shocked to a point of being disgusted. The first one had a price tag of over eighty million dollars. He explored the site further, following a link to the largest super yachts and their owners, it is said that the yachts in this class can cost a billion dollars. Nearly all the people that owned them were members of the Saudi royal family and the royal families of Qatar and Oman. There was a photograph of one of the owners standing with a member of the British royal family. Stephen read about Mears's cousin, a man who had made money in the city of London while working for his family's company, but now spends his time running the yacht company that provides a service for those that can afford it, although not being in the super yacht league. Many of his customers are politicians from different countries, some of the countries are often criticised for their lack of human rights, but Mears's cousin didn't seem to mind about that as he stood posing with the owners of yachts.

There was an ex-prime minister of this country and his wife, photographed with a pop music star on a yacht owned by a Russian oligarch who is said to be a billionaire. Stephen read about chartering a yacht, it is all managed by the company and comes with a full crew, and there was a list of destinations to give the interested customer some ideas. The photographs depicted opulence, the word 'luxury' was used frequently and the men and women looked healthy and wealthy with the crews smiling and happy to serve; all for just over a million dollars for one week. It showed scenes of sunbathing, swimming in the pool and of practicing golfing skills by hitting balls into the sea from the deck of the yacht. Stephen followed links taking him to information about one of the many *rock stars* who owns a yacht, the one that was with the ex-prime minister and his wife. He regularly throws parties and has a select list of people that get an invite to join him on his yacht that costs millions of pounds and has a full-time crew. It seemed to Stephen that they were mainly in the entertainment industry, although there were exceptions. Stephen did smile at the irony as he looked at a photograph of a so-called *bad boy* of rock music, holding a glass of champagne with his wife and child on the deck of the yacht speaking to the owner and other guests who had their wives and young children with them.

Stephen followed a link to an article that was critical of the wealthy people he had been reading about that strut around flaunting their elite status. The journalist had made a documentary, which

Stephen found and watched. The 'clients' who buy the yachts are business people and their politician friends or associates, some are regarded as tyrants ruling over a country that can't sustain the poor that live there. A yacht is seen as a symbol of power and is a place where major decisions to initiate and finalise deals are made and done. The documentary told of how, 'the main players in business, politics and the media controls and furnishes this world from the glitz to the gutter.'

It showed how rock stars are guests on a yacht owned by a construction billionaire who has been investigated for giving support and having dealings with violent, tyrannical heads of states. The man's wealth has grown massively because of securing lucrative contracts to do building work in their countries. Stephen read about one of the rock stars, a person made more famous for his charity work than his music. He has amassed a fortune of hundreds of millions of pounds singing about parts of the world where people suffer in poverty, but ironically enough it is in those parts of the world that the man who owned the yacht he was on had business dealings in.

Stephen watched a film about tax havens in which Mears and his family were featured. Mears's father has businesses and property on an island that is a well-known tax haven. The film went into how there is a great divide between the indigenous people and the tax exiles, with the ordinary folk barely able to survive, let alone indulge themselves in luxury pleasures. The island seemed to be made into a giant amusement park for the tax exiles, with the same old thing of sun, sea, yachts and lots of lazing around. It mentioned how tax is not being paid by big business and it's an exclusive club funded by something called *corporate welfare.*

Another link took Stephen to an article about Mears with his family and friends relaxing on his yacht, and having moored close to the shore they were hitting golf balls into shallow water. The native children scramble to get to the ball first so they could sell it back to a man who looked after the golfing stuff for the Mears family and his friends. The article went on, explaining how this was great entertainment for the Mears family and his friends as they betted one another which child would get their ball. Stephen looked closely at the photographs of them swinging their golf clubs, and he thought how they looked drunk, and the younger ones were probably high on cocaine, if what he had been reading about these people was true. He had read a piece about Mears's daughter, Sophie, and her lifestyle of self-indulgent hedonism. The journalist really went to town, showing his disgust for these pampered people who lack morals and

127

responsibility. Her activities had been written about in the papers, behaviour that involved taking drugs and pursuing a pleasure-seeking life made up of 'partying with friends.' One of her friends, whose name was Beatrice, had died, Sophie was reported as saying, 'It fucked her mind, completely, yeah? She went on the craziest of trips, and didn't come back, yeah?' The article explained how Beatrice was found dead after snorting cocaine and other types of powder with a young man through a McDonald's straw. She was lying on the floor among the remains of discarded food and take-away cartons, which were scattered on the floor with other debris in a flat worth millions of pounds. Stephen clicked on a photo of Sophie and studied her face before clicking on a photo of her boyfriend, Harry. He did a quick search on him, and unsurprisingly his family are a big noise in the City, and like Mears his family banks in the same havens to keep tax from being paid on their incomes, investments and interests.

Stephen checked his watch and looked around the waiting room, but in seconds his mind returned to Mears, going over what he had read and heard. He thought about the hypocrisy of it all, with their assets, business practices and the way they carry on with their lifestyles. Stephen imagined Mears with his family and friends on a yacht, they are fishing and sunbathing. He imagines Mears and his friends with guns, shooting, they are shooting young children and poverty-stricken adults on the shore from the yacht, and they're all laughing as they shoot the people. One dead body is familiar, it's the young man Stephen shot in Iraq, his broken face and head shattered and strewn on the ground like waste that had fallen from a lorry carrying meat slurry. Among the raucous laughing is also laughter with a lighter tone. It's coming from a cabin below deck. It's Mears's daughter, Sophie, there she was, snorting cocaine, and she's with her boyfriend Harry. Sophie is wiping the remains of white powder from her nose and her eyes widen, giving dramatic effect to how she is feeling and what she is saying. She's speaking, but Stephen can't make out what it is she is saying, and then he is suddenly drawn back to sitting in the waiting room at the hospital. Jessica's voice had stirred him from his imaginings, telling him her name had been called. Stephen walked with Jessica out of the waiting room with the images on the yacht remaining very real in his mind.

29

The surgeon told Jessica they wanted her to come in for a scan and for her to see the oncologist before going home. There wasn't much said, and in what seem two minutes Stephen and Jessica were back in the waiting room. Stephen watched Jessica slump dejectedly in her chair as they waited for her to be called for the chemotherapy and more blood tests. While waiting for Jessica, Stephen went for a walk, his mind always returning to Mears, his friends, the lives they live and the unfairness of it all. In the days that followed Stephen read more about Mears and people like him and he was beginning to find it difficult to remember how he used to think and what he was like when younger. He felt that everything was different, he wasn't the same and the world he lived in then was different. Stephen asked himself, but different from what? He couldn't come up with anything other than a vague feeling of who he actually was.

From what Jessica had read there should have been a date given when the tests and chemotherapy lessened, but she hadn't been told anything. She felt unwell with no signs of improvement, and then there was news from the hospital about the scan Jessica and Stephen had been fearing. The cancer was back, and it was spreading. It was depressing and frightening. A date was given for Jessica to go back in for surgery, and whatever hope they had was gone.

'I knew there was something or they wouldn't have given me that scan,' Jessica said as Stephen read and re-read the letter from the hospital. He couldn't speak, he just looked down at the floor, and then he jumped back in fright gasping for air. The eyes of the bus driver were looking at him from the corner of the room.

'What is it?' Jessica asked him, confused at his behaviour, and Stephen continued to look into the corner of the room as he blurted out, 'Him, his eyes, he's watching me.'

'Who is?' Jessica was now more concerned than confused. Stephen regained his senses, although intending to explain himself with an excuse, he was only able to mumble something that was incoherent.

Jessica watched him before saying, 'On top of everything my husband is going mad.' She continued to look at Stephen as if hoping he was going to snap out of the weird mood he had gone into, but realising he wasn't, she turned shaking her head visibly weakened as she left the room. Stephen watched her leave, wanting to go after her and say something, but he couldn't. He stood as if struck dumb, thoughts flashing through his mind at such a speed he couldn't hang on to one of them long enough to form an idea. Stephen stood motionless, his manner distant, which continued through that day and the days following up when Jessica went into hospital. The situation was worsening, there was no hiding from it, and Stephen felt he was disengaging from all around him. His behaviour at work was brought to his attention, his manager complaining that he wasn't, 'focussing and performing the roles laid out in his job description.' What his manager said to Stephen made no sense to him, he stared at her for quite a while before saying, 'And what makes something important in your life?' She told him what he said didn't make sense, and that she was only concerned as his manager with how he, 'performs his role at work.'

Stephen decided not to go into work and didn't bother telling them that he wasn't ever again. The day of Jessica's operation came around, and every day both Jessica's and Stephen's resolve, and any attempts to remain positive, had diminished to a point where they were going through the actions in a state of feeling numb punctuated by sharp flashes of upset and fear.

30

The surgery didn't work. They were told soon afterwards, although Stephen already knew by the mood of everyone around Jessica, and so she was sent home, but not to recover, only to wait for death. The faintest of hope was given of there being a slight chance of survival for a period of time if Jessica took part in a clinical trial. A nurse from the team looking after Jessica visited them at home, she talked about trials, what to expect and how to apply to get on one. It was a last chance action, but they were desperate and would try anything. A few days later an ambulance was sent to take them to the hospital to meet someone who was going to tell them about what trials were on offer and if Jessica was able to apply. They were taken to a room where there were three people who explained to Jessica how leading cancer charities are involved in aiding people to take part in a trial, and that there are advantages and drawbacks with clinical trials. An advantage is that one can have treatment not yet available and might have more scans, tests and time talking with a specialist than if not on a trial.

Jessica was told that one has to remember there are risks involved as the research team do not have extensive information about the drug being tested, even though, the team will monitor the patient carefully and stop the treatment if negative effects are flagged up. There are different phases of clinical trials, the earliest trials test treatments and drugs that not a great deal is known about, therefore extreme caution is taken and only small amounts of a drug are used primarily to see if the drug reaches the cancer and how the cancer cells respond to it. The team examine how the drug behaves in the body, basically to see if it performs as it did in laboratory studies. The patient will have extra scans and blood tests to monitor the drug, even though bad side effects are unlikely in the first phase because only a very small quantity of the drug is used, although there are risks as the amount is still large enough for the possibility of the patient to benefit from it. Trials are used in some cases as it speeds the process of experimenting with a drug when testing on humans rather than animals, because a more accurate response will be found. There are different phases following 'phase one' with more people used on each phase and a higher dose of the drug with constant testing, monitoring side effects and how the cancer responds. The final phase is when a drug has proved successful and has been granted a licence, but is trialled to gain further information on risks, side effects and how well it works on large groups of people.

It was apparent they had discussed Jessica's case as a trial had already been selected for her to go on. It was also obvious, by their manner, that there wasn't going to be a lot of time for Jessica to decide whether she wanted to take part in the trial and their attitude became less soft as they pressed for an answer as soon as possible. Jessica nodded, telling them she didn't have to go away and think about it, and that she was grateful for any help she could have. The room fell silent for a few seconds before one of the people said that they can offer a place on a trial for women with ovarian cancer that has come back or has continued to grow after chemotherapy and surgery, and that the trial is at the stage of phase one. Jessica was told what the trial involves, the likely risks, the side effects and information on check-ups and blood and tissue tests. Jessica and Stephen swapped glances as she was being told about the trial, the words 'phase one' had hit them both very hard.

The meeting ended with Jessica being given a leaflet having information about the trial she was going on. She was told that she can withdraw from the trial any time she wanted to and will continue to receive treatment relative to her stage of cancer. Stephen and Jessica left without asking any questions, they were in a state of shock and fright. The health professionals watched them leave the room, just like they had watched others leave, people in the same situation as Jessica and Stephen, each feeling and believing they are to be treated separately because they are unique and that their life is special.

The following week passed in what felt like to be a dream, or trapped in an airtight room where oxygen is gradually being leaked out. The hospital contacted Jessica to tell her she is always in control and that she had volunteered to take part in research, but can drop out anytime she wanted to. Jessica was asked if she had any questions that she would like answers to, and was reminded there wasn't a guarantee of a successful outcome. She was told it is research and although it would be great if she did personally benefit from the trial, the research will benefit people in the future and that this process is the safest and best way to develop new treatments in order to help people with cancer. Stephen and Jessica went to the hospital for an appointment. Jessica signed a statement giving her consent and was told about the drug being tested and how long the trial was planned to last, which was three months. The drug used on the trial was to find out how well it stops the cancer coming back by blocking an enzyme that allows cancer cells to regrow.

Jessica and Stephen lay in bed talking the night before the trial was going to start. It was a start of yet another journey, each one more disastrous than the one before. It was dreadful. They spoke about possible side effects, whether it will be painful or dangerous and could the test drug trigger another illness. Stephen watched Jessica as she spoke. Poor Jessica, she was so frightened and nervous, but brave. She talked about how she might respond, of how she might feel and her mood dropped as she spoke about it being a last chance as the people selected for this phase are those with such advanced cancer there probably isn't any chance of surviving anyway.

Jessica fell asleep while Stephen lay awake thinking about their plight, forcing himself not to cry he changed his thoughts to Mears, and almost immediately he became angry as he thought about the hypocrisy of big business and politicians. He turned on his side, careful not to disturb Jessica, she had slept very lightly since becoming ill. Stephen looked at Jessica's face, and while studying her he listened to the faint sound of her breathing as it passed through her mouth and nose. He listened to the soft and steady flow, thinking how fragile life is, for it can stop suddenly, just in a single breath. He thought about how it is simple, the need for air, and how it is nature, how we are all nature, and it's free, but a thing called money decides who can live. Stephen thought about Jessica's ability to breath when the cancer worsens, when her organs begin to fail. He conjured up an image of her lungs, diseased and damaged to a point where they can't function and are unable to draw in breath and maintain life.

Stephen watched Jessica's face, the slightest of twitches flickered across her eyebrow and one of her nostrils raised momentarily. He thought how she looked at peace, away from the continual worry that filled every day of her life from now on. He was beginning to get upset, he couldn't let her go. Tears filled his eyes, but didn't break, no longer careful of his movements he leaned over Jessica, and wrapping his arms around her he pulled her close to him. He drew Jessica into him, wanting to get at the cancer and feel it for himself, to share her pain and actually know what this awful thing growing and spreading inside her was really like. Jessica woke, at first with a start, but then relaxed when finding she was embraced in Stephen's arms. On hearing the sound of Stephen trying to stifle the sound of sobbing, she rested her face against his cheek and whispered in his ear, 'It's okay, love, it's okay – I love you too.'

31

Stephen told Jessica he had taken his holiday time when she asked him why he wasn't at work. Stephen felt bad because telling lies was something he had never done before, but then again, he was feeling different from how he had ever felt before. Jessica stayed in hospital for two nights, but she wasn't expected to have any more overnight stays, just appointments to check her blood and have tests for all the other things. When at home that evening, Stephen researched Luke Mears's charity, Support and Development – For Those That Served. The name of the charity had eluded Stephen and he was just curious about it. He found articles critical of the charity and of how it was under investigation, but 'miraculously' a case against it was dropped. The writer of the article sarcastically added that it surely couldn't have been the influence of the chancellor of the exchequer, Luke Mears's brother, and his influential friends that helped to stop the case going to court.

The charity had impressive support, from the Chancellor himself and others in his party, yet they had remained quiet in the face of accusations that had been supported by an examination of tax details, claims of good work being done and other findings. The writer finished the article by saying how the public are being defrauded with misleading claims of how much of the charity's proceeds are going to actually help ex-service people, and it looks like the charity is going to close down as fresh evidence had been uncovered of money going to companies that the chancellor's friends and supporters of the charity have interests in. Recent examination of the charity's records, its activities and bank accounts show an enormous amount of money having been spent on flying Luke Mears's friends and business associates around the world to stay in hotels that are set in luxury holiday locations, but not only that, a number of the flights were flown by a company called Apati, a private jet company in which Luke Mears holds a substantial amount of shares. He had actually started the company, but passed over the operating of it to a company owned by an old school friend. His 'old friend' carries on running the company and the exclusive concierge service it provides for the super wealthy. As well as providing a private luxury jet, Luke Mears uses his contacts to arrange adventures and parties in places most other companies can't.

Stephen followed links taking him to Mears's friends who holiday, own properties and have businesses in the Cayman Islands. He read how the islands, and places like them, are used by the wealthy who play to different rules. There was an article about a tax that has recently been imposed on the island, but affects only expatriate workers, which would hit lower wage earners, especially in the tourist industry, while not affecting the wealthy who use the island as a tax haven, because corporate incomes and those holding foreign bank accounts are not taxed.

Stephen looked at a photograph of Luke Mears, his face showing arrogance and greed. He continued to stare at Luke Mears's face for quite a while before following a link to articles exploring Luke Mears's involvement with companies that are involved with mining in Iraq and Afghanistan. He read how Iraq and Afghanistan were described as countries having 'the most promising mining, materials and mineral markets in the world – at present untapped, but ready for investment.' Luke Mears has interests in a company that is setting up exhibitions in European cities and rich countries in the middle east to entice investment in this area. One of the companies Luke Mears is involved with had the remit of 'problem solving' in terms of companies obtaining licences in order to allow them to explore and exploit natural resources in Iraq and Afghanistan.

Stephen looked at a documentary that explained how governments and companies are working hand in hand to set up conditions for companies to be involved in the entirety of industries and services. The logo on the cover of a prospectus for one of Luke Mears's investment companies says, 'Take the chance to be involved with this exciting opportunity.'

The documentary maker had researched the chancellor Graham Mears and his brother's involvement with companies, and there were many of them that covered the whole area of investment in Iraq and Afghanistan from start to finish. The different companies are involved in mining and all its aspects to extract minerals from producing steel, providing cement plants, all areas of building and construction and phosphate and fertilisers. There are companies that provide solutions to problem solving in all related areas associated to the industries involved, as well as investment companies and professional services that include law firms, banks and advisory and consultancy services. Although, the largest participant is the government that will work with these international companies, therefore connections are made between government ministers and different people representing the companies and services. Another article was about investment opportunities in Afghanistan and how companies should act quickly to have the chance to be in control of the extraction and management of Afghanistan's natural resources.

The country is said to have the second largest amount of copper deposits in the world, as well as having an abundance of lithium, iron and other highly valued minerals and metals.

Stephen's phone rang, breaking his concentration from what he was reading. It was Jessica's friend, Sharron, he had forgotten to let her know how the situation with Jessica was going. He apologised to her, but when she asked if she could visit Jessica, he was firm in telling her Jessica didn't want to see anyone other than close family members. Stephen was aware of feeling detached from what was going on as he spoke to Sharron, it felt like he was an observer or watching a film knowing the characters were not real. When finishing the call, he remembered that he had intended to stop at his parent's house and speak to his mother, and he was also going to phone Jessica's mother. Stephen decided not to ring them, he just didn't feel like going over the same thing, but not getting in touch when he said he would didn't enter his mind. This was something he was doing more and more, and when thinking about it, he thought how it was out of character for him to act in this way.

Stephen continued to look things up online, but changed his search because reading about companies that invested in Iraq and Afghanistan was making him feel angry and sick. He hated Luke Mears, his family and all of them. This thought stayed with him as he unconsciously began researching Iraq, looking for anything about where he had served. One link took him to a discussion that was critical of the U.K.'s involvement in Afghanistan. It ridiculed the government's justification for sending troops to Afghanistan so that girls can go to school, when really, it's all about opium, arms and minerals. The writer of the piece wrote, 'You can hear the business leaders speaking into the politicians' ears "let's get poor people to kill poor people so we can make loads of money – the reason has to be simple, because the people are simple."' The piece ended with saying how 'dumb' most people in the army are, but even so soldiers should be treated with more respect by the people that send them off to do their 'errands' and return home suffering Post Traumatic Syndrome Disorder and homelessness.

A journalist had interviewed people who had served in battle and experienced face to face fighting. An ex-soldier spoke of how his relationship with society has broken down. His actions have caused him to question the authority that directed him to kill people, which has had no effect at all on the objective that he was told was the reason why he was sent to fight in the place that he did. The strongly felt beliefs he had have changed as he cannot justify what he did in the name of bringing justice and peace to the country he fought in.

Stephen thought about what he was reading, the man said what happened was illegal and immoral, and that he was suffering what is called *moral injury*, which is about guilt. It is about killing people and not being killed, and knowing you shouldn't have killed those people. The journalist wrote about how, for many men that had experienced battle, there has been a shaking and destroying of one's values and beliefs. They now question what they once trusted, like their superiors in the army, the army itself, the politicians, the government and the media. The army instils faith in its soldiers by saying they are morally justified to carry out the orders they are given, and together they are unbeatable and are always right in doing what they are doing. When that trust and belief in that power and authority is shown to be false by unmitigated evidence, that is when dishonour, feelings of violation and guilt set in. This causes deep psychological damage as these ex-soldiers feel deceived and suffer *moral injury*. Some go as far as taking their own lives because they judge themselves to be bad as they have taken the lives of innocent people. The hypocrisy and contradictions distort world view of a person who once felt the protection of a system when in battle knowing it is physically dangerous, but morally safe. That has now changed. Some ex-soldiers feel they can't explain how they feel and nobody listens. One ex-soldier said that it would be better if one's community came together and shared the grief and guilt as one, because, after all, the soldiers are, ostensibly, representing that community.

The journalist looked at the question of when murder is acceptable and asked, 'Is it only when the authorities say it is?' He highlighted the factors involved in what has become known as *moral injury*, and examined a situation where, predominantly, young men return home from experiencing severe conditions, have engaged in extreme violence and have witnessed shocking images and injustice. Mix all this with confusion and disillusionment with once held values about authority, and feelings of betrayal from the country and people in general. The ex-soldiers had once felt secure in feeling they belonged to a respected force, together in union with others, and that their actions were justified and even blessed by higher powers to pursue and deliver what they were told to do. Their lives are now blighted as they suffer PTSD, commit out of character actions, violence and even murder. The article finished by saying how many ex-soldiers who experienced fighting in battle become dysfunctional and unwanted. Many of them

137

slide into an illusory world in order to escape their reality, aided with drugs and alcohol their feelings of alienation increase.

Someone had written on this subject, and he didn't hold back in laying blame on politicians and big companies. He was vehement in pushing the point of how the British government have left a disastrous situation in Iraq by pulling back troops and leaving a trail of social conflict, poverty, a shortage of hospitals and resources to care for the sick and ill, along with orphaned children living in a traumatised state. While in this country, the government continue to take away from the health service with things like bed shortages and not having money for cancer treatment, but having plenty of financial help for the interests of big companies that are out to profit from the hell created in Iraq. To add further insult, most of the companies avoid paying tax in this country, a situation created for them by their politician lackeys. As Stephen was reading the article he thought of Ray, the homeless ex-soldier and the things Ray had said to him.

Deciding to finish for the night, Stephen began to close down the computer, but an article on one of the news feeds caught his attention. It was about a member of the royal family wearing a maternity dress and how the shops sold out overnight as people bought the same style of dress. It described how the country was in a 'frenzy' as people wanted to buy the same style and colour, but it seems it has sold out nationwide, just ten hours after the princess was seen wearing the dress on the television news.

Stephen turned off the computer and looked around the room, hearing the silence settle clearly in his head.

32

The trial lasted only two weeks. Using a word such as *devastated* to describe how Jessica and Stephen felt would be to assume there was something to shatter. Their lives were already destroyed, and this let-down was met with such stoical graciousness by Jessica, that one of the nurses at the hospital went into another room and cried. Jessica didn't get as far as taking the drug that was being trialled, she had the first course, which was platinum-based chemotherapy, but the cancer didn't shrink, which meant she couldn't continue to the next course of the trial and take the drug being tested. Stephen and Jessica had an appointment with the consultant at the hospital just days afterwards, his manner was firm and concise in the way he imparted information to them. Jessica was told in very straight terms that time was running out, and as far as he, and his team, could see, there wasn't anything else they could do. That was it, in a hard and bitter nutshell. The only option left was palliative care. He spoke with regret of how there had been funding cuts, and he added that although that isn't the whole the story, and not wanting to get into a drawn out, and unneeded, discussion on the state of cancer treatment and the politics surrounding it, there were treatments available, but not on the NHS.

Jessica looked down at the floor as the consultant explained to her how it is now just a matter of time, and very quietly, and bravely, asked how long she had left. The consultant's head dipped to one side, as if moving away from unpleasant weather, and shook it slightly as he looked up at the ceiling. He said it wouldn't be weeks, it might be 'many' months, although it was hard to say exactly, but there are treatments 'out there' that have prolonged people's lives. Stephen thought how he had heard the term before over the years of people 'buying a few months,' and now it was in his life. He couldn't look at Jessica, nor could he speak as his mouth was thick with emotion that fogged his brain and froze his thoughts. He couldn't think, it was just as if clouds were crashing into one another in his mind. Stephen had to really concentrate to take in the what the consultant was saying as he spoke about a drug that had shown to produce better results at holding back growth and deterioration than drugs used in this country by the NHS. It had been fully clinically trialled and is licenced for use in Europe, the United States and countries in Asia, although it isn't available in this country. The consultant explained how the NHS is not funding the drug because of the 'cost effectiveness' of it. He let what he was saying sink in before continuing. 'It's the way in which they measure it,' and he explained how the drug wouldn't cure, but, 'hopefully' prolong life. The consultant noted the desperate expression on Jessica's face as she was told of the possibility of prolonging her life, he had seen it many times. Jessica asked him, 'Would you try it?' He nodded readily, although gave an uncomfortable shrug of his shoulder when Jessica asked how much it costs, and winced as he told her it is very expensive, and added quickly a question that answered itself, 'You don't have private health insurance?'

The consultant nodded solemnly as both Jessica and Stephen shook their heads despondently and he continued to talk. Stephen didn't hear what he was saying, he just stared the floor, his mind going over unformed and jagged thoughts as he squeezed Jessica's hand, and she squeezed his.

33

Jessica and Stephen were given information regarding private health, names of clinics and of a doctor for her to discuss the possibility of taking the drug that has had good reviews, but isn't available on the NHS. They were going to try it regardless of the money. There was a lot to read about the private health industry, how it works, what's involved and the cost of having it. Stephen didn't like Jessica immersing herself in the details of the private health industry, he felt she had enough to worry about without adding more stress. It seemed that in many, or most, cases, treatment, whether it be on the NHS or private, is usually the same. Tests and certain treatments can be done more quickly privately, but some cancer treatment, for example with something like radiography equipment, is too expensive and might not be available in private hospitals. Although, there are options available with private health treatment that are not available on the NHS. Stephen read about the largest private healthcare provider in the country and how its services are paid for with self-paying patients. It is funded by people that have personal or company insurance and the NHS, which the company gets a lot of its work from, but has been criticised for not delivering an inadequate service in many areas. There are reports of financial priorities over patient safety, unnecessary surgery, poorly maintained equipment, issues of infection control and basic cleanness.

The living room was silent, both Jessica and Stephen were concentrating as they were reading about the health system and the information the consultant had given them. Jessica looked up and said, 'God, look at us, before it was to do with IVF clinics and doctors, and now this.' Stephen looked at Jessica, nodding, thinking of the right thing to say. Jessica continued, 'It's a two-tier system – the whole thing is rotten, and it stinks of corruption.'

Stephen just looked at her, an overwhelming sense of helplessness had struck him dumb. Jessica went on, 'If it isn't enough for a person's life to crash down and break into pieces – to be diagnosed with a fatal illness, and then the frustration when you're told there is treatment, but, oh no, it isn't available because of financial implications – money, bloody money!' Jessica looked around the room before saying, 'Don't they care about how people are suffering?'

Stephen thought about what Jessica had said, and he looked at her. She was different from the Jessica he knew, her face now haggard and bleached with fear and pain. He thought about how money has the power to give or take away hope and life itself, or the people that have control over the money do. Stephen began to think about big business and the greed of those involved with it and of how they are given knighthoods, go on television and are spoken to as if they're respectable people, responsible and committed to this country and the people that live in it. Stephen thought of how they are only interested in financial profits as they go around with pompous smiles while denying good and honest people the chance to live.

'Oh yeah, "fiscal austerity,"' Jessica said, 'That's what it's called – you see, because people are living longer, that's another reason therapies and medicines are cut because the costs aren't sustainable – that's the justification, when it isn't the case at all.' Jessica spoke to Stephen about what she had been reading the last few days, telling him of how there have been breakthroughs with research that has given hope and is regarded as very positive. There are treatments that have a different approach to tackling the cancer. She went on about how many of the new drugs are part of treatment called immunotherapy, or biologic therapy, which is a treatment that boosts the body's natural defences to fight the cancer by using substances made naturally that improve or restore a person's immune system function. These are modern immunotherapies, although it's expensive, which excites people who invest in the pharmaceutical industry, but is depressingly worrying news for patients who aren't fabulously wealthy or covered by some incredibly comprehensive insurance scheme.

Jessica spoke at length on this subject, and Stephen watched her, again noticing how tired she was, how drained and worn she had become, so fragile, and it had happened very quickly. She spoke about the new drugs, 'immuno-oncology,' and how they are changing the way cancer will be seen as many people who have tried all other treatments have been kept alive a significant amount of time with these new drugs. The findings are so positive it is predicted that cancer might very well be seen in the future as just another chronic disease, such as diabetes or HIV. People with advanced cancer, 'People like me,' Jessica said, will have the chance of surviving far longer than what is common at present, even though cancer will be a common disease because of the aging population, but it will be something, to a great extent, that can be treated. But, then again, Jessica explained, if things also go as predicted, which is the immuno-oncology

142

industry being fuelled on a principle of great financial returns for investment, it will create a scary world of the haves and have nots far more blatantly than now exists.

As Jessica spoke Stephen watched the bones in her face playing gently under her skin, which seemed to be nearly translucent. He thought how strong she was, meaning her essence, what she actually was, and he loved her all the more as he thought about it. Jessica talked about advances in genomic science that aims to target the treatment by pinpointing the gene rather than a general sweeping approach, as exists in traditional chemotherapy treatments of cancer. Stephen thought how she had become so learned, she had been forced to become so educated on the subject as she spoke of regulations, giant insurance companies and the influence they have in the pricing of drugs. The prospect of massive profits had companies salivating for their share as potential markets open in developing countries, people will be living longer and there will be a growing middle class with the wealth to pay for the drugs. Although it could be different, as Jessica explained, the price can be reduced, but that would be an anathema to those whose principal value is greed and are interested only in the constant pursuit of profit. 'The love of money,' Jessica said, 'as they say, is at the root of all evil.'

Stephen and Jessica read the profiles of doctors working in the private sector and the comments made by patients. Jessica remarked how it was all very sales-like in presenting an engaging image, which prompted Stephen to read out loud what he was looking at, '"Free carpark, friendly staff and relaxed atmosphere" – I should think so, and it shouldn't be just because people are paying extra for it, that's what it should be anyway, free carparking, friendly staff and a relaxed atmosphere, Jesus, it's somebody's life we are talking about.'

They read how the price of drugs was rocketing, seemingly not only down to branded drugs being expensive, but also because of shabby buying skills existing in the NHS. It has been reported that the NHS pays over the top prices without looking at alternatives or engaging in negotiation. Jessica spoke about how drugs are being targeted where the system feels there might be more hope in making better use of strapped resources, but at present patients are re-mortgaging their homes in order to pay for treatment. People are selling personal possessions, they are borrowing and begging in the desperate struggle to stay alive, in some cases only to have a few more precious months of life with loved ones.

34

A letter arrived explaining details about Jessica's day-case treatment, the date it was to begin and the costs involved. Jessica slumped in her chair with distress as she said, 'One thousand pounds for day-case fees – for about two hours – Jesus Christ – oh my God.'

Stephen read the letter, studying the breakdown of costs, the price of using a bed to administer and monitor the infusion of the drug, the drug itself, observation of the patient and the administration costs; it would come to thousands of pounds a month.

'It's impossible, no way can we do it,' Jessica said. Stephen looked at her, she was in shock. He looked around the room with the pathetic hope that there might be a pile of money hidden away that he didn't know about. Jessica went on, 'There is no promise of it working – and anyway, we know I'm not going to be cured, so why bother? Why bother when we're only looking at a small amount of time – if I'm lucky?'

Stephen dropped to his knees in front of Jessica, gently taking hold of her arms he leaned into her as he spoke softly, telling Jessica how he loved her and that every day he spent with her mattered to him. He wouldn't allow Jessica to talk about the money, he told her they were going ahead with it, and that was final.

A couple of days before Jessica's treatment started, Stephen was reading about health companies and cancer treatments, but his attention was drawn to related articles examining an investigation into senior politicians and their involvement with companies in the private health business. He read how a former health secretary had taken a job with a consultancy that gives advice to companies in setting the prices they charge the NHS for drugs. Another former health secretary had many jobs in the private sector that are connected to the NHS, one of them being a consultant to companies that are putting in tenders to the NHS for services being outsourced to private health providers. There were many examples of politicians being involved in this area, some have been reported as saying how the NHS is a 'business' that offers 'exciting opportunities for investors.' Stephen read how the NHS is being sold piece by piece to companies with connections to top ranking politicians. He became angry when reading about the amounts of money involved, one contract for a county's NHS cancer and end of life services were sold off to a company for billions of pounds, and one of the company's directors is a senior politician.

Stephen began to search elsewhere, although still related to politicians, with one link taking him to a company that organises the hunting of animals in South Africa. He was shocked to read about wealthy people who pay a lot of money to take part in a thing called 'trophy hunting' and of how it is a legal and a thriving business. Stephen looked at photographs on the sites and watched a film of how lions are kept in cages and are hand reared. The lions are used in the tourist industry for tourists to pet, and pay to do so, and then the same animal is killed by a person who had paid many thousands of dollars for the privilege of doing so. The practice is called 'canned hunting' because the animals are shot and killed in a confined area they cannot escape from. Stephen looked closely at the faces of the lions, thinking how they are such wonderful creatures, and here they were being used in this way, and it was legal. Stephen thought how it was wrong, but it was more than wrong, because the word didn't go anywhere close in explaining and describing such a disgusting thing to do.

There were other animals, also reared in controlled areas with the specific purpose of being a product in an industry that, Stephen thought, only Man could think of doing. It sickened him, really making him feel sick in his stomach, and a tightness gripped his throat as anger replaced sadness. He was angry because of the spite and cowardice displayed by what he saw as inadequate people in killing the defenceless animals, and also with business people behind the whole activity making money from such depraved intent and actions. He read of how the industry was organised, the people involved in it and the numbers of certain animals left in the world. It upset him when reading about the elephants, rhinos and all the others, he was also infuriated and frustrated at a sense of weakness he felt for being helpless and unable to do anything about it.

What sickened him was the power these obscene people had, and that laws were shaped to accommodate the activities they wished to do. Just as it was with the health industry of the country he lived in, the country he was always so proud of and willing to lay down his life to protect. Stephen read with interest how people who reside in the Cayman Islands fly to South Africa and take part in the sick activity known as 'canned hunting.' He read how they fly to

South Africa on chartered private jets, which made Stephen think about Graham Mears's brother, and whether he had anything to do with this *business*.

Stephen followed links to other articles to do with hunting and the people that take part in it. He watched a documentary about rich and powerful people, their connections with one another and how hunting brings them together; the title of the film was called, 'Thrill of the Kill.' A 'beater' from northern England, who was interviewed in a pub, spoke about the different people from aristocratic families around the world that come to the 'shoot' where he did his 'beating,' which was on the Duke of Northover's estate. He said, 'A lot of them have links to our royal family, I think the Duke's son is a Godparent to one of the royal children.'

The 'beater' spoke about one of the people who flies to this country to take part in the 'shoots.' He is the grandson of a European fascist dictator who was in power during the nineteen thirties and forties, and his family have strong and historic links to the royal family in this country. He is a 'regular visitor' who comes to shoot animals in this country, and as Stephen watched the film, he was thinking of how the man's family were against this country in the last world war. His grandfather's regime had an awful name for the way they treated the ordinary person who tried to challenge the grim inequalities that existed in their country, and here they are, inviting him over to shoot animals in our land. Stephen shook his head as he went over what he had just been thinking and the words he used, 'our land.' As if it was 'our land' Stephen thought as he listened to the 'beater' talk about the grandson of the fascist dictator, and how he will say, 'It's been a bad drive,' when referring to the amount of grouse killed on that day's 'shoot.' The 'beater' being interviewed said of the grandson, 'He's a killing machine, lands his private chartered jet, shoots, then flies out, probably to another shoot in another country. He once did three hundred days of shooting in one year.'

Stephen looked the grandson up and quickly found several photographs of him. He was dressed in hunting clothes in all but one of them, under a few of the photographs was the title 'Killing Machine.' Stephen read how, in the world of grouse shooting, he's known to be a 'top shot.' The article went on about his shooting techniques, the guns he uses and how since a child he had been to thousands of 'shoots' and that he lives to shoot. It named the different countries he visits to kill animals, which can be up to six in a single week. On reading this, Stephen wondered what this man actually did for a living. 'Nothing,' he said to himself, because his sole pursuit is only

146

to indulge himself in whatever pleasure takes his fancy. Stephen began to think how the whole world is nothing more than a playground for these people. A playground they own and control, and the more he read about the hunting activities of these people and the different animals they kill, he thought of how there seems to be no end to these peoples' depravity.

That evening, as Stephen was getting into bed, he began to think of what he had been reading earlier in the day, about the hunting, and he thought about Graham Mears, his family, their friends and associates, and their involvement with private healthcare. Stephen went over what he had read about politicians with links to private companies that take over NHS services to make a profit. He thought of reading how many NHS experts feared this would have a dreadful outcome for patients, and they are being proved right in thinking so. Some commentators raise the question of there being a conflict of interest when senior politicians support a bill to replace services supplied by the NHS, and then get contracts for private health companies they are connected to. Stephen thought about two of Graham Mears's close associates that have links to private health companies and how the whole affair is blatant corruption.

With these thoughts drifting through his mind, Stephen fell asleep, but woke with a start and realised he was shouting. Jessica had woken him, pulling on his arm, she was saying, 'Get the man out of your mind.' Stephen asked her what was happening, and she told him he had been shouting out Mears's name, 'And lots of mad stuff.'

Stephen noticed how the front of his tee shirt was soaked with sweat. 'It's the way of things,' Jessica said, 'You, we, nobody can do anything about it – God, Stephen, this is bad enough without you acting crazy.' She attempted to turn on her side, but the pain and discomfort was too much, so she shook her head and slapped the pillow before settling down.

35

Jessica started the treatment. She was in hospital most of the day, but only for a couple of hours actually having contact with someone and taking the drug. The overriding concern for Stephen and Jessica, despite Jessica being so very ill, was money. Both Jessica's and Stephen's family wanted to help financially, but were absolutely shocked when told how much the treatment costs. Jessica was just too weak to explain to everyone how expensive the treatment was, and she asked Stephen to tell them, primarily her mother, his parents and Sharron. They all wanted to help, but the more they asked, the more it put stress on Jessica.

Jessica and Stephen looked at possibilities of paying over a period time with a private healthcare card, which is like a credit card that has a credit limit of twenty thousand pounds, and the amount is paid back in instalments. Stephen read how there are no deposit or membership costs, and it has zero per cent interest for the first twelve months, in which time one pays monthly payments of five per cent of the total amount. After the twelve months the remainder is paid off in one lump, or interest is added if continuing to pay the amount off monthly.

The credit card idea was rejected because it wasn't enough money to cover the costs of Jessica's treatment. Stephen adopted a sarcastic tone as he read how the card can't be used to pay for items such as newspapers and meals, but Jessica stopped him, her voice was raised and angry, 'Okay, Okay – I don't like it either, I don't like it at all – and it's me who's to blame for looking at this stuff.' She stared at Stephen, 'There's no need to read it in that cynical manner, I know it's crap – I didn't want to drag us into this, to use all our savings and borrow more, to pay horrible company bosses money so they can buy luxury yachts – I know, I know, and I know what you're going to say about rich people owning these companies and that they don't care...' Jessica broke into tears.

Stephen looked at changing their mortgage lender with an idea to re-mortgage their flat in order to meet the costs of the treatment. Jessica didn't like it at all, but something had to be done, the costs were enormous and frightening; and they were rising daily. After doing some research online, and asking for advice, Stephen decided against re-mortgaging and to take out a loan instead, as loans offered a longer time to pay back the amount borrowed. He settled on what he believed to be the best deal, which was a secured loan secured against their flat, but it was difficult to broach the subject with Jessica. Her life was ebbing away and she was trying hold on to the things she had in her life as much as she possibly could. Jessica's mother wanted to contribute towards the costs, as did Stephen's parents, and even though they were in a better financial position than Jessica's mother, the amount was astronomical and beyond just a few thousand pounds to help them out. It would mean Jessica's mother and Stephen's parents having to use their homes to pay for the costs, and Jessica was adamant that wasn't going to happen. Stephen was aware Jessica knew she wasn't going to live long and didn't want to waste their money and bring them trouble late in their lives. Her bravery was too much for Stephen to cope with, and it sickened as much as it angered him when thinking of the likes of Graham Mears and the other corrupt hypocrites, some of whom kill innocent animals for fun, just because they haven't got it in them to do anything better.

A couple of weeks went by and Stephen took his chance to ask Jessica to sign the form to secure the loan. Jessica signed it; she was so concerned with what she was going through she didn't have the strength to question other matters. Jessica's mother visited every day, and Chris, Jessica's brother, came along with her just the once. He spoke about the places he had been, how he loves 'extreme sports' and enjoys going to other countries with different cultures. Jessica's mother wanted to stay overnight, which wouldn't normally bother Stephen, but her attitude was changing, she wanted to have more involvement with caring for Jessica. Stephen knew it was understandable, and he had to be sensitive in the way he handled it, but Jessica didn't want her mother in their flat all the time. Stephen was beginning to think Jessica's mother didn't have confidence in him to care for her daughter, and it agitated him. He didn't tell Jessica, she had enough to deal with, but he noticed how on a few occasions Jessica's mother had snapped at him. Stephen also felt she gave him a look as if he was strange, and he once asked her if something was wrong, but she just shook her head, although the look remained on her face.

Stephen's parents also visited, but just for a short while to say hello. Stephen noticed the stress on his mother's face, she kept asking him if he was okay, which irritated him. He told her that it was Jessica who was ill, but she wouldn't let it go, and if not asking him she would look at him in a way as if there was something wrong. Jessica's friend, Sharron, came to the flat, the shock on her face when seeing Jessica was like a blow to Stephen's stomach.

One evening, as Stephen sat in the living room listening to Jessica's mother talking to Jessica in the bedroom, he had a sudden impulse to go out. He could hear her clearly as she spoke to Jessica. There was a tone to her voice that said things were under control, as much as they could be, because she was there seeing to everything. At any rate, that's what Stephen thought. He watched her when she came into the living room, busying herself, folding clothes and sheets, placing them neatly on a chair, going about *duties* that only she could do in a proficient manner, because Stephen wasn't as able as she was. She hardly spoke to him and the longer Stephen watched her the more uncomfortable he became. He attempted to initiate a conversation, saying how tired Jessica was when she came back from the hospital earlier in the day, but Jessica's mother responded by saying under her breath that it was understandable. Stephen asked her if she minded if he went out to get some air, and without looking at Stephen she said it was up to him and it didn't bother her, but to ask Jessica because that was the important thing.

Stephen left the house. He couldn't have felt lower than he did. Jessica was deteriorating, at a rapid rate. Stephen thought of this as he walked, not bothering to button up his coat to keep out the chill wind, and he just walked with no destination in mind. It had been nearly three weeks since the treatment started, but it felt like a lifetime, and everyday Jessica was getting weaker. Stephen couldn't think anymore, he was conscious of a constant trembling inside his body, and it felt like his teeth gave off electric shocks when they touched each other. His mouth was always dry, his breath short and his eyes itchy with the bones in his face aching. He got on a bus, held his travel card against the pad, walked down the aisle and sat down. Stephen froze. Fear seared through his body. The bus driver's eyes were staring at him in the rear-view mirror. They were the same as before, dark, unwavering and full of revengeful intent for what Stephen had done, which was to kill this man's son. Stephen shook his head, violently, trying to shake images and thoughts from his mind. He stared down, but he couldn't escape, the young man he shot in Iraq was lying there, his head broken with his brain splatted across the floor; but it couldn't be, not on the floor of the bus. Stephen kept telling himself it couldn't be, it was only in his mind, he was tired, confused and upset, his mind was playing tricks, conjuring up bizarre thoughts and images. He looked out of the window, but jumped back, startled and scared. It wasn't Stephen's reflection in the window, but the bus driver's face. His eyes were staring at Stephen with increasing intensity. Stephen had to get off the bus.

He rang the bell and stood by the doors at the centre of the bus and holding his breath he summonsed the courage to look at the driver. It was a young woman. She was a plump girl in her early twenties with a pleasant looking face, going about her work; there was no man staring into the mirror. It didn't exist. It was in his mind. He was losing his mind. This is what Stephen was thinking as he got off the bus, and as he walked along the pavement he thought of The Beatles song, and immediately the tune and words came to him, 'Nothing is real.' Stephen tried to concentrate, to think about himself, a *self* he had never before encountered or knew that existed, and he was frightened as he thought about it.

36

Jessica was weakening, but they decided to continue with the treatment. The costs were fantastic, Stephen checked and saw they had already spent forty thousand pounds. He hid anything to do with the costs away from Jessica, and where once she was so sharp it would have been impossible to hide something like this from her, it was apparent that she was now losing concentration and didn't have the strength to take an interest in things. The following two weeks went by with Jessica going to the hospital for treatment and her mother staying at their flat more often. During that time Stephen was feeling increasingly distant and detached from what was going on in his life. He read online about a meeting that was to do with poverty and how the government is corrupt in working for the interests of the wealthy while making life wretched for the poor and ordinary working people. The meeting was called Class and Power. Stephen took a note of the date and where it was taking place, fully intending to go along.

While Stephen was reading about corporations, the amount of money they spent on marketing, the importance of presenting the right image and branding, a link with Joe Tara's name came up. An article had been written about the amount Joe Tara charges for corporate speaking, and that his agent said, 'Joe's a phenomenally successful broadcaster with a winning image, definitely a plus in promoting a brand – his selling power is evident.'

Stephen thought about Joe Tara and the most important aspect about him was his ability to sell. He *was* the salesman Stephen had heard him talk about on the radio interview. Everything about him was to sell himself. To 'pitch one's wares,' as Joe Tara had said, and there he was, the *celebrity* he was also talking about, selling brands for big companies. Stephen thought about why a big company would hire someone who is critical of big company practices? But of course, as Joe Tara said in that interview, the public have confused and 'foggy' minds, and the big companies know, that in the main, the public respond to a successful name with an appealing image they wish to aspire to be like, rather than what they actually say.

The article lampooned Joe Tara as being a self-styled revolutionary, and 'voice of the people' who stands up against inequality and exposes big business corruption. Yet, he finds no contradiction, or hypocrisy, which after all is one the main accusations he aims at his targets, to buy a twelve-bedroom mansion in the heartland where the type of people live that he purports to despise, or they would like to live if they had enough money. Joe Tara obviously does have the money, as Stephen read, 'Not only can he afford the eye watering price for the house, he is also intending to spend an extra couple of million on renovating it so that the all modern emperor cave fits his opulent and self-indulgent desires. The house is only a couple of miles from a Royal residence, and who knows, maybe squire Joe Tara will soon be dressed in the correct equestrian attire and invited to take part in a hunt. Although, for this champagne socialist, twelve bedrooms aren't enough as he is keeping his town pad in a trendy part of London.'

The article concluded with a taunting criticism of Joe Tara's involvement with business projects that encourages investments from his wealthy associates that utilise tax havens with deals giving generous tax breaks and large profits. Stephen continued to read about Joe Tara, following a link from the article he had just been reading, and again it was highly critical of him. Joe Tara has set up his own agency to negotiate his own fees for corporate speaking at conventions and other functions. The article explained how it's a good way to keep more of the money by cutting out a middleman, but his agency is also sold to other celebrities to negotiate on their behalf what their fees and conditions will be.

Joe Tara is judged to be an A-list celebrity, which means his earning potential is in the top bracket when hired for speaking engagements, corporate functions and conventions. The amount he receives varies, but for just one night's work he commands a figure a lot of people would like to earn in a year. The amount rockets for major A-list celebrities, and it seems Joe Tara is getting into that bracket as he targets corporate events where a six-figure fee is common. Mixing with guests and having photographs taken with the bosses helps to get a company valuable column inches in the main newspapers and magazines, which is the kind of exposure that would cost more if they went down the orthodox advertising route, plus having the added bonus of brand approval from a *cool winner*.

On reading the amount Stephen gasped. It really did take his breath away, and a sick feeling formed in his stomach. He read the names of other so-called *A-listed* celebrities, that ranged from chefs to ex-politicians before closing down the page and following another link to do with Joe Tara. It was about Joe Tara hiring an old ship, having a famous maritime history, in a dry dock for a party. After the party his guests were chauffeured in 1930's American cars to a new sky scraper building where he had hired the top floor for his party to continue where the guests could look out over London at night until the light came up at dawn. The guests were from varied backgrounds, ranging from pop stars, actors, international entrepreneurs and high profile legal corporate figures. Stephen looked at photographs taken at the party, studying their faces he saw them as greedy, hubristic and rich, but there was something else, something Stephen couldn't quite identify. The feeling he had gave in to words like *empty* and *fake*. Stephen felt they lacked real substance, and he saw ingrained in their faces a great sense of fear, which he thought was probably constant in their lives as they were scared of losing their position in the public eye. They were terrified at the prospect of no longer being accepted in a world occupied by, what they assume to be, an elite. It was the *high society* they craved to be part of in order to define their difference from *ordinary* people. It was superficial, their whole essence appeared to be so, but then, Stephen thought, that is what they peddle, that is their business; superficiality. It isn't reality. It is pretence. It is an act, and that's what they do. They are actors, whether it be singers, comedians or actors. They exist in a milieu that needs money to perpetuate it, so they mix with money people, it's very simple. That's where the financial investors come in, the venture capitalists who are always looking for pickings, as a vulture will do.

There was a photograph of Joe Tara standing with a man who was described as, 'the guru of entrepreneurial start-up companies.' He was quite young with a stylish haircut and a broad smile on his face, he and Joe Tara were standing next to a young member of the Royal family and his fiancé. They were all smiling as they stood on a stage. The prince was giving out awards to individuals and companies that had been involved in charities helping young homeless people, and Joe Tara was one of the comperes at the awards. The article told of how he had the young prince and his 'gorgeous' fiancé in fits of laughter during the night. Tired of reading about Joe Tara, Stephen searched other stories, one was about the wealth of modern celebrities and how some of them can become fabulously rich in a short time when compared to entertainers from years ago. The reasons for this being so is because things have changed so much in terms of technology, marketing and the significant presence celebrities occupy in modern societies. The piece told of how the opportunistic celebrity has a broad portfolio that includes endorsements of products such as fashion, perfume, hard and soft drinks, film rights, royalties, restaurants and investing in the newest technological advances such as apps that bring the fans closer to the celebrity. There were examples of different actors and the amount of wealth they had amassed, with one comedian who was said to have had over a hundred million pounds, and there was a list of the diverse companies, products and projects he invests in.

Stephen turned the computer off and looked around the room as if searching for something. His attention was drawn to a photograph on the shelf, it was a photograph of Jessica and him taken about three years earlier. He picked it up and looked at Jessica, at her smile, the fullness of her face and he thought of how she would have had cancer back then, but now she has been ravaged by it. Stephen studied his own face, noticing how he was smiling in a carefree way. He took the photograph with him to the mirror that hung on the wall and looked at his reflection. It didn't look like him. The face in the mirror had changed from the one looking out of the photograph, it was gaunt with eyes deeply set in hollows staring at doomed prospects. After putting the photograph back on the shelf Stephen walked into the bedroom and looked at the two photographs by his bed, one was when he was in the army and the other one was taken on his wedding day. Stephen picked up the one of when he was in the army, dressed in uniform, he then looked at the one when he got married, the person was the same, older but the same. He was tall and slim, smart and erect, well built across the shoulders and his face looked strong, showing a pleasant smile. Stephen was shocked when thinking of how he looked now. He looked again at his reflection, looking closely, studying the lines around his eyes and the way his mouth appeared weak and showing hunger, reminding Stephen of a wild animal that had been cornered and was frightened for its life.

37

Another two weeks passed, not that Stephen was that conscious time, and it was decided to end the treatment; Jessica's condition was worsening rapidly. Stephen was at her side, holding her hand, and even though she was so ill, Jessica was concerned for him. She noticed that some of the things he was saying didn't make sense. One of them was when he spoke about the two of them going on holiday and how he would teach her to become a strong swimmer. She put it down to stress, and tried to change the subject by saying very faintly how stopping the treatment, 'ended their money worries,' but it hadn't, although Stephen couldn't really care. Two months of private treatment had cost ninety thousand pounds, and as much as Stephen tried to accept it was a ridiculous amount of money, he couldn't take in the significance of the situation.

Stephen had forgotten about his job and didn't answer when they tried to contact him. He just wasn't bothered and didn't care when reading a letter telling him that he had been suspended from his position as a Revenue Officer. Most of his savings had gone, but that didn't concern him either, his mind was occupied with Jessica and obsessed with Graham Mears. He couldn't stop thinking about Mears, his associates, hypocrisy and of how the wealthy crave more and more money and power to the detriment of people, honest people who just want to get on with their lives. Stephen's parents noticed how he had changed and Jessica's mother told them how Stephen seems, 'Out of touch and not really there.' Although, she held back what she really thought, which was feeling that Stephen was letting her daughter down.

Jessica's mother moved into Stephen and Jessica's flat fulltime to help with the care that Jessica needed, which was increasing as she deteriorated. Stephen wasn't sleeping with Jessica, she had become too ill, so he slept in the living room and Jessica's mother slept in the other bedroom. The sofa was the intended makeshift bed for Stephen, but he was too tall and found it uncomfortable, especially with his back, as it didn't take much to trigger off discomfort and pain. He placed pillows, cushions and blankets on the floor, for someone that had spent time in the army, especially engaged in battle, it was a warm and dry home comfort, although sleep wasn't something that came easily, and it was never restful when it did. One night as Stephen tried to sleep, he stared up at the ceiling with thoughts rushing through his mind, but they stopped all of a sudden and intensified into what felt like to be a hard ball, and then the ball splintered into what Stephen imagined to be shards of glass that cut though his head. The pain was terrible and he lay awake for hours, but just when he was dropping off to sleep, he heard the order shouted by his Sergeant, 'Shoot him.' Stephen heard a blast of gun fire, and realised it was him firing the gun. He was back in Iraq, at the scene of the explosion, he looked down, and there was the young man, dead, and the awful mess coming from his broken head, but there was something else, it was a buzzing sound, like a huge swarm of bees, but the sound was coming from people, old and young people, village peasants. They were walking towards him, hatred showing in their faces as they wanted revenge, and the buzzing sound was getting louder the closer they got to him.

Stephen woke up, his breathing heavy and his mouth dry. He lay on his back, not wanting to sleep he placed his hands behind his head, sleep was becoming too much of a frightening place to visit. He looked up at the ceiling, listening to the night sounds that exist in a house, or flat. Although there were now other sounds. He tried to hear Jessica, thinking how she might be restless, in pain, and scared. There were also the sounds of Jessica's mother, moving about the bedroom, going to the bathroom, checking on Jessica and switching lights on and off. Stephen closed his eyes. It was all too much for him, he just lay still hoping his mind would allow him to have some peace.

A young woman, who was more like a girl, was speaking in a posh voice, 'Yeah we're going on a trip,' and Stephen said, Well, let's hope you get what you deserve, after all it's a long way to the jungle in Africa.'

Stephen is in a room, it looks like a young person's bedroom, a young man is also there and he too speaks in a posh accent, 'Yeah, right,' he says and points an imaginary rifle at the girl. 'Lion or zebra? I've shot a giraffe, but a lion would be really cool.' The girl laughs and pulls a face. Stephen realises it is Graham Mears's daughter, Sophie, and her boyfriend, Harry. They are both high on drugs. 'Look at you, getting all excited,' she says to Harry. Stephen watches them. He looks at the imaginary rifle Harry is pointing around the room, and for a split second he sees a young man in the army, a flashback to Iraq, a comrade of Stephen's from his regiment. The young man is standing behind a broken, dusty old wall for protection from enemy gunfire. He is giggling at a stupid joke he's just told, holding a rifle in front of his body, he looks up, the sun bleaching his face as he laughs, and as there's a sound of gunshot, half the young man's head

157

flies to one side, blood has instantly covered the front of his body as the rifle drops to the ground. The young man reels to the side, in the direction the piece of his head went, and Stephen looked at it as it landed on the ground, already covered in dust. Stephen's immediate thought was of how the piece of scalp and bits of brains were covered so quickly in dust, and he wondered why he had thought that as he watched the young man's body collapse, as if in slow motion. Loud shouting from Stephen's Sergeant broke the scene and he was back in the bedroom looking at the young man, Harry, laughing as he fired the imaginary rifle, and Sophie is laughing at him. It was a drugged laugh, she was pulling faces, a response showing her highly charged emotions. She opened her mouth wide, as if laughing, but there wasn't any sound of laughter, just her pulling a face, and her mouth stretched even wider, unbelievably wide to a point where it wasn't possible. And Stephen woke up.

Stephen lay on his back with his eyes wide open as he thought about the dream with his comrade in Iraq. He was killed only feet from where Stephen was standing, and that happened for real, but how odd to dream about being in a bedroom with Graham Mears's daughter and her boyfriend. A heavy feeling came over him as he thought of himself as their servant. His role was to take care of them, like a butler, and jump when they say jump. He didn't like it, the thought of being in a position where he had to take orders and run around after people like them. Yet, that's what he had done in his life, just so people like them can continue to live a decadent lifestyle with luxury and opportunities that people like him, and all the others that serve them, will never experience.

The thought unsettled Stephen and he tried to think of something else, and from, seemingly, nowhere he thought of the time he didn't turn his phone off when waiting for Jessica at the hospital. He realised it was probably the first time in his life he had disobeyed an order, and he knew why. It was because, subconsciously, at that time he was developing a disillusionment and distrust in the authorities and what he had been told in his life. The experience he and Jessica had with private health had really hit him when discovering the same people who said there isn't the money to fund treatment, were actually making money out of a situation they were part of creating by investing in health companies. These people, the politicians, who hold highly influential positions in the government, are the same people who also financially prosper from making weapons, pharmaceuticals and building contracts that come about because of war, the wars he had been involved in, and his comrades, some now dead, injured or living on the streets with broken minds, and there he was, the loyal soldier, throughout his life, from the scouts to the army to working in the tax office, obeying orders and bound to his duty to serve the establishment, a ruling order, which he has learnt isn't always what it professes to be. Stephen thought of how situations are created for these people to exploit and prosper, and in the process to use naïve people like him, because that is what Stephen now considered himself to be. He felt used and deceived by blindly accepting what he was told were the facts and truth. As a young boy he wanted to support that system, to be loyal to it, and in doing so offer his very life, only so unscrupulous people can financially gain and preserve a position of power that will furnish their children's position in continuing with the way things are. Stephen thought of how there is really nothing, or very little a person can do about it. The system has all areas covered, with the media, law, education and so on, primed to protect the order of things in a host of subtle and not so subtle ways. The meek, the humble are told that their placidity, honesty, loyalty and grace are attributes that will be rewarded, for they are far greater and meaningful than materialistic lust, or seeking status, power and positions of influence, for those that crave these things will surely be left with nothing, because they weren't rich at all, in any meaningful way.

Stephen smiled at what he was thinking and shook his head, slowly at first, and then more vigorously as he nearly laughed out loud. He stopped shaking his head and letting his thoughts settle, he looked at them as if they were written on a board high on a wall. He began to nod his head, agreeing with what he was reading, and the more he read the more he nodded his head until he was nodding violently. Stephen gritted his teeth and his face distorted into a mask of disgust and anger, and as if staring at an enemy, he growled aggressively as he sat up and shouted, 'Traitor.'

Stephen stared at the wall in front of him, having shouted had released tension and his breathing slowly calmed until he was taking deep breaths. His eyes intensified, it was as if a fire had been lit in them, and focussing on a point on the wall, he nodded to verify what he was thinking was true as he uttered the word, 'traitors,' and all the while the fire in his eyes continued to burn.

The living room door suddenly opened and Jessica's mother came in, she wanted to know what the matter was. She repeated her question, wanting to know what was wrong with him. Stephen remained sitting upright as he looked at her, not knowing what to say. She looked at Stephen, studying him, and then said impatiently, 'Think about Jessica – she doesn't need anything else to worry her.'

Stephen slowly lay back, saying quietly that he was sorry. Jessica's mother watched him as questions went through her mind before closing the door.

38

The following two weeks could only be described as very hard and extremely upsetting. There had been disagreements with occupational therapists that developed into arguments. Their aim was to keep Jessica at home, but as much as it was difficult to admit, the adequate care Jessica needed just couldn't be given at home. Love and caring just wasn't enough when wanting to give Jessica the most safety and comfort possible. It was decided that Jessica should go into a local hospice. Waves of dread surged through Stephen's body on hearing the name of the hospice. It was a place he had given money to in the past and bought raffle tickets to raise money, the hospice, as far as Stephen knew, was run by a charity, but worked with the local NHS. The words Stephen kept hearing was, 'palliative care,' the rest of what was being said, meaning the details, was increasingly becoming a blur to him.

'There aren't any other options available,' Stephen heard Jessica's mother say to his mother and father, while they were all in the living room of his flat, having just left Jessica at the hospice for a couple of hours while she was being examined. She went on, talking about a 'care pathway,' which, she explained is a practice that aims to alleviate unnecessary suffering by making the patient as comfortable as possible and to stop invasive tests that won't do any good as death is imminent. She took a deep breath and braced herself before saying, 'The aim is for the patient to die with as much dignity as possible,' and she looked down at the floor as if trying not to associate such glib words with the importance that her daughter means to her.

The living room remained silent after Jessica's mother left, until two words broke the stillness. 'How long'? Stephen's mother asked him in a quiet, flat tone. Stephen shook his head in a gesture that said he didn't know, although he was told by a doctor at the hospice that it might not be longer than a couple of weeks, maybe less. He wasn't able to accept it, and shook his head again when asked by his father if they had told him anything. His parents looked at one another, their concern was growing for their son's state of health. Stephen stood up and said he was going to the hospice, his mother and father spoke quietly, asking Stephen to send their love to Jessica and to look after himself. Stephen checked in his pocket before leaving the flat, he was looking

161

for a piece of paper that had the address on it for a meeting he was going to that evening, the one he had read about online called Class and Power.

39

Stephen had sat by Jessica's bed for three hours, holding her hand and watching her. Jessica's mother joined him an hour after he arrived at the hospice wanting to know why he hadn't said anything to her when he left the flat. After all, she drove and could have given him a lift, but Stephen shrugged as if it wasn't important and the matter was left at that. Jessica wasn't speaking, she only nodded and sometimes forced a smile when Stephen said something to her; it was obvious how fast she was deteriorating. A doctor, accompanied by a nurse and a care worker, came to Jessica's bed and spoke to Stephen and Jessica's mother about the examination Jessica had earlier. Jessica's mother nodded attentively, following every word being said, but Stephen looked down at the bed, shaking his head very slightly at something he was thinking about.

Stephen checked his watch, and standing up he looked at the people around the bed as if just noticing they were there. He told the doctor about the meeting he was going to, and the name of it, and as if to prove what he said was true he took the piece of paper from his pocket and showed it to all of them. Jessica's mother looked embarrassed and then furious as Stephen said, 'Someone needs to do something about the things that are going on – there are people who get our votes and support who are working against us.' He stopped and nodded at what he had said before continuing. 'I'm not going to lie down and accept it, I've got a duty to do what I can for my wife – who knows, maybe we can turn this thing round, it's another battle, and we'll grit our teeth, put our heads down and take on the fight.' He looked directly at the doctor and paused for a second before saying, 'Do you want to come with me, this affects all of us you know, and having a doctor on our side can only help.'

The doctor nodded benignly, the smile on her face showed an understanding to the situation as she told Stephen that she was busy and had things to do at work. Jessica's mother forced herself to remain silent, and not tell Stephen to be quiet because he was talking a lot of rubbish. They watched Stephen leave after he kissed Jessica and said goodbye to everyone around the bed. Jessica lay back, tears forming in her eyes as she thought of how Stephen had changed. It hurt her that she will die and her husband isn't the person she had loved so much, and still loved. It hurt her because she knew that inside him there was still the kind, lovely man she had met. Stress had torn his mind apart, and because of this, she had been robbed of saying goodbye to the man she loved. Although Jessica's mother didn't share her daughter's empathy for Stephen, all she saw was her husband going to pieces at the time Jessica needed him the most.

40

The meeting was underway by the time Stephen got there. There were people of different ages, although each generation wore similar clothing. As Stephen looked around at the different people, a thought occurred to him that he would never have gone to something like this before, but it disappeared almost immediately from his mind. He was focused, there was a purpose and he had a feeling that he was on a mission. A few people nodded at him and Stephen nodded back, unaware that the majority of the people at the meeting were treating him with suspicion. They thought he could be an undercover police officer making observations. Wooden chairs were put in rows, they were very old fashioned, just like the hall the meeting was taking place in, which had a little hatch leading to a kitchen where tea, coffee and biscuits could be bought. There was just going to be one speaker and the rest of the evening was made up with informal discussions. A man in his middle forties stood on a small stage and began to speak. After briefly introducing himself and welcoming everyone to the meeting, he rushed into why he had become involved in politics and his interest in the history of politics in Europe since the beginning of the twentieth century. He spoke about the present government and of the way they are governing the country, saying, 'More and more we're seeing the merging of the state and corporate power – Mussolini spoke about this, he said fascism should be called corporatism.'

Stephen thought about the grandson of the fascist European dictator he had read about, the man who killed animals nearly every day of his life for pleasure, who was a friend of, and connected by blood, to members of the royal family and wealthy people in this country.

The man was talking, but Stephen hadn't been listening, his mind was wandering, thinking of those people hunting animals, killing innocent beings just for amusement. He began listening to what the man on the stage was saying, who was working himself up the more he spoke. 'They call it austerity measures, which basically means cutting benefits from poor people while handing out massive payments to their business friends, and letting them operate without paying tax. Trillions are hidden away from state tax by the global elite who exploit cross-border tax laws and offshore accounts from poor developing countries where the people see no change in their poverty ridden situation.'

The man continued, and Stephen concentrated on what he was saying as he moved from one subject to another. 'Accountants working for corporations work as consultants for this government, they give advice on setting up a structure benefitting private finance, much of which is bankrolled with taxpayers' money.' As Stephen listened, he thought of what he had read online and he wanted to speak to the man about what he was thinking. The man was concluding his talk about public money going into private hands, 'The underlying system is ignored, scapegoats are made of individuals and big media coverage pushes the facade that it's just the greedy few ruining it for everyone and laws are being upheld. Big business has historically benefitted from government funding to start companies with research and development costs, nearly all major industries have subsidies and bailout support, yet profits are folded back into private pockets while the financial burden due to the damage done to the environment has to shouldered by the tax payer – the poor working person subsides these crooks for God's sake.'

People clapped, the man had finished and everyone stood up, mingling in small groups or pairs, mainly talking about what had just been said by the speaker. Stephen stood on the edge of a group and listened as they were talking about companies using tax havens and the government's relationship with the rich. People were impatient to talk over one another, eager to say their piece. A young man spoke of companies with links to the government who are getting contracts to do NHS services and provide resources. 'They're selling off the NHS to their friends,' he said, but the conversation switched subject and Stephen watched them as they spoke. He wanted to talk about Jessica, but he just couldn't bring himself to do it, so he listened and watched the people around him.

'Look at the negative effects of tax avoidance has on this country,' a man in his fifties said, and he went on to say how money is lost that should be put into the NHS. 'Our greatest institution,' he said and a young woman interjected and spoke about how rich 'tax dodgers,' along with crooked oligarchs from other countries, invest in property in London, and so much so it has pushed the price of buying a home out of reach for ordinary people. 'It's divided worlds,' a man said, 'one person's life in sweatshop hell is another's money making heaven.'

The young man who spoke before said, 'You see, tax evasion is illegal, tax avoidance isn't, and let's face it, if you had the power to avoid rather than evade tax and stay within the boundaries of the law, you would, wouldn't you?' The young man turned so he stood facing Stephen, he was

166

passionate about what he was saying and finding a person that was listening to him increased the intensity of his delivery as he spoke. He told Stephen that tax avoidance undermines and erodes democracy, but also diminishes the country's commitment to producing services, such as the NHS, which affects the quality of people's lives. He said, 'And what does the chancellor say when asked about funding for our health service? Oh, that's right, he says there's no money in the pot, while he and his friends sit back and laugh, counting their increasing bank balances while families are destroyed because their loved one can't get the treatment they need – with things like cancer and everything…'

What he had said caused Stephen to feel as if everything around him had come to a sudden halt and all sound disappeared. 'What's that?' Stephen asked the young man. He looked at Stephen, thinking of what he had said, he was confused and shaking his head he said, 'What do you mean?' Stephen stared at him before speaking, 'About the health service, and people with cancer – what was that you said?'

The young man shrugged, as if claiming innocence to some offence, and said that he was talking about money that is hidden away which should be going to fund the NHS. Stephen nodded, calming down, and the young man recognised that the heat was leaving Stephen, but it left him feeling uncomfortable. He took a deep breath and nodded at Stephen as he walked away. Stephen watched the young man as he joined another group, but then his attention was taken by a man talking in the group he was standing next to. 'It's because of the conditioning we are subjected to through the media, when someone talks of *welfare* it's common to think they're talking about benefits for single parents, the homeless, the unemployed or the ill, physically or mentally, but there's another form of *welfare* paid out by the government, and that's called *corporate welfare*.'

Stephen remembered reading about it, but he didn't have time to think where because the man continued talking with evangelical zeal in wanting to impart his knowledge with Stephen who had caught the man's attention. 'Billions of pounds is paid to companies in the form of subsidies, loans, grants, and the public think these are private companies financing themselves, when it's not true – take the railways, billions of pounds is given to subsidise that industry – given to people who then avoid paying tax back into the country that has bank rolled them.' He looked at Stephen, 'Some of these companies pay less tax than the grants they've received from the government – the one parent family is vilified and people who claim benefits are demonised in

167

shabby so-called television documentaries, but it's nothing more than propaganda.' The man went on, saying how the government uses distractive strategies to hide what is really going on and people fall for it. 'Oh yeah,' he said, 'there's tons of data on the disabled, the old and the ill who are presented as *claimants*, people who are, supposedly, a *drain* on our country's resources, but there's nothing available about the super wealthy.'

The man's eyes probed Stephen's face, as if urging him to acknowledge and seriously consider what he was telling him, because it was important for Stephen to find out information about it for himself. He told Stephen how the government taxes the population further in order to gain the loss in revenue due to tax not being paid by the rich and big business people, and that they all belong to a self-serving club looking after their interests. The man said, 'And in fact, this club, or system that enables the wealthy to get away without paying tax, and all the other perks they have created for themselves, is world-wide. A global system has been created by the wealthy for the wealthy where multinationals can take advantage of tax havens in poor countries, and if this *financial secrecy* ended it could end poverty in poor countries and provide services in advanced countries.'

Stephen found it mind numbing, the statistics, the *facts* and all the information. Another man intervened, ready to take over from the last one in informing Stephen to what was going on in the world. He spoke of how the rich don't act in a responsible way towards the society they have benefitted from, let alone reimburse the tax payers that have funded their business projects through corporate welfare. 'Forget about the one parent scrounger getting a house and money to feed her children,' he said, 'that pales into insignificance when compared to the handouts big companies receive.' He went on, telling Stephen about the CEO of a large bank who wrote about how there has always been too much government involvement, so the more we limit the role of government the better off we will be. The man said, 'He was talking about himself and his wealthy friends of course, but then only two years later his bank received a twenty-two-billion-pound handout, give or take a few billion, because his bank had failed and his government buddies got the tax payer to cough up and support them.'

The man looked at Stephen, as if waiting for a response, but all Stephen did was nod in agreement with what he was saying. 'It's run by big business for big business,' the man said, 'the government chase the snappers and leave the whales, because they swim with whales, excep they're really sharks – it's hypocritical and with these people, morality doesn't exist in their pursuit for money.'

Stephen thought back to the man in the tax office and what he said to him about the tax office not going after the rich. 'You're just a maggot, like the rest of us – all slaves picking on each other because we can't have a go at the slave masters – the real criminals get away with what they're doing, because they run the show.' He saw Stephen as a coward, just as Stephen had thought the young man who threw him out of the cinema was a coward because he knew it wasn't him that was whistling. Stephen thought about what the man in the tax office had said to him. Anger burnt in the pit of his stomach, and it nearly boiled over, but his attention was taken by two harmless looking faces belonging to a young man and a young woman who wanted to speak to him.

They were dressed in nearly identical clothing and Stephen noticed how their faces were free of deep worry and concern, because that part of life hadn't yet etched itself into the contours of their fresh features, leaving indelible stains and bruising that tells of hardship and injustice. Stephen was listening to what they were saying as they spoke to him, but he couldn't help thinking it strange how they were so laden down with such weighty and complex matters, and how knowledgeable they were for people that looked so young and unworldly. He compared them to himself, he was older, had fought for his country, yet was for more naïve in these matters than they were, but he then considered how they were from backgrounds where they would go to university and have the opportunity to study these things. They took it in turns, one speaking for a while and then the other, endorsing what the other was saying by adding to what had been said, as if providing further evidence in a court trial. They told Stephen about corporations and the loopholes in avoiding paying tax by declaring huge amounts of pre-tax losses, yet pay more than the supposed loss in share payments to their staff. They spoke of shifting money through foreign 'sister' companies and channelling money through countries where they don't have to pay tax. The young woman's face shone as she spoke about offshore trusts and how one of the poorest countries in the world is used as a tax haven and has one seventh of the world's wealth hidden there. She told Stephen how over twenty-seven trillion dollars is hidden there from the system that has laws and policies in place to protect the rich in getting away with this practice, and that only token gestures from both companies and governments are made in a game of showing that the system is working.

169

'No prosecutions are made,' the young man interjected, eager to tell what he wanted to say to Stephen. 'The HMRC only follow up small time avoiders, the tax system is deliberately made so complicated and the lawyers working for the rich easily find loopholes to put their clients in the clear.' He went on, telling Stephen what he had heard the others saying, about how the system has been designed to be in the favour of the wealthy with tax relief schemes and tax breaks for investing in certain businesses. He explained how politicians and big business are working together to further their interests and have created a massive industry out of tax avoidance, and because of this, hundreds of millions of pounds aren't paid into the revenue, which means less money for valuable and essential services.

Stephen nodded, and wanting to change the subject he told the young woman about members of Mears's family and his friends paying thousands of pounds to take part in canned hunting. He told the two of them how he had read about it, and this sparked an enthusiastic response from the young woman who spoke of how, 'Mears and the rest of them' have had privileged opportunities not afforded to the average person, and how they believe they are the chosen people, which is supported by the schools they go to that tell them they are part of an elite few and everyone else is a lackey for them to use in this pleasurable experience called life, which for the most part is little more than an amusement park for these people, all paid for by the ordinary people who don't experience their luxurious lifestyle.

The young woman looked like she was going to explode as she said, 'God – Mears's daughter, and that niece of his, Clementine, or whatever her name is, the model – Jesus, it's so infuriating that an empty-headed parasite like her should be given space in a mainstream magazine to expound her dim witted views. When defending her rich lifestyle she said, "Cream rises to the top," and "life is a hunt, there are naturally the weak and the strong with predators and prey." They're a bit Nietzsche in their thinking, except, of course, they're neither physically or mentally strong, it's just that the system has been designed and maintained for them to occupy a place of ascendency in society – God, she would struggle getting a zero hour contract job in a burger bar if she didn't come from the background she does – it's all institutionalised and mapped out.'

Stephen looked down, thinking about what she had said, and then he noticed they were looking at him. The young man asked him if he was okay, Stephen realised he must have been staring into space and become absent, which was something he had been doing a lot of. The young

170

woman smiled at Stephen and asked him if he was going to the demonstration. Stephen told her he didn't know about a demonstration, and she told him it was called Class War and the objective was to raise awareness to the growing divisions in society between the rich and the poor. He asked when and where it was taking place and told her he would try to come along. Stephen decided to go home after talking to the young man and woman, he had to get back and he was finding the conversations to be all pretty much the same. A thought passed through Stephen's mind as he left the hall about how long the people in the meeting had been talking about the same thing.

41

Jessica's mother was staying at the hospice for the night, so there wasn't anyone at home when Stephen got there. He watched television, flicking through channels looking for something of interest, and then stopped his search on seeing a programme that was being repeated from earlier in the evening. It wasn't the programme itself that caught his attention, which was about cooking and baking cakes, and how some cakes look like the person that baked them, it was the person presenting it, Jay Turn. Stephen remembered the first time he saw her, and of how she went on about celebrityism being 'dross' and that it contributes to a culture that is stupid. Stephen thought about what a man said at the meeting he went to that evening, 'Distraction strategies – so people aren't aware of what's important and the government can get away with what they want.'

Stephen turned the sound off on the television and went online to look up Jay Turn. There was a lot of stuff, but Stephen wanted to read only about her and not the *work* she does or has done. Her real name is Helen Kempsey, but she thought it comical to base her stage name on the word male chauvinists use for a woman, a 'bird,' so she used the names of actual birds, a Jay and a Tern. She spells Tern as Turn because that is the name used when a performer gives a short performance, as in, a comic turn. Stephen felt his chest tighten, his mouth was dry and shifting in his seat he exhaled in an effort to clear the feelings of anxiety, but it grew worse as his stomach burned and his hands began to tremble uncontrollably. The nervous anxiety gave way to a feeling of anger, a deep anger and hatred at what was making him feel this way.

Her parents were described as, 'interesting,' in that her father was an academic, a professor in Business Analytics, while her mother worked in business, co-owning her own company that provides 'Business Planning Managers' to companies. The word *business* was used frequently, and it gave Stephen a sick feeling. She was brought up in a quaint little village secluded in the Warwickshire countryside, going to a prep school before becoming a 'boarder' at a renown private school for girls, and then to a top university. When at university she was described as 'talented,' 'strong willed' and, 'always ready to challenge conformity.' It said that she had a couple of jobs when leaving university as a bar person and working in a shop, but after doing a few 'stand up' sessions, that went down very well, she decided not to go into a profession.

Stephen re-read the sentence about her time working behind a bar and in a shop, he thought it patronising the way the work was described, as if unimportant and something far beneath a person like her. From her early stand-up gigs, she developed into a known comic touring the country, and then later appearing on television, at first as a guest on different programmes until getting her own show. Over the years she has written, directed, been involved in charity work and although, 'maintaining her beliefs,' has, 'softened' and not only appears on, and presents television programmes away from comedy, she also produces them. The programmes have names like, 'Who's Garden Shed'? 'Guests Houses in Provence' and 'The Whiney Wine Show.'

The names of the programmes 'Jay Turn' made Stephen feel angrier, he thought it all reeked of condescension and the people making such rubbish had only contempt for their audience. She sat on panels, judging new writers and young directors, and was described as, 'Always looking for something fresh and challenging.'

Stephen looked at her with the sound on the television remaining off, noticing the way she spoke to *ordinary* people, *the public.* Her deceitful act easy to see, for some reason more so when watching her antics without sound. He thought about how he had come to realise that all media people are fakes. 'Nothing is real.' He thought of the words. She was wearing a tee shirt, a designer anarchy piece with the logo of a chic company on the front that has turned street protest clothing into branded fashion wear. It was a replication of a similar shirt Stephen had seen her wearing when she was younger and making her way in her chosen career many years ago. He had seen old films of her, noticing how she was very busy with her hands, and moved quickly on her feet, darting in different directions like a little bird as she fired out a salvo of spiel filled with anti-government rhetoric. Stephen noticed the audiences, nearly always white middle class and being a type of person, usually woman and many of them dressed in a similar way to Jay Turn. In reflection, it looked more like a political convention of like-minded people, with her being the orator who sanctions their beliefs and values. Stephen had monitored her career from post-student gigs to glitzy, corporate events. Her presentation changing subtly along the route, the clothes at first sight appearing the same, but less coarse and more refined in projecting a sympathy for her proclaimed causes. Her body language now more relaxed and confident, gone is the twitching, speedy delivery of speech and fast pacing around as if trapped in a cage. Now he is out of the cage and in a position of authority, and looking very cosy and at home with it as

173

well. Stephen thought how the whole thing was an act. Of course it was, only the painfully naïve could not see that, but people who are in a position where they are rendered credulous can become a target for dishonest people who wish to gain from them. This is the case for people in many situations, whether because of health problems or losing one's job, it can set a person on a course he or she would not have pursued, especially if not having support. And that's where these confidence tricksters come in, gaining a person's trust in making her or him believe they are something they are not.

Stephen saw it as all the same, whether it be a comedian, a politician or people setting themselves up as therapists or *healers*. It is to have something to peddle in the, 'market place,' as Joe Tara said in that radio interview, a product that is used in their quest to get what they want for themselves. He thought of the people that are struggling in life, it could be an illness, poverty or searching for an identity in a society that has confusing and complex demands, and these charlatans are there to give answers to their problems. Stephen turned his attention to the television, watching Jay Turn, noting her facial expressions as she went through the motions, but her eyes gave it all away. They were hard, as though set in stone, determined and grasping. 'Fuck you,' Stephen shouted at the screen. It was an involuntary outburst, and he jumped to his feet, but as he did so, a pain in his back took his breath away. He crouched in front of the television and shouted at the screen, 'My wife is dying in a hospice, she has cancer – she won't be alive for very long – funny, isn't it? But you see, it's real – and you aren't – fuck you.'

Stephen remained crouching in front of the television for a while, staring at the screen before calming enough to turn away and sit down. He sat still, his mind racing, unable to settle he could almost hear what was rushing through his brain. It was like two soundtracks playing simultaneously, one of racing cars and crashing sounds, the other like music used in films to go with troubled emotions and fear depicting endless nightmares. Stephen shook his head, trying to clear it, at first just a little, but then aggressively.

He looked at the so-called Jay Turn and remembered how he had read that she was good friends with Joe Tara. Stephen began researching Joe Tara and thought back to when he discovered how much it was to see comedians that supposedly have a social conscience, yet charge a fortune to see them. They do corporate work, sell themselves as a brand and live in luxurious places, and seemingly only mix with other successful people that are wealthy. He looked on different sites and read different news pages and articles. One journalist had written an article that was sceptical about the 'bright new wave of entertainers,' her main target being Joe Tara. She wrote of how Joe Tara's real name was Mourib Amir and is married with a young daughter. Coming from a Pakistani background, he was born in England and went to an expensive school before going to Oxford University. His parents were business people working in law and politics in Pakistan before coming to this country. He has an older brother who is a well-known film producer, and his other siblings are doing well in their chosen careers, owning property made up a large part of their interests. Although, there is a blemish on the family's name. His sister was involved in a case of financial impropriety involving her company's handling of administrating a trust fund, and Mourib has also been in the news for using a variety of tax avoidance schemes. It went into details of how one of the schemes worked, but he defended himself, saying how he put his affairs in the hands of his tax advisor and accountant, and glibly commented, 'I'm not a raging materialist that hunkers after more money – the work I do with charities shows where my sentiments really lie.' But the article pointed out that Mourib has also been criticised for his involvement with companies that invest in unscrupulous businesses in the middle east where there are appalling human rights issues.

Stephen followed links that led him to information on 'Joe' and his charity work. One article was about a charity that both he and 'Jay Turn' were associated with that involved entertainers raising awareness and money to address poverty in the developing world. Stephen looked at the photos of Joe and Jay with other *celebrities* performing and reporting in foreign lands. He looked closely at their faces, thinking how they all looked greedy and manic in their lust for publicity, and shook his head at the irony when reading how that particular charity has come in for criticism by certain politicians in a country where it operates for not actually doing what they claim to do. Stephen read that the charity was being investigated for tax impropriety. Another article related to 'Joe Tara' was critical of his wife, Meesha, who was a well-known model in Pakistan and has been used to front top of the range brands in fashion wear and perfume. She has set up her own brand of perfume and had recently been criticised by an animal rights group because her perfume is tested on animals.

It was all too much. The hypocrisy, the deceit, the aggressive nature of these people in their craving for wealth, fame and power. It made Stephen feel sick. He thought about 'Joe Tara,' and

175

the films he had watched, and how he did what has become his trademark departure from the stage, waving like a child going off to school for the first time saying, 'Ta-ra, ta-ra' in an overly pronounced Northern English accent. Stephen watched a clip online of one of his shows, talking to the audience about how his childhood and teenage years were tough, coming from a Pakistani background and living in a hard, depressing post-industrial Northern town. He spoke of how there was a lot of racism and people were 'limited,' but there were funny moments, like the people who came into his family's corner shop, and when they were leaving would say, 'ta-ra, ta-ra.' 'Joe' lied, saying what they were saying confused his mother, and she would say after they had gone, 'What on earth are they talking about?' This made the audience laugh.

Stephen read how Joe, or Mourib, thought Tara would make a good stage name, because of it being an everyday expression it gave a familiarity. 'Joe' said he used the name, 'Joe,' because it's a name that epitomises the average man in society, in a kind of everyman way. Although the article went on to say how the name Tara was actually used by him for another reason. Tara in Sanskrit means, star. Stephen thought of how contrived it was, making out he's an average Joe, yet thinking of himself as being a star. And it was all a lie. It was all made up. The poor immigrants with their corner shop. A fabrication. Stephen thought about it. Did it matter? Does anyone care? And he said the words, 'Nothing is real.'

Stephen had never been interested in these kinds of people before, not really noticing who they were because they hadn't attracted his attention. He had never really been interested in the usual entertainers, let alone those claiming allegiance to a political stance that criticises and challenges mainstream perceptions. In fact, he hadn't heard of them. And now he had. He had been drawn to their existence because of what had happened in his life, and he thought of how they weren't who they said they were, but who is really anyone, and is anybody who they say they are? Is nothing as it appears to be so?

Time passed, the television screen was showing another programme, equally as inane as the one before it. The so-called Jay Turn was talking to *ordinary* members of the public, between giving a sly look at the camera to express feelings of incredulousness or mock horror at what they were saying. Stephen looked down at his computer and researched the word, *delusion*. He said the word out loud, nodding slowly as he did so, and repeating the word he stared at the television screen as if it didn't exist.

176

42

Jessica's mother entered the flat the following morning, having spent the night at the hospice. On opening the living room door, she saw Stephen sitting on the sofa with the computer on his lap, and although the television was on, the sound was turned off. He had just woken, and she thought it was probably her that had woken him. She didn't say anything and closed the door, but not before shooting a frosty look at Stephen, who looked down at the screen and continued researching what he was looking at before falling asleep. He was researching meetings for ex-servicemen and had been on a site specifically for his old regiment. There was a group run by a charity that met up in a venue only half an hour from where he lived, he saw the next meeting was in six days and decided that he would go along.

Stephen had a shower, and on seeing Jessica's mother had gone into the kitchen he slipped into the bedroom she was sleeping in to retrieve some things he had been thinking about. He asked her how things were at the hospice, but she didn't want to speak and was curt, saying no more than Jessica is dying. Stephen left the flat to make his way to the hospice, he had to catch two buses or take the train and have a long walk; he decided on the buses.

The hospice made an attempt at making the environment peaceful and comfortable, but it couldn't disguise what the place really was. Stephen watched a metal case being wheeled, in what seemed to be a surreptitious manner, around the corner of the building. He knew there was a dead body in the case. Nothing was said, it was just something that happened in the building of soft furnishing, soothing colours and calming music. It is a place of soft smiles and gentle voices, and always there was the wheeling of a metal case taking the body of a former patient away to the mortuary. Stephen shuddered when seeing Jessica's body in the case. He looked up at the sky; but he couldn't see anything.

Jessica was getting worse, some days she didn't speak, as was the case on this day. She slipped in and out of consciousness, her eyes, when open, looked up at the ceiling, although all hope of finding something had long gone. Stephen spoke to her, whether she was awake or not, holding her hand he spoke about things they had done and said to each other. He stayed all day, sitting by Jessica's bed and then having a walk around the building, inside and outside. Sharron came late afternoon, just as Jessica's mother arrived. The two of them went off together and spoke, looking over at Stephen as they went. Jessica was unsettled by Sharron visiting her and told Stephen to ask her not to come again, and then she closed her eyes. Stephen watched Jessica, he tried to think of something to say, and he tried to think of how he felt, but he couldn't, everything felt so distant and removed.

Stephen left the hospital that evening, leaving Jessica's mother by her daughter's side. He had told Sharron what Jessica's wishes were, although he wasn't subtle in the way he told her, which caused Jessica's mother to give him a stern look, showing exasperation at his behaviour. He went back home on the buses, his mind reflecting on all things internal, but he then looked at the driver's rear-view mirror; he was back. The dark eyes were staring at Stephen, they were damning him for having murdered the young man in Iraq. The eyes belonged to either the young man's father, his uncle or a man sent to curse Stephen.

Stephen sat rigid, fear turning him to stone as his mind raced back to Iraq. 'Shoot him,' the rasping voice of the Sergeant echoed throughout the bus, and Stephen looked up at the rear-view mirror, but the eyes weren't there, it was the shattered and bloodied face of the young man he had shot. Stephen jumped up from his seat, pressed the bell and stood in front of the doors, telling them to open, willing them to open, at first under his breath and then loudly until he was shouting.

The bus finally stopped and Stephen got off, oblivious to people looking at him he began to walk, his breathing fast and shallow, his mind racing with a buzzing sound that caused him to shake his head and shout out for it to stop. He tried to calm himself, trying to think of something to concentrate his mind on in an effort to still its incoherent rambling, and from seeming nowhere the tune of Strawberry Fields Forever drifted softly into his mind, calming him as the gentle introduction of the song slowly wound itself through his very being. His breathing slowed and became deep and even, the buzzing, flashing images and disturbing sounds cleared and it was as if he had turned a corner and entered another world. It was a world free of suffering and pain. His senses were sharp and insightful, nature was bristling with its colours and sounds. He became immersed in its natural beauty, and the air was so fresh he could feel the hairs in his nostrils cool to the presence of it. It was beautiful. 'Let me take you down,' the words in the song had a meaning. They were guiding Stephen to a place, a place that was secret, but open to

179

everyone if they only knew how to get there, and he was going there. It was as if he had been chosen, and Stephen wondered why he had been chosen, and the words, 'nothing is real' floated into his consciousness. He was smiling, he was happy and said hello to people as a euphoric feeling grew inside him.

The feeling of elation and freedom had waned before Stephen got home. He sat in the living room staring at the television, which wasn't turned on, but he continued to look at the blank screen. Stephen began to look things up online, wanting to find out what boy's names there are in Iraqi. He wanted to find a name that he felt might have been the name of the boy he killed, and he looked at the meaning of the different names, imagining what kind of person the boy was, and while doing this he thought about Jessica's mother and why she slept at the flat even though Jessica wasn't there. He wondered why she didn't go to her own home, but he wasn't to know that it was Jessica who had asked her mother to stay in the flat to keep an eye on him. Jessica was worried about him, having noticed how his behaviour had changed and the strange things he was saying. When her mother admonished Stephen for not being supportive, Jessica told her it was not his fault and that he was ill, but she knew somewhere inside him he was still the lovely, kind loving man he had been before.

Stephen changed his search online, looking up forums discussing soldiers that had fought in battle situations. He read how soldiers use sarcasm and *humour* in battle situations as a strategy to avoid addressing and expressing one's deeper feelings and emotions. Someone had written about the percentage of soldiers that didn't fire their weapons at the enemy during the Second World War, and deliberately aimed to miss. Stephen thought back to the time when he shot away from a person, which was probably rare, because it was different from the Second World War as there were people on both sides that didn't want to be there, while in Iraq the *enemy* definitely wanted to fight.

There was an article about ex-soldiers making up a group that is alienated from the principles of mainstream society. It examined how like-minded individuals who feel neglected by societal standards band together and develop their own sense of identity, sharing experiences not known to most people in society they often feel others do not understand or care about them. They can be seen as different and sometimes labelled as potentially dangerous people who one should be wary of because they can be unpredictable. Research shows that ex-soldiers develop self destructive habits and exhibit aggressive behaviour because of a result of trauma and having experienced extreme violence. They have used guns, killed people and carried out actions not experienced by the vast majority of people in society. It's as if they need to be socialised back into *normal* society from a world where they did and experienced *abnormal* things. Ex-soldiers that had been in battle situations are a group of people distinct from others in society, and they will often identify themselves as different because of having shared something only others that have been in battle will know. They are comrades, often resentful about the way they have been treated, but proud, which bonds them closer to one another. Some ex-servicemen that display aggressive or strange behaviour can be viewed as belonging to a subculture, which is ironic considering they were protecting the norms of society.

The article went into how there are a large number of ex-soldiers in prison and how they often find it hard to settle in civilian life. Stephen read how there isn't as much support and guidance as one might think for people who have defended their country. The ex-soldiers, primarily those having been in battle situations, develop problems sleeping, habits where they use alcohol and drugs to nullify intruding and disturbing thoughts and feelings, and using violence becomes a regular response against those they see as threatening them. Stephen thought about ex-soldiers feeling estranged from what they were supposedly protecting and how there doesn't appear to be much understanding or respect for them. He asked himself whether people like him wanted respect as he read more around the subject of ex-soldiers returning from war and feeling outside of things. A researcher wrote about how the harder the battle is the harder it is for the ex-soldiers to feel part of the society they return to. When in battle situations they experience a sense of comradeship through sharing feelings, experiences and situations that bond them to an identity that is private, personal and special only to them. Stephen identified with what the ex-soldiers told the researcher about feeling used and rejected from that which they fought for, and risking their lives in the process, which the researcher pointed out is a massive irony that isn't understood. The point was reiterated of how many ex-soldiers find it difficult to join a society they have been apart from, which makes resettlement very difficult.

Stephen thought about Ray, he had been thinking of him more and more, and he thought about his experience on the bus earlier, and then from nowhere a feeling cut through him of how separate he was from others in society. He thought of that area in the hospital where he sat

181

outside the chapel, and remembered how the corridor had a deserted feeling. Stephen felt himself to be like that part of the hospital in that he felt aside from what is going on. It was a sense of abandonment, like an outcast and with it came a nasty feeling, like he was an undesirable person.

He couldn't think straight and shook his head as he tried to make sense of what was going on. There was Ray, the eyes in the mirror, the way he felt, the music in his head, Jessica dying, and he then thought it might not be happening. None of what he thought was going on has really happened because he had been in a sort of dream. But he knew he wasn't in a dream, and he then thought that maybe he had occupied someone else's body and was living, feeling and experiencing what that person is going through.

Stephen tried to clear his mind, but a powerful thought caused him to seriously consider that he might have been in an accident, and he tried to remember if he had been. Was it a car crash? He didn't know. He asked himself why was he thinking he was occupying another person's life. It didn't make sense. He told himself it's a ridiculous thing to think, and in fact it's a mad thing to think. Stephen thought about the word *mad* and said the word out loud, repeating it over and over.

43

Stephen had spent the whole day at the hospice, and during that time he was thinking of the ex-servicemen meeting he was going to that evening. He sat by Jessica's side, wearing his army beret, holding Jessica's hand he looked at her, his mind unable to settle as it was bombarded with thoughts that didn't stay long enough to form into something he could analyse. Jessica's mother was present for much of the time, she didn't mention Stephen's beret, in fact they didn't converse beyond the briefest of acknowledgements. Her concerns about Stephen had escalated because of what she had seen earlier in the day. She had gone to Jessica and Stephen's flat to pick up her things, as she wasn't staying there any longer, and saw some unopened letters. She knew she shouldn't look at their mail, but Jessica wasn't able to read them and Stephen was acting so strangely she decided to anyway. What she read took her breath away. There were two letters from his work, one saying that his position at the tax office had been terminated and three letters regarding a loan that had been taken out. One of those letters was a complaint about Stephen not contacting the company as had been arranged, and it had the amount of money that was owed. It was so great, that when reading the letter, she had to sit down. Her relationship was frayed with Stephen's parents, because of the way she had spoken about him, but she had to talk to them as this matter had to dealt with.

Stephen's parents visited Jessica that evening and asked her mother if she knew where Stephen was. She told them that she didn't, but asked them to go into a room where they could speak without Jessica hearing. When in the room she told them about the letters she had read and how Stephen's behaviour was making things worse. She also told them about how Sharron had visited her and spoke about the time Stephen came to her house and the way he acted. 'He frightened the children,' Jessica's mother said, and she told them about Stephen wearing his army beret and asked them why would he be doing that. She continued to go on about Stephen to such an extent that his parents felt she wasn't so much concerned for Stephen, but criticising him. Their response was one of silence, which was broken when Stephen's mother spoke quietly in a solemn tone, 'He was always a good and honest boy, and so it is now he's a man.' When finishing what she had to say, she and Stephen's father walked towards the door and left the room without looking at Jessica's mother: a definite rift had now developed between the two families.

44

The meeting was taking place in a room at the back of a pub. Stephen entered, wearing his beret. He looked around at the people in the room, nobody else was wearing a beret, although some had ties bearing the name and symbol of their regiment. He introduced himself to a couple of the men and one of them called over a man who helped to organise the meetings. He was easy going with a ready smile as he asked Stephen about himself, but Stephen's manner was serious, ignoring pleasantries he came across as edgy when telling the man of the places he had served in. Stephen spoke about how many people fired their weapon away from people, not wanting to shoot them when in battle. 'I did,' the man said, and he looked closely at Stephen, but it was as if Stephen hadn't heard what he said as he carried on, telling the man what he had read about soldiers in the second world war and of how many of them didn't want to kill people they had never met. 'But it was different where we were,' Stephen said, and he then talked about what goes through one's mind and the thoughts one has when in combat. The man Stephen was talking to was uncomfortable, he felt Stephen was manic and more than probably suffering mentally, but he wasn't in the mood to deal with it. He pretended that someone had caught his eye and told Stephen he had promised to speak to him, he then walked away after wishing Stephen 'all the best.'

A small group of men standing close to Stephen shook with a burst of laughter; he decided to join them, standing on the outside of the group. One of the men noticed him and, while stepping to one side to allow space for Stephen to join them, he introduced himself. They were friendly, making light of what they were talking about, but then the tone lowered respectfully as a comrade who had died was remembered. Stephen began talking about suicide and the number of ex-soldiers that kill themselves, especially the ones who had been in battle and had experienced terrible things. He went on, saying how he had read about research that found a major problem facing ex-soldiers is something called *moral injury* and it's that which is the main reason why ex-soldiers suffer. Stephen explained to the men what he had read, and of how being told to do something one knows is wrong and immoral is more harmful than seeing and experiencing terrible things. He told them how it's to do with the injustice and becoming aware that you've been used by shameless people in authority, like politicians, their wealthy friends and the leaders

185

in the army itself. One of the men started a completely different conversation with another member of the group, and the others joined the conversation in an effort to break away from Stephen's bleak ranting. Stephen turned to the man standing next to him, capturing his attention, and spoke about Mears and what Ray the homeless soldier told him about their gun and the General probably having shares and financial interests in re-designing it rather than getting a better gun off the shelf. But the man wasn't listening, he was just looking at Stephen, as if studying him before taking his chance and joining the conversation with the others.

Stephen felt on the outside, although not noticing the odd looks some of the men were giving him as he walked around the room. He noticed two men standing quietly by themselves, they looked like good friends who had known one another for years. Stephen introduced himself and the men reciprocated in an affable manner, but within seconds Stephen began talking about ex-soldiers who find it difficult when returning to family life. He carried on, talking about how many ex-soldiers are unable to hold down a job, especially those that had been in battle. Not allowing the two men time to speak, he went on, talking about ex-soldiers feeling alienated, unwanted, rejected and outside of the general flow of things in society. He spoke about the number of ex-service people that are homeless, of the problems there are with alcohol and drugs and of how he met a man whose life is now ruined because he fought for his country. The two men watched Stephen, not able to join in with what he was saying, because he wasn't engaged in a conversation, he was venting pent-up emotions. Stephen continued, talking about Ray and of how he opened his eyes to the way things really are. He said, 'I could tell you loads of things about the way politicians and their friends abuse this country and the people in it – they have no loyalty whatsoever to it or the people.'

Stephen talked about how the system enables the rich to avoid paying tax, yet chase the poor, and how governments give taxpayers money to big companies. His speech was fast and intense, and it was obvious that he was only speaking to himself and probably wouldn't have heard another person talking to him. He stared through the two men in front of him, his speech slowing down and becoming softer in tone as he talked about Jessica. He spoke about the IVF experience, and then the cancer, private healthcare and of government ministers that have investments in private health provision. He speeded up as he spoke about their hypocrisy and cowardice, of how the wealthy use the poor and anything else for financial gain and personal pleasure, and then he talked about canned hunting and the people involved in it.

One of the men placed his hand on Stephen's shoulder in a kindly manner, which stopped Stephen talking. He told him in a calm voice that he and his friend had seen someone they hadn't been in contact with for a long time and that they would speak to Stephen later. The two men smiled as they walked away, again, wishing him the 'best of luck.' Stephen looked around the room, a heavy, dark feeling weighed him down as he watched men in groups or pairs talking and laughing; he felt very much out of place.

Stephen left the meeting, feeling irritable and frustrated he talked to himself about how the men at the meeting didn't understand what was going on, and that they were ignorant to how they had been used. He spoke to himself about how things over the years have never changed as he made his way to the hospice with intentions of staying there the night.

45

Jessica's condition had deteriorated, doctors, nurses and carers stood around her bed with great concern. Stephen and Jessica's mother were standing behind them, Stephen was wearing his beret. A doctor asked Stephen and Jessica's mother to go with him as he wanted to speak to them. They went to a vacant room and once in there the doctor turned and closed the door. He remained standing as he told them it was only a matter of time before Jessica died, and that time could come any moment. Jessica's mother broke down while the doctor spoke about increasing the morphine Jessica was having. The doctor got her a chair, and as he did so he regarded Stephen with a quizzical look. He had experience of witnessing the responses people have to being told their loved one's death is imminent, but with Stephen it was different. It wasn't so much that Stephen was shocked into stillness, it was more that the news had triggered another train of thought in his mind that he had to pursue and deal with. The doctor couldn't think what it was, but had to let that thought go as he was dealing with more pressing concerns.

What the doctor wouldn't know, was that on hearing his words Stephen's mind became inflamed with anger that was directed at the comedian Joe Tara. Stephen wanted revenge. He wanted to avenge and fight back at the wrongs in the world and take it personally to those that he saw as deserving it on behalf of the innocents that always seem to suffer; and Joe Tara was the person he saw as worthy of having his wrath directed against him.

Stephen went home after hearing the news from the doctor and sat in the living room researching Joe Tara, he found his agent's name and the address where his office was. He planned to visit the agent's office with the hope of finding Joe Tara being there. Stephen also searched for where Joe Tara lived, but such information wasn't easily available, although he did see that Joe Tara had a couple of shows in town during that week.

The next morning, before going to the hospice, Stephen decided to write a letter to Joe Tara and take it to his agent's office, which was only thirty or forty minutes away from where he lived. It took several attempts until Stephen was pleased with what he had written, and then he sat back to read the letter one more time.

'Dear Joe, (I'm calling you Joe even though it isn't your name, but if I called you Mourib you might not like it because that isn't the name the public know you as) I've enclosed a photograph of myself when I was first sent out to Iraq, I look very

much the young soldier don't I Joe? By looking at my face you can see that I'm tanned and healthy, and very proud to be serving my country, but I have to tell you, Joe, I don't look like that now. You see, Joe, that photo was taken before I was involved in what they call an 'incident,' which means I was in a vehicle that was blown up by an IED. (Improvised Explosive Device – or you might have heard them called a roadside bomb, Joe) I was injured and one of our men was killed, but my Sergeant told me to shoot a boy who was standing by the side of the road, so I did, I shot him in the head and it made an awful mess, Joe. His brains were splattered all over the ground, and you know what, Joe? I'm certain he had nothing to do with it, but I shot him all the same, because I was told to. I think about that boy all the time, Joe, about his family and who he was, and I know I shot an innocent person. Strange, isn't Joe how we do what we're told? And believe what we see and hear, but you know that's not the case, don't you Joe? Because you're not an honest man, no, no, not at all.

My wife is dying of cancer, Joe, and there's nothing anyone can do about it. I got a loan out to pay for private healthcare, because the treatment we were pinning our hopes on isn't available on the NHS. You see, Joe, too many rich people are getting away without paying into the system and things like the NHS suffer, which means poorer people suffer, and all the while our leaders are lying to us. They want us to fight for them, but the reasons they give are false, because it's all about money. And you see, Joe, I think it's the same with you, except you're called a comedian and they're called politicians. I would like to meet you Joe and talk to you, man to man and tell what I think. Who knows, maybe we will meet sometime, or our paths might cross in one way or another. I'm going to sign off now Joe, because I'm losing my thread, if you know what I mean.

Yours sincerely. Stephen Dale.'

Stephen was happy with what he read, and as he was putting the letter in an envelope, he decided to ring Joe Tara's agent. He asked if Joe Tara was in the office, and when told he wasn't, Stephen asked if he could speak to his agent. The person on the other end of the line told Stephen that the agent wasn't in the office either, and then Stephen asked if they could give him Joe Tara's address because he wanted to know where he lived. He was told that they do not give confidential information about their clients to someone they do not know. Stephen then asked if Joe Tara would do a concert in aid of people that have cancer. The person he was speaking to told him she didn't organise Joe Tara's bookings, and that he would have to talk to his agent. Stephen said goodbye and decided to visit Joe Tara's agent before going to the hospice. He had a phone call from Jessica's mother as he was on his way to the agent's office, but didn't answer it on seeing who it was from. When he didn't answer Jessica's mother then rang Stephen's mother to ask if she had seen him because Jessica was getting weaker by the hour and he should be with her. Stephen's mother told her she didn't know where he was and that she had been trying to contact him herself. The phone conversation between the two women was short and their manner was reserved.

Stephen stood on the pavement outside the agent's office and looked up at the windows before ringing a bell. A buzzer sounded and Stephen opened the door that led to a narrow staircase, which went up three flights of stairs before reaching the office he was going to. He entered, after tapping on the door, and strode purposefully up to the reception desk. The young woman sitting behind the counter appeared to be younger than her age, looking more like a frightened little girl at seeing the scary man wearing an army beret staring at her. There was also a young man in the office, sitting behind a desk and looking too shocked to move he just stared at Stephen as he asked the young woman if he could see Joe Tara's agent. The young woman told him that his agent wasn't in the office, but Stephen didn't give her a chance to finish what she was going to say as he sighed irritably and handed her the letter he had written. 'Not very honest, is he?' Stephen said, and the young woman looked at him, not knowing what he meant. 'Joe Tara,' Stephen went on, 'Joe Tara, it's not his real name – that's what I'm saying, not very honest is it?' The young woman didn't know how to respond, she just shrugged and shook her head slightly. Stephen said, 'Don't know who to believe do we? But I *know* my wife is in a hospice dying of cancer, that's something I know is real.'

The young woman was terrified and scared of what Stephen might do next. She watched him as he spoke about the government, Mears and his business associates, corruption, private healthcare and then Joe Tara. The young man sat rigid in his chair, too frightened to move as he also

190

watched Stephen, and the young woman maintained a show of appearing interested in what Stephen was saying.

'It's not his real name – you know that?' Stephen said, and he looked at the young woman as he waited impatiently for her to answer, but he didn't give her time to form the words she was struggling to find. 'No, it's not his real name – he should be careful, telling lies about who he actually is – there's a lot of people suffering out there, a lot of good people, honest people, and they're getting let down, they're being lied to by politicians and they don't need entertainers lying to them as well – I mean, what can anyone believe? You know? Is anything real?'

A man appeared from a back room to see what was happening in the office. He moved in a slinky manner, but stopped suddenly on seeing Stephen as alarm and suspicion replaced his former self-assured attitude. It was too late for him to slither back into the room where he came from, because the man in the army beret had seen him, so he remained in the doorway. He looked sly, having fine features he was very slim and presented a delicate disposition. His clothes were fashionable and worn to accentuate an identity that was aimed at being feminine.

Stephen said to the young woman, 'You take me, I was Iraq, and I hate to say it, but I killed a man, well, he was really only a boy – younger than you I would say, anyway – yeah, I killed him, and he was innocent – he wasn't involved in anything. I've given it a lot of thought.'

Stephen stopped speaking and contemplated what he was saying, but then suddenly turned and looked at the man in the doorway. He stared at him for a few seconds and then turned his attention to the young man at the other end of the office before returning to the young woman and continuing to speak. 'I shot him because I was told to.' He stared at the young woman. 'And there he was, dead on the floor, his brain splatted in bits of bones, blood and flesh, which was his head and face – was, until I pulled that trigger – and I can't get it out of my mind – because someone told me to do it – and that's what people do, you see? They do what people tell them, and they believe what people tell them – even when those people are lying.'

Stephen looked at the young woman, his expression might have been asking for an answer to the madness of it all, but her young unblemished face remained still with her soft eyes levelled on the man standing in front of her.

191

'Do you know what I mean?' Stephen said, and while this was taking place, the man in the doorway had surreptitiously phoned the emergency services and was leaning back as he spoke quietly into the phone, giving the address and telling them it was an emergency. Stephen turned and looked at him. 'What are you doing?' He snapped, 'Are you phoning the police?'

The man quickly dropped the phone to his side and said he wasn't phoning the police, but making an important call to a client. Stephen walked towards him and said, 'Why do you want to phone the police?'

The man's devious nature went naturally into play as he lied, placating Stephen, telling him that he was going to phone the police but changed his mind, and he said, 'When I realised that you're a nice guy and just upset, I thought I would ring Joe Tara's agent and ask him if he could come over.' Stephen stared at the man, who didn't give Stephen time to think as he asked if he could help in any way. A servile smile appeared on his face as he glanced deceitfully at the young woman.

Stephen stared at him, his mind racing as he said, 'I don't trust you – you've phoned the police, you sneaky bastard – well, fuck you.' He took a step towards the man who froze in fear, but Stephen stopped and looked at him. He shook his head as he said, 'No, no, no, no – got to get out of here.' Stephen walked towards the door and left the office repeating what he had said.

The man in the doorway stumbled into the room and dropped with total relief onto a sofa that was opposite the reception desk. The young woman came out from behind the counter and the young man walked towards the other two on shaky legs. The young woman said to the man on the sofa, 'What do you think he would have done if he knew you were Joe's agent?' The man fanned away the question and said, 'Hopefully, the police will be here soon – lock that door.'

The young man took a key from behind the desk and locked the door as the young woman looked at Joe Tara's agent with admiration. She said, 'I'm so proud of you, the way you spoke to him, you're so brave – you deserve a medal.'

46

Stephen stood at the side of Jessica's bed wearing his beret, his parents were standing next to him and Jessica's mother was sitting in a chair. Jessica's brother, Chris, had gone away for a short break, which had upset Jessica's mother because she thought Jessica might not be alive by the time he got back. She hadn't spoken to Stephen since admonishing him earlier on for not getting back to Sharron. Her sad gaze moved from her daughter to Stephen, and as her look hardened, she said to Stephen's mother, 'Why is he wearing that bloody beret, what help is that? For God's sake.' They looked from her to Stephen, who hadn't taken any notice of what she said. He continued to look down at Jessica, every now and then shaking his head very slightly.

Stephen was staying at the hospice that night, but went out in the evening with a plan to confront Joe Tara who had a show in town. He walked around the building Joe Tara was appearing at, surveying it carefully for points of exit, and was told of a door at the rear of the building where the performers leave and often sign autographs for fans waiting outside. Stephen walked around to the door he was told about and saw a group of people politely jostling one another to be nearest to the door, that was open and guarded by two men. The people in the group were holding autograph books, pens and some had books in their hands, books with Joe Tara's face on the front. One of the two men guarding the doorway told the small crowd to stand back and be, 'respectful,' which they did, for all of a few seconds before surging forward to be close to the door, some finding themselves further away than they had been, while others feeling lucky to have jockeyed themselves into a prime position. Stephen pushed himself among the gathering of *fans*, not being too aggressive, but assertive in getting to where he wanted to be at the front. One of the men guarding the door looked at Stephen, his curiosity causing him to study the man wearing an army beret and he nudged the man next to him, alerting him to Stephen. The two men swapped glances that conveyed a shared thought that the man in the beret seemed different from the others. People were approaching the doorway from inside and the two men told people to calm down. One of the men watched Stephen, noting the blank expression on his face, how he didn't look excited and that he wasn't carrying any kind of book to get an autograph, but was determined to maintain his place in front of the door.

A few people came through the doorway, walking quickly, saying hello to the crowd, mostly in a patronising manner, then shouts of 'Joe' came from the crowd and they pushed as one to get closer to the doorway. The two men had a job on their hands pushing them back while remaining composed and *professional* in their work. There he was, Joe Tara, standing in front of Stephen. Words didn't form and it was as if all thought in his mind had frozen. All Stephen did was point at him and say, 'I know you – I know you, you're a liar you are, you're a liar.' Joe Tara looked at the man wearing a beret and glanced at the two men at the door, as if to check it was safe to leave. He began to walk, thinking of what his agent told him earlier about a 'crackpot' that had been in the office that day wearing an army beret. People were thrusting books towards him, some he took and signed, returning them only in the direction of the crowd and not to the people that gave them to him, and all the while he was mindful of the odd-looking man in the beret, as were the two men at the door. Stephen walked after him, repeating what he had said before, 'You're a liar you are, you're a liar.' The two men stepped in between Stephen and Joe Tara, blocking him from making any attempt to physically do anything.

Joe Tara walked out of the alley running by the side of the building onto the main road where a cab was waiting for him. Stephen followed, the two men standing in front of him as he shouted about how he fought for his country and his wife is in a hospice dying of cancer. He shouted at Joe Tara as he got into the car, 'You're just like the politicians and the rest of them – that's not even your name, Joe Tara, that's not your name, you liar – why do you lie?'

The car drove off and almost immediately the crowd dispersed, leaving only a few people who watched the cab drive away. The two men were looking at Stephen, who was also looking in the direction of where the cab went. 'On your way mate,' one of them barked, his manner having changed to overtly aggressive. The other man repeated what his associate had said, and they stared at Stephen. Their look was hostile and holding a hope that Stephen might start trouble, because that is what they really enjoy. Stephen didn't take any notice of them, it was as if they hadn't spoken to him and he turned, looking troubled and frustrated as he walked away. 'Weirdo,' one of the men shouted after Stephen, but he didn't turn, he didn't hear him, he was thinking of Ray, the ex-soldier. He wanted to speak to Ray, and he decided to go and look for him.

Stephen went to the station area where he had seen Ray, but he wasn't there, and he couldn't find anyone to ask if they had seen him. He searched out grubby recesses of all kinds, including doorways and subways and asked the homeless and lost if they had seen Ray, some waited long enough for him to give a description, while others were too disturbed and shook their heads not wanting to hear what he was saying. The night had worn on, only the stragglers, some of them making a hasty dash to the railway stations in order to catch last trains. Stephen carried on looking, desperately wanting to find Ray, as if Ray held answers to matters that were causing Stephen distress.

He stood outside a fast food place, looking through the window to see if Ray might be in there. Two men were sitting on stools inside at the window facing the street, they were talking about Stephen. One of them was pointing at him and they both laughed. The man who was pointing got off his stool and opened the door, remaining in the doorway he said to Stephen, 'Nice hat, man, you playing at soldiers, yeah?' Stephen looked at him with no intention of answering. The man went on, feeling it safe to do so. 'You like playing war games, soldier? Is that it? You play games with your soldier friends, or maybe you play by yourself?' He laughed, looking at the man inside the window for support. He continued, 'You big brave man killing all those little children, man – you big brave soldier, yeah?' Stephen turned and walked away, and the man shouted at him, 'You prick, you go play your little soldier games with your silly little hat – you too much coward to be soldier, real soldier, you prick – fuck off.' The man's voice faded and was lost within the collective urban noise that engulfs all sounds, whether they be mechanical or the emotional cries of people, it is all the same to a thing or being without a spirit that cares.

Stephen stopped walking on seeing a man in the entrance of a subway folding out a cardboard box onto the ground, just like laying a fresh sheet and blanket when making a bed. He was taking things from a battered old shopping trolley and placing them next to the cardboard bedding. One of the things he took from the trolley was a clear plastic shopping bag stuffed with paper, which looked as if it was to serve as a pillow. Stephen noticed something inside the bag which made him look closer. It was a Christmas card with a picture of Father Christmas waving merrily, his face full of warmth and good cheer. Stephen looked from the card to the man, only momentarily considering the irony of it all. He asked him if he had seen a man called Ray, and described what he looked like and that he is an ex-serviceman who had served in Afghanistan. The man stopped

195

what he was doing, but didn't look at Stephen, he stared at the wall, hoping Stephen would go away and leave him alone. He eventually turned and faced Stephen, but only to stare at him without speaking. Stephen nodded, and just as he was going to say something, the man widened his eyes as he said, 'Ex-serviceman? Who do you work for? The CIA, MI5 – Mossad? What you doing, hunting him down?' His crazed eyes blazed as he looked at Stephen and then around where they were standing, as if looking for someone. 'Who are the feds, man – yeah?' He said with a devilish grin, 'I mean, really, who are they?'

The man pointed his finger indiscriminately in the direction of the street, 'You know, probably everyone walking around here, man – look!' He pointed at a young woman, who looked as if she was probably on her way home having had a meal or a drink with friends after work. Stephen looked at the woman and thought how she had missed the last train, but then she might be getting a bus, or a cab, or maybe someone was picking her up, or even she was driving herself. The man's voice broke Stephen's thoughts. 'Yeah man, I'm right – I'm always right,' and he nodded at the young woman as he said, 'She with you?' A crafty expression filled his face, and thinking he had blown Stephen's cover he said, 'You two working together? Or are there more?' He looked all around, crouching low and tapping his nose he pointed at Stephen. 'You're not gonna get me that easily, baby – don't think I've got this far without knowing what you guys are up to,' and he made a gesture of holding a pistol and fired it at Stephen, 'What you gonna do, shoot him? This *ex-serviceman*, as you say.' The man began to laugh, which grew into hysterical laughter that nearly doubled him over. He gripped his sides and spoke in between laughing, 'What's he done? Run off with some secrets? And he's gonna sell them to the Russians? And your ass is on the block for letting it happen – oh boy, oh boy – I've seen this so many times, man, they got to start training you guys seriously, I mean, you come here all the time asking me questions, and you 'ain't got a clue what it's all about.'

The man stopped laughing, and placing his hands on his knees he leaned forward and looked at Stephen with an air of melodrama. 'I've got enough to do covering my own ass without having to tell you what it's all about so you can save your ass, only to come back and blow me away.'

Stephen had heard enough, he decided to leave, but the man became aggressive and stepped towards him. He shouted at Stephen, 'Don't come round here asking questions and looking over my property, man.' He held up a piece of wood with a board nailed onto it, EAT PITZA HERE was painted on it. He shook it at Stephen and shouted, 'Get off my property, man, leave us alone, man – go away and work for your leaders – the big gangster guys, yeah? Everyone knows the story – it's all about killing innocents, in the factory farms to the open concentration camps you guys call democratic countries – so get the hell out of here – you understand?' Becoming increasingly angry, he shouted, 'Go back to where you came from, tell them I ain't buying your shit, man – killing innocents, that's your game, man.' He took a step towards Stephen holding the advertising placard in his hand like an axe. Stephen began walking backwards, watching the man carefully he nodded and said under his breath, 'It's okay, I understand, I understand – I know what's going on.'

It was nearly three in the morning when Stephen got back to the hospice; Jessica's bed was empty. She had died an hour before he got there. Jessica's mother was sitting on a chair in the corner of the room, her voice lifeless as she told him when Jessica had died, and that she had seen to things like contacting the undertaker and signing forms. She told Stephen he wasn't capable of dealing with such things and had told the staff that he wasn't. The room was quiet and still, having the feel that all previous energy had been extinguished from it. Nothing was said as Stephen looked at Jessica's possessions lying on top of the bedside table, but he turned quickly away when seeing her wristwatch. The flat, hardly recognisable, voice of Jessica's mother stirred depressing fog that had settled in the room. 'I gave up wondering where you were. Don't worry, I'll deal with everything, you haven't been managing your personal and financial affairs so I shouldn't think you'll be able to manage matters that have to be seen to with Jessica.' She looked at Stephen, but not getting a response she continued, 'There's a lot of things to organise, and from what I read in those letters you aren't in any fit state to deal with any of them, and I'm not going to stand by and have poor Jessica's name dragged into a complete mess.'

She stared at Stephen, but he wasn't going to answer her. He pointed his finger down at the empty bed as if confused as to where Jessica had gone. Jessica's mother looked away with a stifled cry, but not able to hold it in, she blurted out through sobbing how Jessica had suffered and tried and fought so hard, and he wasn't there to give her support, but only made matters worse.

Stephen continued to look down at the bed with an expression that said he was not able to comprehend what had happened. It was too much for Jessica's mother, she turned, holding a handkerchief to cover her face she left the room weeping.

48

Jessica was told about having cancer at the end of September and she died the end of May. Stephen thought about the dates over and over as he sat on the sofa in his living room. Jessica's mother didn't want Stephen involved with organising the funeral or anything that had to be taken care of, such as going to the civic centre, registering Jessica's death and get the death certificate. She was seeing to everything, although matters to do with Jessica and Stephen's building society account had to be put in order by him. A week had passed and Stephen hadn't done anything, which prompted Jessica's mother to find out if she could take control of her daughter's financial affairs, because as far as she was concerned her son-in-law was obviously incapable of doing so. A solicitor told her it would be complicated and suggested she could make Stephen keep to a time where she would meet up with him and then go to the building society together. She asked Stephen's mother if she could help her, even though their relationship was now very cold because of the way she had spoken about him.

Stephen's parents visited him after getting the call from Jessica's mother. It was difficult to track Stephen down as he rarely answered his phone and was out of the flat a lot of the time. He hadn't showered or dressed when his parents arrived, although it was midday and he looked terrible. His mother asked him if he had been up all night, but he avoided giving straight answers to questions his parents asked him. They told Stephen how Jessica's mother is overcome with grief and is worried out of her mind over the loan and settling matters with the building society. Stephen's father lost his temper and shouted at him, he wanted to see the building society details and in frustration grabbed Stephen's wrists and shook him. It made no impact on Stephen and he refused to show any details of the loan or his building society statements. Stephen's mother was so upset she gave up pleading with him and began to cry. She told Stephen how they were worried about him, about the way he looked, the things he was saying, his behaviour and they wanted to help him but he just wasn't the Stephen they always knew. They asked him to move in with them and together they would work towards dealing with things, and that he should contact the doctor to get some help during this time.

The tension between Stephen and his father calmed down, he agreed to go to the building society with them and apologised for things that didn't make any sense to his parents. It was as if he wasn't grasping the importance of the situation and talked in a jumbled manner of how he was trying to understand them, but what they were saying and asking of him was vague. His mother saw that Stephen's condition was worse than she had thought and decided to phone his doctor later that day and explain to him what was happening with her son.

Stephen's parents left his flat, the lingering look on his mother's face staying with him after she had gone. He sat on the sofa and tried to concentrate, trying to think clearly about what they had been talking about, and he began to cry, feeling upset at letting Jessica down, and also her mother, but he couldn't get a clear image of Jessica in his mind. It was as if she was part of something that once existed, but was now distant and not relevant in his life. She just didn't seem important and as much as he tried, he couldn't help but think this way, although a part of Stephen was telling him he shouldn't be thinking about Jessica's mother like that, but then Stephen suddenly jumped up from the sofa, shouting out, realising he was confusing Jessica with her mother.

49

It was early afternoon outside Joe Tara's office and Joe Tara's agent emerged from the building. The office is in a busy part of town where all kinds of business and activity goes on amid the traffic, pollution, noise, people on the move and people out of the game, but though all this, Joe Tara's agent stopped moving as if he had been shot on seeing the man wearing an army beret. It had only been a couple of hours since Stephen's parents had visited him and he was still feeling distressed and sad, but he was also extremely anxious. Stephen took a couple of steps towards the thin, sly looking man, who wanted to re-trace his steps back though the doorway as Stephen said, 'Have you seen him yet? Did you tell him I would like to talk to him about some things?' Joe Tara's agent didn't respond, he just looked at Stephen who was now only a few feet in front of him. 'My wife died,' Stephen said, but all the man could do was to nod, his sneaky nature emphasised as a weak smile formed on his lips. He was looking for an escape route, he wasn't just uncomfortable, he was petrified.

'Her funeral is tomorrow,' Stephen said, and the man nodded, squeezing his insipid smile even tighter. Stephen asked him where Joe Tara was, where he lived, did he come to the office very often and did he know him very well. The man began to talk, his eyes unblinking as he stared at Stephen all the while, telling Stephen he didn't know Joe Tara very well at all, and he knew nothing of his personal life because 'Joe' was a private person. Stephen told him that 'Joe' wasn't his real name and did he know this. The man nodded slowly, looking away from Stephen as he thought of something to say. 'Well, you know, he's an entertainer,' he said with a simpering but careful smile, 'Oh, don't ask me, these artists are a law unto themselves – I just do the paperwork,' and then nodding more confidently at Stephen he said, 'God, you know, I'm really nothing to do with them – it's just work, I could be working at Tesco or somewhere.' He then broke into a little girlish giggle, which calmed his nerves to a degree as his eyes darted in all directions.

'Yes, but it isn't funny,' Stephen said, which turned the man to stone, and Stephen went on, telling him how people are dying in hospitals, in their homes and on the streets and they shouldn't be because there is the money to save them, but our leaders choose to make financial profits for their friends in business. Stephen spoke about Iraq, the young man he killed, how it's always the innocents that get hurt and suffer and that 'Joe Tara' shouldn't be adding to the deception that's already out there, especially as he's a comedian and says he's on the side of people living in a world run by hypocrites. 'I mean,' Stephen said, 'what can anyone believe, it's like nothing is real.'

The man agreed with Stephen, his obsequious manner causing him to squirm against the door he was standing in front of, but saying nothing a pathetically weak smile froze on his face. Stephen told the man what he thought, getting things off his chest brought him some relief, even if it was for only seconds.

Joe Tara's' agent also felt relief when Stephen walked away, breathing deeply his feeble smile turn into an expression of determination as he phoned the police. Stephen drifted from walking around streets to getting on busses, their destination was of no concern to him. As evening turned into night Stephen was somewhere in the suburbs on the other side of town from where he lived. He sat on a bus, staring at the driver, having convinced himself he had seen him in a village in Iraq. When the bus reached the terminus, Stephen waited for the last passenger to leave and then approached the driver, asking him if he came from Iraq. The driver shook his head, regarding Stephen with some suspicion, but no great caution as being spoken to by strange people was an everyday experience in his job. He told Stephen his family came from Pakistan, but Stephen carried on talking to him, telling him his wife had died and the funeral was the next day. The driver stopped what he was doing and looked at Stephen, nodding sadly he said Stephen should go home and rest. Stephen told him she had cancer, and that there is treatment if one can afford it, and repeated what he had before regarding politicians, business people, corruption and immorality.

The driver was a caring man and he patted Stephen's arm as he got off the bus, with Stephen following him talking about Iraq, how he was injured and how he had shot a young man who was innocent. The driver had to go into the garage, but before walking away he looked into Stephen's eyes and wished him all the best and for him to take care of himself. Stephen walked around the different bus stops in the station, talking to people, telling them what he told the driver. Some people listened, some looked sympathetic while others looked away, but all of them looked at the beret he was wearing.

50

As Stephen was getting ready for the funeral, he had a phone call from the woman he and Jessica had met who 'facilitated' the yoga sessions they went to, she wanted to know if they had considered coming back to the classes. Her manner was so pushy she wouldn't allow Stephen to explain that Jessica had died. He listened as she told him how the classes had been, 'Revised and are now guided with a gentler sensitivity.' Stephen finally told her Jessica had died, and as she finished offering her condolences, she told him about a therapy centre called Peaceful Glade and that it might be of help to him. She told Stephen that she would talk to the woman who runs the company to tell her about him. 'She is incredibly sensitive and empathetic,' the woman said, 'Her insight into trauma is quite fascinating as her energy to heal is beautiful.' He told her he would think about it, and before finishing the call she gave him the address of the centre, told him two more times what it was called and said, 'The first session is half price.'

Stephen wanted to carry Jessica's coffin into the crematorium, but there had been instructions from her mother that he shouldn't be allowed. Stephen's mother calmed him, talking to him quietly, but in a firm tone that it had been organised and he wasn't to upset things. She told him to think of Jessica and that she wouldn't want him to get upset. He sat with his parents, refusing to take off his beret, and he was shocked when his mother told him that Jessica asked for certain songs to be played at her funeral. She hadn't mentioned it to him, and nobody else had said anything about it to him, but he couldn't concentrate on the subject as his mind strayed elsewhere while watching the coffin being carried into the chapel.

A reception had been organised by Jessica's mother, Jessica's associates from work were there and some of her personal friends, including Sharron who was mindful to keep out of Stephen's way. Stephen appeared as being dazed. To be in shock was understandable, but there was something else about his manner that caused others to feel apprehensive, and all the while he wore his army beret. Stephen didn't talk to anyone, his mind kept returning to a nagging feeling, which was that although Jessica was dead, he felt there was something important that had to be completed in order to make the whole affair final; but he didn't know what it was.

51

Stephen stood in front of a building that had a plaque on the wall with the words Peaceful Glade, he had rung the centre the day before and made an appointment. He was guided into what was called the 'consultation room' by a woman who had the air of a person working in an environment that entailed corporate-like professionalism. Stephen wasn't really listening as she reeled off information about the courses and services on offer, his attention was taken by the expensive interior design in the place. She spoke about different therapies, counselling and guidance that is given when following a self-help approach to take care of 'emotional health' with things such as meditation, yoga or having a massage. The woman talked about booking a session with an art or drama therapist and, 'Explore ways to be creative which helps engaging positive feelings and calming oneself through personal expression.' The centre had books he could buy that give help, advise and support in all areas of one's life. She spoke about learning new ways to cook with healthy nutritious food that heightens one's mood, and to educate oneself to eliminate harmful products such as sugars, artificial chemicals and saturated fats from one's diet that make one lethargic and depressed. Stephen was told about dance classes that are run by 'qualified teachers,' and when telling him about a 'qualified councillor,' the woman said, 'She is amazing, and she will give you guidance in learning ways of releasing endorphins that will give you a natural positive feeling, and to just engage with what is around you in nature, yeah? You should read one of our books that guides you to be aware of your uniqueness and place within nature – look up at the sky, sit and look at trees, slow your breathing and relax – yeah? We'll guide you on routines that won't hurt your body, but definitely boost happy hormones and a sense of well-being.' She smiled and showed Stephen a thin pamphlet of no more than two pages, but before talking about what was in it, she said to him, 'Oh, you can take this with you, it doesn't cost anything.'

Stephen looked at a box of tissues on the table, they were the same make as the tissues that were in the hospital when he and Jessica spoke to the woman about her cancer. The word *industry* came to his mind as he thought about the *props* and procedures that are part of the *industry*. The tissues, the books, the medication, the hourly segments filled with therapy talk. It was just like a mechanic in a garage, in a place of work surrounded by the accoutrements of their trade, or *profession*, for these *therapists* like to be called *professionals*. They refer to themselves as being so, and there is the evidence hanging on the wall, the qualifications in a frame, awarded by an organisation, the accreditations to prove that they are.

Stephen looked at the woman, all of it felt to him like it had happened a long time ago, meaning Jessica and her contact with these people, the therapists, healers and the rest of them. It had become an extinct memory somewhere in his mind. It had gone, and also gone was any need to try and understand what was going on and what they were talking about. The woman watched Stephen as he sat in front of her, he looked to be in deep thought. She noticed his untidy appearance, his staring eyes, his wired manner; there was something about him that was beginning to scare her. She smiled, but Stephen did not smile back, he was tired of it all, the caring smile they all had, it sickened him; he saw it as fake. He was done. That was what he thought. Finished. Stephen was sick of the jargon, the appeasing facial expressions, the ingratiating manner, and then there was the question of money; there was always talk of money. He remembered hearing how money spent in this area is an investment in one's personal health, well-being and future happiness in the great pursuit to *move on.*

The warmth of the room was making Stephen tired. He felt heavy, exhaustion weakening his body his eyes closed as he thought of healers and therapists. They were smiling, like sales agents gathering at a convention, holding portfolios to their chests, talking, talking, talking and talking, and changing what they are saying as new language becomes fashionable, leaving what was said before as redundant, but it is okay, because they have *moved on* as the *industry* moves along creating new opportunities for new people to pursue careers. The sales people looked different, they were politicians, they were laughing, faces infused with greed, gluttonous people with no principles their hard features emphasising their arrogance as cruelty poured from their mouths.

Stephen was in a hut, he looked around and saw there were beds, and Graham Mears was standing by a table wearing hunting clothing and holding a rifle, as was his family, they were all holding rifles and laughing. Stephen looked at Mears's brother Luke, standing next to his sister, Amber and his son, Sam, and there was his daughter Sophie with her boyfriend, Harry. A few other people were also in the hut, friends of Mears they were also dressed in hunting clothes and holding rifles. They were in Africa to do some canned hunting. Stephen was their valet, a servant brought along to keep an eye on them as he knew about guns, and being ex-army he was disciplined and subservient to his masters. They were at play, enjoying themselves, and Stephen had to keep quiet about the way he felt, with killing innocent animals, fenced in so imbecilic psychopaths could kill them while they drank alcohol and took different types of drugs. They were the leaders, these were the people in authority, this is what the establishment looked like. Stephen had difficulty breathing, the people in the hut intimidated him, he was mindful of their power and propensity to wield merciless violence. He was detached from them, as if they were on a film he was watching. They started to leave the hut, talking to one another and laughing, oblivious to Stephen's presence. He shut and locked the door when they had left and turned to watch them putting their rifles in a container on the back of a large bush vehicle, that was driven by a black man wearing rags.

They all climbed aboard the vehicle and Stephen followed, nobody took any notice of him as he got on. He looked down and saw the driver's legs, which were nearly bare because his trousers had been worn to mere threads, and he drove barefoot. Stephen pointed his rifle at Mears's friends. They looked at what he was doing and laughed, laughing at his impotence, because he was a man having no power or anything they regarded as worth. Stephen pulled the trigger and started shooting everyone on the vehicle. They screamed, and Stephen loved the feeling it gave him, watching them screaming in fear. There was Harry, trying to escape, but a bullet tore into the back of his head, skull bone and blood splashing over Graham Mears and his sister. Sophie sat frigid with fear, but the bullets undid her tight posture, her face and shoulder separating into bloody lumps. The driver looked up at Stephen, and Stephen acknowledged him with a smile, but this didn't calm the driver who stared at him even though Stephen was telling him he was safe because they were the same, they were both servants to these disgusting people that are morally corrupt. Mears had escaped. He had jumped off the vehicle, all the others were dead, and Stephen started to follow him, jumping off the vehicle…

Stephen woke with a start. He had shouted out, 'My back.' The woman was staring at him, she was frightened and didn't know what to say.

52

Stephen's parents came to his flat at nine thirty in the morning, they had come to take him to the building society. It was a surprise visit, having previously spoken with the building society his mother had arranged an appointment for Stephen. She told them how Stephen needed support in managing his affairs as he was unwell, and she explained how he was injured in Iraq and that his wife had just died. Stephen didn't offer the resistance his parents thought he would, the loan and building society didn't seem to bother him because he was preoccupied with a demonstration he was going to that afternoon. He told his parents how the demonstration was important as it was about the government cutting money to the NHS and creating poverty in the country. His parents felt Stephen wasn't facing things and that he was in denial because he couldn't cope. They felt he needed help, his experiences in Iraq and now Jessica had triggered emotions that had rendered him incapable of coping. Stephen's mother phoned his doctor again to press the importance of seeing her son, they were worried about the condition of his mind and that he would get lost in a state of unreality.

The meeting at the building society was a disaster. There was an enormous amount of money outstanding with the loan, and payments on Stephen's mortgage were going to be jeopardised as it looked like the flat was going to be seized to pay the money that was owed. Stephen wasn't concerned, he stood up during the meeting, approached a member of staff and asked her if she knew Jessica, but his mother had chosen to go to a different branch from the one where Jessica worked.

Stephen had never been to a demonstration before, the atmosphere felt to him like it was happening in another country and foreign. Groups of young people were all dressed the same wearing completely black clothing, some with their faces covered and some banging drums. There were people who looked like they worked in the health service or were showing support from other unions carrying banners, and there were just ordinary people wanting to make their feelings known about the situation. Separate from everyone else were others that were dressed in black and in a style to identify themselves as *rebellious* political demonstrators, and it was this faction of the crowd that made the most noise. They weren't just walking in an orderly manner and making their point, but shouting and chanting slogans against the establishment in general, as well as provoking the police who kept a close eye on them.

The demonstration had a set route that was planned to finish at a point where there would be speeches made, but the organised atmosphere changed into hostile protesting when reaching the final destination. It was led by the people dressed in black having a stylishly unorthodox appearance. Stephen got caught up in a part of the crowd that was targeted by the police. They were pushing and shoving people, a policeman pushed a young woman backwards, and when she shouted at him he said, 'There's other places I'd like to be – I'm only doing my job,' which prompted the young woman to shout at him, 'Yeah, and that's what the Nazis said when they were throwing kids in ovens – only doing my job – but who in their right mind would want to do that job?'

A violent shove from another policeman sent Stephen backwards and he lost his balance, falling to the ground he let out a scream of pain, it felt like an electric charge had shot through the base of is spine. Getting to his feet he picked up his beret, put it on and shouted at the police that he was just standing there. 'Well move,' came the reply, shouted at him by a large policeman, and 'Keep moving or I'll shove you again.' The policeman's voice grew deeper and louder in tone as he couldn't hide his lust for wanting to engage in violence. The young people dressed in black shouted cliched comments at the police about them being fascists, but Stephen didn't see it like that. He felt betrayed, and he thought of what the homeless ex-soldier Ray had told him about Queen Elizabeth and her speech at Tilbury. Everything else he had been thinking about and learned in the last year flooded through his mind. He thought of how there has to be order, but it was wrong how the police were behaving, and why shouldn't he be standing there? After all, that's meant to be what people like him go to war for, to preserve liberty, but he had found it to be very selective in who has rights, privileges and freedom. His thoughts ended abruptly as he felt a breath-taking thud in his chest that sent him reeling backwards. Stephen was nearly knocked unconscious and completely disorientated. Yet again he found himself on the ground, but now there were people falling over him while others were trying to get him to stand up as the noise had louder and more aggressive. With the help of others, Stephen managed to get to his feet and grab hold of his beret as it was kicked along the ground in the scuffle. His first concern was to get out of the fracas as he shoved his way to the periphery of the commotion, and then a bit further until he was free from the crowd.

A group had also disengaged themselves from the trouble, wanting to have nothing to do with what the demonstration had become. A young woman said to Stephen, 'I'm sure the so-called anarchists are fifth columnists – it undermines the whole purpose and importance of why people are demonstrating.'

Stephen spoke to her about how nothing is as it seems, and then he told her about Joe Tara, the entertainment business and how it is full of deceitful people telling lies in order to get the fame they've always wanted 'They are just like politicians,' Stephen said, and the young woman agreed, saying, 'Good analogy,' and she went on to say how celebrities are more important than politicians because they are more meaningful to many people in society because they relate to them, and therefore politicians use them, as do big companies like banks. 'It's a big business with big money involved,' the young woman said, and then she spoke of how the agents of celebrities are particular in what brands or type of politics they advocate. She said, 'They would definitely not want to be involved in promoting baby milk powder for a company that has previously been found to have been selling products to women in undeveloped countries that has blinded their children Their personalities are used to persuade their followers to engage with a product, and if they have millions of followers it's a big catch for a company, and it's very useful in politics as people believe them more than they do politicians.'

While talking, they had walked away from where the demonstration was held, and then the group that the young woman was with went into a pub. She stopped by the door and told Stephen about an anti-war meeting and where it was taking place, 'Look it up,' she said as she was disappearing into the pub. Stephen walked to a train station, caught the first train that came along and twenty minutes later he was walking down a high street. He stopped on seeing a leaflet pinned to a tree, t was to do with a Spiritual church and advertising that there was a meeting that evening. Stephen decided to go along, it was only a couple of hours from the church service starting and by the time he got there it wouldn't be long to wait. Stephen didn't normally go to church, but he thought there might be something in it as he had been speaking to Jessica every day and felt she was with him all the time.

On entering the church, Stephen looked around at the people that had gathered there, and his first thought was of how many of them looked lost. The people running it were friendly, although making it plain to Stephen they would like him to make a donation, even if it was a small one. Stephen had a brief chat with a woman before the service started, telling her it was his first time, and she told him it was good to keep an open mind and that most people came because they have suffered the loss of a loved one and want to communicate. 'To say goodbye,' she said, 'To want closure in knowing those that have passed are happy and in are still with us in spirit, although not with us physically.'

The service was short with everyone seemingly impatient to get it out of the way and start with what they had come for, which was *healing* and *communication* with those that had *passed*. There were four *healers* and people queued in front of the one they had chosen. The *healers* placed their hands on the heads of the people in front of them and ran their hands down their backs, their shoulders and down the front of the body. The recipients were told to breathe slowly and deeply; Stephen declined the invitation to take part in the ritual.

After the *healing* the *spirit communication* got underway with a *medium* who was a middle-aged man wearing a cheap suit and very worn shoes. All *communication* was, apparently, conveyed through the man's *guide* who, according to the man, was an 'Aztec King.' Those that were picked out by the man looked regulars, mainly women and what they heard from the man was a standard reply from the 'other side,' such as, 'enjoy your life,' 'don't worry, I'm happy,' 'you do too much for others, think of yourself.' Each *message* was a variation of the one before, the only stumbling points came when particular information was wanted. One example being when the man said, 'Brown shoes, he's saying brown shoes,' but the old lady that wanted contact with her late husband shook her head and said, 'He didn't have any brown shoes, he hated them.' Another time when a *communication* was floundering, the *medium* turned it round by making light of it. He put his hand over his mouth in mock shock, as if his *guide* had said something suggestive and said in old-time music hall style, 'I can't say that.'

Stephen watched the man, and he looked around at the people that had come along with hopes of releasing themselves from the heartbreak they were enduring, even if it was for a short while. He felt it all too sad to think about.

53

Stephen picked up the two envelopes on the mat by the front door. One was from the building society, which he discarded immediately, and then he opened the other one. On seeing it was a circular from a utility company, he tore them both up, walked into the kitchen and put them in a waste bin that was flowing over. While waiting for the kettle to boil, Stephen stared at it in deep thought, he was undecided whether he should go to Joe Tara's agent or travel to a town about a hundred miles away where Joe Tara was performing. He had a desperate need to communicate with Joe Tara and had written another letter that he wanted him to read. Even though Stephen knew he was a fraud and a hypocrite, he wanted him to use his influential position to raise awareness of the threats to the NHS and the involvement of corrupt politicians.

After deciding to take the letter to his agent, Stephen made a cup of tea and took it into the living room. He searched on his computer for information about psychics and mediums, the experience at the spiritualist church didn't impress him, but he wanted to pursue this area. There was something not in place, he felt there was a piece missing in the jigsaw that was his life, and he didn't know what it was. He had a feeling that maybe, just maybe, Jessica was trying to contact him, to speak to him and say something, and if they could communicate the jigsaw would be complete.

His search brought up different people, nearly all women, who professed to be spiritualists, mediums, healers and those offering 'life-coaching.' There were some that had nearly all bases covered by their supposed ability to read 'tarot and angel cards,' communicate with the spirits of animals that have 'passed' as well as animal bereavement counselling. Most did 'readings' on a one to one basis, in groups and on Skype. Words such as, 'intuition,' 'growth' and 'journey' were used and each site had testimonials saying how 'accurate' the medium was; there was also a tariff giving the different prices for 'readings.'

Stephen read what one of the *medium's* said on her site. 'A proficient spiritualist, medium, can provide much needed peace, closure and comfort that will bring fulfilment as one engages with one's spirituality and explores a journey that is there, but just needs guidance in unlocking.' She went on, saying how all kinds of people go to her for all kinds of reasons, whether it be health, love, or relationship concerns. She also helped people take a fresh look at their career, their potential and how to take a direction that leads to work that is fulfilling and meaningful. Staying on the subject of work and money, she said that people may be addressing issues that have become obstacles in furthering their business plans, so spiritual guidance could help them make decisions that direct them towards their goals and objectives. She spoke of how people contact her about family issues, 'Whether it's having to care for an elderly relative, issues around children or it maybe to do with drugs or behaviour that is destructive and tests the strongest partnership – and also maybe a partner has been unfaithful.'

Another *medium* spoke about how loved ones that have 'passed' leave signs to let us know they are still with us. Examples were given such as signs in dreams, often called a 'spirit visitation,' or it could be a bird pecking at your window. It is common for spirits to use coins or small objects that have a significance to a person and the person that has 'passed.' Stephen settled on a psychic called Angelina Eris who lived quite close to him. He made an appointment to see her and during the brief chat he had with her on the phone, she asked him to bring an item that was personal to Jessica and belonged to her. After making the call Stephen left the flat and went to the office of Joe Tara's agent.

Joe Tara's agent looked through the slats of the venetian blind onto the street outside, he was watching Stephen who was standing on the other side of the street holding the letter he had written. 'Oh my God,' the agent said in a voice that rose to falsetto, and with his voice suddenly changing to low and flat, he said, 'Don't let him in.' He turned from the window and saw the young woman and man staring at him, their looks pleading for leadership. 'Shall I phone the police?' The young woman asked him, her face appearing ten years younger than it did twenty seconds earlier. The agent spoke quietly while looking out of the window, 'No, not yet anyway, they weren't too pleased last time.'

'He doesn't do anything though,' the young man said.

'Not yet,' the agent snapped and he looked with contempt at the young man, who nervously examined his fumbling fingers. The agent slowly returned to looking out of the window, and then jumped with a start. 'He's gone!' His voice sounding more surprised than relieved, and then all three of them jumped as a buzzer sounded.

'Shit, that's him,' the agent said as they looked at one another. The office had been struck silent, the only sounds being that of muffled traffic and just the occasional blast of a car horn. Besides those sounds there was nothing, and just as stillness was beginning to settle, the buzzer sounded again. 'Shit,' the agent said, and the young man let out the breath he had been holding in. 'Don't do anything,' the agent said, 'He'll go away.'

'Did you see that film about stalking last night? The young woman said, 'What was it called…'

'No!' The agent barked at her.

She looked hurt as she said, 'But it was really interesting…'

'I don't find that nutter in the beret very interesting,' the agent cut in. 'Being famous attracts attention, whether one wants it or not. I was telling Joe the other night that army boy had been here wanting his address and ranting about politicians and the health service, and of how the wealthy find it entertaining to kill animals that are confined in a space – canned hunting, or something he called it.'

'That sounds terrible,' the young man said, but all the agent did was give him a long withering look.

Stephen remained at the door of Joe Tara's office for a while before finally giving up. Pressing the buzzer one more time, he put the letter in the mail box and left.

54

Angelina Eris showed Stephen into her lounge, noting his army beret as she did so. She invited Stephen to sit at a table and watched him look around at the different artefacts in the room, as if expecting him to comment on them, but he didn't. She took her time before sitting down as she looked at Stephen and processed her thoughts. Stephen was considering the cost of coming to see this woman, it was expensive and his money was running out, but he thought it would be worth it if there was the faintest possibility of having some contact with Jessica.

'I became interested in mediumship after my partner died. I felt lost, confused, angry and all the emotions associated with bereavement. I went to a counsellor, but it didn't, feel right? I knew there was something else? I knew my partner was still around me, I could feel his presence...' Angelina Eris spoke continuously, and she went on, telling Stephen how she sought the services of a medium to contact her partner and became involved herself in becoming a medium. It was a lengthy and detailed background of her 'journey' to how she became a professional medium. Stephen looked at her closely when she told him of how, through meditation, she connected with her main Spirit Guide who was a famous African warrior. She told Stephen that people come to her for many reasons, although the most common one is to hear from loved ones that have 'passed.' Angelina Eris went on, and on about 'helping others' and 'giving guidance.'

She stopped talking and looked at Stephen for a few seconds before continuing. 'I am a spiritualist medium – I work closely with angels – I always preferred the company of spirit children when I was a child. Their love was so unconditional, not forced and prescribed, or false, just honest, natural and true.'

Looking into Stephen's eyes, she said, 'And Stephen, I hope to help you with your spiritual growth and journey.'

Stephen looked at her, a horrible sinking feeling formed in his stomach and heavy tiredness filled his head. Her voice was as it should be, sympathetic and soft, there were the props, books, charts, the scene set for a *reading*. Stephen thought of how language is used that really says nothing if you analysed it separately from the setting. He thought it bland, open-ended and repetitive, because there is nothing to say, so they use jargon to confuse and mystify the recipient. Stephen noticed how they always flatter by saying things such as, 'you're a good person,' 'you're honest,' 'you're well-intentioned,' 'you care too much about others' and 'people don't understand you.' He saw them as nothing more than generalised statements that can be applied to most people. Stephen thought how the healers, mediums and therapists were all the same. He wanted it all to stop. He felt sick and tired of everything he had heard and encountered. The woman in front of him was talking, he knew that because her mouth was moving, but he couldn't hear what she was saying. Stephen didn't want to hear what she was saying. The word, *deceit* came to his mind, and for a fraction of a second temper nearly rose in him as thoughts of Jessica flashed across his mind. His hearing returned, and without concentrating on what she was saying, Stephen watched her rather than listened.

'So, if this is new to you,' Angelina Eris said, 'You could be, well, maybe a little shocked and overwhelmed. So, how does one find a guardian angel? Well, it's perfectly normal, they are a natural part of life, existing in many religions and belief systems, and have done so for thousands of years. Angels are celestial beings, and no, they don't show themselves in a human form. Loved ones pass over and can become guides to others, but with angels it's different, they haven't existed in this life form we understand as a human form. Consisting of celestial energy, they have particular functions, if you like, in helping, supporting and guiding us. As I'm sure you've heard, even if you're not au fait with this area of understanding, there is a guardian angel, our own angel that keeps watch over us, giving us advice on what direction and choice to take or make. To return to the question, now we have more understanding of it, how do we find an angel? Well, Stephen, it's remarkably simple, and because it is so simple, it's probably the reason many people haven't found the way because they've overlooked what is all around them, all the time.'

Stephen nodded, watching her carefully, noticing the changes in her facial expressions, the way she used her hands in artistic shapes to explain herself and the way she nodded to affirm that he agreed with what she was saying. 'And with you, Stephen,' she said, 'It's important for you to connect with a loved one that has recently passed.'

It was a while since she had spoken, but Stephen hadn't noticed she had stopped speaking, and he repeated the word, 'okay?' a few times to gain his attention. Stephen couldn't remember if

215

she had asked him something and was waiting for an answer, and all he could do was nod at her. She reminded Stephen that she had asked for an item that belonged to Jessica, and as Stephen took her wedding ring from his pocket, she asked him if he knew what psychometry was. Stephen shook his head and mumbled something incoherent as a reply. She told him it means psychometric measurement, and explained how holding a personal item belonging to the deceased person can give a connection to the person who has 'passed.' She said that the personality of the person is felt as the essence of the person remains on items close to them. Stephen looked down as she went on, saying how it is a good way of communicating with those that have 'passed' as information is conveyed through vibrations imbued into the item by emotions and past actions. Stephen gave Jessica's wedding ring to Angelina Eris and watched her as she looked at it and closed her eyes. 'She wants you to know she loves you Stephen,' she said, and then added as she nodded at him, 'She's not in any pain Stephen, she wants you to know that she's okay.'

Stephen looked down at the table as Angelina Eris spoke. 'She's by your side, all the time – she wants you to know that – she's standing there now Stephen, look to your left, there she is, can you see her?'
Stephen looked to his left, and continued to look at the empty space in front of the wall for a few seconds before looking at Angelina Eris. Her smile grew wider the longer Stephen didn't say anything, and then he brought the *reading* to an abrupt end. He stood up as she was talking, way before the time was up, but her composed, smiling manner didn't change, and continuing to smile she looked at a little dish on the table for him to put the money in, as she had asked him to do before the 'reading' started. He put the money in the dish and left the *medium* who called herself Angelina Eris without saying anything.

Stephen didn't give much thought to the experience, and nothing would come when trying to conjure up a clear impression about the woman called Angelina Eris. The experience had gone extinguished from his mind as something having no importance whatsoever.

On the kitchen table were six unopened envelopes, they were from the building society. There had been a letter relating to the debt that Stephen did open, but on seeing who it was from he didn't bother to read it. Someone from a company related to the debt had visited his flat, but as he wasn't in, they left a card. The company were making threats, but Stephen didn't see them as threats, he understood their actions as part of a general and growing vendetta that was building and conspiring against him, and the reason it was happening was because of the knowledge he had acquired over the last few months about what politicians really get up to.

Stephen's GP had rung him several times, he answered on the doctor's fourth attempt and spoke to him, being wary of what it was he wanted. The doctor told Stephen there were things he wanted to talk to him about and for this reason he would like him to come to the surgery. When Stephen asked him why, the doctor said he could help him cope during, 'this very difficult time.' Stephen told the doctor about making a complaint against the company that set up the loan, telling him how he had written to them and sent one of his wedding photographs with the letter. He also wanted to complain about the private healthcare. The doctor told him it was a difficult process, but would go over it with him if he came to the surgery. Sensing how the matter of private healthcare was of great importance to Stephen, the doctor used it as a reason for him to come to the surgery. He explained to Stephen how there isn't a standard complaint procedure with private healthcare, and complaints are made to the individual hospital or clinic where one is being treated, or was treated. The doctor kept Stephen's attention, telling him about in-house complaints systems, and that there are various organisations, such as the Patients Association that might be of help, but he would explain in more detail when he came to the surgery. Stephen thanked him and said he would come in as soon as possible.

The doctor watched Stephen enter his surgery, barely recognising him as the same man he had seen before. Stephen's mother had told him about Stephen and what had happened regarding the debt and the way he has changed. Stephen sat down, took off his beret and holding it between his hands he told the doctor about making a compliant regarding the private health company. The doctor noted how he used the words 'injustice' and 'corruption' as he spoke about exploitative methods used to extract money out of desperate people. Stephen began to talk about Jessica, of how she suffered, of her hopes of having a baby were crushed and the money involved in having IVF treatment, and then the cancer. He told the doctor about the Chancellor of the Exchequer, Graham Mears, and what he learned about him and his associates, of corruption and dealings with big business, the lies they tell and the pretence they hide behind.

The doctor watched Stephen as he spoke about the arms industry and the people involved with it who are hypocrites and nothing more than mass murders of innocent people. Stephen talked about religion, the royal family, the way ordinary people have been exploited and used so people can maintain power and control while making money. He mentioned Joe Tara and then the medium, Angelina Eris, telling the doctor how, 'nothing is real.'

The doctor waited for Stephen to finish, thinking how disturbed he was, and when there was a lull in Stephen's tirade he talked about bereavement. He spoke of how shock and upset can, and does, alter a person's normal pattern of behaviour for a while, and then he said, 'I've asked you to come in to discuss making a complaint, but also because I'm concerned about you, Stephen. I wouldn't profess to be knowledgeable about the treatment of PTSD in cases relating to those returning from places of war and conflict, although, maybe all of us in the health profession should be. Like many people, I've read and seen documentaries, and of course, I have experience of treating patients suffering forms of depression and anxiety.' The doctor spoke in a candid manner, telling Stephen that, in his opinion, from his experience of treating patients with anxiety, a spell of medication does help, and that he was thinking of medication from the SSRI type of drugs.

Stephen's immediate response was to tell him that he didn't want to take, 'drugs,' but the doctor's manner was sharp as he told Stephen that he doesn't prescribe 'drugs,' but, 'medicine.' He spoke of how the basic principles of the Hippocratic oath were still observed to in its modern form, and is relevant in upholding ethical standards with intentions of only doing good, and not harm, to one's patient. The doctor said he would prescribe a small dose, 'initially,' and then see where they go from there. He asked Stephen about his time in the army, and said that because he wasn't Stephen's doctor when he returned from Iraq, he didn't fully understand the details of what happened to him. He said, 'The benefits massively outweigh the negatives with this medication. The anti-depressant, Sertraline, is, I believe, best suited for you. It is used to treat anxiety and depression and has had positive results in cases of PTSD. Now, read the little information slip that comes with them to familiarise yourself with the possible side effects, and we'll meet in a couple of weeks to have a chat and see how things are going.' He finished by telling Stephen the medication can take over two weeks to take effect, 'So, a little patience is needed.'

The doctor watched Stephen as he looked down at the beret he was fidgeting with between his hands, and as he did so a look of vague curiosity showed in his face as he said, 'Okay Stephen?' Stephen looked up and nodded, and the doctor went on, 'The SSRI'S, which is short for selective serotonin re-uptake inhibitors, have, as I told you, been successful in treating depression, anxiety and PTSD. The medication you have been prescribed has the generic name of sertraline. Now, the medication works, basically, without getting overly technical, by balancing chemicals in the brain.'

He looked at Stephen as he spoke, noting how he wasn't listening to him, but occupied with some other matter. 'There has been research that found people with PTSD appear to have different amounts of particular chemicals, which are called neurotransmitters, in their brains than people without PTSD.'

Stephen looked at him, unmoved by what he was saying. The doctor continued, 'Experiencing a war situation can, and does, affect people at the time, soon after, and sometimes a long time afterwards. PTSD is sometimes triggered by another trauma, seemingly unrelated, but a trauma all the same in that it is a cause of massive anxiety that one feels one has no control over – your wife's illness, the struggle she had and then ultimately her death can be understood as overtaxing

219

what were already frayed nerves, although you weren't aware of how strained they actually were.'

Realising Stephen wasn't going to say anything, the doctor said, 'I feel comfortable in prescribing this medicine, Stephen.' Looking from the computer screen to Stephen he nodded reassuringly, 'Go home and try to relax, and we will arrange for you to come in and see how you are getting on – with the medication and yourself.'

Stephen looked at the doctor, his expression changing from blank to unconvinced. The doctor continued, 'So, just take one tablet a day – we'll start on 50 milligrams, and as I said, it will be about two weeks before you should notice a difference, so it's important to keep taking the medication, even though you might think they're not working – and we'll meet up, see how the land is lying, and change the dose if we feel it needs it.'

The doctor sat back in his chair, and while looking at Stephen he thought how Stephen appeared so detached from what was being said to him. He said to Stephen, 'To grieve is a normal, a natural part of life, but to suppress emotions and block out what is upsetting can be seen to cause deep problems. The use of medication, in this case antidepressants, can be of use, although not for a long period, and I must say, I believe bereavement therapy could well be of help for you – you see, there's a large body of thought that believes medication will hide the emotional pain, but when the medication stops, the emotions that haven't been fully addressed and completely felt will still be there and have to be faced.'

Stephen looked down at his beret as the doctor asked him if he was in touch with someone from the forces, such as a counsellor, and when Stephen shook his head the doctor began to write on a piece of paper as he spoke. 'There is also the debt, Stephen – your mother told me about it.' He looked up, forcing a smile, 'That will be something else we'll be discussing, but for now, let's just take our time – yes?'

57

Stephen left the doctor's surgery and took the prescription into the nearest chemist, and while waiting he was overcome by a feeling of euphoria, it was a feeling of exhilaration when thinking about Joe Tara. A warm glow spread in his stomach. It was a feeling he hadn't felt for years. The last time was when involved in battle and news came through that all was safe, meaning he and his comrades could relax. He decided to visit Joe Tara's agent's office, and promised himself he would go to where he was doing a show and wait outside for him again. But then he changed his mind, thinking what was the point, and then a silly, fanciful thought flitted through his mind that he should throw a can of red paint over Joe Tara. Red symbolising the blood of innocent people, and animals, that suffer in this world because it's controlled by sneaky two-faced people like him. He wondered where that thought came from, but he found it amusing and it gave him a sense of relief.

A few days went by and Stephen found it hard to sleep, he thought it might have been a side effect of the Sertraline he was taking. His thoughts, because of lack of sleep, were less clear and he felt nervous. One afternoon, as he was sitting on the sofa at home, his phone rang, Stephen answered it, even though he didn't recognise the number. The voice on the other end was female and soft. It was a woman from the NHS regarding his visit to the doctor; she was ringing about bereavement counselling. Stephen hardly said anything as the woman gave him information regarding counselling and where it took place. She spoke about stages of bereavement and told Stephen that it isn't a sign of weakness to ask for help, guidance or support, and in fact, 'It's a sign of strength and an acknowledgement, even if subconsciously so, that you need to move on.' Stephen asked her what she meant by 'move on,' and that he thought it was a stupid thing to say. 'Move on where?' He asked her, and he said, 'It's my experience, it's not like buying a new car.'

The woman spoke quietly, telling him how it is natural to feel angry and irritated by things, words, what people say, even the train or bus being one minute late or the television not changing channel in a split second. She told him to try not to fight and challenge everything, and that to move on isn't to erase cherished memories or forget the person one loved, but it's a process of learning to live one's life to the fullest. She talked about embracing change and to, 'Grow stronger and engage in understanding feelings you might never had been aware of.'

The woman went on, talking about being happy, fulfilled and to follow interests while knowing you will always honour the one you loved and lost as you venture forward. Stephen listened to the tone of her voice as she spoke, rather than the words she was saying. Her voice reminding him of dry cake, and he imagined her facial expressions, nearly uncomfortably precise in showing sympathy. The soft, arid voice carried on, talking about how his mind will get jumbled in adjusting to life without having Jessica, but with time the grieving takes, 'Less emotional energy as one puts one's energy into new things as one begins to move on.' She continued, telling Stephen how his feelings will become less intense and just to accept the chaotic order in his mind as deep upset will cause this. She spoke of how he will be angry with others and the loved one that died, but with time the pain will decrease. While talking to Stephen, she was writing a note for his doctor, saying how she thought Stephen might need a more in-depth course of therapy.

Stephen mumbled, 'goodbye' and terminated the call. It was as if he had never received it and the woman talking to him had never existed. As he put the phone in his pocket, he decided to go out and try to find Ray, the ex-soldier, hoping he would have better luck during the day.

58

It was late afternoon when Stephen left the flat. He started his search where he first saw Ray, but having no luck, he began to look anywhere, asking people that were homeless or looking down at heel and out of luck if they had seen him, giving them a description, but most shook their heads, others were suspicious. Stephen was conscious that these people were aside from *normal* life, and a large part of their existence was taken up with fear. He went into a pub, not having drunk alcohol for years he wasn't going to start again now. Ordering a cup of coffee he looked in the direction where people were looking, which was up at a screen on the wall showing a football match. Stephen took his cup of coffee to a table and sat down, he wasn't that interested in football and knowing nothing about it he shrugged his shoulders and nodded in agreement when a man said to him how 'rubbish' one of the teams were. Stephen looked around the pub, at the people, the furnishing, the menu on the table he was sitting at, and for a second it seemed to him as if he was on a film set. It didn't feel real, and panic exploded inside him.

Stephen calmed himself and stood up. He spoke to a few men up at the bar, one of them had said something about football and the conversation quickly got onto the money footballers earn. Stephen spoke about the government and corruption, the NHS and money made from wars. The men looked at him, noting his army beret. 'It is what it is,' one of the men said, but Stephen asked him what he meant and the atmosphere became uncomfortable. Stephen left the pub without giving any thought to his brief conversation with the men at the bar, in fact, it was as if he hadn't met them. His mind was set on finding Ray, and as darkness came in shadows that eventually replaced the light, Stephen felt more comfortable. The workers, shoppers and day trippers had gone home or were on their way and Stephen was aware of feeling a sense of relief, because he felt that he had become like the people he was now talking to, in being aside from *normal* society.

The back alleys and service roads behind the large stores are usually unseen areas by the hordes of shoppers and visitors to the cities, and at night they are even more hidden and can take on a foreboding atmosphere. Stephen wasn't bothered by any feelings other than finding Ray as he walked by cages of flattened cardboard boxes and passed metal shutters pulled down and locked for the night. He stopped walking as he reached a small side street and saw a strange looking old man, who was standing with his hands pressed together in prayer and bowing at a group of pigeons scavenging on the ground in some rubbish. Stephen watched him for a while, and he noticed Stephen looking at him, but continued all the same. When Stephen asked him what he was doing, the man smiled and nodded as he spoke, but his English was poor, making it difficult for Stephen to understand him. The man told Stephen he was offering a prayer for the spirits of the birds and that they may live the life they are doing so at present in peace and without too much fear and pain, and that their next life will bring more comfort. Stephen nodded, not really knowing why, but thought what did he know and maybe the man was right in his thinking. He asked him if he saw the pigeons as important, and what possible part do they play in the lives of people. The man held his arms out to his side and told Stephen that we are all spirit and that we are all part of one, the pigeons, the cats, dogs, the animals people eat, human beings, all of them, the rich, the poor, the strong and the weak, all are equal. The man looked at the pigeons and said, 'These are untouchables in animal form, that is what they have been born into, despised and destroyed without pity by many people, but they are children of God, and if I can bring God's love to them in any humble way I can, I have done, what I believe is my duty. The man who is proud does not fear these birds, for what do the proud care of the weak? They are seen as unimportant, but even the proudest and most powerful man is nothing when judged next to God, who looks over those men of power as he does these pigeons – for they are the same, they are his children.'

Stephen took a step towards him with deep thought showing in his face. The man watched Stephen closely as he began to speak, his words coming slowly. 'I wish you were right, but I don't think it's so – no, I don't think that's the way of things. The country is run by hypocrites – the world is – big business, and they all lie. They're full of deceit – look at Joe Tara, even people like him – more deceit. Nothing is real – it's all about money, it's not about being honest or the truth – I don't think most people know what the truth is.'

'Is knowing the truth important to you?' the man asked Stephen, his voice quiet and his manner serene.

'Yes, it is,' Stephen replied, 'It was always the most important thing to me, but from what I've seen and been finding out, I didn't know what it was even when I thought I did.'

The man looked at Stephen, his kind face creasing as he nearly smiled, 'Following the path of truth is the gateway to heaven,' he said, and he looked closely at Stephen to see his response.

'Where does being honest and wanting to act in the right way get you?' Stephen said, and he told the man about his experiences, of being in the scouts, of respecting those people in authority as principled that work for the betterment of mankind. He spoke about the army, of getting injured, and then about Jessica, the IVF and then the cancer. Stephen told him about private healthcare and how it is just a moneymaking business for wealthy people and their politician friends who don't care, and that the same people start wars to make money. He told the man it is always the innocents that are killed and suffer.

'I was wrong, about everything,' Stephen said, 'I did my duty without thought. I was programmed to do it without really thinking – from an early age.'

'But you are thinking now,' the man said. Stephen waved his hand, dismissing what the man had said and told him it's of no use now because it's too late. Stephen looked around where he was standing with disgust as he said, 'I can't understand why there aren't more people getting back at these politicians and their type because of the way they've behaved – they lie to the ordinary person and laugh at them because they see them as fools – it makes you want to pick up a gun, because they *are* the enemy.'

The man held his withered old hand up in a gentle gesture and said, 'No, that is not the way. You are on the right path, to be conscious is the way. To be aware and conscientious in fulfilling your duty to your best ability – dharma, to perform your duty, take responsibility relevant to your position – it is difficult because of distractions, but you are a good man. There are false teachers who spread delusion, but you seek the truth – you are an honourable man for there are many who don't want to know what truth is, because their minds have been perverted – but not you.'

Stephen looked away from the man with a pained expression, and all the while the man watched him closely. He said to Stephen, 'Everything is Maya – what we see isn't real, it's an illusion, as everything doesn't remain the same because it is in state of constant change, appearing as one thing, and then another as a mass perception for seeing it as such develops.' The man took his time as he spoke. 'Those that consciously present an untruthful appearance is to knowingly act against one's dharma, which makes a bad person, and he or she will reap what karma will bring

225

back to them. All are of spirit, each having a part, although only temporary, but all are part of the same energy, all are interconnected and as one moves another shall feel the effect of the other's movement, and as one thinks another will be influenced by the other's thoughts – one is all and all is one – there is no escape, only to fulfil one's obligations – one's dharma. The aim is to free ourselves and reach moksha – to be released from samsara, the cycle of birth, suffering and death.'

Stephen looked from the man to down at the pigeons. His mind began to wander, but the man's voice pulled Stephen's attention to what he was saying. 'I will pray for your wife, Jessica, and you – what is your name?

Stephen told him, quietly, and then added, 'I know you mean well, but I've seen with my own eyes how the weak and helpless are treated, sometimes you have to fight back, it's not fair.'

The man looked at Stephen, feeling his anger and frustration, he said, 'This journey has to be experienced – you are a good man, please do not seek retribution, for you will have failed – let God decide, let him make his judgement upon those that engage in the ungodly practice of pride.'

Stephen shook his hand and bowed as the man bowed his head to him. He then turned and walked away from the man and the pigeons, thinking about the man's beliefs and contrasted them with the arrogant, greedy bullies who seem to run the world. He also thought about the desolate loneliness suffered by people that meant and mean well, like the old man but have fallen to the side of *normal* life. He thought about the pigeons and the fear they must feel, and the spite and animosity felt towards them by many people. Stephen thought about his life; a life that had been shattered.

59

Stephen watched the bus move slowly in traffic that looked irritable and tired, reflecting how the people felt inside the vehicles, most of them on their way home having been at work. Stephen never thought about the job he had at the tax office. It was as if it had been expunged from his mind. He didn't give any thought to the debt, ignored letters from the building society and the few times there was a knock on his door he ignored that as well. Stephen was seriously considering buying a tin of red paint and throwing it over Joe Tara when he came out of a theatre he was performing at. He imagined doing it, and seeing the shock on Joe Tara's face, and Stephen would shout at him, 'You're lucky it's not your blood.' But all thoughts of Joe Tara vanished as he got on a bus. He was sure it was the same driver that had been looking at him in the mirror. Stephen's insides chilled and his mouth dried, and when taking a seat his full attention was directed on the mirror. His breathing was short and his hands were sweaty as he looked at the driver's reflection; he had to get off the bus. The eyes looked out of the mirror at Stephen, the same eyes he had seen before, staring and cursing him to hell for what he had done. Stephen got off the bus, taking a last look at the driver as he went, and there they were, his eyes, staring at him.

A man was standing on the pavement holding leaflets that he waved every now and then in the air as he spoke about Jesus Christ and the need to have God in one's life. His appearance was unkempt and he talked continuously at people as they passed by. Nearly everyone ignored him, yet he carried on speaking at the empty spaces left before the next person walked by. Stephen watched him, thinking how it didn't seem to matter to him that people looked the other way when he spoke to them. It was all the same whether they listened or not, he just went on speaking, reciting words he had repeated many times before. The man's eyes had an intensity that gave strength to the rest of his being, just as his physical appearance looked shabby and beaten by what he had encountered in his life, his eyes did not. They had a purpose, sharp and penetrating they snatched hold of a subject, be that a person, what someone had said or an idea he was thinking about, and he examined it with a drilling stare. Stephen noticed the man's shoes, they were worn down, the heels completely so at an acute angle, and they were scuffed with a slit separating one of the soles from the upper. Stephen looked into the man's face guessing his age, which he thought would have been about thirty, and he then thought of the man's origin. His family, or he, had probably come from Africa at some time, his features were strong and at times looked proud. Stephen thought about the man's ancestry, of who they might have been, maybe proud warriors, and maybe forced from their homes by companies that the likes of Graham Mears are associated with.

The man looked at Stephen and said, 'Be saved my friend, repent, believe and live with Jesus – be saved.' He offered Stephen a leaflet, which Stephen took and the man said, 'Come to a service – all are welcome in the house of the Lord.'

Stephen looked down at the leaflet as he walked away, hearing the man's voice as he told people to embrace the Lord and be saved.

60

Stephen checked online the place and time of the ani-war meeting that the young woman at the demonstration had told him about as she was going into the pub. He read about the meeting and what someone had written about the 'system' needing war in order for the rich and powerful to make money and maintain the status quo. His mother had visited him that afternoon, wanting him to come and live with her, and she also wanted to know if he had spoken to anyone regarding the loan and his mortgage. Stephen told her he had important things to do, but when she asked what they were, he became withdrawn and told her it wasn't the time to talk about such things. His mother left his flat, her frustration and worry growing, she wanted her son to sort things out, but also to be given help and support.

The meeting was in a large room at the back of an old building, which looked like it would have been a significant place in the community, like a village hall, years ago before the progression of urbanisation. Stephen entered and saw a sign inside the doorway telling people they can bring their own refreshments, but alcohol wasn't allowed. He spoke to a man and woman who were seated beneath the sign, they were part of the organisation that was holding the event. They asked Stephen if he had been to their meetings before and gave him some leaflets. Stephen thanked them and walked around the hall, unaware that people were looking at his army beret.

A young man with a deceitful face sidled up to Stephen and said, 'We know who you are man, it's obvious you're undercover.' He smiled sneakily as he said, 'Christ man, you wouldn't fool anyone, I mean look at the way you're dressed,' and he looked Stephen up and down, examining what he was wearing with a contemptuous curl of his lip. Stephen told him that he didn't know what he meant, and feeling confused he said, 'Are you laughing at me?' The seriousness of Stephen's manner alarmed the young man so much he stopped sneering and looked around himself for possible support. 'I don't know what you mean,' Stephen said, and looking directly into the young man's eyes he said with a touch of hostility, 'What do you mean? What are you saying?'

Well, come on man,' he said, but the young man wasn't now so confident, 'Anyone can tell you're a cop, or something,' he added with a sly smile.

'Something?' Stephen said, although he felt it didn't sound like him that was asking a question. The young man began to back off, and the further away he walked the braver he became, the sneer on his face returning as he said, 'Don't worry, we can pick you out – easily, oh yeah, just as long as we know you're here.' He nodded as he turned, but the relief of being out of Stephen's physical reach was patently noticeable. Stephen had unnerved him, he was scared of him with his intense, but also detached manner, and Stephen continued to look at him as he walked away. A middle-aged man approached Stephen and told him he had heard what the young man had said, and not looking completely relaxed himself about Stephen he spoke about how it is common practice for undercover police to infiltrate dissident groups, and for that reason many people are wary of newcomers, especially with an unknown history and looking out of place. Stephen thought it was ridiculous, but didn't say anything, and the man continued, telling Stephen how the police have become very skilled at mixing in with groups and even have personal relationships with members who they are spying on, and then feed any information they have gained back to their superiors.

Stephen looked around at the people in the room thinking how everything seems to be part of a fashion. They were dressed alike as others of a different type dress alike, presenting a style declaring their identity. Whether the group or type wear expensive designer clothes and jewellery, it was the same with the people at the meeting, young or old, they wore similar clothing, had similar hairstyles and the same way of speaking. Stephen looked at the amount of people that had ponytails and were wearing headbands, large jumpers and baggy trousers made of rough material. Their presentation was a statement of who and what they were, which was a person who is critical of mainstream values.

Stephen stood by the side of a group and listened to what was being said. A young woman was speaking, her pitch and manner was that of a lecturer delivering a well-rehearsed script. 'Oh, the theatre of war that the rich produce and direct uses ordinary people as unpaid actors – everyone has their costume to wear, army uniforms, some with fancy gold and silver on the lapels to show they're the principal actors, but the writers and editors stay behind the scenes with the producers making a new war for pernicious productions limited, where it's the same old people that win and the same old people that lose and blame one another for what's happening to them.'

She went on, saying how the world is trillions of dollars richer than it was a year before, but who would notice because everyone feels life is getting tougher and cash is tighter. She spoke of the contradiction between what the mainstream news broadcasts and the daily life experiences of the ordinary person. The young woman caught Stephen's eye as she was talking about how people are confused and shocked by the amount of wars that exist, and she directed what she was saying at him. 'Not when you realise it's designed to be that way, this world has been turned into a market place that benefits those with the power – the natural world, the people and animals living upon it are exploitable products, and war is created for profit.'

Her words were pointed and aimed at Stephen because of his army beret, but he wasn't conscious of what she was doing, and she continued, talking about how banks generate money within the economy because of the interest paid on massive loans needed to fight wars and the re-construction money afterwards. She then spoke about the 'working class' being used to fight 'rich people's wars,' and she pointed at Stephen as she spoke. 'This is what our armies protect, the privileges of the rich and their positions to continue treating us this way, read for yourself what's happening with the arms trade – the construction of wars,'

Stephen still didn't realise she was talking about him, and then his attention was taken by a man who started to speak about the ecological chain effects caused by war, and of how the ecological damage affects everything and everyone. He said that it causes the displacement of people, which creates homelessness, poverty and disease, 'But who cares if it ruins people's lives as long it makes a financial profit for the companies and their investors,' the man said, and he went on, 'The land is battered, bombarded and poisoned when the infrastructure is attacked – bridges, power supplies, roads and rail, they are bombed and destroyed, and water is poisoned. When the war is over the earth is left sick, and people suffer as a consequence. The political influence and lobbying on behalf of arms companies is well known, there is massive collusion between politicians and arms industries, and the pharmaceuticals and all the other industries as war is given legal status by the politicians. Law is perverted in the interest of these people – if you make the laws to sanction your activities you have it pretty well sewn up.'

Stephen turned away and looked at a group of people that had gathered near him, one of them, a middle-aged man said hello to Stephen and started talking to him about how the royal family are used to lobby for the arms industry. 'It's an industry they've been involved with over the years,' the man said, and he added how they prosper from arms deals as do other royal families in the world. He told Stephen how leading members of our own royal family are sent to places on earth known for exhibiting the very behaviour that we are told is the reason why we go to war, which is to fight tyranny, and when there they don't try and talk them out of their cruel, bullying behaviour and actions, but use flattery and their influence to sell arms to them. The man said how they are heavily involved in an 'evil' industry that prospers the rich and brings inhuman suffering to the poor and ordinary people in this world. He said, 'To have an allegiance to organisations that strive to work towards peace, harmony, and a world with inequality is one thing, but to have loyalty to an authority that does the opposite is self-destructive for the world, the people and all things upon it – why would ordinary people support such insane gangsterism? Why would a decent, honest person with good intentions want to offer their life in service to fight and defend these people?'

Stephen was disorientated. The man didn't stop talking, it was a barrage of words with no pause for conversation with others to take place. He went on, 'We need an establishment, of course we do, we need authority, laws and rules. Of course, it's nothing to do with anarchy, it's just decency and wanting a better place to live in for all living things – not only now, but in the future. We want a world that we can be proud of and content in knowing we are using our knowledge to create something good rather than what we have, which is constant war and misery and poverty for large sections of the world, and an environment destroyed so a tiny minority of people financially profit. Yeah, the royal family, they're involved and personally profiting from the arms industry. Some of these weapons are banned, and our media make a big thing of the atrocities caused by other regimes yet we, the world's policeman, as we like to say, use horrific weapons, knowingly to kill and mutilate innocent people now and in the future because of the effects of weapons like depleted uranium.'

A young man interrupted, adding to what the man was saying, 'The queen is a master insider trader, and because of her position she is armed with knowledge of other countries' plans, their positives and their pitfalls – and that puts you ahead in the game of dealing at the rich end of world trading, especially arms where there's great financial profits to be had, and the royal's wealth has grown considerably over the years due to their investments – they've made billions, and that's in an age of *austerity* – remember that when you can't get seen at your local hospital.'

232

The other man carried on, 'The royal family, the wealthy, they've become richer from involvement with stuff like uranium and other toxic metals and chemicals. She doesn't care about her devoted, subordinate subjects getting ill, let alone people and their children in other places. They use cheap psychology of presenting a face to the public of being even a little eccentric, and to be seen as *out of touch* with *reality,* having *way out* concerns for the natural environment, when the real reality is they have no concerns at all, their primeval lust overrides everything, and that's power – their interest in green politics, caring about where we live and nature – bah! It's not even a sick joke – their concerns are only for themselves and the maintenance of a political system creating laws that favours their desires. Oh yeah, as I say, they pay lip service by getting involved with fatuous campaigns to save the environment, yet invest in stuff like uranium, which is a component in arms, and one that has produced massive returns for investors…'

The young man interjected 'Especially those who are in there at the beginning and given the nod of what to invest in and when – like the royal family.'

The other man nodded in agreement as he continued. 'Weapons tipped with depleted uranium are hard enough to pierce a tank – or a busload of school children, and the after-effects pollute the world – it's an insane act of self-destruction – the world will be contaminated, food and water poisoned and babies born with their immune system damaged. The foreign office requests senior royal persons to butter up leaders in countries with terrible human rights records, but don't worry, it's all about money – and, oh, by the way, the arms we sell to these people fund those *evil terrorists* that *our* army go and fight. Designed? How dare you think of such a thing.' And he added sarcastically, 'Not our wonderful leaders – surely not.'

The young man nodded, in competition with the other man to address their audience, which was Stephen, but the older man continued to speak. 'The uranium used in shells pollute and poison the earth, so if a person hasn't actually inhaled the dust of this stuff, they will consume it in their food and water as it will be contaminated, because all food ultimately comes from the ground that has been poisoned by the use of radioactive and toxic weapons. The result of low level radiation is a cause of leukaemia in children, and the rates are spiked in areas where these weapons have been used, along with other horrendous effects such as congenital malformations, malignancies, heart disease, malformations, and women are reported to suffer high rates of

233

miscarriages and sterility – so the worms are now radioactive and mutant – mutant worms – "only a worm" some people might say, but worms are more important than humans in keeping this planet breathing, without them, nothing grows.'

The young man finally took over, speaking fast. 'There's a cover up by this country, and others in releasing the statistics, and there isn't anything in place to clean up the contaminated areas. To say it doesn't exist is a huge lie and denial of the truth – so much for pretending to care about children in areas of the world that are under threat from the *terrorists*....'

The other man cut in, 'They scream in the media of the shame and inhuman treatment of children, when we kill and injure millions of them, and the ones that aren't yet even born to live a miserable existence in poverty and serious ill health.'

The two men started talking amongst themselves, and as Stephen watched them a third man approached Stephen and said, 'What we need is action, direct action.' The man continued to speak, but Stephen didn't hear what he was saying because what he had said brought to his mind Ray, the ex-serviceman, and what he had told him as he gripped Stephen's shoulders and stared into his eyes, 'Action, we have experienced action – they haven't – we need to bring it home to them,'

Stephen's mind cleared, 'We have to act,' the man was saying, 'What's needed is action, not words – actions speak louder than words,' and again the man's voice vanished as Stephen reflected back on thoughts and experiences. He thought of his scout days and what he read in one of his books about those that act on seeing something wrong, such as stepping in when someone is being bullied, giving aid to a person if they fall in the street, helping an old person, and if they are infirm to do their shopping, because it is in the *deed,* the *act*, anyone can say words to pretend they're a type of person only to fool others by giving a false impression of themselves.

Stephen suddenly became aware that he was talking, he was speaking to the man about a need for people to take action against, 'Our leaders and bring it home to them – to those that are lying and using us.' He went on, talking about the difference between troops who saw combat and those that didn't, and its significance in relation to alcoholism, drugs, crime, homelessness and suicide.

Another man stood by Stephen's side, watching him closely as he spoke about Graham Mears and his involvement with private health companies. He was absorbed by Stephen's passion, but mainly by his anger as he watched him, and looking Stephen's beret he asked him if he had fought for his country. Stephen told him that he had and where he had been. The man said, 'And you've realised that you were used – you were really serving the interests of big companies.'

Stephen nodded and the man said, 'People are conditioned not educated, and there's a difference. The system wants malleable tools, not thinking individuals – that would be far too difficult to control,' and he gestured for Stephen to move away from the group. They walked to the side of the room and stood next to the wall. The man nodded at Stephen's beret, 'Still proud of the regiment though? The boys you served with?' Stephen told him that he was, and opened up, telling him about Jessica, the private health companies, the politicians involved with them and of how there isn't any honesty, and all the while the man watched him, his gaunt, unshaven face turning slightly as his sly eyes widened at thoughts he was having.

The man licked his lips, and looked around to check nobody could hear what they were saying before speaking to Stephen in a confidential tone. 'There are ways to get back at these people – all is not useless, don't give up, because that's what they want you to do – but we have power, and that's what they're scared of.'

'But it's everywhere,' Stephen said, 'Everything is like this – I don't know, it just seems impossible, as I say, it's everything – take things like comedy, and this Joe Tara.' He went on about Joe Tara, his lifestyle, his wife, their conniving ways and of hoodwinking people, making them believe he's something that he isn't. Stephen told him about going to the agent's office and the time he waited outside the theatre when Joe Tara was rushed into a car. The man was becoming more interested, his eyes were nearly feasting on Stephen as he studied him in a detailed observation while Stephen was talking, anger showing as he told the man how he would like to know where Joe Tara lived.

The man stepped back, a tight smile formed on his scraggy, dishonest face as he told Stephen there were ways to, 'get at these people.' He spoke about the 'connections' he had, that he belonged to a group that is 'active,' how he can get information on the dark web and that he would get him Joe Tara's address in town. He asked Stephen if he had heard of an anarchist group called Conflict for Freedom. Stephen told him he hadn't and the man said, 'You were a soldier for the enemy, but now you've woken up to what's really going on, and it must hurt you, a good man like yourself.'

Stephen became reflective, talking about the young man he killed and of how he thought about him, knowing he was just an innocent person standing in a street where he came from. 'An innocent man, it is always the innocents that get killed and used,' Stephen said, and the man watched Stephen with intense interest. Stephen then smiled and told the man how he had thought of throwing red paint over Joe Tara, and he shook his head. 'Red paint?' The man said, 'What's that about?' Stephen said he would like to hit him with something a lot stronger, which he wouldn't be able to wash of.

'To fuck him right up?' The man said, and Stephen looked at him, his expression solemn with underlying menace as he said, 'Yes, I'd like to really hurt these people,' and he spoke of how he lay in bed at night imagining he was in the Cayman Islands hunting down Graham Mears and his family, just like they kill innocent animals for fun. The man watched him, closely, and then turning towards the wall he told Stephen it could be a reality, to shoot or kill these people because through the group he belonged to he had access to all kinds of weapons. Stephen looked directly into the man's eyes and asked if he could get explosives. The man nodded, a smile breaking on his face as he told Stephen about getting him what he wanted, and that Joe Tara's address and explosives wouldn't be a problem. He arranged to meet Stephen at another Anti-war meeting at the same place where they were, and he told him when it was.

Stephen looked around the room, lost in deep thought, and watching him as if having made a stimulating discovery, the man breathed in with excitement. Stephen noticed the sneaky young man who spoke to him when he came in earlier. He was standing between, but just behind, two people watching Stephen, and he began to nod with a devious smirk appearing on his face.

61

Stephen received a letter and a text for him to go to the doctor's surgery, it was for the following day. The doctor watched Stephen carefully as he entered the room and sat down, noticing there had been a change in his appearance since his last visit. He asked Stephen how he was getting on with the Sertraline he was taking, while taking note of how Stephen looked dishevelled and the distracted look on his face. Stephen told the doctor he hadn't noticed any great difference with the Sertraline, only that maybe it was responsible for him having difficulty sleeping. The doctor nodded and asked if he had pursued the bereavement counselling, but Stephen shook his head, making it plain he didn't want to discuss it. He told Stephen that he had spoken to his mother and that she was very worried, and would like him to come home. The doctor asked Stephen about the building society, if he had contacted anyone from the army, had he made any headway with the complaints he wanted to make and then he mentioned the debt.

Stephen wasn't listening, his mind was elsewhere. It looked like he was having a conversation with himself as he stared down at the beret in his hands, but then he suddenly looked up at the doctor and began talking about the world of therapy and counselling. 'The industry of talking – the industry of death. Vultures waiting, ready to swoop, not on the actual corpse, because humans are too deceitful for that, but on the emotional remains suffered by loved ones – *helping* and *supporting* them with the practical things where money is involved, like funerals, paying off companies for contracts that have to be cancelled, yes, there's the financial costs, and the money to be made by those people *pitching* their *product* in emotional care. The therapists and counsellors, creating careers and businesses, using insincere language from the religious to new philosophies that are in fashion.

'What happened with Jessica was worse than war – that's simple, with Jessica you can see the snipers, but they make out they're your friends – they've got smiling faces, lots of hugs, feeling your pain – empathy, helping, supporting, but it all has a price tag, because nothing's for free, not if you're unlucky enough to fall into the hands that reach out of a sewer where the private caring industry lives – I can't even be bothered to think of a name to describe them – it's just wrong.'

Stephen stared at the doctor, 'Yes, these therapists – I've seen the look on their faces when they realise you aren't going to cough up the money – the light goes out and the warm smile is packed away for another day and another sucker. Their farewell is a lot colder than their greeting – and they're all so sincere, and they all want to help you, and they keep coming in on you like waves – like waves that break into nothing when they land on the beach, that's the way it is with their promises, turning to nothing once the money has been paid, because the magic ends and another promise is pulled out of their hat.'

Watching him closely, the doctor thought about Stephen's anger and the words he was using. 'It's disgusting,' Stephen said, 'These people who use people, but have no loyalty towards them.'

The doctor asked Stephen what he meant about 'loyalty' and would he explain it to him so that he could understand. Stephen spoke about his time in the army, of how he was a loyal servant to the country and the people in authority, unquestioningly, but he was wrong. He told the doctor how the rich and members of the government use tax havens and are happy to allow our public health system to deteriorate, and that the system is set up to serve them while ex-servicemen sleep on the streets and aren't really listened to because, 'It would blow the whole thing apart if the truth came out – the real injury the majority of ex-soldiers who were in action suffer isn't because of what they did, saw or experienced, it's a moral injury – what really gets them is the deceit and the lies and the hypocrisy, and they were part of it, thinking they were doing something else – well intentioned people killing innocent people.'

Stephen talked about his experience of killing an innocent young man, and then his wife not able to get treatment because they live in a country that has medication, but it's only available for the rich in a land that is wealthy. 'The people we give our lives for,' Stephen said, 'Who profit from private health businesses, and wars. Oh yeah, "faithful and loving people."' Stephen went on, telling the doctor about, Queen Elizabeth's Tilbury speech and of how he was taken in as a young boy – deceived, when in the scouts, having faith in authority, prepared to give his life for his country. 'I spoke to an old man,' Stephen said, a Hindu I think, but that doesn't matter – he was praying for pigeons, and he told me about a thing called dharma. I don't understand it, but it's also about karma – it's bigger than what we think it is, the greedy men who start wars and create poverty so they can make money, but the pigeons are better off, they're just going through the experience of life, being born, living and dying, while the greedy, self-important people have

238

fear, and they hurt and make money out what they can, but they're still scared, and their actions will come back on them in ways they're not aware of, because ultimately we are all one sharing the same experience – life. They are cruel uncaring people who have the power to create a state of delusion, but there is reality, it's life, being born, living and dying. The man told me that I might feel deceived, but it didn't make me wrong as I acted in good faith, because life is bigger than the plans of greedy men. He told me I was right in wanting to do my duty, he said that is the way, that is good dharma and it is good for all other living creatures.'

Stephen stopped talking and looked down, re-engaging with the internal conversation he was having earlier. The doctor had been making notes as Stephen was speaking and also writing out a prescription for him. He watched Stephen engaged in his internal conversation, and clearing this throat to get his attention the doctor told him that he was increasing the dose of his medication and they should arrange the next appointment. But Stephen ignored what the doctor was saying and started to talk about canned hunting, how it's organised, the people involved it, like Graham Mears, his brother, his family and friends and he spoke about the Cayman Islands and private jets.

'Maybe we'll continue this conversation the next time Stephen,' the doctor said, cutting across what Stephen was saying, and he watched Stephen as he stood up and put on his beret. He shook the doctor's hand and said something the doctor didn't catch as he left the room. As the doctor watched Stephen leave, he thought about his behaviour and how there are studies that confirm the link between taking SSRI antidepressants and mania. Stephen's behaviour was certainly manic, but then the doctor's thoughts were diverted to his car, which was at the garage and was being delivered to his surgery later that afternoon.

239

62

Stephen looked at the unopened mail that he had dropped in a pile on the sofa, but his thoughts were elsewhere and not to do with the mail, the building society or the debt. Stephen stood up, and as he did so a leaflet that had been lodged between the cushions fell to the floor. It was about the church that the man in the street had given him. The name of the church was F.A.R – Faith and Redemption. There was a meeting that night and Stephen decided to go along, just for something to do more than anything else.

'Remember, nobody can see the kingdom of God unless he is born again,' a man said to Stephen, and he added, 'Transform yourself through accepting Jesus in your life.' The man who said this was in his sixties, wearing cheap clothing, but presenting himself as a smart professional in a suit and tie with his heavily worn shoes shining. Stephen looked at the light reflecting in the man's glasses and glistening on his sweaty forehead. There were children's toys and furniture pushed to the sides and corners of the hall in which the meeting was taking place. People stood in groups behind rows of chairs where they would sit when the speaker started. One person spoke about being baptised and reborn into a transformed existence, and a discussion started about people being miraculously healed from pain and disease, even cancer. Stephen watched the person carefully who said that. He was a short man who had a habit of turning his head to one side as he spoke, and Stephen noticed how he avoided eye contact when speaking to him. Stephen interrupted the man and asked him if cancer could be cured, which caused him to stop what he was saying. He looked at Stephen for a few seconds before answering, as if summoning the strength to substantiate what he had said, but Stephen wasn't convinced. The man went on telling Stephen about a woman who came to the church who had cancer and it looked like all was lost, but he prayed for her, as did other church members and she was healed. He spoke about other cases of people being healed and of how he and the others in the church pray for people Stephen nodded, tired of everything he had heard he spoke with obvious cynicism 'A miracle? I was God?'

A young man pushed close to Stephen, and said as he looked at his beret, 'Yeah, when I was cured, I knew that God is the real deal.' Stephen didn't respond, which caused the young man t become excited as he continued with a hint of aggression, 'Yeah, come on man, I've never had anyone die for me except Jesus – think about it, dude.' Stephen looked at him and the young man nodded to confirm what he had said.

A voice sounded close to Stephen, he realised it was his own, but it didn't feel to him like he was saying the words he was listening to. The voice said, 'How do you know?' The young man braced himself, and just as he was going to answer, Stephen cut in. 'I'll tell you what I know for sure, I knew men who died for you – or thought they did.'

Stephen stared at the young man, but he wouldn't meet Stephen's gaze, and Stephen began to talk, words coming from his mouth without thinking. He spoke about Graham Mears and his family, the hypocrisy of politicians and those involved with big business, Jessica and private health, and he went on, not listening or caring what others wanted to say. When he finished, a man said to him 'It's all about following the spirit of the Lord, and the bad will have to explain themselves to God when their time comes.'

'That's what they want you to think,' Stephen said, 'To remain silent while knowing about the wrongs that are going on – everyone's either stupid or scared.' One of the church people said they would pray for him, but Stephen turned towards him, his anger evident as he said, 'It's easy just to say words, it's in the action that reality exists, on the battlefield, in hospital budgets, murdering people to take over their land – this what really affects people, it's safe to just talk in mumbo jumbo world where nothing happens – nobody seems to care – lay down your lives for God, for Queen, for King, for leaders – and we shall all share in the rewards of your efforts – yeah, sure, that's going to happen only when those with power want it to happen, but it doesn't work that way.'

Stephen didn't wait for the person, the vicar, priest or whatever he or she was called to speak. He left the hall, getting on the first bus that came along, not knowing and not caring where it was going. Stephen changed buses, speaking to people who watched him warily as he spoke about the hypocrisy of politicians and Jessica dying. He told people he was searching for a bus driver, because he wanted to tell him that he was sorry for killing his son.

63

Stephen's mother came to his flat and asked him why he wasn't answering her calls, but he was difficult to get at. He told her that he had 'chores' to do, but would be in touch when things settle down. Stephen was evasive and a lot of what he said didn't make sense. Two days had passed since Stephen saw his doctor and his mother wondered what he was really doing for Stephen as he appeared so distant and his behaviour was getting worse.

The following day Stephen went to Joe Tara's agent, it had been nearly two weeks since he had been there. The agent had changed the way they let people into the building, this was because of Stephen. People now had to identify themselves, say where they were from and the reason why they wanted to contact the agent. Having seen a young woman going into the agent's building, Stephen stood by the side of the doorway, his back against the wall waiting in case she was going to come out. Once through the doorway, a person had access to the different companies that were housed in the building. The young woman did come out of the doorway and Stephen slipped in. He made his way up the stairs and getting to the agent's door stopped on seeing an intercom. Stephen cursed, this was something new, becoming frustrated he knocked on the door. There wasn't an answer, so he knocked again, this time harder. The voice of the young woman spluttered through the intercom, asking who it was. Stephen said he was a courier and had a parcel. She asked who was it from and what was it. Stephen took time thinking of something to say, and the voice asked him what company he worked for, which stumped him even more.

'Who is it please?' The voice asked, but Stephen couldn't answer. He couldn't breathe and his head began to spin. Stephen thought he was going to faint, and in an effort to calm himself, he tried to take slow breaths, but it felt to him as if his throat had contracted and he began to hyperventilate. He became dizzy and stumbled, stopping himself from falling he held onto the frame of the door. The artificial sounding voice asked a question, but he couldn't hear what it was saying. Stephen wanted to get away, and although his legs were giving way, he started to walk down the stairs, but getting only halfway down he fell. Realising he was falling Stephen threw himself to one side to stop tumbling head first. He clattered down the stairs on his back, his army training instinctively employed, he placed his hands behind his head. When at the bottom of the stairs he attempted to stand, but a pain so sharp and vicious in the small of his back forced him onto the floor. Stephen cried out, he couldn't help it, but his immediate thought was of his beret. It was on the floor next to him. This brought him some relief, but the pain was terrible. The door to his left opened and a young woman stood in the doorway, looking shocked at seeing him on the floor.

'Oh my God, are you okay?' She asked him, and Stephen managed to nod. 'What happened?' She asked Stephen. He began to answer, but didn't continue when seeing she realised it was a stupid question. Stephen was trying to stand, the pain nearly unbearable, but he was forcing himself to get up and get out of the building. The young woman stepped towards Stephen and helped him to his feet, her manner changing as she looked closely at him and his beret. She looked carefully at Stephen as he limped through the doorway and into the street. Watching what was happening from the landing, standing in a position where they couldn't be seen from the bottom of the stairs, was the agent and the young woman.

64

Stephen went to the anti-war meeting. The same people were there from his first visit and the same couple were sitting by the door. They welcomed him like an old friend. Stephen felt it was like a cult, or even something innocuous like a club for people having the same interest, such as a model railway society, and nothing more. He walked around the room, the sneaky looking young man was there looking at Stephen, but he ignored him. He heard conversations about imperial forces stripping Africa of its natural resources, someone else was talking about the royal family's involvement with tyrannical regimes, another person spoke about the setting up of puppet governments and arming mercenaries to kill indigenous people wanting to protect their way of life.

Stephen thought how many of the older people looked a bit mad and out of kilter with mainstream society, but a lot of the younger ones were different. They were hungry for opportunities to pursue their own ends, and this might be little more than a product to do so, a steppingstone on the path of their career. Stephen thought how they're educated and might have contacts in jobs with status and influence in something like journalism or publishing. Their manner and speech was slick, some of them reminding him of Joe Tara and that type of person. Stephen spoke to a young man standing near him, who jumped as Stephen had caught him unawares. He spoke to him about comedians like Joe Tara and how they are fakes. A few people turned and listen to Stephen. A young woman said she liked Jay Turn and that there are some good comedians.

'Jay Turn is a fake,' Stephen snapped, 'She lies to people, like Joe Tara, even they're names are fake for fuck's sake – making out they are something they're not, taking the piss out of the public, they're just like politicians, they're the same type of people.'

Stephen felt anger building inside him, and he unintentionally shouted out, which not only shocked some of the people near him, but also frightened them. He felt like telling them they hadn't put their lives on the line and seen friends killed or horribly injured.

'I shot a bystander,' Stephen said, his voice raised, 'He was an innocent person, because someone told me to – that's the kind of person I am.'

Most of the people turned away, some swapping looks, but a girl of about seventeen years of age stayed where she was standing, looking into Stephen's face, as if searching for a clue that might give her an answer to what she was thinking. She was like a medical student studying her subject, but her enquiry concluded with just a look of confusion. The man from the anarchist group was at Stephen's side asking him if anything was wrong.

'This is all wrong,' Stephen said, waving his arm around the room. The man watched Stephen, noting how his eyes were intense as he looked around at the different groups of people and the ones retreating from him.

The man said, 'Did you check us out on the net? CFF.' Stephen didn't know what he was talking about. 'Conflict for Freedom,' the man said, but Stephen shook his head, dismissing what he had asked him. The man stepped close to Stephen and spoke into his ear, 'I've got what you asked for – but not here.'

Stephen looked at him without any change of expression. The man sensed there had been a change in Stephen, he seemed different, but he wanted to see through what he had come to do. He told Stephen that he had 'the stuff' in a car parked nearby and for to Stephen to come with him. Stephen complied, without saying anything he followed him outside and walked to the car. The man talked all the while as they walked to the car about the aims and philosophy of the 'anarchist' group he belonged to. Stephen got into the car, his face more waxwork than human, which was beginning to unnerve the man as he showed Stephen the explosive that was wrapped in a bag. He then gave Stephen a slip of paper with Joe Tara's address on it.

You okay dealing with that?' The man said, looking down at the explosive. 'Oh yeah, no problem there, I know what to do with this,' Stephen said, his voice steady as he looked down at the bag. The man asked Stephen if he needed backup and that he would like to 'work' with him, but Stephen shook his head, his manner so firm and determined the man knew he wouldn't be persuaded. He asked Stephen for his number or how he could contact him, and again Stephen shook his head, not looking at the man, but at the address on the slip of paper. Stephen pulled the handle to open the door, but the man stopped him by placing his hand on his arm. 'If something happens, you know, obviously you don't say where you got it from,' he said, and he smiled, but his smile faded because of the way Stephen was staring at him. 'But I don't know who you are,' Stephen said, his face impassive with eyes flat and dead. Stephen got out of the car and walked away.

65

Stephen went home. He was weary of the people he had been meeting and thought of how they all sounded the same, many of them wanting to impress, but it was empty and the others were lonely or ill. His thoughts didn't remain on the people at the meeting, or the others he had met since Jessica became ill, it was on the explosive. He looked at it thinking of his own experiences when dealing with explosives. Stephen had been given extensive training on the subject and knew how to detonate with a pressure pad. He put the explosive in a drawer in the bedroom that Jessica's mother had been using, and while doing this, he saw one of his old scout books. Taking it out of the drawer, he looked closely at the book, and then sat on the bed and began reading it. His interest was taken immediately as he read about standing up for the weak, which was illustrated in a story where a bully was brought to task by a scout for picking on smaller boys. There were stories of performing good deeds for those unable to help themselves, of showing courage even if one is scared because it is the *right* thing to do. It gave examples of putting principles into action, an endeavour one has to see through if one is true to the character of a good and just person. Stephen read how a scout that has passed away is said to have 'gone home.' It has become traditional to show this by using a Native American tracking sign of a circle with a dot in the middle, a sign that has been engraved on Baden Powell's grave in Africa. He put the book down, thinking of honour and loyalty and how there are people in authority who have none, which turned his mind to Graham Mears and the Cayman Islands.

Stephen went into the living room and researched the Cayman Islands and about getting a job there. An idea came to him of finding out how to get employment on the Cayman Islands and confront Graham Mears when he visits there. Stephen read about opportunities for investors and the privileges given to the wealthy who can afford to invest in businesses, but he wanted to find out about employment for a person like him. He thought that jobs in tourism or hospitality would suit him, and his background of having been in the army would hold him in good stead. There were strict rules about getting a work permit, but the hurdles and details were so confusing Stephen decided to check it out at a later date. He began writing a letter to Graham Mears, having the idea that he would personally give it to him when he met him in the Cayman Islands.

Stephen phoned his doctor's surgery the next morning and left a message. What he said was a rambling rant about Graham Mears, corporate welfare, the royal family, the arms trade and private health companies. He also said how there could be a 'greater power' and maybe it can guide him to take vengeance on Mears and people like him because of the wrongs they have committed. Stephen said that it could be this 'power' that is directing him to get a job in the Cayman Islands and meet Graham Mears personally, although at the moment he just wanted to give Mears a letter that he had written, but maybe this 'power' would want him to kill Mears.

The doctor listened to Stephen's message later that morning with concern creasing his forehead. He rang Stephen, but not getting an answer he left a message for him to phone the surgery.

66

A few days passed, Stephen didn't contact the doctor and neither did he get in touch with his mother. There hadn't been any contact between him and Jessica's mother and he ignored the building society and anything to do with the debt. During the previous two days Stephen travelled only to a local park, a few minutes' walk from his home. He sat on a bench, thinking, trying to calm a trembling feeling inside him, and all the while his teeth felt like they were giving off electric shocks. A band tightened around his head, at times so hard he thought his eyes were bleeding. He knew there was no going back. One day Stephen decided not to go to the park, his anxiety was increasing, thinking all the time people were looking at him, and maybe even worse, planning on taking revenge for what he had done to an innocent person. Stephen had read how ex-servicemen feel alienated and he had been thinking about it, but his thoughts weren't clear or consistent and everything in his mind just became a woolly mass of jumbled words and disparate thoughts. He felt like an outcast, despised and abandoned because he had done wrong.

Stephen went out, he couldn't stand it any longer in the flat, to be alone with thoughts that were cursing him. He didn't know where he was going, but then it had become a common thing for him to travel aimlessly on trains and busses. He went to Joe Tara's agent's office, although didn't try to go in, the time he fell down the stairs had put him off. Stephen stood outside the building, and then he caught himself shouting. He was shouting up at a window he guessed was the agent's office, People looked at him as he shouted about Joe Tara being a fake, but he didn't take any notice of anyone else. It now felt to Stephen as if he had slipped into a zone reserved only for those that are rejected, hated and damned. He had become disconnected from everyone and everything else, and he liked it. Stephen felt safe with this new feeling. It was the best he had felt for a long time. He felt that everything was sorted out and in its place. 'As it should be,' he would often say to himself, because he was now set on a course with a purpose, and it felt good as if giving him a feeling of being free at last. He lost track of time, it didn't have any meaning to him anyway as he wandered the streets speaking to people, sometimes not knowing what he had said and never bothering if they spoke back to him. The hours and days went by, travelling miles on trains and buses, and late at night when the buses were empty, he spoke to the drivers, continuously, often nothing more than a stream of babble.

250

67

The television was on in Stephen's lounge, a man was being interviewed by a woman in a setting that could be an office. The woman said, 'This medication can, has done, change a person's personality, and quite significantly as well. It is well known in this area of research that SSRI'S address neurotic and depressive moods, but often the negative thoughts are replaced with thoughts of wanting to be more outgoing and socially expressive. This newborn extroversion can show itself in bizarre ways that will shock others that know the person, because his or her behaviour and thoughts are totally out of character.'

As the man started to speak, his name and title appeared on the screen, Psychiatrist. Dr Bernhard Devlin. 'Well, it's a case of Pandora's box, once opened it can ignite a process of very complicated illusory thoughts – it can be seen to be primarily about inhibitions. So, it can act in a contradictory way, in that antidepressants are generally thought to be prescribed to deal with mental states causing distress to a person. Although, it is widely recognised that certain antidepressants, primarily the SSRI type of drugs, have the potential to arouse pre-determined dispositions, by which I mean, the manifestation of hidden feelings as the control over behaviour one might be having inhibitions about is relaxed, therefore exposing the hidden, repressed and suppressed potential. Psychoactive drugs dull, to a more or lesser extent, emotional responses to stimuli, but can also be seen to weaken one's restraint over emotions not previously manifested.'

The woman watched him, nodding slowly and thoughtfully as she began to speak. 'And from the research that's been conducted it can be seen, although by no means in the majority of cases, but more than just a slight percentage, that when taking medication, such as Sertraline, one's world view changes, and the altered view increases to a point where one's perception towards something or someone, changes and bizarre, but also dangerous, behaviour can follow. There are studies in the United States that show how people with no history of violent behaviour prior to taking SSRI's have committed violent acts, such as killing a family member, and for example, a great number of the school shootings were perpetrated by people having been on antidepressant drugs.'

Man: 'That's correct, there were concerns in the late 1980's when the SSRI'S were fully rolled out. It is a drug used to repress thoughts that disturb and depress a person, but can trigger the deepest feelings that have been dormant which are destructive to the individual, those around him or her and to society.

Woman: 'So, just as an illness can trigger psychotic behaviour, so can taking an SSRI drug?'

Man: 'We have found that to be the case, there is evidence of triggering uncharacteristic feelings, especially when there has been a trauma in conjunction with taking SSRI medication,'

Woman: 'And so, it would be correct to say that an underlying pre-disposition is an important factor, and that should be investigated before prescribing an SSRI type of drug?'

Man: 'Yes, most certainly in order to gain an understanding of the patient's history and to be mindful of a person's level of anxiety when at first prescribing the medication. A matter I would like to draw attention to is the subject of the connection between PTSD and psychosis or schizophrenia. It is something I have researched and have found the medical industry, the GP's, often overlook, presumably because of a lack of education on the matter, or maybe, rather cynically it could be said that governments do not want any statistics of this sort to be revealed. But what has been found, is that young men, soldiers, returning from battle with PTSD that was developed in combat, are often in their early twenties, which is the peak age for developing schizophrenia. Getting the correct diagnosis at this time, when a young soldier has returned home exhibiting symptoms of PTSD is imperative for administering the correct treatment.

'There is research on the connection between stress and people who have experienced deeply traumatic situations with developing schizophrenia and states of psychosis. The young man, and it is usually young men in front line action battle conditions, returns home traumatised by what he has experienced and is diagnosed with PTSD, and treated for just that. Yet, the circumstances that caused the trauma aren't dealt with separately, and so the stress, as I say, can lead to psychotic behaviour, but the medication used for treating PTSD is not the correct approach because different medication is used in the treatment of schizophrenia and psychosis. It is to understand the co-occurrence of a stress disorder, such as PTSD and schizophrenia or psychosis so, putting it plainly, the treatment of only the PTSD leaves the psychosis untreated, and to simply increase the dose of a SSRI to modify behaviour and anxiety, is not appropriate or accurate treatment. It can have devastating effects, because, as we have spoken about, the outcome for some people is destructive and sometimes very dangerous for the person, those around them and indeed others in society.'

He looked around the room, as if searching for something, and then turned to the woman.

Man: 'There is research that says there is a link between PTSD and dissociation, which can vary from being mild to severe, where one feels detachment from one's surroundings, and there is depersonalisation, where one feels detached from one's self, meaning from one's body and mind – and from one's physical and emotional feelings. Other conditions related to this are derealisation, where one's external world feels unreal – but, however it shows itself, the person suffers a loss of reality. Now, Post Traumatic Stress Disorder and symptoms of psychosis do co-exist with the sufferer having hallucinations, paranoia and delusions, along with many other conditions such as abnormal thought processes and periods of mania.

The man stopped talking and his mood became sombre as he looked down at his hands.

Woman: 'We are letting these people down.'

Man: 'Yes, we are letting these people down. The medical profession, politicians and society, we aren't treating these people with the respect they deserve. We have found that doctors increase the dose of SSRI'S as anxiety increases, and maybe increasing it again, and it is at that point when uncharacteristic behaviour and strange thoughts shortly follow. We believe that if destructive and strange thoughts had been subliminally existing, yet kept suppressed by inhibitions, the increased dose of an SSRI drug shrugs off those inhibitions and unleashes that underlying predisposition to crazy, uncharacteristic behaviour.'

The man looked at the woman for a few moments before continuing.

Man: 'And indeed, it can show itself in very bizarre ways.'

Across the room from the television, Stephen was sitting in a chair, but he wasn't listening to the conversation between the man and woman, because he was asleep. He was dressed as an Arab, wearing the known terrorist style head dress and a sheet around his body.

Stephen sat on his bed looking into the wardrobe mirror. He was dressed in his Arabic-like clothing with a fake suicide vest strapped around his middle, the vest consisted of small water bottles filled with rice. He had been staring at himself for over two hours, not once looking away from his reflection, but time had no meaning, his mind was filled with a continual sequence of words and music. He listened to the words and music as if they were separate from him. Sometimes the words were singular and random, at other times strung together in short statements. They were said in different voices, some in a strict tone as if giving an order, others were in different accents and some sounding like slogans from adverts Stephen saw on television when he was a very young child. The music changed from choral singing to The Beatles song with the line, 'Nothing is real.'

Police flank the doorway of a large building in central London. A large, expensive car pulls up outside the doorway, Graham Mears gets out of car. A man breaks from the crowd, the scene is on live television. The camera zooms in on the man breaking from crowd and heading towards Graham Mears, it is Stephen dressed in his Arab-like clothing; he is holding a plastic bag in his left hand. The television presenter remarks on what Stephen is wearing, pointing out that a dollar sign is drawn on his shaved head. The presenter says, 'It looks like it's been drawn with red lipstick.'

Back on the ground. We hear ear wireless communication between police, an order is heard, 'Shoot him.'

Back to the on the television. Stephen is shot. The presenter says, 'He's been shot – he's been shot – he's down.'

Back on the ground. There are shouts of, 'Don't go near him, stay back – stay back – the vest – what's in his hand?'

A dog moves towards Stephen, smelling the body, a policeman also studies the body through binoculars, He shouts, 'They're fake, the bombs, they're fake, but what's in his hand? In the bag?'

The television camera is trained on Stephen, the presenter explains that the body maybe booby trapped so people are staying clear. 'The police are evacuating people from the area – what a tense moment, and it shows just how professional and prepared out security services are, and thank God for that – our lives are literally in their hands, and fortunately, because of their skill and bravery no one has been hurt – Graham Mears has been ushered into the building. We'll wait here to see what's happening – it's all very confusing, and shocking, and unfortunately it is now a part of everyday life – which brings it home how much we really need our security services.'

Back on the ground. A policeman gives orders to wait until the bomb squad get there to check all areas, look for other bombers and any suspicious packages. 'He might not be a lone wolf,' the policeman said, 'Bomb disposal are on their way – the army are coming now, evacuate the area – people and traffic – make it secure.'

The dog pulls at the plastic bag Stephen is holding and the dog handler calls the dog. The dog runs towards the handler shaking the bag, the contents of the bag spill out onto the ground. Two items were in the bag, a framed photograph of Jessica and a sheet of paper with writing on it. This causes the television commentator to become excited. He says with added enthusiasm, 'Two things have fallen out of the bag, we can't see what they are, but we'll have a close-up on them very soon and we should then be able to find out then. In the meantime we've been told a police cordon is being set up and they are assessing the area, and also the army are on their way – my oh my, this is a shocking and terrible scene, which is very frightening, but thankfully nobody is hurt, as we know of, that is, and let's hope and pray it stays that way – and again, thank God for the security services, the men and women in the police and the army, we owe them so much gratitude, and I know, we all respect every single one of them very much from the bottom of our hearts, because when you actually witness something like this....'

Back on the ground. The piece of paper flutters across the road until a policeman puts his foot on it, judging it to be just a sheet of paper and not of any harm. Adjusting his glove, as if to give him protection, he picks up the sheet of paper and looks at his superior who is waving him over. The senior officer takes the piece of paper, and at first holds it away from himself, mindful that it could be coated in some kind of poison, but eventually disregards those thoughts and reads what is written on it. What was written on the paper had been done so in large capital letters.

As a young boy I was in the boy scouts, I valued duty and honour as virtutes to aspire to, with honesty and kindness. As a young man I served in the army, but unfortunately got injured in Iraq by an IED. Even so, I am proud to say I had the honour of meeting and working alongside colleagues in battle who were brave and honourable. It is in a situation like that when a person finds out what trust and friendship really is. I was a proud boy scout and serving my country was a thing I wanted to do, without question. My wife, Jessica – see photograph – died of ovarian cancer earlier this year, we couldn't afford treatment that might have helped in the early stages, but it wasn't available, to people like us. I took out a loan, just how much she didn't know, because she didn't want me to spend our money – that would leave me in trouble after she had gone, that was the kind of person she was, beautiful in all ways. I would have done anything for her to be well. We tried for a baby, and ended up having to pay for private treatment, until we were told Jessica had cancer – she had the operation but it didn't work, and after treatment we were told there was no hope, although there was medication that is not available on the NHS. She had private treatment, but Jessica died.

I have not held a gun for a long time, Mr Mears, unlike you – you shoot guns at defenceless animals, when you go on expensive shoots to kill creatures far more worthy than you could ever be.

You, your family and friends have financial investments in health companies, and money which should be going to the NHS is being put into companies you have investments in. You and your type see the health and well being of people as just another thing to make money out of.

I want to give this letter to you, to let you know – although I doubt if you care – how people are affected and how lives are ruined by people like you, who are only interested in the pursuit of money – it makes me think you are pure evil.

The police officer walks over to where the photograph of Jessica lay on the ground and picks it up, ignoring a voice shouting, 'Sir' as a warning for him to be careful. He walks up to Stephen, ignoring calls for him to take care, and leaning over the body he looks from the bottles of rice to Stephen's face. His eyes settle on a large hole blasted into the left side of Stephen's chest. The police officer looks at the letter, focusing on a small drawing at the bottom of the page of a circle with a dot in the middle. He looks closely at it, an old scout himself he nods grimly, and says quietly, 'Gone home.' Kneeling by the side of the body, he places his hand on Stephen's head. Tears form in his eyes as he looks to the heavens, and then looking at the building Mears had gone into, his face hardens with contempt showing beneath the tough and resolute features of his face.

Watching the events unfold on television, in a stylish apartment, in an expensive part of town, is Mourib Amir, his wife and their young child. 'God, he's a nutter,' Mourib Amir says.

His wife, Meesha, looks at him, 'Is he a terrorist?'.

'Or a prank gone wrong – either way he's a nutter – or was,' Maurib says as he looks down at the child who is on the floor playing with a knife she had picked up from a plate. 'No angel,' he says in a soft voice, 'Don't do that baby.' He picks her up, and she offers resistance as he playfully wrestles her onto his lap.

'He's dead, isn't he?' Meesha, says.

Mourib looks at the television. 'Seems like it – there's a lot of nutters out there, bit of luck it's the one that's been bothering me. No Anaisha.' He holds the child close to his body to stop her squirming from his hold and pretends to bite her ear.

'God, I can't help thinking about her,' Meesha says, looking at Anaisha. 'What society is this for her? All the different dangers and these weirdos and sickos walking the streets.' She looks at the television and makes herself more comfortable before continuing, 'I really think we should re-consider about making that move we were talking about.'

'Aw, honey bear,' Mourib says, – I know, but my office is here, my business associates, most of my family – it's not that easy.'

Meesha looks at Anaisher and sighs reflectively, 'I know, but what about her – her safety, and her mind,' gesturing towards the television she says, 'Of having to live among these kind of people.'

'But she doesn't, and she won't.' Mourib speaks in a more assertive tone. 'Security is good and it's going to get better – we're safer here than if we were living in a quiet village in Goa.'

He looks at Meesha, dropping his head he continues to look at her with doe eyes, something he does on occasions when intending to get his own way.

'Stop worrying,' he says, 'Poppet here needs the best education and contacts with people that cut it – it doesn't happen in chill out zones.'

Meesha looks at the television, picks up the remote control and turns the volume down. Mourib Amir watches his wife thoughtfully before picking up the remote and turns the television off. Meesha tells him she was watching it, but only offering a shrug as an answer he says, 'It's just negative stuff – these people have nothing to do with us. We know the story, but it's always been the same.'

Mourib Amir stands up with his daughter in his arms, he kisses her cheek and nuzzles into her neck as the little girl tries to squirm away. Meesha smiles contentedly as she watches the two of them. 'Oh yeah,' she says, 'A package came for you earlier, Ludwika put it on your desk.' Mourib looks puzzled and gently puts his daughter on the sofa. 'Okay, I'll get it,' Mourib says as he is leaving the room. He walks past photographs of himself on the walls, some are of him accepting awards, some to do with charity work and there are other photographs of him on stage with the name Joe Tara behind him in lights.

Mourib returns holding a parcel, he nods at the television, 'You know all that stuff on there, all that anger and nutjobs – a lot of these people are just plain thick – they believe any crap that's easy for them to understand. A lot of it is jealousy, wrapped up in political excuses, or to do with religion – or some rubbish.'

Meesha looks at him, uncertain of what he's talking about.

'Well, you know,' he went on, 'The haves and the have nots, the aggrieved, different beliefs and crap – it's part of life. It's natural, there aren't any reasons or, anything – it's just the way it is, you get a bad deal, you make a good deal, and if you don't, well, it's tough shit. We're all in control of our decisions.'

'What's brought this on?' Meesha says, shaking her head and smiling.

The *trouble* in the world, that's what I'm talking about – there's the facts, and that's it, but people want answers to the way of things.' He shakes his head, 'Remember I told you about that *oly man* in India going on about renunciation, you know, that old thing about giving up material things to reach a spiritual life?'

259

Meesha lazily curls her legs under her body, 'No you didn't,' she says, but quickly adds, 'You probably did.'

'Yeah,' Mourib says, 'He was called a Sadhu, meant to be a wise and holy man – I met him in India when opening that school for homeless kids. He came to give his blessings and we had a chat about homelessness, poverty and all things beautiful, and I said to him, 'You know Saddo, the meek shall inherit the world – if it's okay with everyone else.'

Mourib nods as proof that he did. 'These people are ridiculous,' he continues in a sarcastic tone, lampooning an Indian accent and rolling his eyes, 'Follow a spiritual path to reach enlightenment and release from this worldly life preoccupied with greed and delusion – and remember, enlightenment will never be achieved if one consciously practices bad dharma.'

He drops the accent and says with a smirk, 'Or some such nonsense.'

His mind goes back to that time in India when he was there as a representative for a well-known charity that people from the entertainment industry are involved with. The charity had provided money for a school and medical centre in an area with meagre opportunities and little support for the impoverished people who lived there. Mourib is standing with children and adults who have gathered outside the school to celebrate its opening. After posing for photographs, he walks away from the other people in a manner as if disconnecting himself from the whole spectacle. An old man approaches Mourib, he is very thin and looks fragile, although there is strength in his clear eyes that fix onto Mourib as he takes a detailed look of him. Mourib had been told by someone at the school that the man was known as a holy man. He is called a Sadhu, a Hindu priest who wanders from place to place offering spiritual guidance and support to those that need it.

The old man presses his hands together in front of his face and bows to Mourib Amir. He says, 'It is a very good thing the charity has done, to help people that are in need, I thank them,' and looking more closely at Mourib he adds with scepticism, 'Joe Tara.'

Mourib Amir looks at him, barely able to conceal his contempt he mutters dismissively, 'It's all part of the job.'

The man looks at him, 'No, I said the charity, meaning the people that gave their money, with respect, I didn't mean you.'

Mourib Amir doesn't like what he said and shrugs, 'Suit yourself.'

The man studies him judiciously, 'You are a clever and wealthy man.'

'True,' Mourib says.

The man speaks slowly and quietly, 'There is no hiding place from one's actions and thoughts – and arrogance doesn't go unpunished – it doesn't matter if nothing happens now, we are all bound by interdependence, our action's will influence the actions of another man he has never met, but is connected to – the past, the present and the future are all connected – we are not in control, it is too big and beyond our comprehension.'

'I'll take your word for it,' Mourib Amir says, 'I don't really think about it,' losing patience he checks his watch, 'All I know is, it was cash that built this school,' looking away, he speaks under his breath. 'And not you lot with your philosophy and claptrap.' He turns towards the man, 'No disrespect to you, but how much money did you chip in for this school and medical centre? Yeah? I've heard all the stories, but it's money, the people here are poor, they need big business, companies to come here and shake the place up.' He looks away, speaking under his breath, 'And I know what team I want to be on.'

They look at one another for a few seconds.

The man looks directly into Mourib Amir's eyes before turning away. 'But, be careful,' he says, and adds quietly as he walks away, 'Reap as you sow.'

Back in his lounge, Mourib Amir returns to the present. He looks at Meesha, 'He told me to be careful, yeah, he said it as a warning, or even a threat with all that, you reap what you sow business.'

Mourib says mockingly, 'I was terrified, from his wrap-round old sheet of clothing to his worn out cheap sandals that some peasant probably gave him – I knew he had a twenty mile walk to where he was going – I drove off in a Mercedes,' winks at Meesha, 'That's karma for you, wonder what he did wrong?'

Meesha shakes her head at his joking. 'You didn't offer him a lift?'

Mourib Amir looks up, striking a mock meditative pose, 'Nah, testing this karma thing, aint I.'

Mourib looks at the paper the parcel is wrapped in before taking it off and dropping it on the armchair. 'It's a box!' He says, weighing it in his hands. 'It's pretty heavy – hope it's Charlie, or cash.'

Meesha looks at him disapprovingly.

He opens the box. 'It's soap, six balls of soap.'

He shows them to his daughter, 'Look, angel – pretty colours.'

Mourib takes off the plastic cellophane wrap, 'Mm, and a nice smell.' He takes a small card from the box of soap, before putting them on an armchair, and reads what is written on it. Mourib looks confused as he says, 'It's the way of things.'

'Who is it from? Meesha says.

'Don't know, doesn't say,' Mourib shrugs. Tired of the mystery, he drops the card on an armchair, 'Probably get a call saying what it's about – most likely your mad auntie.

Anaisha slides off the sofa, and reaching out she toddles towards the armchair with the soap.

Meesha says, 'Don't put them in your mouth darling.'

'Soap,' the little girl says.

Looking over his shoulder as he is leaving the room, Maurib stops in the doorway and looks at his daughter as she places her hand on one of the balls of soap. He watches her with a smile on his face because she is having difficulty releasing it from the packet. She finally grasps the soap and lifts it... Stephen's bomb explodes.

Printed in Great Britain
by Amazon

17969584R00149